LADY FEBRUARY

Year of the Sword Book Two

DAKOTA KROUT

MOUNTAINDALE
PRESS

ACKNOWLEDGMENTS

I will never stop being amazed by my wonderful readers. You all make my life so much more fulfilled and awesome.

A massive thanks to all of my Patreons, who help me make this book the best it can be, and a specific thanks to William Merrick, Samuel Landrie, Garett Loosen, and Zeeb!

PROLOGUE

"What do you *mean* she's coming here?" Baron Thursday the Twenty-Second boomed at the runner that had just skidded to a stop in front of his wagon. "*Why* is Lady February coming here? I've paid my taxes! W-why is she *doing* this to us? We haven't done anything!"

The runner shrugged and started stretching right in front of the Baron, whose eyes went cold. "You're one of her lackeys... no one else would show this level of disrespect toward a member of the peerage! Guards, grab this man and put him in a cell until he learns proper-"

"Baron Thursday." The cool, crisp voice of a young lady cut through the orders and made the man himself tremble. "The issue is the fact that you are correct. You *haven't* done anything. You leave your people to fend for themselves, while you hide away from dangers and threats in your fortified home."

"I *pay* my *taxes!*" the Baron roared, pulling both himself and a halberd out of the wagon. "You dare to come after me on the road, only because you know that you would never even get through the gates if you came to my home! My job is not the defense of the realm, my House provides the lifeblood of *trade-*"

Once more, the crisp voice cut him off. "I challenge you for possession of your Wielded Weapon."

"N-no! I refuse to be like the others!" Baron Thursday clutched at his polearm in a way not dissimilar to a wealthy lady clutching her pearls when being robbed.

"Take the *challenge,* or do I need to pry your weapon from your broken fingers?" The young woman stepped onto the road in front of the wagon, coming to a stop next to the runner that had arrived only shortly before her. "Just like everyone else, you can either hand over your weapon now or prove your worth by defeating me. Otherwise, I'll leave you broken on the side of the road and *still* take the Wielded Weapon."

"Never!" Spittle flew from Baron Thursday's twisting mouth, and his eyes were bulging as he stared down the Lady of the Month, ruler of District February. "Guards, kill them both! Spare no expense!"

Barely an instant passed before giving the order, and every Vassal began throwing a vial or weapon at the two people blocking their path. The wealth of House Thursday was on full display as the consumable items exploded into a kaleidoscope of colors and effects. Bottled lightning exploded outward, melting the packed dirt of the road and instantly refreezing it into glass.

"Should never have left the House." Baron Thursday sighed at the mess that the road had become. He turned to get into his wagon and glanced at the driver. "Double speed until we're back to safety."

His blood ran cold as Lady February's voice rolled into his ears. She was *not* amused. "Fourteen Vassals, sixteen guards, two thousand and fifty-six cultivators under your command. Your duty is to protect the *ten thousand* mortals living in your barony, at the very *minimum.* As of the last report, your defensive force has killed: one. Just *one* monster. Over six *months.* It claimed the lives of thirty-two people before a cultivator crushed the creature's skull. What did you do after this? You repossessed the land and homes of those people for unpaid rent. I judge you guilty of negligence, as well as treason against your rightful ruler."

Baron Thursday watched in horror as Lady February sprinted across the glassed section of the road and drove a fist into the face of his Prime Vassal. Her seemingly innocuous silk gloves had transformed into behemoths of metal and gems, gauntlets that were each nearly a quarter the size of her entire body barely weighing her down as she followed through on the attack, which brought the Vassal to the ground and could have easily crushed his skull like a grape. Instead, the man was only knocked out as she moved on.

Almost entirely unable to defend themselves, the Vassals fell one after another as they attempted to protect the Baron. For a reason unknown to them, not a single one was slain, only rendered unconscious. Too soon, it was Baron Thursday's turn. He swiped at the teen with his halberd, intent on bringing her down for the good of his House. She easily dodged, her short skirt swirling up to reveal practical exercise shorts underneath.

Two hits followed. She hit him; he hit the ground.

"As punishment, you will be stripped of ninety percent of your total wealth, which will be distributed as needed in the District. You are no longer a Wielder of House Thursday, just another money-grubber that does anything to stay ahead." Lady February kicked the defeated man to roll him onto his side, not wanting him to drown in his own fluids. "If you want a chance at rejoining the Aristocracy, you have until the end of the month to prove your worth. Join the Tournament of Reallocation and *earn* your position."

She scooped up the halberd and started walking away, only pausing to collect the runner out of the tree she had tossed him into to save him from the initial attacks. Looking back at the fifteen people she had defeated in under three minutes, she shook her head and grumbled.

"Look at where *hereditary* transfers of power got us. This District is diseased, and I *refuse* to let us degrade any further. The last five years is just the beginning."

CHAPTER ONE

The air sizzled with pent-up energy as Grant shot out of the barrier, landing with a splash in February. He spent a long moment on his back, looking at his status sheet, then pushed himself up with a groan. "I hated that so much… but it *was* really neat to cut through the barrier like that."

He was still struggling to believe that he was free from January. Since the barrier was erected a millennium ago, *no* one got the chance to travel, apart from the Lord of the Month and a select few merchants of House Thursday.

<Better than staying in January and getting assassinated for your position,> Sarge chuckled away to himself. <By the time you see anyone from that District again, they'll quiver in terror from your blood-soaked aura. Killers and Kings alike will tremble before your fury.>

"Sarge! You're alive!" Grant stared down at his feet, which were currently ankle-deep in silty water. Exhausted, muddy, and on the run, it was hard to imagine crowds of people fleeing before him. As he scanned his surroundings, he could see that he was at the bottom of a hillside covered with water-filled terraces, and a raincloud had chosen that moment to welcome him by dumping its contents across the terrain. "What am I standing in?"

<Of course I'm alive! I'm the best sword trainer in existence! *Bwahaha!*> The explosive reply startled Grant. <I will admit, there was some comfort in the emptiness as my spirit was enlarged and filled with new information. Back to the topic here... have you never seen a paddy field, farm boy? Seems right up your knowledge base.>

"Can't say that I have. Back in January, the crops were corn, wheat... basically anything that could be ground up and turned into bread or cake. You were empty? What does that mean? Are you feeling okay?" Grant ran his hand along the carpet of green shoots in wonder. "Also, what are paddies, and why do they grow in water?"

<Your ignorance precedes you! I see your limited logic hard at work. I'm fine. At any rate, they grow rice here, on the slopes there is ample rainfall to fill the terraces. Yet... these fields are untended. They're actually starting to rot. Where are the farmers?> Sarge stopped speaking and showed no signs of continuing, so Grant simply gazed around to determine the answer for himself.

While he was standing there and taking in nature, the rain shower slowed and petered off. The flooded terraces glistened in the midday light, sheets of glass reflecting the azure blue sky of a glorious *February*. Only the sensation of his feet slowly sinking into the soft silt brought his mind back to his current situation.

Grant's knuckles were white as he realized that he currently held February Twenty Nine outstretched, ready for battle. He hadn't been sure what to expect when he stepped through the barrier in a random location, but now the tension in his arms and shoulders was fading. The trip had only lasted an instant, but his mind was filled with confusing images and patterns that swiftly faded away.

He was just starting to sheathe his sword when he heard distant shouting carrying over the breeze. Squinting down the hill and past the paddy fields, he spotted a smattering of buildings and specks of people nestled amongst the trees. He couldn't make out any details from where he stood, but the specks appeared to be running from something! "Are those people in trouble? I need to help! Who knows what ravenous monsters or terrible Wielders inhabit February?"

<Recruit, get down there on the double!> Apparently, Sarge was satisfied with the attempt. <What are you lazing around for? Those people might need your help! Let's get over there and show them what we can do!>

"I'm on it!" Grant paused and squinted at his sword. "Hold on; this was my idea from the start."

<*Move* it, you sorry excuse for a sword-slinger!>

"I'm already going, and it was *my* idea to help them in the first place!" He waded through the paddy field as fast as possible, but made better progress upon reaching the edge of the waterlogged area and climbing onto dry land. There was even a path that wound lazily through the fields towards the hamlet below, and he started moving as quickly as his feet would carry him.

Soon he was able to make out details of the figures escaping from the town. They wore tight clothes: pants with the bottom half of the legs missing, paired with short-sleeved tops. What really bothered him was the numbers plastered across their tops. Had they been branded like cattle? Were these people only known by their numbers? The ruler here must be terrorizing the population!

Grant picked up his pace, muscles protesting at the rough treatment, but he had to help them! Drenched in sweat from his exertion, he stumbled towards the first of the figures. "Are you —*hurk*—in need of... do you need help?"

"*Move!*" The slim person running along the path darted to the side and dodged past the bulky obstacle that was Grant. "What are you even *doing*? You're going the wrong way on the track!"

Grant watched the stick-like villagers sprinting past with great pity in his eyes. "Those poor people... they're starving!

Maybe their food stores were destroyed by monsters? I can help you, you don't need to run away!"

The people streamed past him. They all wore firm and resolved expressions, but none of them seemed sad or afraid. Had they simply given up and decided that it was their fate to be treated like this? The poor things! He considered trying to match their pace and ask questions, but he doubted he'd be able to run as well as keep a conversation going for any length of time.

Shouting and puffs of smoke rose amongst the trees and buildings, and Grant started toward them right away. "That must be where the troublemaker is."

The crowd of escaping villagers thinned as he climbed a path and passed a waterwheel. His breathing was labored, and he struggled to inhale raggedly. The Early Spring Medium armor he had purchased back in January constrained his movement. "Is the air *thicker* here? It's so *hot*!"

Around the corner, villagers bearing identification numbers were corralled behind a rope. There was a huge *bang*, and a puff of smoke drifted into the air as they stormed out of the enclosure towards him. Rather than risk getting trampled, he dodged to the side and watched the group speed past.

The faces were a blur as they moved, but he thought he could see... smiling? The people were having *fun*? This didn't make any sense. Why would fleeing people be having fun, and where were the attackers? He needed answers. Grant stepped into one of the side streets and off the main path and simply watched the people moving and going about their days. He couldn't find anyone who wasn't running slowly or bouncing along well-maintained paths. The strangest thing was still the fact that every single one of them was *smiling*.

Could it be some kind of poison? This was clearly unnatural.

Grant's breath was taken away as he gazed past the running people. The slowly rotting paddy field terraces, buildings, and forested regions were replaced by an expansive vista.

At the bottom of the slope, grasslands stretched as far as the eye could see; it reminded him of home, and that *terrified* him. He approached one of the nearest runners—a woman in short trousers and a tight top—who bounced along a path; she appeared to be one of the few people not wearing a number.

"This one begs your pardon... are you in distress?" Grant ran alongside the woman, whose ponytail was flicking to the side as she bobbed up and down in what Sarge informed him was perfect running form. "I heard a bang and saw smoke... then these runners bearing numbers across their-"

"Sprinting Saints, where did *you* crawl out of?" She wrinkled her nose as she examined Grant's large form covered in mud, blood, and sweat. "We're training for the end-of-February Reallocation tournament, and you're distracting me from my physical cultivation. Are you going to compensate me for the lost time, or will you leave me alone?"

Grant had no idea what she was talking about. She wasn't eating anything? He needed answers. "What are the numbers? What do they mean?"

"That means they're competing for a place in the main tournament. Each runner is given a number for easy verification and only the top runners will get through to the next round. Move away, please!"

"Just to be sure... you aren't under attack? No one is forcing you to run?" Grant tried one last time.

"No! What gave you that idea?" She stifled a laugh and took a deep breath to get her breathing pattern back in sync. "I'm a jogger."

"Oh. I didn't realize. I thought you were a human." Grant searched for any of the tell-tale signs a monster should have, but she seemed normal... just tiny. "Can you direct me to a human settlement?"

The woman stopped and bounced on the spot, kicking up her heels while giving him a strange look. "Where are you from? How can you not know what's going on... and pardon the rudeness, but why are you so large? I've never come across an individual that was so... grand."

"Grand?"

<She's trying to see if you're sick or just lazy, Grant.> Sarge's enhanced voice crashed into Grant's head, making him wince at the sudden mental shout. <Right now, you're only strong in character; she's used to men that are strong in body.>

"Well, you're a smidge more, uhh, *horizontal* than the average Februarian." She smiled brightly, a strange look in her eyes. "I meant no offense."

Feeling a strange need to impress her, Grant shook his head and smiled. "I'm not from February. I've just arrived from District *January*."

"Oh? Did you come via Hajimeni? Why didn't you take the merchant road, the one the caravans take?" Her footfalls hadn't slowed at all as she ran in place, but she was clearly becoming agitated that she was still here. "Listen, as interesting and rare as it is to meet a foreigner, I need to keep going now. I'm not going to toss away my chance to join the Nobility!"

"So that you can finally get access to food...?"

"Food? What does the Nobility have to do with *food*?" She stared at him as if he were crazy. "Becoming a Noble is the highest achievement anyone can ever aspire to in this life. Being the shield that protects the people? Who wouldn't want to have that sort of power and responsibility? *Everyone* is doing anything they can to place in the tournament."

Her description of a Noble almost made him laugh aloud, until he realized the final part was even more stunning. "*Everyone*? Wait, so *anyone* that joins this tournament has a chance at becoming a Noble?"

"You really *are* new here. Everything has come to an absolute halt. Every single business and individual in the District has stopped functioning, and has become focused on gaining a Wielded Weapon to change their fates..." She trailed off with a longing look at the road she had been running along.

"That explains the rotting fields, I suppose. The tournament… do you think you can win it?" Grant really wanted her to do well, since she seemed really nice.

"No one wants to *win*. They want to *place*." At his question, she shook her head and looked around cautiously, and her smile dropped away. "The winner will become Lady February's sparring partner."

"That doesn't sound so bad. A really good training partner sounds kinda nice?" Perhaps he shouldn't have opened his mouth.

As soon as he had spoken, she rapidly backed away and started running, calling over her shoulder, "I… I have to go. I can't let my heart rate drop too much, and I have another fifteen miles to do before my aerobics class. Don't… don't ever tell anyone that you want to be the sparring partner of Lady February. You might die."

"Wait!" But the jogger was already gone, bounce-fleeing along the road. Grant dropped his eyes to the ground and growled out a sigh. "I don't understand this place at all."

CHAPTER TWO

Grant walked along the side of the main road, trying to figure out what to do next. 'Joggers', apparently some subspecies of humans, were passing him on either side. Some smiled, and others waved as well when they passed. After the first hour of this, the super positivity was wearing on him. It seemed forced, wrong, unnatural. It didn't help that there was apparently something here that made people look really similar; he could have sworn that *this* person had already run past him with a smile and a wave *seven times* on this strangely springy road.

He was used to January, where the most exercise anyone got was lifting a heavily laden fork from their plate to their mouth. It was hard to believe that he had defeated Lord January, taken his power, and traveled through the barrier to February within the last few hours. Grant grumbled as his stomach clenched, and he winced as he realized that he hadn't had a decent meal since he'd left the Leap sanctuary in the sewers under Castle January.

"I better find somewhere that sells food. I think Time can be spent in any District, so I should certainly have enough to get me through in the short-term." Even the thought of biting into a juicy steak was making his mouth water. "Sword Expertise—no, Sword *Grandmastery* now—will probably fight me if I go overboard, but I'm sure I can find *something.*"

"You, on the running track! You're going the wrong way!" a carriage driver yelled while pulling up next to him, strangely on a road that was right next to the one he was walking on. That turned into a caravan of carriages snaking its way from the grasslands, one that was apparently never-ending. A group of energetic runners bounded out of the carriage, whooping and hollering as they pumped themselves up for their upcoming races. To Grant, they looked painfully thin, a stiff breeze capable of blowing them over.

"Hey! Look at this guy getting out there and doing the right thing!" One of the new arrivals ran over and slapped Grant on the back. He, like all the others, was wearing a strange pair of silk gloves that went almost to the elbow. "Keep running, my dude! You are wildly impressive to come out here and better yourself like this, and I would *love* to be your pacer to help keep you motivated!"

Grant nodded and gritted his teeth, not entirely sure what was happening. In January, people thought he was weird for training with a sword and performing any weapon cultivation, but here, he was seen as... what? A child that needed help just to do some minimal training? The people of February were friendly enough, but it was clear what they thought of his portly physique.

The people jostled him until he finally turned around, and then a crowd of people ran alongside him, hooting and hollering as they pushed him to pick up the pace. Whenever he started to slow or tried to leave what he found out was a road made into a circle, they would beg and convince him to stay and keep going. It was only when he was foaming at the mouth and the sun was getting low in the sky, that his 'pacers' let him go; even though they went back onto the track and kept going.

"I... need... food." Grant slumped onto a bench and took

out his money pouch. "Five Days and three Hours… must find steak and water. So much *water…*"

Taking a moment, he tried to plan out his financial situation. A loaf of bread back in New Dawn was supposed to be five Minutes, assuming he wasn't scammed by a shopkeeper. Here, in the town apparently named 'Hajimeni', he couldn't imagine it would be different. At least here, people seemed overly friendly, so he shouldn't be scammed or forced to buy snot-coated bread!

<Don't forget that sack of Time that Sir Friday handed you before we left. Haven't checked it yet!> Sarge reminded him cheerfully.

Grant pulled out the sack and counted out a series of coins that came out to a solid seven Weeks, more Time than he had ever earned in his life. With a happy bounce in his very sore feet, he got up and headed back towards the center of the village in search of a shop or tavern. The thought of a bacon-wrapped steak and cold milk kept him placing one foot in front of the other. He felt like he'd never start moving again if he stopped, so he continued to press himself onward. The stress, hunger, and tiredness of the past few days were catching up with him.

Finally, a tavern loomed ahead. He licked his lips as he approached; this was exactly what he was looking for. Grant could hear chatter coming from within, apparently this was a popular place, going by the sheer number of competitors that had entered. Some were sweaty, likely in search of a good meal or bath, others seemed fresh and in search of an energy boost before… night time training or some such nonsense?

Ivy covered half the quaint building, which he only noticed because he had to push through it as he went through the entrance. His stomach was *screaming* at him. It would take every shred of willpower for him to keep from going overboard tonight. Looking around the abundantly popular tavern, Grant was shocked beyond belief. There was no wild boar on a spit, with fat sizzling and dripping as the meat spun.

In fact, the only scent in here was the light scent of sweat that came off people that exercised regularly. Where was the wheaty smell of ale? Fresh-baked bread? …The vinegar of pickles?

His brain struggled to comprehend what he was seeing instead. People were drinking from glasses filled with a thick green substance. A server came around, stared at him for a moment, then ran back and brought him a large mug filled with the 'drink' everyone else was going to town on. "By order of Lady February, any person such as… yourself… that is clearly working to better themselves is to be given physical cultivation resources for free at least twice per day. Here you are, on the house!"

Grant was in a state of numb shock, completely out of his element in this culture of strange people. He thanked her and took the mug, sniffing at it tentatively. It smelled just like it looked: a glass full of freshly cut grass. Wrinkling his nose in disgust, he went to put the un-sipped glass down on the table. He looked over at the bar and gasped as he saw this drink advertised, with the price clearly displayed.

"*Sword Saints*! One Hour for a drink of *grass*?" He snatched up the glass just as it touched down and lumbered over to the server that had given him the noxious substance. "What in Lord January's name do you call this?"

"Lord *January*?" The server smiled uncomfortably as Grant waved the precious liquid around. "That, sir, is our most popular recovery drink. The special blend of plant matter and powdered monster proteins aids recovery and increases muscular endurance over time. It's called 'Beastly energy drink', or 'Bed' for short, since it is most effective if you do physical cultivation all day and drink it right before sleeping. It was designed by Lady February herself."

"I don't want to 'Bed' myself, I want to *treat* myself after a really difficult month!" This statement received more than a few laughs from the tittering bunch of competitors, who were downing the pungent drinks as if they were shots of whipped cream at a Noble feast. "Where is the *food*? Something solid that I can bite into?"

"On the other side of the bar you will find pre-packaged ready meals." The server pointed, but her expression seemed to suggest that he would be less than satisfied with what he found.

"Okay... that's... thank you." Grant hurried over, hopeful that he could find something to enjoy. He had defeated Lord January and taken his position less than a day ago, and he needed to *celebrate*! As it turned out, the small boxes on display were only a *teensy* bit more appetizing than the grass drinks. He picked one up and examined it warily, struggling to make out the words. Growing up as an abandoned orphan on the farm, he hadn't exactly had a chance to develop strong reading skills, though words and language intrigued him. "Sarge, *tell* me... that is, I could use a hand here?"

<Heh.> Grant scowled as soon as he heard the first inkling of Sarge's laughter. <I would like you to know that I'm absolutely *delighted* with the selection of food here. Imagine how fast you'll be able to swing me through the air when there's less wind resistance from your arms!>

"Are you *kidding* me? How can this be safe to eat; listen to this!" Grant picked up the box once more and tried to sound out the words. "Queen-noa, chee-ah seeds, go-gee berries? I feel like I'm reading a poison recipe. Maybe an assassination plot, some kind of Regicide in the works?"

<Those are *more* than safe, they're *good*. These foods are considered 'superfoods'. Exceptionally nutrient-dense foods, filled with vitamins, minerals, and other health-enhancing benefits.> Sarge's voice darkened, and Grant felt chills run down his spine; something fundamental had changed in Sarge when he got upgraded with Sword Grandmastery. When he spoke, power rolled along with his thoughts. <This is good, because you don't have *time* to be weak, Grant. Don't forget your mission, or what happens if you fail. Today is February first, and that means a full one-twelfth of your time to live has *expired*. I think following along in this District might just save your life.>

"I… I just wanted to eat an actual meal." Grant lowered his head as the stress of the last few days settled in on him. "Is that so much to ask?"

<Around these parts, apparently so.> Sarge outright laughed at Grant's kicked-puppy expression. <You're outta luck, big boy. Go drink your wheatgrass shot and figure out how to survive off it for the remainder of the month!>

"No. I'm gonna at least have something to chew on…" Grant looked at the sign and almost choked when he saw the price: two *Hours*! His only choices were the 'free' one Hour grass drinks, or the wildly expensive box of nuts and berries. He could afford it, for now, but couldn't bring himself to hand over such a vast quantity of time for such a… "Wait! There's chicken on the menu! It's… *five* Hours for a boiled chicken breast? *Why?*"

"*Sir*, just so that you don't get yourself into *trouble*, please allow me to explain." The man behind the counter looked like he could lift Grant into the air and tear him in half like a sheet of paper. Grant had no idea how he hadn't seen this person until now. "Lady February has decreed that all protein sources for the population be lean meats, and all food has to be approved by food scholars known as 'Royal Nutritionists'. That means all food sources are controlled by Lady February and her Vassals directly and are guaranteed to help you remain healthy. Decrying this order is a *finable* offence. If you are unhappy with the cost of the food, let me be the first to inform you that the fine is far more hefty."

Grant stared at the man and tried to think of anything to say. Eventually he simply nodded and walked back over to the glass of grass and monster parts that he had originally abandoned. "If I can't eat what I want, might as well eat for free."

The server smiled at him and gently gripped his sweaty shoulder. "I'm glad you decided to get on board. Would you like to enhance your drink for only thirty Minutes?"

"What would an additional thirty Minutes get me?" Grant

stared at her hopefully, surprised that she didn't seem to mind his body's stench or moist clothing.

Seeing a chance for an up-sale, she beamed at him. "A long-life herbal energy drink. All proceeds from enhanced meals will go towards the charity, Pacers for Trainers. They're a group of Lady February's roving Vassals who find people that are struggling in their health journey and encourage and help motivate them."

His mind flashed to the strange people that had bothered him all day. "Those were all *Vassals*? Lady *February's* Vassals? They looked like they were going to beat me up if I stopped, so I guess it makes sense that they…"

He didn't finish the sentence; the server's eyes were already the size of dinner plates and looked ready to pop out at any moment. Her hands clutched her tray, and she seemed as though she were ready to punch him in the face. Gulping nervously, he pulled out the Time and handed it over with a quiet, "I met them today, and they helped me a lot. I don't mean to be so ungrateful, I'm just not used to all this…"

He waved around the room, and the server huffed and snatched the Time, briskly leaving and returning with a fizzy cup of purple tea. She slammed it onto the counter for him, leaving again as soon as she had. It was only at that moment that Grant realized there were no chairs in this place. Everyone was standing as they ate or drank, clearly doing what they could to continue their training in their down time. Even the people that he had originally thought were sitting were actually in a chair *pose*, braced against the wall.

Grumble.

His ravenous body demanded *meat*, in any form. Grant unhappily stared at his green 'Bed' and purple tea. He held his nose and downed them both as rapidly as he possibly could, noticing right away that the glasses were designed to look large, but held only half of the actual content he had been expecting.

Nutritional needs met. Do not ingest any other foods for at least three hours, unless heavy exercise has been undertaken.

He stared at the message, startled that the shot of grass and… monster powder… was enough to set off the intake warning. His stomach wasn't satisfied, even if Sword Grandmastery seemed to be. He needed to get out of this place and find a spot to sleep on all the changes that he was running into. Was *every* District going to be so wildly varied? It made sense; a thousand years of nearly zero contact was certain to make people different culturally, but this much from just January to February?

<Listen.> Sarge seemed almost… embarrassed? <I was integrating the new training information and creating plans, as well as assessing how your training progressed under my previous ability. It was determined as: not very well. With that said, now that I'm fully up to date… there will be significant changes coming to the way we do things.>

"All of it is to become better and survive, right? Then… as much as I may complain, bring it on, Sarge. Glad to have you back to normal; screaming laughter in my head seemed a little bonkers." After trudging back outside, he found that the sun had officially set on his first day in District February. Grant walked along the cobbled streets, his stomach still rumbling. "Since I'm here… should I try to qualify for the tournament? It looks as though, so long as I 'place', I should be able to meet and fight against Lady February. I can use the entire month to train, then participate in the tournament and try to win legitimately."

Bang!

Grant flinched as some kind of powdered monster horn was tossed into a fire and generated a small explosion and puff of smoke. He looked over at the track, where people were *still* training, and shook his head. "Do they *ever* stop?"

Feet thundered on the road, and he sucked his stomach in as the tightly-bunched group passed. He didn't need to worry too much; the runners were only focused on winning the race, but some clearly treated him like a new and interesting way to train agility as they dodged around him in ever-more-acrobatic maneuvers. Once they were out of sight, he continued on in search of somewhere to sleep for the night.

The glowing candlelights of the Hajimeni Hotel welcomed him in the distance, the only place he could see in the entire town that was well-lit besides the training grounds. He picked up his step and hurried towards the hotel excitedly, until he got to the entrance and was greeted by a 'No Vacancies' sign. "Aww, come on… wait… maybe they have a restaurant in there?"

"Please stop right there." A burly man blocked his path as he moved to enter, "Do you have a room?"

"Um, no. I just want to eat in the hotel's restaurant. I assume it has a restaurant?"

The man crossed his arms, showing off bulging muscles due to his formal shirt with the sleeves ripped off, and making Grant wonder what the dress code was at this place. "It does, for guests *only*."

"Can you… make an exception?" Grant rummaged around in his money pouch, taking out a shiny one Hour coin.

The man didn't say a word, only shaking his head and shooing Grant away. With a long-suffering sigh, he walked away from the welcoming lights that were now practically mocking him. The issue was repeated throughout the village. It turned out that the rooms here had been booked out *months* in advance. How could he expect to find a place at such short notice?

A jogger was stretching against a wall, her foot propped on top as she cooled down. Grant took the opportunity to approach, hoping that maybe she could direct him to somewhere he had missed. The last jogger he had spoken with had been really nice; maybe this one was as well? He decided to shout out, not wanting to be mistaken for an attacker.

"*Hello*! I was wondering if you could help?" The woman glanced over at him, her face hidden in the long shadows, and went to stretch her other leg. "I need to find a place to sleep, and maybe somewhere to eat? Do you know any open bakeries?"

"Oh, it's you again." It turned out that the woman *was* the same one he had come across earlier, though now she looked decidedly more tired. "There are no free rooms at this time of year, and certainly not when a tourney is on. What's a bakery?"

"Are you *serious*?" Now it was Grant's turn to laugh. "A place that makes bread? Cakes? Pastries?"

"Oh, that would do it then." She nodded as if he had just explained a great mystery. "There *is* no bread in February. Pasta either; not for *years*. Empty carbs like that are a big no-go."

"You're... you're messing with me, right? *Everyone* eats bread. It's the main source of food for the people of January." He raised a single hand in a 'please' position. There *had* to be bread.

She kept working her legs, though now he had more of her attention. "They're... more *your-sized*, I assume?"

"Well... no, not really. I'm actually so thin that I've been driven away for looking sickly, or like a beggar." Grant hadn't wanted to admit that, but he was glad it was out in the open, so he could find out if these people were just playing mind games with him. "Look, I just want to eat something tasty to cele-brate... um... coming to District February."

"Listen, if you've already been to a store or restaurant, and you don't like what you found there, I really can't help you. I think wheatgrass shots are the most tasty cultivation booster, so... can't help you, except maybe try a Bed? Those are pretty good, too. Hey! You never compensated me earlier! After you made me slow down and chat, I took two minutes longer than my predicted time to complete the circuit!"

The accusation brought Grant up short. "That's... my fault?"

"It's against the law to inhibit someone's training if they are working to better themselves. If I'm *slow*, I'll never win my race and progress to the main tournament! You can't just make people lose the chance to be their best self, and then not pay for their services." Now she was standing with her hands on her hips and clearly working herself into a fury.

"Oh, come on. I just got here and needed help. You can't

blame me for that." Seeing her hard look, Grant started to get angry. "If a one-minute talk is enough to make you lose out on your chance, that's not on *me*. Maybe you just need to train harder."

She gave him a sarcastic once-over. "What do *you* know about training?"

"What do I know about...? I'll have you know, I've spent *weeks* training with the sword!" Grant unsheathed February Twenty Nine, and the blade rang, its song echoing off the walls of the cobbled streets. He swished the blade in artistic patterns in an attempt to impress the fatigued jogger. He walked closer to give her a better view, the light of a torch reflecting menacingly off his eyes and sword.

She screamed and backpedaled, "Stay away! *Help*! Someone!"

"W-what?" Grant looked at his sword, his balanced position, and realized that they were having a misunderstanding. "No! Oh, I'm not attacking you, I was only showing you-"

"Help! *Help*! I'm being attacked." The lady darted off down the cobbled street at breakneck speed. Doors to hotels and shops slammed open, and various people streamed out, their eyes searching for the source of the commotion.

"Regent's frozen-" Grant bit off his curse as he hurried to hide his sword and self.

<You *do* have a way with the ladies, don't you?> Sarge's voice was a welcome and familiar presence, but even so, now was not the time.

"Sarge. *Please*."

<So touchy. I *was* going to let you know that I was going to give you special dispensation for not training today, considering that you went to the effort of eating such a healthy meal and doing some serious physical cultivation. Maybe I should change my mind? We haven't run through Sword Grandmastery training yet...?>

"S-Sarge! You know I didn't mean it. I'm just starving and tired is all." Grant chuckled nervously as he hurried along the road perpendicular to where the screaming jogger had run. Far better than directly away, in his mind. Less chance that people would come directly after him.

<Actually...> Sarge let the words hang in the air for a beat too long for comfort. <You're a Lord of the Month now, Grant. It's about time you started acting like one. Tonight is the last time your exhaustion will sway me.>

Grant bolted away, not wanting the attention of the guard, especially if he hoped to participate in one of the events. He darted down the first side street he came across and resigned himself to the fact that he wouldn't find a room for the night, or another meal. He heard the sound of horses nickering and reluctantly climbed a nearby wall. At the top, he came face to face with a chestnut bay that snorted and sniffed at the hand he presented. Grant smiled, having always been more at home amongst the animals than with people.

After stroking the horse's mane and letting its head nuzzle against his hand, he crept inside the stables. It stank of dirty hay and unwashed beasts. In the darkness, he tripped over a couple of buckets, making a racket as they tipped their murky contents onto the grimy flagstones. Off-balance, he narrowly avoided landing in the spreading slick. The stable wasn't well-kept, but at least it was somewhere he could hide out for the night.

In the other half of the stable, he could make out the outline of carriages. Earlier that day, they had taken competitors to Hajimeni, and tomorrow would probably leave, taking the runners with them. He considered forcing his way into one and sleeping there... but he had no idea what would happen if he was caught, so he unrolled his bedroll and settled down on a layer of fresh hay for the night.

As he stretched out on the bedroll, hands propped behind his head, he reflected on the events that had led him here, the most important of which was saving the Leaps. Yes, the quest 'Heal the World' was more important to him on a personal level, because if he didn't, he'd die at the end of the year, but even so... it filled him with a great sense of pride knowing that he'd brought change to January. *Maybe* there was hope for the people of January, and it would all stem from him making the hard choice to push forward through the pain. He really wanted to see the changes since he'd killed Randall and defeated Lord January.

If the District *didn't* change, he would go back and burn it to ashes himself when he had the power to do so.

Name: Grant Monday
Rank: Lord of The Month (January)
Class: Foundation Cultivator
Cultivation Achievement Level: 11
Cultivation Stage: Late Spring
Inherent Abilities: Swirling Seasons Cultivation
Health: 184/184
Mana: 9/9

Characteristics
Physical: 89
Mental: 34
Armor Proficiency: 44
Weapon Proficiency: 66
Cultivation resources detected: purified monster meats. Physical and Armor cultivation is increased by 10% for 2 hours.

Wielded Weapon: "February 29"

Weapon Inherent abilities:
1) Weapon Absorption: This sword has the ability to absorb another Wielded Weapon's power, taking its ability into itself. Restriction: Only one weapon per Monthly series.
2) Weapon/Armor Synergy: When the Wielder is equipped with armor, this sword increases in potency and gains power. Increase is capped at the Wielder's cultivation stage or average armor stage, whichever is lower. February 29 is now considered an 'Early Spring Medium' sword. Current maximum damage is: 8 (5.5 from weapon cultivation, 2 from weapon

stage, rounded up.) Damage type is 'piercing', or 'slashing' depending on how February 29 is used.
3) Time is Space: you now have access to any of the powers of February Twenty Nine, no matter where the Weapon is. You may also call your Weapon to you, so long as you touch upon a place in the world where it once was while in your possession. Cost: 25% of mana pool.
4) Locked

He wondered how Duke Friday was getting on after he'd told Grant to flee. He hoped the man had taken over and instilled some order, but who knew for sure? He knew that it would likely be a long time before he returned to January, if ever, so he may never learn the answer to that question. There was *one* more thought in his mind that was tearing him apart, after a day of being around people that were stronger, faster, healthier, and *far* more intense than he was.

How would he, only one month into his journey, compete against people who had spent their entire lives training and preparing for specific competitions?

CHAPTER THREE

"What's happening!" The blasting of horns had just wrenched Grant from a deep sleep. A snare drum made a rat-a-tat noise as he rushed to roll up his bedroll and stuff it into his pack.

"*Hey*! Who's over there?"

Footsteps crunched through the hay, and Grant panic-yelled, "Sorry, I took a wrong turn!"

"No one is allowed to be in here. Get on your way before I call the guards!" Grant barged past the elderly man wielding a pitchfork. He considered hanging around to help the man with his chores; from the state of the stables, the old man was struggling. Sadly, Grant didn't have the time to make that happen; he needed to go investigate the cacophony of noise.

Not far from the stables, spectators squeezed into the narrow streets, craning their necks for an opportunity to see the marching band as it passed by. Grant had to jump to see over their heads in order to catch glimpses of the brightly dressed band members, hammering on drums, blowing into horns, and playing other instruments he didn't recognize. There was no explanation as to why so many people were up at the break of dawn, but this was February... the people were a little *different*.

Unable to get a better view of the band, Grant decided to leave the packed streets and find an alternative vantage point. Walking along a parallel side street, food vendor carts came into view. His stomach reminded him that he hadn't eaten breakfast, and he scampered over hopefully to the nearest stand, still somewhat wary after last night's episode in what just *had* to be a health food shop.

<Grant, I need to tell you,> Sarge chuckled darkly as he imagined Grant's forthcoming despair, <I'm once *again* delighted with the selection of food on offer.>

Grant's heart sank and his stomach rumbled in protest. Laid out before him were low-quality protein shakes, orange slices, and strangely crunchy-looking grains. He pointed to a small bar. "How much for one of those?"

"Good morning, young man, and what a *wonderful* morning it is, too! This nutritious granola bar can be yours for only one single Hour! A bargain at any price, but even more at this one!" The skinny vendor was wearing shorts, a tight top, and an orange headband. He looked like he was ready to leave his stand and join a race.

"Those are your best prices?" Grant backed away from the stall instantly. "Sure, a… bargain. If you don't mind me asking, are you taking part in one of the matches?"

"Oh? No, no. I just enjoy the atmosphere. I would take part, but I broke my ankle a few years back during a race." The vendor looked down sadly at his leg. "I was in the lead as well. Could have won, if that root hadn't jumped out of nowhere and ended my chances. Well, back then the rewards weren't for positions in the Nobility, but you could still impress a Wielder and gain Vassalship."

"I see." Grant's stomach clenched and he inhaled sharply before waving at a different section. "How much is one of those pink drinks?"

"Gum-tree protein shakes are two Hours. Get it while you can. They'll sell out by lunchtime." The vendor reached for the mug as if the sale was a done deal.

"What? You can't be serious!" Grant's head spun at the exorbitant prices of food in this area. "Water! Simple *water*. How much to fill up my water skin?"

"That will be forty-five Minutes." Grant's mouth hit the floor. He was lost for words. "This is no ordinary water. It is spring water from Mount Yama. Rich in minerals. Perfect refreshment for the aspiring athlete."

"You're pulling my leg, aren't you?" Grant looked around, assuming that he was talking to an actual thief, but people were actually *lining up* behind him after the vendor had listed his prices. "You probably filled your tank from one of the paddy fields up the road!"

"I wouldn't *dare* do such a thing." The vendor's smile vanished as the people around Grant gasped at the accusation. "I'm an honorable food vendor, here to serve the citizens of February! All prices are approved by Lady February's council, and all food and drink sources are *required* to meet rigorous standards. If we are found to be cheating someone, there is nothing at the other end, except never being able to make a sale again! The price for one of our bars and enough spring mineral water for your waterskin is *two Hours*. Take it or leave it!"

Grant's eyes flitted between the various unappetizing choices and the angered crowd. "I meant no offense."

The vendor glared at him and pointed at the people behind Grant. "Make your selection and be on your way."

Grant handed over two one-Hour coins to the unsmiling food vendor. He held on tightly to the second coin, unwilling to part with it in exchange for some *water*.

"Let *go*!" The vendor stumbled backward as Grant released his grip. "Before you go, would you like to enhance your meal? All proceeds go to the charity, Run with-"

"I will certainly *not*!" Grant scoffed at the idea of handing over any more of his swiftly dwindling coins. The food vendor shook his head in pity as he filled up Grant's water skin.

"Here. *Enjoy*."

Grant took his tiny portion of food and escaped the rapidly

growing line that had formed behind him. Several runners glared at him as he made his way towards the end of the street, finally able to get across, now that the band had vanished into the distance.

"Mommy." A toddler tugged at her mother's hand. "Why is that huge man standing in the road? Is he part of the parade?"

"No. You stay away from him. The poor soul is clearly unwell." She looked over at Grant and winced, hurrying to pull the child away before they decided to ask more awkward questions. "Throw a coin to him. Hopefully, he'll find a way to get better."

An Hour coin was flicked at him from the *child*, which he quickly snatched out of the air and pocketed. Embarrassing as it was, money was money, and he had no problem accepting it, though he did wonder what everyone was doing to be so incredibly wealthy around here. He felt a stab of pain in his chest at the way people perceived him. They saw him as someone to pity, for the exact *opposite* reasons as his life in January. His head hurt, and he decided that he needed to sit down.

After pushing through the lingering spectators, he headed toward a statue with a plaque that read 'Lord February'. Thankfully, the gleaming bronze statue was clear of spectators and even had a small bench that the people seemed to evade as though it were ground zero for a plague. To Grant, it was too good an opportunity to pass on.

"I hope you don't mind, fellow Lord, if I make myself comfortable? At least I know what the Lord of the Month looks like now. Strange; I thought people were talking about a 'Lady' in charge?" The statue didn't answer as he settled in on the bench to catch his breath and eat the… food. The bar was bland and disappointing, tasting more like tree bark than an edible meal. The water was surprisingly cool and refreshing, quenching his thirst completely and making him feel more awake than he had the entire previous day. "Alright, maybe there's something to be said for high standards for food and water."

With his hunger very *temporarily* satisfied, he found that he was enjoying himself and the break from fighting or training. The early morning sun cast long shadows. The shadow of the statue moved inch by inch as the sun lazily made its way higher into the sky. He nearly dozed off, but a thunder of footsteps rapidly approaching brought him back to full attention. From his place by the statue, he would have an uninterrupted view of whatever or whoever was about to emerge from around the corner.

Grant shaded his eyes as he focused past the banner highlighting the name of the event, the 'Pre-Tournament Mega Marathon'.

"Here she comes!" a front-row spectator screeched excitedly. "I can't believe she came *here!*"

Grant had no idea who 'she' was, but the din of rapidly approaching feet intensified until the sound filled the square, countered only by clapping and cheering from the crowd. He couldn't help but feel excited as he waited for the swarm of runners to appear.

"There must be *hundreds* of people running through here!" He could feel the vibration through the statue, glad that he was watching rather than participating in the huge river of bodies that must be charging along the road. The cheering swelled to a roar, and Grant noticed a pink-haired woman come into view, sprinting towards him. As the lady approached, he realized that it was a runner wearing a number plate with a stylized 'one' on it, and she was wearing perfectly white gloves that went up to her elbows.

Her legs were a blur, knees pumping hard as she blazed a path directly toward the statue. If Grant was reading the signs correctly, she would have to go around the statue and exit from the north of the square. This would give him a moment to view the first-place runner, and he was starting to see why people got so into the tournament; this was somehow *exciting*.

"If I could run like that, I'd make my way across February in a matter of days." He just *had* to find the ruler of February somewhere out there within the district. At least he now knew what to look for. Grant's eyes flicked up at the statue, then back to admiring the runner.

He wanted to be able to zoom around like this; he'd be able to cover the miles with ease in search of his target. The nearly *fluid* woman barreled toward him and took the corner as wide as possible, not even slowing down. Grant waved down at the speedy woman from the bench at the base of the statue, unable to help himself from being carried away by the wave of excitement passing through the crowd.

"Go, pinky, go!" As the pink-haired, glove-wearing woman passed, she flashed a glare at Grant sitting next to the statue. A tingle shot through him as her awareness briefly fell on him; he blushed and felt strangely privileged that he had been noticed… and then she was gone. There was a collective sigh from the crowd as she exited the square. Grant looked around, still able to hear the rumble of pounding feet but unable to see more participants. "Where are the rest of the mega-marathon runners?"

At least five minutes later, the second-place runner stumbled into view. The man who approached the statue looked ready to collapse at any moment. He stopped to take a drink that was offered, his arms trembling as he downed one of the green 'Bed' drinks. After a few deep breaths, he worked up the energy to continue. The sweaty, exhausted mess of a man ran after the pink-haired woman. Even to Grant, it was clear that he'd never win the race. At this point, *he* could run faster than this twig of a man.

Once the second-place runner had exited the square, most of the spectators started to disperse, the entertainment apparently over. Grant hopped to his feet and approached the nearest person. "Please pardon my intrusion. Is it all over? Were there only two runners?"

"What? No! *Thousands* take part. The rest will pass through here throughout the morning. You can't have a mega-marathon with only two runners!" The man was edging away from Grant, bouncing on his toes. He was clearly energized by seeing the runners and was about to go do his own routines.

"That... makes sense. Where is everyone going?" Grant looked into the distance, hoping that he'd be able to see the impressive runner once more.

"People are only interested in seeing the first two competitors." The man started moving faster, but Grant tried to keep up with him and continue his information gathering. "Please back off a little, buddy."

Grant couldn't contain himself; he ignored the concerned tone from the man he was inadvertently stalking. "That guy... the shaky one, he was running slowly. *I* could have beat him, so why was anyone interested in seeing him?"

"I have... doubts about your ability to defeat him in long-distance competitions." The man was obviously doing his best not to insult Grant but was still trying to subtly escape. "After ninety miles, he was almost completely spent."

"You're joking," Grant deadpanned, but the other man simply shrugged. "Ninety *miles?* How long is the marathon?"

"One hundred miles exactly." The man pointed right at the runner that was competing and running nearly drunkenly. "That's why we wanted to see the second person. First place was never in doubt, but whoever steps over the finish line right after Lady February is guaranteed to at least *place*. That man is a future Wielder for certain, and is going to be a Noble that might eventually control the area we live in."

Grant was astounded by the information, completely uncertain how he should be feeling. "That... was Lady February? Is she the Lady of The Month? The pink-haired one? She looked right at me... I had no idea who she was. Maybe she recognized me, somehow?"

"What is there to *recognize*, you-?" The man forcibly halted himself and took a few deep breaths. "Look, kid. She looked at you because you were *sitting* at the feet of the statue. That's a Very Bad Thing for you."

"Why does that matter?" Grant looked up at the benevolent

face on the statue, wondering at the same time why the man had enunciated the warning so clearly. "He seems like a nice guy, and how can there be a Lord *and* Lady of the month? Are they married? She seemed almost my age, so that kinda-"

The man sputtered so hard that Grant thought that he was having a fit. "That's the statue of her late *father*, the previous Lord February! Sitting on the bench of the man who hated the lazy is seen as a direct challenge. He started changing this District ten years ago, and *sitting* there means you think you have contributed enough to society that you feel you can relax even under his watchful stare! If she sees and recognizes you, I'm sure she's going to challenge you to prove that you had the right to be sitting in her presence, at the foot of her father, no less!"

Grant could do nothing but watch the man storm off, his mouth open and his face as pale as a sheet.

CHAPTER FOUR

The majority of the crowd dispersed, the main event clearly over. Only a few people hung around to watch the next batch of sweaty, shaky competitors pass through the square. Even so, the people overflowed with energy and excitement. They were friendly and enthusiastic, but Grant still felt wildly out of place around them. He decided to try to take stock of the information he had gathered and re-center his thoughts.

"All these people are serious physical cultivators that apparently have a cultivation method. Does that mean that every single person in this District is a cultivator? At least a physical cultivator? I can't tell if they do weapon, armor, or mental cultivation. Heh; being so narrow-minded, I *doubt* they do mental cultivation."

<Oh, *wise* one,> Sarge broke into his thoughts. <The mental cultivation characteristics you've gained have almost entirely been gained by increasing your Cultivation Achievement Level. Actually, only your weapon cultivation can be said to have really benefited from cultivation directly, at more than *double* what you've been getting passively.>

"Well, I have no idea what that looks like, so I can't exactly-"

<I'll let you see so that you can understand the abject failure that you showcased in District January.> Sarge grumbled for a moment, then a screen popped up as he finished with, <We're gonna need to do way, *way* better than we did.>

Weapon Cultivation: 18 bonus characteristics, 364 hours spent cultivating

Armor Cultivation: 8 bonus characteristics, 329 hours spent cultivating

Mental Cultivation: 8 bonus characteristics, 330.55 hours spent cultivating

Physical Cultivation: 7 bonus characteristics, 290 hours spent cultivating

<As you can see here, you've absolutely been *wasting* your time. Look at these *atrocious* numbers. There are eight thousand, seven hundred and sixty hours in a year!> Sarge stopped and waited for a reply from Grant, but the young man was only confused.

"But... if there's thirty-one days in January, that means there's only..." Grant tried to put together the numbers, and the silence began to stretch. "C-carry the eleven...?"

<Seven hundred and *forty-four* hours, Grant!> Sarge barked into his mind. <If you're training all four of the methods simultaneously, that means you *could* have achieved two thousand, nine hundred and seventy-six hours of cultivation last month! That's nearly *three* Cultivation Achievement Levels, and you only earned *one*.>

"But what about sleep?" Grant begged the sword, but Sarge wasn't having any of it.

<I was clearly too easy on you, but with all the training devices I now have access to... that will no longer be an issue. You can sleep peacefully when you're dead, Grant. If you aren't working nearly every single *second*, that'll be in three hundred and thirty-four days. Tell me right now what you want: to take it

easy and keep complaining the month away while all of your opponents get stronger, or to get out there and become a true competitor for the position of Calendar King?>

"I was only making a joke..."

<Well, *stop*. The punchline to that joke is your *life*,> Sarge heartlessly demanded. <You have your work cut out for you, and you need to get moving. Today is February second, which means that after today... you only have six hundred and forty-eight hours to cultivate this month. If you somehow managed to make it happen, you could get two and a half levels from cultivating alone!>

Grant was quick to deny his claim. "Sarge, that's not *possible!*"

<Did I ask you if it was possible? No! I said it's time to go train! Go do what you did yesterday, and run on the track for the rest of the day. Now, make your choice! You wanna half-heartedly move, or do you wanna->

"Sarge." Grant clenched his fists and stopped to look skyward. "I... I want to be a true contender."

The sword seemed to consider something, finally giving Grant an order, <To help *facilitate* your training, my training simulations will be active all day long. You'll be under *constant* attack. To help you identify whether the situation is real or fake, any monsters created by me will be a bright orange. Wear your armor as you run, and make sure your sword is out at all times.>

Time remaining to begin training: 5... 4...

It was only at that moment that Grant realized he had been standing right next to the multi-mile running track. He got on it and started running—also making the countdown vanish, to his great relief. Grant pulled out his sword and maintained a balanced pose as he ran slowly, trying to ensure that he'd be able to maintain this pace for the... rest of the day? Grant slowed down, and the countdown restarted. "No slacking off at all? Not even to maintain?"

<You can maintain this pace the whole time you're moving.

I know your body better than you do.>

Feeling very put-upon, Grant looked off to the side as he ran up a hill, getting a great view of the road into the distance. Far off, he was *sure* he could make out a tiny pink dot zooming along the main road for a few seconds before it was too far away to be noticeable any longer. As he ran, a pair of smiling joggers bounced past. With a small burst of speed, he joined in alongside them. "Lovely day for a run, isn't it?"

"Perfect. The weather is warming up nicely, now that February is coming into ascendance." The woman who spoke took a sip from her bottle and wiped the green liquid from her lips. "Mmm! Can't get enough of this stuff. It works wonders. Stops me from hitting the wall."

"The wall…?" Grant looked along the path, unable to see any obstructions. By this point, he'd only jogged a few hundred yards, but his legs were already starting to feel the burn. "That drink sure is… something. Certainly not like anything I've ever come across. If you don't mind me asking, why would you hit a wall? Are you doing some kind of weapon cultivation?"

"Haha, you are so *funny*!" She gazed over at him, not finding a name tag or number. "'What wall', *indeed*! You're right; with appropriate training and pacing, we *should* never hit the wall. The reality is often much different, isn't it? I'm glad you joined us; I see you understand that when you are doing a long run, you should take a pace that allows you to hold a conversation. Great for training your lungs and breathing patterns."

Grant couldn't reply, as his body was forcing him to heave for air. The guy jogging along with the woman saw his predicament and chimed in to give the teen a chance to even his breathing. "You should try getting some Bed in you. Gets you in the *zone* and really aids recovery! Say… any chance you're planning on competing?"

Notice! Competing in an event will reduce the time needed for running each day by two hours! Winning *a competition will grant additional rewards.*

"Yes! Absolutely I will! Where do I sign up?" Grant jumped

on the opportunity to escape the monotony of his feet pounding on the pavement.

"You... *haven't* signed up?" The pair shared a confused look, and the lady winced as she let him know the facts. "Every event is usually booked up months in advance. Get down to the stand near the start line? I mean, I don't think you'll be able to get a spot, but you never know." The jogging man glanced at Grant, then his running partner, and jerked his head to the right, as if to signal something to her. "We'd better be off. We should... increase our pace. That was just a recovery mile, and we're doing interval training. Good luck; maybe we'll see you around!"

The cheerful couple waved and picked up the pace, having hung back to chat with him. As soon as they left, Grant stumbled to a standstill, his head spinning from the exertion of keeping pace with the joggers. "Why is this so hard?"

<Because you aren't used to it.> This time, since Sarge's voice held no anger, Grant listened closely as the sword started lecturing. <Your physical cultivation is *maxed out* for your cultivation stage, Grant. The fact of the matter is that you *should* be able to utterly *dominate* any of these people. That man was no older than twenty-two, and *not* a Wielder. He's only a Method Cultivator. If he had done physical cultivation, started five years ago, and used your cultivation manual for *twelve* hours a day, he'd be at Cultivation Achievement Level twenty-one, and have accrued five hundred and forty-seven points of physical characteristics.>

"That... is way more powerful than I am. Like... *so* much more powerful than me." Grant couldn't even fathom that kind of strength, except by thinking about the power Lord January wielded.

<Heh. Knew that'd scare you.> Sarge chuckled to gently put Grant's fears at ease, <If they're all using a publicly available cultivation method, and they can all understand it, that means it must be the *most* basic of basic methods. I'd estimate them getting... perhaps a *quarter* of the characteristics that you

achieve per level. That'd also mean that they gain a characteristic for every one hundred and sixty hours of physical cultivation. Someone might be at level twenty-one, but they'd be sitting at around one hundred and forty physical characteristic points at the top end.>

"Sarge, none of what you're saying is help… oh." Grant had a moment of inspiration just before Sarge gave him the answer. "The changes likely *started* five years ago, even if Lord February started shifting the mentality of the District. If they made this method available, how long did it take for everyone to get it? To learn it, and put it in practice? Until these foods and recovery drinks became commonplace, how many people could actually cultivate that method for a full half-day?"

<*Now* you're thinking. It's likely that this reached its peak within the last year or so. Keep running; that's enough of a break.>

"Okay…" He caught his breath and watched the joggers disappear into the distance. "I have to find that event they mentioned. They pointed at that side path; here's hoping they weren't trying to get rid of the competition—*ahh*!"

The newly-christened Lord January was taken to the ground by a massive, hairy spider. Its beady eyes stared death into his own, and its bright orange fangs ripped into his abdomen. Grant's blood splattered across the track… and then he found himself on his back, alone and unhurt, aside from a rapidly-healing bruise on his rear. "What by all the Sword Saints was *that*?"

<*That* was part of your training program. As it turns out, one of the great failings of Sword Expertise was that you could always discern reality and illusion. It let your mind wander, and you only needed to focus when the world around you went grey. Isn't this so much more *exciting*? Now you can *always* be in the true mindset that you could die at any moment!>

Ignoring the sadistic sword that he had no choice but to obey, Grant shakily got to his feet and followed the sound of excited chatter on the side path. As he followed the road to its natural end, the smell of freshly cut grass assaulted his nostrils: the telltale sign of the Bed drinks.

The sensory explosion led him to a packed area where Joggers quaffed their beverages. A runner wearing black gloves that rose to his elbows was there, proudly displaying a token that guaranteed him entry to the main tournament. Other runners fawned all over him, treating him like a highborn Noble holding court. Grant approached a clapping teenage girl, her hair dyed the same shade of pink as Lady February's. "Excuse me; what's the big deal? Why are people going crazy over him?"

"That's Windsprint Friday!" She turned to Grant, her clapping never once slowing down. "He's the first person in the last three years to come so close to beating Lady February in the thousand-meter dash!"

"That's…" Grant looked at the man, not recognizing him at all. "When did he race against her?"

"His event was a few days ago, and he's doing a District-wide motivational tour. It's incredible, isn't it?" The girl turned her eyes back to the lanky, near-skeletal man, and sighed adoringly. "He lost by only forty-one seconds!"

Grant shook his head in confusion. "Isn't that… a huge loss in a race?"

"You clearly don't understand." Her voice was firm as she replied; evidently, she was upset that Grant was getting in the way of her excitement. "It's an *awesome* achievement; he closed the gap by over a *minute* since he first started training. His accomplishment earned him the position of her Herald! No one else is trusted to deliver the most important news as quickly as he is. Not only that, but because of him, there's hope that someone will manage to beat Lady February someday!"

"Thank you for the information." He glanced at her nametag. "Sara? Can you point me in the direction of the information booth? I want to sign up for a preliminary event and… do I get a nametag and number there?"

"You're here to compete and better yourself? *Really?*" She squealed and clapped harder, jumping up and down in happiness. Eventually, she managed to point toward a banner near the mass of runners. "I wish you the best in your fitness journey!"

Grant pushed through the crowd, wearing a real smile for the first time today. After seeing what she was capable of, he didn't honestly believe that he could fairly defeat Lady February after only one month of training. Still, no one would ever have believed how far he had already come. He struggled to believe it himself, but here he was, in February and on his way to sign up for a *race*, of all things! "Hello! I'd like to-"

"*You* again?" The girl with the ponytail, who he kept bumping into, was manning the booth. "Don't do anything strange! I'll scream! I had *nightmares* last night after you waved that sword at me."

"That was a misunderstanding, I swear! I'm here… I want to take part in one of the preliminary events." Grant gave up on trying to explain himself and simply pushed right into the main point.

"You… *can't* be serious. Look, you're holding up the line." Grant turned around, but it was obvious that he was the only person waiting to be helped. Rubbing at his head, Grant decided to be as forthright as possible. He looked just above her head and read her name tag as it appeared, then met her eyes. "Look, Miko, right? I just want to race, and… better myself? Isn't this just you turning me away because you think I can't win? Does it *matter* to you if I lose? Won't I come out on the other side as a healthier person?"

His words shook her confidence, and Miko's expression softened. "You… okay. Who am I to impede your journey, even if you started out as a creep? Let me check the roster." Ignoring his wince, she thumbed through a sheaf of paper containing hundreds of names, numbers, and race details. "Sorry, doesn't look like there are any openings for standard race packages."

"Look for a non-standard one?" Grant shrugged helplessly, not really knowing how to handle this situation. "Sword Saints, I can't believe I'm standing here arguing to get *into* a race."

"Okay, I think I've got one…" She stated after flicking through the pages. "There is *one* spot. Comes with a deluxe race package. That'll be two Days; you want it?"

Grant thought about it, but he had really been hoping for a method of reducing his training *today*. "Is there anything… sooner? I don't want to wait two whole days."

"What? Oh. I see the confusion. No, the preliminary race is tomorrow at seven in the evening. The top two positions from every heat go through to the main tourney. The entry *price* for that slot," she laughed as she finally got to take a minor revenge for him chasing her with a sword, "is two Day *coins*."

"I… see." The color had drained from Grant's face. "The prize for winning is entry to the main tournament? Anything else…? Maybe a cash prize?"

"You look like you've seen a ghost." Miko's smile started to vanish as Grant's eyes seemed to deaden. "No cash prize for the preliminary, but the deluxe race package entitles you to unlimited Beds on the day of the event, spring water, and snacks. You just have to display the coupon to one of the food vendors."

<Time for training! You had your chance to get into events, but you failed to make it happen. Get back on the track and prepare yourself for all *sorts* of ambushes!> Grant almost jumped out of his skin at Sarge's interruption. Usually, he waited until Grant was alone, or at least in dire circumstances. <I'm so *excited* by the possibilities! I don't know why it never occurred to me that if you are constantly on guard, that will count as mental cultivation. Having complete situational awareness is absolutely ideal for a Swordsman; today will be *fun!*>

Grant made his excuses, much to Miko's self-satisfaction, since he didn't book the spot, and started hustling over to the long-distance running track as soon as a timer appeared in his vision. It was frustrating that he was controlled by his sword, and not the other way around, but he had to admit that it was only Sarge's training that had kept him alive to this point. "Can we avoid the spiders tearing into my intestines this time?"

<Nonsense. How do you ever expect to become a master

Swordsman if you don't train as if the battle is real?> The sword laughed at him, a metallic tinge in the sound making Grant shiver. <Besides, when you are experiencing pain, that will increase your armor cultivation efficiency far more than just *wearing* your armor!>

"Are you telling me that you're *intentionally* going to be causing me pain?" Grant idly considered simply throwing the sword away, as he had at least once a day since he had first picked it up.

<Only until you can stop every monster that comes at you head-on, in an ambush, sneak attacks, assassinations...> Grant didn't say a word as Sarge rambled on, listing all of the possible ways he could be attacked. He simply got on the track, pulled out his sword, and started running. Over the course of the day, as monsters seemingly spawned out of nowhere and tore into him, Grant continued mumbling a phrase that slowly became a mantra.

"Three hundred and thirty-four days, then cake for a month! Three hundred and thirty-four days...!"

CHAPTER FIVE

Three hours into his 'run', Grant was sweating freely. Heavy breathing was matched by a steadily increasing pulse. He could feel the pounding of blood as it pumped through his veins. This was *not* a fun experience, but he couldn't give up yet; not while he still had energy. He wanted to, but being browbeaten by his sword—and killed over and again—was a wonderful motivator.

He lifted his feet higher with every step to stop them from dragging along the dirt road. The flat section was an order of magnitude more challenging than the occasional downhill section. Grant's lungs and legs were burning when he came across a bridge that crossed a wide, lethargic river. The cool water sparkled in the light, and fish flopped on the surface. He wanted nothing more than to jump off the bridge and into the water... until he saw movement under the surface.

Knowing Sarge was up to something, he *sprinted* across the bridge, making it to the far side just as orange tentacles launched up and smashed the bridge to bits behind him. Grant was struck with flying splinters and logs, and it felt like one of his ribs had broken. <Aww. Was I really that transparent?>

Looking back, Grant half-expected to see a mess of shattered wood, but the bridge was in perfect condition. No tentacles in sight, either. "I *really* don't like that you can do that now."

<Too bad that you can't stop me, isn't it?> The instant rebuttal gave Grant pause, and then he started to laugh.

"Yeah... yeah, it is," he agreed ruefully—just before he screamed. He looked down to find a fuzzy orange snake pumping venom into his ankle just before his vision went dark. A few moments later, he was blinking sand out of his eyes and working to get to his feet. "It *really* is. Snakes? Seriously?"

<Not every threat to your life is the size of a carriage, Grant.> The deadly seriousness in Sarge's mental voice forced Grant to accept what he was saying. <I wasn't joking when I said you need to have constant and *perfect* awareness of your surroundings.>

After the bridge, he had two choices: continue along the main road, or take the path alongside the river. Knowing that there would be far more tentacles than he wanted to deal with if he stayed near the river, he chose the main road. Now that he knew that there would be tiny things attacking him alongside the normal stuff, Grant's eyes were constantly roving. He spotted several ambushes, sunbathing critters, and bright orange bandits. Too often, he failed miserably and ended up 'dying'; the main perpetrators of this were giant spiders that somehow just *appeared* without warning.

"Is this really *fair*, Sarge?" the young cultivator finally exploded, his resentment hitting the boiling point. "Where are they coming from?"

<Trap spiders,> Sarge curtly explained. <They're too real of a thing. They live underground and spring out of holes at high speed to take down their prey.>

"These things really exist?" Grant's blood went cold. He hadn't 'survived' a single time against the spiders. If this situation was *real*... "How do I fight against them? I can't *really* always be holding out my sword, not if I'm ever going to be around people."

<That's a good point. Okay... training opportunity! Put me

away; we're going to be practicing 'Iaijutsu', a combative quick-draw sword technique that is unique to swords like February Twenty Nine.> Sarge slowly started walking Grant through the steps of the technique, and Grant found that he was *very* talented at doing it incorrectly. They trained with it as he ran, during breaks, and when he could barely breathe. Sarge didn't allow him to stop until he had actually managed to perform it… functionally.

As soon as Grant had the movement somewhat practiced, *all* the attacks on him became sneak attacks. If he couldn't kill the monsters that jumped at him nearly instantly, he 'died'. Needless to say, within the next hour he had stopped bothering to even clean the dirt from the road off his face after he 'came back to life'.

Grant's lungs and legs were on fire. He half-ran, half-stumbled forward, his poor running form replaced by a desperate need to struggle onwards. Despite his heart beating its way through his chest, he wanted to learn and improve. He wanted to be the best, and he wanted to *prove* it to everyone. His run was cut short as he caught his foot on a rock and tumbled head over heels, coming to a spread-eagled stop on the dusty earthen road.

"I… can't do any… more." He sucked in deep breaths and choked on the dust. "I also think I'm now terrified of spiders. I can't fight any more right now."

<No… I don't think you can. Nutrition, rest, and mental strength are almost as important as your level of physical cultivation.> Sarge's voice turned consoling and cheerful. <Good work for now; let's take a long physical break.>

"More rest sounds good," Grant agreed wearily.

<Since you can't do more *physically*, let's keep your mind warmed up! Let's discuss nutrition and mental strength. Planning, managing time, and being disciplined is your priority. You're going to have to make sacrifices if you want to perform optimally. I know it doesn't seem like it, but training isn't about *not* enjoying your life, but about setting boundaries and

balancing the amount of time spent improving and recovering.>

<These elements, along with an appropriate training plan, should be able to rapidly improve your physique to match your cultivation.> Sarge patiently let him digest that information. <As you reach higher cultivations, these become less of an issue. When you can heal any damage done to yourself in mere instants, like Lord January could, you can get away with a lot. Back to the main point: let's start easy. Plan: what did you have for breakfast?>

Grant lifted his sword and looked at it. "Sarge, you know everything I do. I had a bar and mineral water."

<Yes. Listen, this is going to sound counter-intuitive, but you'll need way more food than that.>

"What!" The sword couldn't get another word across as Grant grunted, "Food here is *ludicrously* expensive! Besides, won't that slow down how I'd 'match my physique to my cultivation'?"

<Not if you follow the training plan that I craft for you. Right; back to learning. Let's start discussing major muscle groups! *Ohhh…!*>

Grant cast his eyes down at his toes as Sarge sang about triceps and ligaments for the next five minutes or so. His poor feet ached from the punishing effort he'd been putting them through, and he wasn't sure how much more they could take. Sarge let out a roar of laughter as he pieced together what Grant was likely thinking. <Don't worry; training like we did today is almost *all* that you'll be doing this month! It's gonna hurt a *lot*! Remember, even the most flawed lump of steel can be smelted over and *over* again… until it can be molded into an efficient weapon. That's enough resting; I think I hear *rattlesnakes!*>

As it turned out, Grant had collapsed almost exactly at the halfway point of the track, which meant he got to run the same amount of distance to get back to Hajimeni. He 'died' fewer times, but that was only due to Sarge sending fewer monsters at him because of his inability to function properly. "Can't... I *won't* give up. It's only February second; I have plenty of time to train. Just gotta... put my trust in Sarge. He's gotta know what he's doing. I'll be... the first new Sword Grandmaster in a thousand years!"

The path back up the road to Hajimeni was certainly more challenging than the way down. He hadn't realized exactly how far downhill the road had taken him until he needed to get back *up*. Grant kept moving. He kept battling and dying, but he kept *moving*. The world around him was hazy, and his brain was telling him that he was slowly dying of lack of oxygen, which was why he missed the first time he completed his sword technique perfectly.

The bright orange spider had been pierced through the brain and his sword had been returned smoothly to its sheath, and still, Grant did not notice, simply working to continue putting one foot in front of the other. Sarge wanted to compliment him, but he knew that if he interrupted Grant's focus, it was likely that the young man would collapse for the remainder of the day.

He made it back to the place he had started the intense run, and in his muddled state, he almost continued along the track. Only a familiar voice caused him to stumble to a halt, and he searched around exhaustedly for the sound. Miko was bouncing over toward him and held out a thin binder. "Looks like you've been working hard, Grant! I'm really impressed; I hadn't expected you to actually be so committed. I was wrong to treat you poorly. Here, this is your race package. The number you've been assigned is 'two nine two'. The number will stay with you throughout the events, if you, um... show up."

Grant blinked at her, looked at the number, then back up at Miko. "Two nine two...? February Twenty Nine. It's... *ideal*. Thank you, Miko."

"I don't know if you know this, but you can get a Bed for free twice a day anywhere that sells them if you either wear your number like this, or show up after clearly exhausting yourself," Miko explained, reminding him of what the server had mentioned at the tavern the previous day. "I really think you should go get one, especially if you plan to be able to compete upon the morrow. You'll need to pay the fee before competing, so hand over two Days."

"You got it." He pulled out the requested Time and handed it over, then turned and started stumbling back to the center of town, deliriously excited to get the cut-grass drink into himself. For *free*, even! How had he forgotten that he got two for free each day? He'd even been hustled by a street food vendor!

"Good luck during the Tumbler tomorrow!" Miko called after him nervously, her eyes distant. "Still can't believe people want to be in those. I'll stick to *normal* races."

"Um, thanks?" As he walked off, he considered going back and asking her what she meant. If the race wasn't normal, then what was it? Why had she shuddered at the end? "I'll be fine… it's a three-mile race. I ran for *hours* today, and if I pace myself better, I'll at least finish. If I could do this…" He held up the race package as he daydreamed about winning. "I can do anything!"

CHAPTER SIX

As Grant hurried to find a Bed—the drinkable kind—he spotted and waved to the jogging couple that had directed him to the sign-up area earlier. He noticed with some disgruntlement that they still looked perfectly fresh as they started yet another loop around the village.

He passed through a narrow cobblestone street and heard horses, realizing that he was right next to the stable where he had spent the previous night. As he ambled by, the old man he barged past that morning was sitting near the edge of the road with his head in his hands. Grant considered moving on and taking in the sights of the town, but... he wanted to be the sort of person that others relied on, and the first step of that was showing that he was willing to be there for them.

"Hello, old uncle. You seem to be having troubles; can I help ease your mind?" Grant slowed as he approached the old man. In the light of day, the stables looked like an artillery spell had hit them. Far worse than he recalled from his night spent there. "Is everything... what happened here?"

"No... *nothing* is okay here. I... can't remember, but I must have knocked a couple of muck buckets over last night." Grant *immediately* remembered the buckets the man was referencing. He also remembered knocking them over as he looked for a place to sleep. The old man lamented, "Oh, what a mess. I try my best, I really do… but when you get as old as I have, *every-thing* becomes rather challenging. Can… I feel terrible asking you, but can you help? I don't have much to offer, but I can give you a bowl of vegetable broth and a protein bar? Hate those things, but practically nothing else to eat in this place anymore."

Quest gained: Do The Right Thing. Clean Up Your Mess (Common)
　Information: You made a mess of the stables when you kicked over buckets of horse manure! Will you do the right thing and clean up your mess? The rewards are minimal, but you will at least feel better about yourself.
　Reward: One bowl of vegetable soup and one protein bar.
　Accept / Decline

"I happily accept." Shame burned through Grant at the distress he had unknowingly caused to the old man when he'd kicked over the buckets. "I have nothing to do besides train, and I can't imagine how this *won't* put a strain on my muscles. Show me the way to the mop, and I'd be happy to clean this up."

"You'll… actually help instead of going off to train? I don't know what to say. Maybe there is still some good left in the world after all? My name is Takato. Grant Monday, is it?" The old man sat down with a thud and pointed to the mop and bucket after confirming Grant's name by reading what was floating over his head. "Fresh water is in the trough. Once you're done in here, give the carriages a quick rinse?"

"What?" Grant peered past Takato to where the muck-encrusted carriages were lined up. There must have been at least ten. "How did that…?"

Old Takato sighed and put his feet up on an upturned pail.

With his hands clasped behind his back, he instantly dozed off. "This counts as physical cultivation, right, Sarge?"

<I'll allow it.> Sarge's words cheered Grant up immensely, so the sword made sure to add a caveat. <We'll call this your breaktime.>

The sun was deep into the horizon by the time Grant had finished his grueling task. Takato continued snoring loudly until Grant moved closer, startling the old man awake. "Huh, wazzat? Oh! *Look* at this place! That wasn't too hard, was it, sonny?"

"Being honest, I'd rather not do it again." Grant's frank answer made the old man laugh.

"I like you, Grant." Takato leaned in to whisper, "How would you like to earn a bonus? If you clean my house to be as spotless as this, I'll throw in a *sack* of protein bars. You young-sters need all the protein you can get!"

"Clean your home?" Grant stared the man down. He was swaying on his feet, and his stomach was nibbling on his spine to see if it tasted as good as it looked.

"That's right." Old Takato nodded enthusiastically. "Char-acter-building work!"

"I'll pass."

Quest Complete: Do The Right Thing. Clean Up Your Mess (Common)

Information: You came through and cleaned up your mess. Good boy. Old Takato can rest easy now that the stables are cleaner than they've been in years!

Reward: One bowl of vegetable soup, and one protein bar.

"As you will; not an issue. Follow me, kiddo." Grant followed the hobbling old man out of the stables and into the house next door. "Take a seat."

Grant looked around and was glad he'd turned down the bonus offer. Rather than offend the elderly gentlemen, he made an effort not to inhale the odor as he cleared a seat covered in knickknacks.

"Sorry about the mess. Housework has been a bit challenging recently. Here we are! Your bar and soup." The bowl of soup wobbled alarmingly as Takato teetered towards Grant. "Enjoy! There's no bread to sop it up, unfortunately… not since Lady February came to power."

Grant took a tentative sip of the thin, steaming soup, finding it more than adequate. "Thank you; this is the first hot food I've had in a couple of days."

"Care for a story as you munch on that protein bar?" Takato watched Grant eat with a strange hint of nostalgia in his eyes. "I can tell that you're not from around here, and you match a rumor going around about someone that royally ticked off our fearless leader."

Nearly choking on his bar, Grant tried to get more information about that rumor, but could only nod as he coughed to clear his lungs. "You have the same look about you that my son did, years ago. The desire to do more, to be better. To be *enough*. Let me tell you something right now, young man. You probably have it hard. There's nowhere that'll take pity on you, nowhere you can walk where people will assign you intrinsic *value*. They don't know you, and they won't, unless someone else tells them about you. Even then, they'd just want something from you."

Takato watched Grant eat, a hint of joy in his eyes. "So let me be *very* clear: wherever you are in life, whatever you are doing… it is enough."

Grant's bar was nearly forgotten, a bite half-chewed as this old man directly sliced open old wounds that had festered in Grant's mind since he was a child. Old Takato trembled, bending the thin metal spoon as his hand clenched. "You remind me of my son… and he died alongside Lord February near six years back. They said he had achieved the *highest honor*."

"What happened here?" Grant finally managed to form the words after a long moment where both had been silent.

"Someone killed the Lord of the Month? That thought is just... so foreign to me."

"Oh... Lord February was a physical cultivation maniac. He didn't go down easy, let me tell you." Takato seemed oddly proud of the man that had presumably gotten his son killed. "Change is not an easy thing to create, certainly not sweeping changes that reform and forcibly alter the flow of power and money. Six years ago, there was a coup d'etat that left a quarter of the Nobility slain, and a solid half crippled cultivation-wise. When the dust settled almost a year after that, Lady February was sworn in. She vowed to finish her father's work, to bring the entire District to its highest heights."

"Is that why she trains so hard?" Grant dug for any information that would allow him to have an edge against his opponent. "Are there people still working against her?"

Takato didn't acknowledge the question. "Some say that she took the death of her father especially hard, and put it down to him not training enough. According to her, if he had *maximized* his cultivation time, he'd still be alive."

"Is there anything else you can tell me about her?" Grant pressed the old man, hoping for *something*.

"Not much... I *do* know that she's wildly powerful. Her physical cultivation is impressive, but I'm told that she's a Berserker Cultivator. Her weapon cultivation is what makes her so dangerous, and her physical cultivation lets her keep going nearly endlessly."

"Berserker? I don't-"

<Forgot your lesson from last time already? Don't worry, I can explain in more detail. Time to go, Grant.>

Sarge's interjection made the young man bite back his words, and he stood and nodded at the kind old man. "Thank you for the dinner and story. I'm sorry to leave, but I have to prepare for a race tomorrow."

"A runner! From looking at you, I'd never have guessed!" Grant's heart sank, and he was left blinking in shock as Takato finished his thought. "From your armor, I'd have guessed you were an adventurer! Listen here, lad. You need a place to sleep, you come right on back here. I've got a spare bed."

"R-really? Thank you for your kindness." Grant bowed deeply and left old Takato's residence with a smile and a spring in his step. It buoyed his spirits that the old man regarded him positively.

<Ready to do some *training*?> Sarge broke the silence, prompting Grant to roll his eyes.

"Sarge... I already trained today. The day is practically over."

<There are twenty-four hours in a day, and you only need four hours of sleep to survive right now. Those hours do *not* need to be consecutive.>

"You *can't* be serious." Since he hadn't been warned off food, and in fact had gotten encouragement for it, he went to the Tavern and got his free Bed. He drank it down and walked outside, finding that his legs were *burning*. The thought of sleeping right now made his legs twinge, and he felt that he needed to get some air. He walked out of the town along the springy track and decided to spend some time at the river.

"You know, tomorrow I'll be taking part in the 'Three Mile Tumbler'. I have no idea what I actually signed up for; is there any advice you could offer?"

<Don't take a tumble? Make sure to keep your stance steady.>

"I'm being serious here." Grant groaned as Sarge's attempt at levity failed.

<So am I, Grant. To tumble means to fall suddenly, clumsily, or headlong. It could also mean to perform acrobatic feats such as handsprings and somersaults in the air... but I doubt it in this case.> The sword thought for a moment, then slowly declared, <My advice? Take your time, examine the environment, and approach any obstacles appropriately. I expect that it won't be easy. No offense, but you aren't in the ideal physical condition to take part in a race.>

"I didn't expect it to be straightforward. If it were, there's no way there would have been an extra spot. I can't *believe* how much competition there is just to participate in extreme exercise around here." Grant finally stood beside the river and stared into the dark water.

A shiver ran through him. The night air in February had a bite to it, even if the days were mild and pleasant. The fact that he was a mess of sweat certainly didn't help to keep him warm, so he pulled the leather straps of his armor tight, blocking out errant gusts of wind.

Sarge brought out the bright orange monsters, and soon, Grant's exertion was protecting him from the worst of the chill seeping into his bones. He glanced up at the stars that were brightly visible in the sky, and softly stated his new mantra as his eyes dropped to scan the darkness around him for the tell-tale signs of things in the dark creeping toward him.

"Three hundred and thirty-three days, then a warm bed for a week!"

CHAPTER SEVEN

Thunder echoed across the landscape, startling Grant awake. He couldn't even remember when he had fallen asleep! His eyes popped open, and he found that he had rolled within a few inches of the river. Quickly yet carefully extracting himself from the weeds he was tangled in, he tried to understand what was happening. The sky was clear, so why was there thunder? "Wait! I know this! This is Lady February pounding the ground into submission! She's coming this way!"

He couldn't help feeling excited about the prospect of going up against her, but was a little nervous as to why she would be coming this way. His mind flashed to an option he had, something he had needed to fend off the entire previous day: an ambush.

It wasn't exactly an honorable way of defeating her... but the alternative was to participate in—and win—an extremely arduous tournament against all manner of people putting everything on the line to win. That was a risk he didn't want to take. "This... this might be the way to go."

The clatter of footsteps increased in intensity as Lady February passed underneath the welcome sign of the town and came into view. Grant's stomach churned, butterflies threatening to escape. She sprinted down the hill at breakneck speed. A relentless, unstoppable force.

"Any moment now…" Grant prepared himself. As soon as she stepped foot on the bridge, he would launch himself at her and force her to submit… or see if she could survive the same treatment he had given Lord January.

Then Lady February leaped into the air, somersaulting onto the upper guard-rail of the bridge. Grant couldn't believe his eyes; she had just used the natural environment to *enhance* the difficulty of her run? At the end of the bridge wall, she jumped into the air and laughed as she grabbed hold of a tree branch, using her momentum to carry her forward, and tumbled—in the artistic sense—through the air, landing lightly on her feet.

Grant stood there stunned, completely dumbfounded as his plan unraveled before his eyes. After smoothly landing, she continued on her way, not even breaking her stride as she sped towards the ravine in the distance.

<For what it's worth,> Sarge began with a light cough, <I thought it was a sound, logical plan. Pretty clever, actually, trying to save yourself a ton of time and effort. How were you to know that she'd be more monkey than human?>

"I just can't win. Should I have coated the walls with oil or something?" Grant despaired as he inspected the bridge. No matter how he scanned the area around him, it was clear where people should be *walking*! Running on guardrails? Swinging through trees? Who *did* that? Was she entirely wild?

He had no plans for the morning, beyond whatever Sarge was going to make him do, so he hurried over to the town and collected his free Bed in order to have a boost to his cultivation before the day got started. The sun had barely crested the horizon, meaning that he had at least twelve hours to prepare for the event he was signed up to participate in. "Oh! That's right! Unlimited snacks the entire day of the event!"

He had a bounce in his step as he entered the contestant tent and examined the selection of goods. Grant grabbed three of the berry-and-seed snack boxes, and an additional Bed before going to the counter. The cashier looked at the items, then Grant, and smiled warmly. "That'll be four Hours, sir."

"I have this!" Grant proudly presented his token.

"A deluxe coupon! Now I see why you'll need so many of these." The vendor smiled conspiratorially. "Good luck with your race today! You should grab some energy slimes. We've run out, but I heard some of the food stalls have some stock left?"

"Slimes…?" He shook his head and exited the health food shop, then stuffed the boxes into his pack. A group of joggers ran up, and Grant was struck by a magnificent idea. "*Unlimited* food on race day… hey, guys! I went and bought too much. I can't get a refund… would you be interested in taking these off my hands? Twenty-five percent discount. Whatcha say?"

"Oh *yeah*! Is that a Bed?"

"A box each for us, please!" The runners happily handed over forty-five Minutes each before moving on to consume their snacks. Outside, Grant cackled as he counted his stacks of coins.

"Three Hours, just like that! Maybe I should have been a Thursday; I'd make a great merchant." With nothing better to do, he decided to see if he could make some more money. The smile on the face of the street vendor, whom Grant had accidentally offended the day before, dropped away when he got to the front of the line and smiled brightly. "*You* again? Come to haggle over prices, call me names?"

"Not this time." Grant grinned and presented his race coupon. "I would like to stock up for the race."

"Why… *certainly!*" The food vendor was temporarily lost for words, shocked that Grant was doing a deluxe event. "I admit, I may have underestimated you. What would you like, sir?"

"I'll take those two remaining pink protein drinks, and…" Grant's eyes scanned the products, "five of those bars."

"*Five*! Are you sure? You only need one, *two* at most during an entire day."

Grant glowered and raised an eyebrow. "Five. I'm hungry and I need energy. Does this let me fill up my waterskin?"

"Absolutely it *does...*" the vendor hedged, deflating as Grant handed over the pouch. "You know that I still need to go and restock all my own goods, right?"

The young Lord of the Month ignored the snark and tapped his chin. "Do you have any of those energy slimes? I was told there was some stock left at the food stands, but I don't know what they are."

"We have them; there is also a limit of one per person per day. This is a special formula, imported directly from January. Purified honey; super sweet. One hit of this concentrated liquid during a race fully replenishes stamina with ease."

Grant chuckled to himself as he departed the stand. Around the corner, out of sight of the food vendor, it took no more than five minutes to offload his latest stash. It would take a bit of work, but he was determined to replenish his funds. For the next hour, he did rounds of the square and side streets, offloading bars, pink protein drinks, and recovery drinks to dozens of delighted runners.

He stared at his open money pouch, now filled with over seven Days of coins. He decided to do just *one* more loop of the town, stopping off at the various stands; then he'd be done. "I'll take ten more bars, please, and, oh, one recovery drink!"

The food vendor with the bum leg smiled too widely back at him. "They *are* tasty! Just can't get enough of them? Sorry to say, I don't have ten bars left to give you."

"No worries." Grant waved his token in the man's face. "I'll take whatever you've got!."

"Before that, I think *they* want to talk to you...!" The vendor pointed behind Grant just as a shadow engulfed him.

He spun around on the spot, shivering as he found three House Tuesday Peacekeepers surrounding him. "Pardon the intrusion in your routine, but there have been reports of an unlicensed food vendor selling goods."

"Doesn't my deluxe race package entitle me to unlimited

snacks and drinks during the day of a race?" Grant wasn't offering a challenge to the men; he was legitimately confused.

"For *personal* consumption, and only for what you eat during the same day. Any excess is strictly prohibited. It is clearly explained in your packet." The Peacekeeper pointed at the folder that was jutting out of Grant's pack.

Grant pulled out the paper and blankly stared at the tiny text, trying to figure out what the man was talking about. His face burned crimson as he tried to sound out the intricate text. "Part... participants are re... *required*! Participants are required to arrive at least ten minutes... pree-or... prior? Prior to... com... competition start time?"

The Peacekeepers winced as Grant kept going, realizing that the young man could barely read. They evidently decided to be lenient and let go of the weapons they had been reaching for. "Ah. I understand that you may not have been aware of the rules. We can take you to the guardhouse to properly educate you while you work off the fine you've incurred, or you can voluntarily reimburse the various vendors."

Grant let out a moan and stifled a cry as he opened his money pouch, full of low-value coins. He tipped half the coins into the Peacekeeper's cupped hands, and the man scoffed. "*All* of that. We've made a tally."

The young man tipped out the remaining small coins with a long-suffering sigh. The Peacekeeper shook his head. "What about those, the big Day coins?"

"Those are mine! Look!" He flashed the coins in front of the guard's eyes. "See? The coins are from January."

"Yes; by adding those, you should have fully paid your bad debt. It isn't *my* fault you gave the foodstuff out at a fraction of its value." Grant almost broke down at the heartless demand. He handed over the remainder of his coins, and the Peace-keeper nodded severely. "The matter is settled. Don't come to our attention *again*, Grant Monday."

"Understood." The guards left Grant to his misery, slumped against the wall, penniless once more. Then his eyes popped back open and he sighed in relief when he remembered the several Weeks of Time stored in his main pack.

<You're full of mad schemes, Grant.> Sarge chuckled at the youngster's misfortune. <It would have worked, but you got greedy. That, and the fact that they likely easily identified the 'husky' boy wandering around town, hawking healthy food on the cheap. Either don't be so greedy, or blend in with the locals. This would be a good start to a disguise course, but I don't think you're ready for that yet.>

There was one positive outcome: as Grant walked through the town, he passed many runners merrily munching on cut-price bars and swigging drinks. They gave him the thumbs up as he passed and called out in greeting to him. This brightened his mood considerably. "If nothing else… it seems like I made some friends!"

CHAPTER EIGHT

Bang!

The race was on, and he was off. Grant jostled up against nineteen other competitors as The Three Mile Tumbler commenced. Out of the square, through narrow cobbled streets, and under the 'Welcome to Hajimeni' sign. Even at this early stage, Grant was starting to fall behind the spritely lead runners in their skimpy shorts and tops. His leather armor, although flexible, still weighed him down slightly and restricted his movement.

Even so, this was the first time he was truly competing against other cultivators in a purely physical way that didn't potentially involve death. He was *astounded* to find that Sarge had been correct; even with his extra weight, his physical cultivation easily matched—if not surpassed—a slew of the other competitors. With a grunt of effort, he picked up the pace, firmly cementing his position in the middle of the pack as they started down the slope against the wind.

Here, Grant had a distinct advantage. For once, his bulk proved a boon, rocketing him to the front of the pack and propelling him down the hill. He had to furiously spin his legs to remain upright as his lead extended. The others started to regain ground as he crossed the bridge, and he followed the markers to the right, jogging along the riverbank path. If it wasn't for the fact that he was participating in a race, he might have even enjoyed himself. "Maybe running *isn't* so bad?"

Despite his confidence, his energy reserves were rapidly depleting, and his form was deteriorating. This was a three-mile race, and by his estimation, he only had to keep the pack at bay for another two miles. "Easier thought than done."

Then something *unexpected* happened. The markings veered off the path and into the water, where a series of obstacles provided a new path. Race officials lined the path, clearly there to make sure no one 'accidentally' continued along the main path.

Grant leaped into the air and onto an upturned barrel. It wobbled as he landed but didn't tip over. A series of barrels were placed several yards apart, so he leaped between the various platforms as quickly as he could. For the first time, he was truly glad that Sarge's training had forced him into situations where he'd had to contend with unsteady footing and strange paths.

This wasn't the time to reminisce. The pack of runners had caught up, and a few had even darted past. His muscles screamed at the punishment of playing leapfrog after sprinting a mile. He propelled his mass into the air, and was back on firm soil.

Shortly thereafter, it got worse. The markings once again veered into the path of the water, but unlike last time, the barrels had been rolled onto their sides, providing a challenging moving platform. As he puffed away, arms and legs pumping furiously, he watched the leading group jump and skip over the barrels. They made it look easy as they bounced across the watery assault course, but the person on their heels landed on a rolling barrel that the leader had been on and tumbled directly into the river, since the barrel had been unexpectedly soaked.

"Ah. I see: the 'Tumbler'." It was Grant's turn. He leaped

into the air, and his foot connected with the barrel. As he went to push off to the next barrel, his platform spun. His heart leapt into his chest as the spinning barrel churned the water below. Grinning competitors bounced past as he spun his wheels atop the barrel.

Then he was sinking into the river.

Water rushed to meet him as he entered the frigid flow. He coughed as it shot up his nostrils, and he unintentionally inhaled the liquid. He clawed frantically at the water, terrified of drowning… until he realized the water only reached his knees.

Dripping wet, he went back to the riverbank to try again. After two more dunks, he managed to figure out how the challenge worked. As he landed on the barrels, he immediately jumped and didn't push back against the barrels, forcing them to spin.

The runners were long gone, as were his hopes, but he was determined to at least finish. Back on firm soil, at little more than a snail's pace, he followed the marking which led him across a rope bridge. Traversing the rope bridge was harder than it looked, but it didn't pose much of a challenge compared with the barrels. His vision wavered and his legs were jelly as he stumbled across the final challenge, a cargo net, with the finish line tantalizingly close. He could vaguely make out the sound of cheering, but it was almost drowned out by the blood thundering in his ears.

He clung onto the cargo net for dear life and pulled with every last shred of energy. His foot sank as he attempted to push off and up. No matter what he tried, he only managed to climb three of the rungs in the flexible ladder. Then his body shut down and refused to continue any further. His grip slipped from the heavy rope, and he found himself upside down, legs twisted and pinned within the net. The way the event had progressed, he almost expected a monstrous spider to show up and claim its prize.

What made matters worse was that he'd actually paid two Days to be subjected to this torture, and he was no further forward in his quest to enter the main tournament. He couldn't even sob as he hung there, every movement tightening the ropes around his legs and cutting off blood flow.

The other runners had cheered for Grant as he was extracted from the cargo net by race officials. They commended him for his courage and the determination he'd shown in his attempt to finish the course. "You're amazing!"

"Remember, when you see how far you have to go, make sure you look back at how far you've come!"

A short while later, Grant reentered the town of Hajimeni with no goal or plan in mind. He went to the tavern and collected his last free Bed, chugging it down as someone opened the door and caused a paper to rustle. He turned, not recalling the papers, and walked over to take a closer look.

Fight Night—Tonight in the square. Be there, ya circles!

Ticket Price (1 Day). Free to any competitors upon presentation of a valid race coupon.

"They actually *fight*? Not just trying to speed around and bounce off walls? This I gotta see." Some brutal fighting was exactly what he needed right now. The sun had already set as he followed the flow of the crowd towards the square. He didn't have to waste time trying to purchase a ticket with his non-existent Time, waving his coupon instead.

Late as he was, there weren't many seats remaining. Someone waved and caught his attention. It was Miko, the girl with the ponytail. He plopped down in the seat beside her. "Hey, Miko. Is this seat taken?"

"It is now! I need to know, how was your race? Someone told me that you did *amazingly*!" Miko was practically *bursting* with curiosity.

Grant was confused, but the Bed had really fixed him up, so he was smiling and ready to accept whatever silver lining she was presenting. "What? No, I didn't even come close to winning."

"Don't *worry* about it. The majority of these events require a *lot* of practice. The Tumbler is tricky. I prefer the standard running races, although I still lack the stamina to win a long race or the speed to win a short one. Oh, did you hear the news?" Miko clapped her hands together and waited impatiently for an answer.

"No?" Grant waved at his clothes, which still had river muck drying on them.

"*Apparently*, Lady February is *furious*. Someone *sat* at the feet of her father yesterday and directly taunted her while she was running." Miko's eyes were shining; she was positively bursting to share the gossip. "They're pretty sure he defaced the statue as well!"

Grant swallowed the lump that grew in his throat. His eyes darted around, on the lookout for House Tuesday Peacekeepers. "What do you mean, defaced the statue?"

"It was *literally* defaced. Lord February's bronze nose was cut off and it was found lying by the base of the statue! Oh, look. The fight is about to begin. My money is on Six-Pack Sally." Just like that, Miko practically forgot what they had been discussing. Grant didn't have it as easy, thinking that people were going to be hunting him for something he actually *didn't* do for once.

"Look. House Tuesday is here!" Miko's shout almost made Grant re-moisten his river-soaked pants, but his eyes tracked her pointed finger to the competitor lifting a leg over the rope.

"Oh! Competing!" Grant let out a sigh of relief. He assumed that the Peacekeepers had arrived to take him in for questioning. "Where are their weapons?"

"There are no weapons allowed. It's hand-to-hand combat only, a true test of strength and skill." Miko explained as the fighters' bodies slammed together in a sickening collision of solid muscle. The contestants rained blows down on each other without sophistication. There was no dodging or feinting; the attacks were direct, not subtle in the least. Muscle slammed against muscle. Fists and feet wore each other down, something *certainly* different, and unlike any fighting Grant had experienced before.

"How... entertaining." Grant scoffed as he watched the brutish display. Six-Pack Sally ended the bout, swiping Philip Tuesday's tree-trunk leg out from under him. He slammed down to the mat, giving her the chance to get a headlock in place. Within moments, he pounded his hand on the mat, conceding the match. "Hey, Miko. Do you know when the next preliminary will be? I gotta get through to the main tourney."

The fighters left the arena, and Miko turned her full attention to Grant. "Let me think... There is another 'easy' race like the one today at the next town over, Nandayo."

"What is it?" Grant furrowed his brow at the unfamiliar word.

"Exactly." Miko nodded, adding to Grant's confusion. "That race is at the same time, seven in the evening. It won't be easy to find a ticket at this late in the day, but if you're lucky, you'll find a deluxe race package. There is also a harder tournament, the mid-February one. It takes place near Valentine. Listen, only the top ten percent of competitors taking part in standard events get through to the main tourney. I'm not sure how many go through from the Valentine one. The difference between them is that the standard event has a maximum competitor cap, and the deluxe event isn't limited. *Hundreds* will take part. I think the top ten percent of that whole group go through."

Grant bobbed his head slowly, already knowing what he would likely have to do. Miko recognized the determination in his eyes and offered one last word of advice. "Listen... you seem like a nice guy, even if you are a bit of an airhead. Be *careful*. Lady February is *intense*, and she expects all the competitors to be just as intense as she is. That means the rules change every time to keep competitors on their toes."

"If you aren't ready for that, the strain might kill you."

CHAPTER NINE

Grant absentmindedly watched two more rounds of fighting. Sweaty slabs of muscles clashed, straining to dominate each other as they wrestled on the mat. Grant's troubled mind was elsewhere; his thoughts struggled with what he should do next just as hard as the random fighters were struggling with each other.

It almost seemed that every decision he'd made in February so far appeared to be the wrong one. The ambush of Lady February had gone spectacularly wrong, the 'easy' Three Mile Tumbler had just proved how unfit he was, and attempting to make a profit from his struggles had almost gotten him tossed in prison.

Perhaps it would be best to stick with what he knew? Perhaps he should funnel his time into increasing his prowess with February Twenty Nine? He was a Novice in Kenjutsu, but he was certain that Sarge would be *more* than willing to help him boost his ability. In fact... focusing on improving himself was almost *certainly* the answer for all the issues that he'd been running into. Grant gravely closed his eyes and firmed his resolve. "Miko, I'm going to head off now."

"No problem." She seemed almost sad as she watched him get up. "I'll be here if you change your mind. Remember not to swing your sword at people; that makes them have misunderstandings!"

"I'm just glad we can laugh about it now. Bye, Miko." Grant squeezed past spectators and left the buzz of the square and the cheering crowd behind. With no plan in mind, he wandered the streets toward the stables, his only companion being a troubled mind. Before he had left yesterday, Takato had invited him to stay there as an extra thanks for his work in the stables, and he decided that he was going to take the man up on it.

The house smelled as unappetizing as before, but he couldn't judge the old man, left to get by on his own since his son's passing. He crept up the creaky stairs, the aroma of freshly brewed tea leading him to a bedroom. "This man is truly too kind."

Unlike the rest of the house, the bedroom was in *immaculate* condition. A pot of tea, saucer, and teacup sat on the dresser; clearly prepared well in advance of his actual arrival. He felt strangely comfortable as he poured a steaming cup and sat on the fluffy mattress. The warm tea soothed his aching muscles as he lay down, sinking into the cocoon. One thing was certain… this was going to end up being the best place he had slept in *days*, and he was going to enjoy it as much as possible.

Still, his thoughts on the future refused to allow him to drift off. Eventually, he gave in and started making a plan. "Sarge, are you there? I'm hoping for advice."

<I'm always here to offer you advice now! I can even give you a few warnings in combat if you've done enough training to impress me!>

"Oh? That's good to hear." The fact that he may have new combat utility certainly brightened Grant's prospects. "There is an 'easy' preliminary tournament tomorrow I can enter, and there is a 'hard' tournament in mid-February."

There was a beat of silence as Sarge waited for more information. <What's the question?>

"Entry to the 'easy' tournament will likely cost at least two Days if there are only deluxe race packages remaining." Grant waved at his clothing and empty pouch. "I officially have zero coins. The other option is to train hard and take part in the mid-February tournament."

<It may seem difficult at first, but *everything* is difficult when you are first starting.> February Twenty Nine glinted a golden-red as a hint of bloodlust slipped out and made Grant's heart race. <Follow my training plan, increase your skills and fitness, and then participate in the harder tournament when you're ready.>

"I suppose you're right. The problem is... if I lose? That means there are no other chances to get into the main event. I'll miss out entirely. If I can somehow get in on the easy one, I can at least have two chances of winning." Grant's thoughts started drifting toward that fact. "Sarge, I could lose everything. This might be my only chance at getting a shot at Lady February. I guess-"

<So *what* if you lose, Grant? Don't *guess*. That's what training is *for*. It takes all the guesswork out of doing things correctly. When you are properly prepared, you *know* you will win. If you don't *know*, you'll treat the fight differently than you should.>

Having no choice but to agree, Grant nodded and tried to think his way out of the situation. "You're... right. I'll train hard. But I need *more*. I need an advantage. I'm an outsider that isn't used to any of this culture-"

Sarge cut him off harshly, <Stop there and *think*. What sets you apart from the other competitors?>

"I'm from January...?" That wasn't the answer Sarge was looking for, and it was demonstrated by a small orange rock appearing on the nightstand and *screaming* until Grant stumbled out of bed and stabbed it. He looked at the sword that had practically leapt into his hand. "Oh... I have February Twenty Nine. That rock wasn't a *real* monster, right? Wait. Is that what you're getting at? February Twenty Nine can steal power from a

Wielded Weapon? The ability slot for February is empty... I see. What else, what else...? I have an elemental spell slot, but I have no idea how I could get a spell."

<I like this so far! Challenge Wielders to a fight, get them to admit defeat, steal their power, and make it mine! Ah... *ours*, that is!>

Grant's eyes flashed as he realized that he could only take a single ability per monthly series. "Maybe that's how I can get a spell as well? Return their power if they give me a spell in return?"

<That's what I was thinking. The elemental spell... *that* will be our advantage.> February Twenty Nine shone as Sarge laughed in preemptive victory. <You've already unlocked three of the four abilities this sword has to offer, and you've taken a training program that will bring you all the way to the Grand-master ranks. Getting *another* ability, and a spell?>

<They'll never see it coming.>

Both of them cackled together and started working on their own plans for growing in power. Even so, Grant's thoughts remained tumultuous and refused to slow. "Sarge... can you tell me more about cultivators? How do I get more spell slots? What are the different types of cultivators? You mentioned something about Berserkers, and then called me a 'Foundation' cultivator... can you tell me more about that?"

<Are you *actually* asking me to tell you a bedtime story?> Sarge's voice was strained as he tried to determine how to react. <Should I be pleased that you want to learn, or insulted that you're likely to fall asleep halfway through the explanations?>

"Um... pleased?"

<Cultivation's main purpose is to go against heaven's will and create a body and mind that will withstand the true test of heaven and earth: *Time*.> Grant let out a sigh of relief when Sarge didn't ask any more uncomfortable questions before diving into his lecture. The nineteen-solar-year-old settled in and listened. <As I have told you, a Foundation cultivator is the most difficult task, the rarest, and the slowest. Reaching the

summit, becoming a Dao cultivator, is almost only achieved by old monsters. Their bodies are withered, their beards are grey. In this, we have an advantage that most others do not. You can hunt other Wielders and potentially even achieve what is essentially immortality at a young age.>

<The problem with most types of cultivation is that when you are unbalanced for decades, centuries, millennia... the instability takes over. As an example, take the previous Lord January.> Sarge's tone softened here, and Grant's eyes cracked open to stare deeply into the unsheathed blade that was next to his bed. <He is certainly *not* a method cultivator that only took the path of the physical. He was once heralded as the brightest of his generation, a title not easily gained. We know that the ability of his Wielded Weapon allowed him to cultivate weapon methods easily. This means that he is almost *assuredly* a Trinity cultivator, a person that cultivates at least three methods without conflict.>

"There's a term for that, right? Like the Berserker?" Grant knew that investing into this conversation would bring great returns. Anything that allowed him to have an edge on the competition in the future would be beneficial.

<Correct. A Berserker is someone that cultivates Weapon and Physical methods, and is likely the path that has been taken by Lady February. If I had to guess, the previous Lord January was a 'Monk' Cultivator; a person who cultivates Physical, Weapon, and Mental to enhance close-range combat with powerful spells, buffs, or debuffs.> Grant could imagine Sarge shaking his metaphorical head, the disapproval in his voice was so thick. <However, when the barriers went up and cut him off from those that could compete against him, he began practicing a deviant physical cultivation method. The problem with deviant cultivation is that the method becomes your personality, and it shifts who you are on a fundamental level.>

"So he had access to lots of spells?" Grant was disappointed that he did not think to raid the castle before fleeing the district.

<It wouldn't have mattered.> Sarge stopped that line of

thinking right away. <When the barriers went up, spell slots became regulated, and it became impossible to cast spells of a certain type in the lower districts. In January and February, it is only possible to cast Elemental spells. Using artifacts is a different story, as shown by Auld Leap, which is how House Thursday and Wednesday remained so important to the world. We will discuss higher spell slots at a later date, when you gain access to them, but the essence is: every 'odd' District, you will get an additional spell slot.>

"Then... when I get into March, I'll have access to two slots?" Grant scratched at his hair, suddenly worried that he had gotten fleas from the horses.

<Correct. Elemental, Utility, Debuffing, Buffing, Mental, and finally, Spatial spells. Now, just because you have a slot does *not* mean you can *cast* the spell. They all have a minimum mental cultivation requirement and other prerequisites, similar to skills.> Sarge knew that Grant was about to ask an easy question, so he cut the young cultivator off with, <No, you *can't* get bonus slots for any reason. Yes, you *can* fill a slot with a lower-tier spell. In other words, in District March, you could cast an icicle and also make the earth move as you willed it, but you would need to give up the ability to... purify water, for instance. Not much combat utility in clean water, but it still might save your life in an area where everything's poisoned.>

"Seems like a giant game of chance?" The young man's eyes were barely remaining open. "Just hope you bet on the right spell?"

<Just be prepared for *anything*, and you'll be fine, Grant.>

"Totally reasonable requirement, Sarge." Grant yawned at the sword and snuggled into the fluffy bed. "Last... last thing. How many classifications are there for cultivator types?"

<That's an easy one. Every single combination makes a new class. Four 'method' cultivators. Six 'Duo' cultivator classes. Four 'Trinity'. One 'Foundation', that *might* someday reach the pinnacle and become a 'Dao' practitioner. A maximum of

sixteen cultivator types. Now, there are pros and cons to each…
oh. You're asleep, you brat! How dare you ignore the words that
I, the great February Twenty Nine, have to say!>

Grant declined to answer, a slight smug smile the only hint
that Sarge's words may have reached him in his slumber.

CHAPTER TEN

Morning came quickly, and Grant awoke early with his new plans front and center in his mind. He left the house and quietly shut the door, not wanting to impact Takato's sleep. The man had already been kinder than Grant could ever expect, and he needed to leave before he was asked to help again; he wouldn't have the heart to say no to the old man a second time.

The smattering of Hajimeni's houses against the backdrop of paddy fields and the shimmering District barrier was soon a smudge in the distance. Grant took one last look over his shoulder, a strange feeling of loss impacting him as he realized that he needed to continue traveling across the world for the entire year. Any friends he made would be left behind; any impact he had on a region might never be seen. Shaking himself out of his melancholy, he took a moment to center himself. His destination was Valentine, as was the chance to better himself further.

His trek slowly brought him deeper within the District and across the verdant grasslands. Though he was keeping a lookout for monsters, so far, all he had seen skittering through the long grass were a few rabbits. He'd run after one with the full intent to eat it, but it was quickly evident that they were more than agile enough to escape him. He glared at their flashing tails and remembered Lady February's incredible speed. "Too fast for *now*. Imma eat you someday soon."

There were exceptions. Namely, bright orange monsters that assailed him anywhere from every minute to five minutes, but never longer than that. Getting attacked *hurt*, and even though any false damage done was reverted after a few moments, it didn't stop fatigue from accumulating rapidly. Sarge swiftly noticed because Grant began accumulating injuries more rapidly, but the sword only gave the cold answer of, <The next time you break through a mental cultivation stage, this much will be nothing. Can't get there without doing this, so *focus!*>

A hawk circling high above caught his eye. It soared effortlessly, catching updrafts, completely at one with its environment. The hawk suddenly switched direction. Grant was fixated on the bird of prey as it drew its wing in and dropped like an arrow towards the ground. At the last moment, it lifted its wings to slow down, then flapped them wildly. Its outstretched claws snatched something from the grass before powering back up into the sky. From the look of it, it appeared to have caught one of the rabbits that had been eluding Grant thus far. This made him realize that the grass was probably teeming with life, and he just lacked the means to catch any of it.

"Good to know that was just a normal hawk..." he muttered grumpily as hunger started settling in more seriously. This led to a sudden flurry of aerial bombardments from bright orange birds, and he resolved to keep his observations about nature to himself from then on. "Sarge, is this training supposed to *help* me, or are you literally just trying to mess with me?"

Six fraught hours later, he began to see buildings on the horizon. "That must be Nandayo! I did it! Soon I'll be able to stop attacking random orange *stuff*!"

He was so pleased with himself that he actually found a hidden well of energy and started *jogging* toward the town. Sarge took that moment to show him that his cautious speedwalk had a reason behind it. Instead of monsters every few minutes,

Grant's loud run 'attracted attention', and soon he had a swarm of orange creepy-crawlies after him. Not wanting to 'die' due to his inattention, he hurried to finish them all off. From that point forward, he made sure to slay everything as soon as he first saw it. There was something about a cluster of spiders the size of hunting dogs chasing you that made you feel better about finding them one at a time.

"So... *close!*" A short while later, he drew close enough to make out *details* on the buildings. Their walls were coated in mud, bleached by the sun, and they were roofed in simple thatch. Normally, he would have expected to see farmworkers working the fields, but crops near the buildings withered in the sun, forgotten. The only visible activity was runners bounding along the dirt roads, kicking up clouds of dust.

Grant entered the outskirts of the town. There was no sign identifying it, so he made sure to ask the first person he saw, a man that was hammering colored race markers in the ground. "Excuse me. Is this Nandayo?"

"What is it." The man glanced up and did a double take before wiping off the sweat beading his brow. "Yes. Where else would it be?"

"Well, Bert," Grant checked the man's name with a quick upward glance, "I'm new around here, and I could've ended up anywhere."

"Nah... hard to get lost." Bert got back to work. "You're on a road. Pretty easy system we've got here. You stay on a road, you walk into a town. There's no forks in our roads. Makes people too hungry when they think about 'em. If you got on the road here, and stayed on it, no where else in the District you could be."

"Oh? That's an interesting way of doing things..." Grant mumbled as he continued walking.

"One village every ten miles, one city every fifty. District is two-thousand and seventy-five miles wide, and a perfect square." Bert rambled on as if he had once been a tour guide. "House Thursday laid out the road system and built up the towns. Crazy to think that they're… basically gone now. Huh. Anywho, the twentieth city you'd reach, a little over a thousand miles east of here, is smack-dab in the center of the District, also the District capital city. Where ya headed?"

"Valentine." Grant's skin started to crawl as he had a terrible thought… Bert confirmed it before he could even ask, and Grant nearly sagged into himself.

"Ah, that makes sense. Lots of people headed to the capital for the big tournament. Well, best of luck with that." Bert kept hammering, and Grant started walking.

"Sure, Bert." The young man sighed heavily. "Now I miss ice cream. Slithering swords scraping sheaths… a thousand mile trek to reach the capital? Is that *possible* on foot?"

<If you jog the whole way, let's say about five miles per hour, you're looking at only about nine days of continuous running. We can make it pretty easily before the finals, which should be near the end of the month. We *got* this!> Sarge bellowed in Grant's mind, making him flinch.

"Who even *are* you these days, Sarge?" Grant spat as he moved into town.

<A motivating force for change!> The young man had to hide his grin from the sword; it wouldn't be good to let him know that he liked this sort of treatment. Grant had been craving positivity his whole life, even if it still rankled a little.

The village, basically a collection of ramshackle houses, was smaller than Hajimeni, with far fewer runners bouncing along the dirt paths. The village was clearly nothing more than a brief rest stop, a place for travelers to restock as they either headed to Hajimeni or traveled deeper within the grasslands. With so little to the town, Grant was eager to continue his journey.

He passed the one shop in the center of the village, a health food shop… nope. That was the tavern. He showed his number to the barkeep and was handed a single Bed to slurp down, then looked at the options available for purchase. Sadly… the prices were equally ridiculous here. Even though he had a surplus of Time currently, none of the food was worth stocking up on.

Grant chuckled as he saw a strange little shop on the way out of town, 'Wagons 'R' Us'. The double doors stood open, so he strode inside to see what they were actually selling. "Hello?"

The interior was filled with a multitude of wagons in varying conditions. He liked the look of one with massive wheels banded in shiny steel, with a chassis made of oiled hardwood. It would fit *tons* of carcasses and pelts! This had clearly been designed for hunting, maybe even having originally been a House Wednesday wagon. He paused and tried to remember if that was correct. "Yeah... they're supposed to be monster hunters, right?"

"Be right with you, sir." A bald head poked out from under a wagon. "Just finishing up here."

Grant waited patiently, just happy to get out of the glare of the direct sunlight. He glanced around at the wagons, imagining himself careening through the grasslands, loading up on valuable carcasses. He would skin the animals, save some meat for himself, then hoard a huge amount of Time by selling the pelts and bones. If the weapon shop he had seen in January was any indication, horns were especially sought after, as they could be crafted into weapons and even armor if they were large enough. "I wonder how I can get one of these...?"

"Sorry to keep you waiting. I just have to finish fixing a wheel, and that's not something you want to stop doing halfway through a job!" He wiped his oily hands across his overalls and presented his hand to Grant. "Name's Lucky Leap."

"You're a *Leap*!" Grant gasped in excitement.

"Yeup?" Lucky withdrew his hand and cast a beady eye at Grant. "Ain't no law against being a Leap; there's just not many of us."

"No, no. No issue on my end, I... have a huge affinity for Leaps, is all." Grant held his hands up in apology. "Back in January, until recently, Leaps weren't treated with much respect."

"What can I do for you?" Lucky's easy smile returned. "Got quite a few wagons ready to go. We have delivery wagons, hunting wagons, and bounty hunter wagons. If you're heading deeper into the grasslands, you *need* something to haul food and water along. Only a small town like this every ten miles or so. Most don't have much in the way of foodstuffs."

"You think I need one just for me?" Grant had been about to ask Lucky if there was anyone he could ride along with, but a term he was unfamiliar with caught his attention. "Bounty hunter wagons? What are those?"

"Guardhouses across the district have wanted posters on boards outside. You catch the bounty, return to the guardhouse with the bounty either dead or alive, depending on the required condition, and you get paid." Lucky pointed his thumb at the wagon, "This is for when you return them alive. A cart would work otherwise."

"People are paid to do this? I mean, anyone?" Grant corrected himself after he saw the wagoneer give him a strange look. "Not just House Friday; *anyone* can take bounties here?"

"Oh, I see the confusion!" Lucky nodded briskly, trying to figure out how people just a single District over could be so strange. "Yes, though hunting humans is regulated by House Friday, anyone can claim a bounty. In fact, the top bounty hunters are some of the wealthiest people in February."

Grant considered that for a few moments, but reluctantly turned to the next wagon. "I understand. I'll keep that in mind. What about the delivery wagons? Any fun facts on that? Before you say it... I understand they are for delivering things, but are there any kind of regulations I'd need to know about?"

"Haha, sure are. They're regulated by House Thursday, which has been put under the direct control of Lady February... um, *recently*. She was born a Friday, so tensions are high, as you might imagine. That means some politics if you have one of these, and frequent 'quality assurance' checks when going through a town or city." Lucky cast a meaningful glance at Grant. "That said, you can make a decent living delivering goods for events and races. There is always the need for people to deliver shakes, bars, even some race equipment. The pay is decent, though not quite as much as bounty hunting. Longer routes pay well, but there are risks."

"Risks?" Grant's ears perked up. So far, delivering goods sounded boring and especially tedious. "Such as?"

"Bandits. For some reason, banditry has been increasing in *huge* amounts over the last decade or so. They often target delivery wagons due to the value of their cargo. Drinks and bars are pretty pricey." Lucky shook his head at the thought of any of his precious wagons falling into the hands of a bandit.

"I am… painfully aware of how expensive they are." Grant squeezed his empty money pouch and felt his stomach twinge.

"Ha, did you get fleeced?" Lucky chuckled at the sweaty, pale-faced youngster.

"I couldn't exactly say I was *robbed*, but I did, um, *hand over* a substantial amount of Time in Hajimeni." Grant decided to change the subject before any more could be said on the matter. "Bounty hunting wagons and delivery wagons sound cool and all, but I think what I really need is a hunting wagon. Just a place to pile monsters and bring them into a town or city for selling."

"Suit yourself." Lucky waved at the left-hand side of the room. "Let me show you our stock."

"I know for a fact that I can't afford it, but to help me form a baseline… how much for that one?" Grant pointed to the biggest hunting wagon, the one with the shiny chrome fittings and oiled hardwood chassis. "Does it come with horses?"

"Horses are your own responsibility, but it does also fit non-standard pulling creatures up to the size of a Corpsewolf. That's the 'Huntsman One Hundred', and has a capacity of fifty carcasses, one hundred large pelts, or a combination of both." Lucky turned to lock greedy eyes with Grant, "As for the price… six Months."

Grant didn't say a word, but his pained expression painted a solid picture for the wagoneer. "I should take into consideration that you're a young lad; where would you come up with that kind of money? I don't do this often… but I can sell it for five

Months, fifteen Days. It's worth more, but I need to free up some space in here for a couple more wagons. Before you ask, that is the best price I can possibly offer."

"Do you have anything… smaller?" Grant shook his head and sighed. "I'll be honest: cheaper. Anything cheaper?"

Lucky didn't miss a beat, "Yes, sir. The Huntsman twenty-five, and Huntsman fifty. They can carry a maximum of twenty-five or fifty large pelts respectively. Due to their smaller capacity, they are typically pulled with a single horse."

"You don't offer a… payment plan? By any chance?" Grant laughed weakly, getting only a blank stare in return for his efforts.

"Nope. Sorry. It's Time only. We accept all common currency, Days, Weeks, and Months. Would you like to know the price for these two?" The salesman tone had all but vanished at this point.

"I think I'm wasting your time…" Grant sighed and leaned against one of the gleaming wagons, his vision of becoming a hunter as he was roaming the grasslands fading away as reality set in. "Thanks, Lucky. I'll be on my way."

"Hold your horses, Grant!" Lucky walked up to him and clapped both hands on his shoulders. "I have another option… I'm not sure you'd want it. But if you really need a wagon… follow me around the back of the workshop."

Lucky led them out of the salesroom and into what was clearly a workshop area in the back. They passed tools and broken wagons leaned up against the back wall, coming to a stop before a 'wagon' that was little more than a cart. "Here we are. It might not look like much, but it provided me with years of faithful service. I used it to move tools and parts around."

"How much is it?" Grant struggled to get excited about the cart in front of him, after admiring the gleaming wagons. It had hardly any capacity, and the wood was cracked and faded. Even so, beggars couldn't be choosers, and he was looking more like a beggar every day. "It looks… sturdy?"

"Yes. It's solid. There are quite a few miles left in the old girl yet." Lucky patted the wood, and it creaked alarmingly.

"The price?" Grant secretly hoped that Lucky would just give the rickety old thing away. No such luck.

"Best price, before I change my mind, is two Days and twelve Hours."

"Please, Lucky." Grant had a spark of inspiration, "Would it help if I told you that I saved the lives of almost every Leap in District January?"

"That's cute, but how am I supposed to…" Lucky's eyes widened as he got a notification from the system. "You're… *exalted* with the Leap faction? How? There's so few that… you were serious."

All Grant could do was nod, sure that opening his mouth would only lead to failure at this critical juncture. Lucky slowly nodded, looking between the old cart and Grant. "I am truly honored to meet you, Grant Monday. For you, and my people… let this be a gift, my friend."

"Thank you, Lucky, it-"

The salesman snapped his fingers and pointed at Grant. "You… you're the one!"

"Huh?"

Lucky shook his head, alarmed suddenly. "A caravan passed through here yesterday. The guards were babbling about the destroyed Januarian trade routes, and that House Monday is searching for anyone with information about it. I don't get paid to partake in gossip, but was that you?"

"I did what I had to do." Grant quietly deflected.

"Then… enjoy your new pull cart." Lucky sighed and started to walk away. "Come tell me your story some day."

"Thanks." Grant gripped the cart and started moving, and the wagon *screeched*. "Lucky? The squeal?"

"I won't charge extra for that." Lucky chuckled without looking back. "Don't worry, you won't notice it after a while."

Lucky was wrong. Grant pulled the squealing cart out of Nandayo, kicked the wheel in an attempt to quiet it down, but the blow actually made the noise worse. "If this cart had stats… they'd say 'the cart will let out a high-pitched squeal, alerting all humans and animals within a fifty-yard radius'. Then I'd laugh, maybe do some crying; you never know."

The patter of running feet made him turn around, a hand on the hilt of his sword. A panting Lucky stopped alongside the cart and pulled out a knife. "I thought I'd missed you there! I wanted to give you this!"

He pushed a rusty blade into Grant's hands. "It's not much, but you'll need a skinning knife. I see you have a sword strapped to your side, but you will struggle to use that to skin an animal. Plus, you don't want to risk damaging your sword on a tough hide or bones. This knife is certainly disposable."

"I appreciate that." Grant pushed the rusty knife to the back of the wagon. He stared at the rusty knife and the creaky wood, thinking that they complimented each other well.

With a wave, Lucky was off, heading back in the direction of his workshop. Grant was alone once again, now the owner of a squeaky pull cart and a rusty skinning knife. With no food, and only a single waterskin, living or dying in the grasslands now lay entirely in his hands.

<Interesting choice to be using both hands to pull a cart along.>

"Wha-?" was all Grant could get out before a huge orange spider that was flying through the air on falcon wings slammed into him and tore into his abdomen with a primordial *Scree*!

"*Sarge!*"

CHAPTER ELEVEN

Squeak!

"That's driving me crazy." A herd of hoofstock was startled by the noise, and he delighted in the fact that the stampede temporarily drowned out the noise. Sarge had gone silent for the past couple of miles, which always made Grant nervous.

He was right to be nervous. The ground went orange, and Sarge's cheerfully malevolent voice bellowed out, <Start running! Keep your knees up and lengthen those strides. Run! Look, you're carrying precious cargo!>

Looking behind himself, the young man found three bright orange beauties sitting in the cart, nursing various wounds. <These are three people that you saved, and their lives are in your hands! Prove that they're capable hands, and get your charges to safety! The monsters are coming!>

Grant did as he was told, and was pleased at the discovery that the change did bring benefits. He found that he was able to maintain a faster pace, with each bound seeming easier. The only problem was his sword; with every step, the scabbard collided with his leg. He'd suffered the same issue during The

Three Mile Tumbler, and his leg was still bruised from the constant collisions. <Do. You. *Not* see the problem?>

He jerked his head up and glanced around fearfully, but he saw no monsters closing in. "No?"

<Your *sword*, Grant. I don't want to be slapping on your leg like a drunkard hearing a funny joke! Brace me on *properly*.>

"I don't know how...? Wait, this is on wrong?" Grant touched the scabbard, which hung from his now-overly-large belt.

<Do I have to teach you how to wipe yourself, too?> Sarge growled, then groaned, <Hold. It. Still. Brace the scabbard with your hand, pull the wagon with the other. You're a *cultivator* now, not a farm boy!>

"Yes, Sarge." He did as he was told, and the sword instantly stopped slapping his leg. "Hey, it works!"

Grant bounded through the grass, somehow pulling the wagon along just as easily with one hand as he had been with two. Birds swarmed into the air to escape the intruder careening through their territory. <This, Novice, is called 'running with the sword'.>

As he moved along at a moderate pace, Grant found that it took a little longer for his muscles to begin to burn than the previous day. Then the monsters started appearing. Bright orange hoofstock were now stampeding at *him*, birds were swooping, and he just *knew* that there were going to be ambush creatures on the road. "Defeat them or outrun them!"

It only took a few more minutes before his muscles protested, and he was a long way off from escaping the stampede. He focused on the rhythm of his feet and suppressed the burn in his lungs and legs, keeping an eye on the road for the hidden hazards.

To his surprise, Sarge started offering encouragement and advice. <Looks like the stampede kept going past you! Now that the major threat is gone, slow down. You lack the fitness to maintain a sprint pace for more than a few minutes.>

Following orders as always, Grant slowed to a jog once

more. The expected relief never came. Instead, his breathing became ragged and his head felt as though it had caught on fire. <Hey! Maintain your form! If you let yourself get wobbly like that, your energy will dry up in a flash. You're making far too many unnecessary motions, so *stop* it. Ya think your opponents aren't going to use that against you?>

The first of the 'orange beauties' died at that exact moment to a swooping bird, and the other two began to wail and curse, hurling profanities at *Grant* for some reason. They started hitting him with sticks and screaming at him, to the point that he wondered if the *actual* test was to figure out they were monsters and destroy them. His hand drifted from the sheath to the *hilt* of February Twenty Nine, but Sarge interjected.

<Don't. This is something that really happens. They've lost someone, and the only person around to take it out on is you: they don't know you. Understand this. Accept it. Save them, even if they act like they don't want to be saved. If you let them go, they die... and you fail.> Grant had no choice other than to grit his teeth and bull onward, and soon enough the whipping sticks left him alone.

Then another died from a snake that had somehow gotten on the cart, and the third retreated into silence as he killed the serpent and got back to running. <Build a rapport with the people you're protecting! They *saw* the snake; they just didn't know what to do.>

"I hate this." His eyes were overflowing; every time he looked back at the sobbing lady, his heart broke for her. He *knew* that she wasn't real, but... orange or not, she *seemed* human.

An hour of jogging and fighting later, they reached a tree that grew alongside the road. It was difficult to judge distances out in the open, but he had seen it nearly thirty minutes before, and had been trying to make sense of the terrain. As it turned out, the tree wouldn't help with that at all. It wasn't a mere stump; it was an ancient *giant* of a tree. Standing under it as he was, the light of the sun struggled to penetrate its dense canopy.

An opening stopped him in his tracks. He couldn't see inside but felt the urge to investigate. "Sarge, can I have permission to investigate this hole in the trunk? I think it leads somewhere."

<Adventuring permitted. We will resume your training immediately afterward, understood?> The sobbing beauty froze in place, and Grant let out a huge sigh of relief. He couldn't believe how much of a toll that had been taking on his mentality.

"Yes, Sarge. Thank you." Grant stepped forward, hand on his hilt. Carefully inspecting the area, he found that the bowl of the giant tree was unremarkable. Disappointed, Grant knelt to pluck one blue cap mushroom and two red ones. His plant insight skill was going wild, so even though he hadn't yet discovered a use for mushrooms like these, Grant was sure they would come in handy.

"Well, that was an exciting adventure." He sighed and headed for the opening. A gust of ice-cold wind made his oversized clothes flutter, but the wind hadn't come from... outside? "That was odd."

He swept his sword around in search of the source of the wind. He felt air resistance and plunged his sword into a small knot of wood. A chunk of wood fell inward, creating a hole, just wide enough to fit a man, even one as large as Grant. The aroma of damp and dirt was overwhelming, and something else almost familiar... but he couldn't place the scent. After scrambling down the steep slope, he squinted down what appeared to be a natural tunnel. With the tip of February Twenty Nine leading the way, Grant began moving along the opening.

The deeper he went, the more the tunnel became coated in a sticky white substance. It was everywhere and clung possessively to his armor and face. The skittering of many feet set his senses on edge, and he hoped that it was just his mind playing tricks on him. "Spiders. Gotta be spiders. Sarge... tell me those orange assassin spiders are from somewhere else. Are those native to February?"

<Might be from anywhere, Grant.> Sarge informed him noncommittally.

"I'm out." Curiosity paralyzed him just before he escaped, and with a grumble, he forced himself onwards, pressing deeper into the mass of cobwebs… and then he just flat out changed his mind. The reward, if there was any, just wasn't worth the risk.

Grant sheathed his sword, dropped to the ground, and rolled back to turn around in the claustrophobic confinement of the tunnel. He got to his feet… and his heart nearly stopped at the sight of bloated bodies and hairy legs skittering towards him. The spiders paused in their pursuit to observe their prey. Hundreds of pinpricks reflected at Grant through a multitude of eyes. "I… don't suppose any of those are *orange*, my new favorite color?"

He backed up a step and the spiders realized their ambush was blown. The horde attacked in various ways: leaping into the air, skittering at him, or preparing webbing. Poison-tipped fangs dripped acrid liquid, and Grant realized *that* was the smell he couldn't place. It was so similar to the giant rats in the Royal January Mill, which meant this *must* be the source of the poison used against them! His body recognized the threat, and his muscle memory kicked in. Somehow, his sword practically *leapt* out of its sheath and into the first of the bloated, hairy bodies. The perfect attack halved the first spider and continued on to burst halfway into another. Both died, and the notifications blocked his view for a moment.

Damage dealt: 29 slashing. (Critical!)

Damage dealt: 12 slashing.

Skill gained: Iaijutsu (1/5). This skill is designed for instant strikes, a way to take an opponent off-guard or defend against sudden attacks. You have shown initial mastery! Congratulations!

Tier one effect: When prepared to attack, sword instantly leaves a sheath and slashes or penetrates target, increasing on-hit damage by 10%.

. . .

Disorientated, he flailed around and made sure to make rapid slashes. Dozens of the cat-sized spiders died each second, and Grant screamed as mandibles tried to sink into his arm... only to fail to penetrate. It still *hurt*, but no damage was done, and no poison entered his blood. His armor and armor cultivation seemed to stave off the worst of it.

Damage taken: 0 (10 mitigated)

Now knowing that they couldn't hurt him, Grant attacked with wild abandon. He whimpered as the fangs bounced off his flesh, then retaliated in kind. Soon, the small number of survivors hissed at him and slunk away into the deeper shadows of the tunnel. Heaving for breath as his adrenaline faded, he looked for a notification and couldn't find one. "No monsters in there?"

<Two, actually. You just got them before they could close in. They're set up as assassin-type creatures, with a huge amount of damage and damage-over-time, but very low health.> Sarge pointed out two of the corpses, and Grant swallowed as he realized that the fangs on those were nearly as long as his middle fingers. <Toss the whole bodies in your pack, and let a professional collect the materials. I don't want to get too far ahead of myself here, but I think your coinage troubles are over.>

Grant put the bodies in his pack after stabbing each an additional time, just to make *sure* they were dead. Now he wasn't sure if he should be heading back towards the exit, or deeper within the maze of spiders. He gazed down the deeper end, and just before deciding to turn back... something metallic glinted and caught his eye. "Treasure?"

Rolling around to get himself back on the path of descent, he followed the glint until the tunnel opened into a chamber. It was tall enough for him to stand upright, and at the other side of the chamber, he could make out what the 'treasure' actually was: a mass of bones. They appeared human and were suspended in a rope. The gleam came from a rapier that rotated in the air, waiting to be claimed by a courageous adventurer.

The lure of adventure and the promise of riches proved too

strong, enticing him towards the blade. Before he could doubt himself, he reminded himself that he wasn't defenseless. February Twenty Nine was unsheathed, its blade tested and true against the denizens of this odd dungeon. Grant crossed the gap and approached the mound of bones to find three bodies, each at varying levels of decomposition. A realization made him stop in his tracks. "They all must have come to claim the sword."

"No. I fought the spiders off already... pretty sure?" He considered searching through their belongings, but balked at the idea of disturbing the dead. They should at least be allowed to rest in peace. The sword, on the other hand...! He reached out and plucked the shining blade from the sticky white 'rope'.

Do you, Grant Monday, wish to absorb the power of February 17th, 'Stolen Sunlight'? Accepting 'Stolen Sunlight' will override any previous Wielded Weapon power absorbed in the current monthly series. If not over-ridden by another weapon of the same month, this ability will vanish at the end of the year, unless the quest 'Heal the World' has been completed.

Accept / Decline

"Accept! A Wielded Weapon, here? Done deal." He popped the blade into his pack and started back to the entrance, eager to be free from the claustrophobic surroundings. His sword suddenly became a beacon, blazing with light. Strangely, it didn't hurt his eyes, but he felt it *should* have as it bathed the chamber in lumi-nescence.

It also highlighted a serious problem.

Hiss.

Descending from the ceiling on a rope of white silk was a bulbous spider body, several orders of magnitude larger than its small skittering brethren. Its bulk dropped in an instant and blocked his exit. Above its twelve-eyed head was a red skull and the name 'Snippy the Gleam-Fang Stalker'.

The spider was deadly and *way* above his level. Grant backed up, and his foot collided with the pile of bones, disturbing the grave. Snippy reached the ground and extended its arm-length fangs. They oozed sizzling green liquid, looking more like a pair of long knives wielded by a member of House Saturday than anything a natural creature should have.

<I can paint it orange for you, if it'll make you feel better?>

"That'll make the damage it deals disappear?" His answer was half dry, half hopeful.

Sarge took a long beat to reply. <Maybe you just fight it without access to wishful thinking like that.>

Grant slowly knelt, not taking his eyes off the multifaceted eyes before him. He slowly pulled the rapier out of his pack, then whipped it at the spider. It easily skittered to the side, firing a spray of silk in his direction. He took the opportunity to run past it and into the tunnel, scooping up the Wielded Weapon as he sprinted. Relief washed over him. There was no way the spider could fit in here. He glanced back, hoping to catch sight of the creature… and saw far more than he wanted. It was scuttling towards him, its legs held tightly to its sides as it advanced.

He pounded his legs or scrambled on all fours along the dark, dank tunnel, all while the sound of scurrying legs grew louder in his ears. The tunnel went into an abrupt incline, and he knew he'd almost reached the exit. Grant scrambled up the steep slope, hands chafing as they skated off sharp rocks. Suddenly, he slipped, almost falling back towards the razor-sharp mandibles.

"Only a few more steps, then freedom!" He slammed his sword back in the scabbard and tossed the rapier out ahead of him. The tunnel was abruptly plunged into darkness as the light of the sword was held at bay by the scabbard. "Ahh!"

Snippy uses Gleaming Fang! Piercing attacks have a lower critical threshold!

Damage taken: 7 piercing (13 mitigated).

Pain lanced through his foot, and Grant didn't need to look to know that the spider had pinned his foot to the ground. Dropping to all fours, he braced himself on the floor and kicked in the direction of the creature's eyes. It pulled back, and his pinned foot slid free. Desperately, he scrambled up the last few feet and into the bowl of the giant tree. He sprinted away, ignoring the searing pain coursing through his leg, powered only by fear and copious amounts of adrenaline.

<Back to training; that's the spirit! How was your adventure?> Sarge let out a deep, bellowing laugh just before an unholy *hiss* echoed across the grasslands. Grant peeked over his shoulder to see eight hairy legs lurching out of the opening, along with a multitude of eyes glowing in the dying light of the day.

<Grant, you forgot your cart!> Sarge waited a long moment as Grant continued to limp-sprint further away from the massive-arachnid infested tree. <So… you just don't want it, or…?>

CHAPTER TWELVE

Grant finally calmed down after a solid ten seconds of running —the pain may have had something to do with that—and slowly made his way back to the tree. There were no signs that Snippy had come out into the open, and Sarge had been working to convince him that an ambush predator like that wouldn't leave the safety of its normal hunting grounds. "Sarge... I gotta ask, during that escape... did that spider use a *spell?*"

<No.>

"Okay... yeah, I thought that was just my imagination. I saw-"

<It wasn't a spell, it was a natural ability. Essentially the monster version of a skill.> The full-lecture tone made Grant groan, but that didn't impede Sarge at all. <How is it, do you think, that weapons and armor can be made with such incredible potency and abilities? Why is there an entire Noble House devoted to hunting monsters and collecting materials?>

Grant took a calculated guess, "Because they can process those parts and use the natural abilities to enhance the equipment?"

<It's because they can process—hey! Look at you, using your noggin! Check your status soon; I think you increased your cultivation a little with my methods.> The praise made Grant glow, and he listened closer as Sarge explained, <Creatures naturally cultivate by killing, surviving, laying ambushes, and eating. In fact, most cultivation methods and skills are originally derived from watching nature at work. Any of that remind you of anything?>

"The eating? In use as a physical cultivation method back in January?" Grant was on a roll, so he was making sure to try and get everything correct. He hadn't realized that getting a few words of praise from *Sarge* would be so heady. Maybe it was the blood loss? He risked a glance at his foot but had to look away again quickly. No one wanted to be able to see *through* parts of their body.

Sarge let his concern shine through. <You better get that looked at soon. Let's clean it up while we can; battlefield injuries and the resulting sepsis debuff can lead to amputation or death. Only reason you didn't get a nasty poison debuff was that it went all the way through, but that has its own issues.>

"Amputation?" Grant didn't know this word, but it didn't sound fun at all.

<You could lose your foot. Maybe even the leg, if you're unlucky.>

The straightforward answer almost threw Grant into a full-on panic. "I'm going to die out here, killed by a spider with a stupid name!"

<Get a grip! Wash out the wound and dress it.> Now back at his wagon, Grant sat and rummaged through his backpack, almost cutting himself on his newly-earned blade, and plucked out the water skin. Taking off his boot, he was given a perfect view of the hole in his foot. Without anything to keep it bound together, blood pumped out of both sides, drenching the grass beneath. He gritted his teeth and poured half of his remaining water reserves over the wound. It provided little relief, as blood continued to pump from the wound, swirling and mixing with

the water. He couldn't keep himself from checking his stats, to see just how long he had left.

Name: Grant Monday
Rank: Lord of The Month (January)
Class: Foundation Cultivator
Cultivation Achievement Level: 11
Cultivation Stage: Late Spring
Inherent Abilities: Swirling Seasons Cultivation
Health: 81/184
Mana: 9/9

Characteristics
Physical: 89 (Cultivation Stage Maximized. Gains will be retroactively applied when all stages are aligned.)
Mental: 35
Armor Proficiency: 45
Weapon Proficiency: 67
Debuff: Incised Wound. You have a large, open, untreated wound in a limb. -3 health per second.

<You're going to have to close the wound. If you don't, you'll die! Pay attention to me; you don't have time to be browsing your stats!>

"How?" Grant grimaced in pain as the ground spun below. He felt himself fading away. "I… don't have anything to bind it with."

<Your new ability, Stolen Sunlight! Does it just make light, or *heat* as well?>

"No idea, Sarge. I *just* got it!" Despair was setting in as he watched his health trickle away with the blood that soaked into the ground.

<Wake up! *Focus*; there's a good lad.> The orders were at least kind. <Pull me out and lay me on that hole. We need to try to cauterize that wound.>

Grant put his foot on his sword, his fuzzy thoughts trying to help him remember when he had drawn it. With Sarge coaching him, he activated the ability. "Stolen Sunlight?"

The sword lit up, and the world around him dimmed as though the evening light was draining away. He hissed as the blade heated up, but once more, it seemed that he was immune to any ill effects from the weapon. Then the edges of his wound started to sizzle.

<I got it. Figured it out. Not much heat produced at your cultivation stage, but it's enough if we focus it to the extreme.> Sarge was mumbling frantically. <Designate that as a threat; good thing your cultivation has been increasing... I think that's... *yes!*>

Debuff: Heavy Limp. You have a hole in your foot. Movement speed when walking is decreased by 40%.

<That's not great, but at least you aren't losing blood anymore.> Sarge sighed and noticed the surroundings. <We should get outta here. The scent of blood might draw in predators, and who knows if Snippy stays indoors after hours?>

"You think it comes out at night?" Grant perked up, and a dark rage started to fill his heart.

<Probably. Not much in the way of prey down there. I don't know about you, but I don't know many people that walk into a monster's den and feed themselves to—oh, *wa~ait.*>

"The sarcasm is *strong* with this one." Grant got off the cart and started scooping the bloody dirt into a pile. "I've got bait, and I know where at least one exit is for that thing. Let's see who's better at laying traps."

<Snippy is. *Guaranteed.*> Sarge clearly had no faith in this plan. <Your ability to do anything but run into combat screaming, and run *away* screaming, is very suspect.>

"You don't think that thing will come after me in the dark after I found its nest, killed other spiders, and stole the bait?" Grant scoffed at the mere *idea* that he'd be left alone. "It's coming out, and I'm going to be ready."

He piled as much of his blood-soaked earth in front of the exit to the tree as he could, washed the blood off his body with as much water as he could spare, then climbed up the tree until he was in position above the main entrance into the hollow. Using February Twenty Nine as an axe wasn't his favorite thing to do, but he spent a good half hour beating apart the rotten wood until he had carved a small seat that he could remain on with minimal effort.

Then he simply sat there with his blade pointed downward, ready to fall forward and skewer whatever came out.

Sarge had zero faith in the success of this plan. <I'll admit, as far as traps are concerned, I've never seen anyone use *themselves* as the rock in a rockfall trap. This seems like a very Januarian concept... fall on someone and hope they die? Whew.>

"I'll never feel safe again if I know this thing might be stalking me, Sarge. You want me to have 'heart demons' that impede my cultivation?" Grant was keeping his voice low, focusing on his sword and slowly working his muscles to keep them from falling asleep.

<It's called *trauma*, Grant, and you're *going* to have it. Then you'll keep having it, and oh, guess what? You'll have more.> Though Sarge was being harsh, he wasn't being unkind. <You're growing up on the outside, but going through painful circumstances and experiencing new things is how you grow up on the *inside*. How you deal with those scars eventually defines you. Are you going to let them define you as someone that is afraid, and angry? Or are you going to define yourself as someone that can overcome the obstacles and help others face them as well?>

"Imma define myself as someone that *defeats* my heart demons, Sarge." Grant looked down the length of his blade, which—even without the new ability active—seemed to be drinking in the last of the light. "I'll overcome them so that other people don't *have* to go through this. Just like I saved Leaps in January so they can be free again, I'm going to kill a giant spider so random joggers don't get *eaten*. Sure, there's less philosophy in my approach, but I still feel like I'm going to help a lot of people. Quiet, now."

Evening faded into twilight, then true night. Grant stayed where he was, patiently half-seated on the tree. Hours passed, and his thoughts wavered. 'Lucky' for him, each time his eyes drifted too far closed, Sarge would bellow abuse into his mind.

Then he heard it.

Skitter.

It was quiet, but there was only so silent a giant spider could be in a rotten tree like this. <Hold your breath. *Now.* Put everything you are into the tip of your sword. You are one with the sword. You are not a human on a tree. Put *all* of your presence into the *tip* of your *sword.*>

Maybe it was the sleep deprivation, maybe it was the blood loss, but for some reason, Grant really *understood* how to make this happen. Just as Snippy's front legs reached out of the hollow in the tree, the entirety of Grant's presence faded into nothingness. No bloodlust. No anger or rage. Just a tree, and a piece of metal attached to it.

Nothing to see here.

Skill gained: Stealth (1/9). This skill is the hallmark of the dark, the dastardly, and the desperate. Masters can walk through crowds without being noticed by the people, while Saints can walk through walls without being noticed by reality.

Tier one effect: Active concealment allows your presence to fade and increases critical chance by 10%.

The spider's head came out, and a leg tentatively touched the mound of bloody dirt. A heartbeat later, the two front legs stabbed viciously into the ground, just to make sure there wasn't a body beneath. In that moment of distraction, the tip of a sword fell from the tree above as a gust of wind overbalanced it.

Skree!

Critical!

Damage dealt: 19 piercing. (10 mitigated)

In an ironic turn of events, Snippy was now impaled and nailed to the ground. As it began to thrash, Grant activated Stolen Sunlight and blinded the remaining eyes of the creature. It started to buck in an attempt to throw him off, but his weight, combined with the angle of his blade, forced the monster to injure itself over and over without being able to get free, finally falling to the side as its health went negative.

"I got it! I did it!" Grant lurched to his feet, gasping as his body shook from adrenaline and fear. He stood and waited for something to change, but… "Nothing? I feel like I should get a level?"

<It's big, but it still counts as one kill.> Sarge scoffed at Grant's disappointment. <That's right; today, you killed three monsters. Two of them, you didn't even notice, and the third took you half a day. If that hadn't been *excellent* for your mental cultivation, and the fact that you got a skill out of it, I'd have made you move on by now. There's a good chance that foot gets infected still. Think you can make it to the next town and get treatment?>

"I faced my heart demons and won, Sarge." Grant's eyes were watering as he loaded Snippy up on his wagon. "I can do *anything*."

CHAPTER THIRTEEN

"*Ha!*" Grant stood victorious over a slain rabbit as he waved his sword at the hawk that had killed the oversized animal and been too weak to carry it off. "Get! Shoo! This is mine now!"

The bird flew away, leaving Grant his prey. The human took the creature to his wagon and chopped it up with his rusty skinning knife, then held his sword over a pile of tinder. He angled the blade so that it reflected the sun as much as possible, then magnified the light with Stolen Sunlight. The tinder burst into flame, and he let out a sigh of relief. "Thanks for teaching me that trick, Sarge.>

<Survival is paramount!> Grant liked this gregarious new personality that his sword had acquired after getting to February. <Can't kill things if you're too weak from hunger or frozen stiff!>

"Mm. Still *some* downsides to it," Grant mumbled as he revised his thoughts on Sarge once more. The smell of the roasting meat wafted on the breeze. Grant sat cross-legged, observing the sizzling meat atop the fire. He had to admit, liberating and then cooking his own food was deeply satisfying. The sound of pounding footfalls caught his attention, and he gazed down the road to discover a man pulling a hunting cart at high speed.

Grant gripped the hilt of his sword as the stranger drew near, stopped, walked over, and plopped down beside him. Grant inspected the finely dressed newcomer with a prominent nose. "Who might you be, then?"

"Meat. I'm craving meat. That rabbit will do." The man clapped his hands together. "I'm Waylon Wednesday, and I am carting monster meat to Valentine. I claim need."

"You're trying to rob me?" Grant's hand stayed in the perfect position to perform Iaijutsu. "So, you choose death."

<I can't believe you're still so aggressive about *food*,> Sarge chuckled lightly at him.

Waylon's hand dropped to his own sword, and he rapped his fingers against the hilt of his weapon, irritated at being kept waiting. "Every employee of Lady February is granted one free meal from *anyone*, no matter where they might be. My supplies are for competitors; I didn't have room for my own supplies. Move aside if you don't want to serve me yourself."

"I am starving, injured, and *also* have no other supplies." Grant explained neutrally, not changing his stance at all. Waylon snarled and drew a tomahawk from his belt as Grant finished, "You taking my only food is the same as killing me yourself."

That brought the man up short. He eyed Grant critically, taking in the fact that he didn't yet have a weapon drawn, and the food. "You'll be fine; a few days without food won't hurt *you*.."

The tomahawk swung lazily at Grant to get him to move aside, but its wielder stopped moving as a slightly glowing sword tip pressed against his Adam's apple. "S-so fast!"

"Drop it." Grant was too tired to do anything other than give a simple command. Waylon dropped the tomahawk and slowly lifted his hands above his head.

. . .

Do you, Grant Monday, wish to absorb the power of Waylon Wednesday's weapon, Last Hit? Accepting Last Hit will override any previous Wielded Weapon power absorbed in the current monthly series. If not overridden by another weapon of the same month, this ability will vanish at the end of the year, unless the quest 'Heal The World' has been successfully completed.

Accept / Decline

Grant mentally declined the offer as Waylon let out a low whistle. "I've never seen anyone move their blade like that; well, 'sides Lady-"

"*Gah!*" Grant gasped as golden power washed through him. His foot felt like it was on fire... for a moment. Then he felt better than he had in *days*.

"Did... did you just increase your cultivation achievement level? Right in front of me?" Waylon gasped in relief as the blade was moved from his throat. "*Gross.*"

"You're a Wielder?" Grant looked down at the fallen tomahawk. "What in the *world* are you doing out here all alone? Whaddaya mean, 'gross'?"

"Um. Your flesh just *regrew* in front of me. Kinda off-putting." Waylon regarded the wagon, the sword, the rabbit... and slowly put his hands down. "Also, I'm starving? I was serious, I'm delivering goods."

"Okay..." Grant sheathed his sword and held out a hand. "Sorry, I thought you were a bandit. I got healed up, so I'm less... touchy. Split the rabbit?"

Waylon didn't thank Grant for the meat as both ate in silence. Grant, although happy to share, almost lost it when Waylon said, "Not bad. It could do with a little seasoning."

"I have spider poison if you wanna add it on, or maybe you can smear some ash on it from the fire?" Grant locked eyes with the man, and they both started to chuckle. The release of tension was good for the pair, and they finally started to relax.

"Spider poison, huh?" Waylon idly wondered as they finished the charred rabbit meat. "What's up with that?"

"See the wagon there?" Grant pointed at the rickety rig. "I killed three monsters, and I'm carting them along."

Waylon went to take a closer look, and almost screamed in shock. "Gleam-Fang Stalkers! How are you *alive*?"

"What are you talking about?" Grant started to get a bad feeling, replacing his pride from only a moment prior.

"Stalkers *never* give up once they designate their prey! Unless you manage to kill the queen and start a hive war, they'll keep coming after you. Only way to stop them is to burn out the nest whenever you find them." Waylon stared at the corpses for a few long minutes, then paled as he noticed how *fresh* they were. "How... how long ago did you kill these?"

"Yesterday." Grant's voice was dull as he realized the danger wasn't as far behind him as he had hoped.

Waylon looked like he wanted to run, but he held his ground. "You know where the nest is? You can seek succor from House Wednesday, and they'll issue a quest to burn it out. Where is it?"

"Big hollow tree about half a day's walk back down this road?" Grant's voice was a whisper.

"I know it." Waylon took a few deep breaths. "Okay. *Okay.* This one... it's so big, it *has* to be a queen. That gives us at least until overmorrow till any remaining monsters gather the beasts among them to hunt you as revenge for *regicide*. I'm going to harvest these, then you're gonna come with me, and we are going to run for our lives, warning everyone to get off the road and out of town until a subjugation crew comes through here. This is about to be the most dangerous road in the District. Also, how did you know I'm a Wielder?"

"That's... I am too." Grant's sword sizzled with Stolen Sunlight, and Waylon's eyes widened.

"That looks just like what Paladin Quentin could do in the stories from before the Wielder Wars!" Waylon's excitement didn't stop him from rapidly cutting up the Gleam-Fangs. He tossed their fangs, poison sacs, eyes, and oddly enough, their entire legs on top of his wagon and strapped them under a tarp. "Did you find a lost Wielded Weapon?"

"Yes and no?" Grant wasn't sure what to say that wouldn't sound like a lie or evasion. "This is mine."

"The reward for returning a Wielded Weapon is *unimaginable*, Grant. It'll make the bounty for all *this* look like legumes." Waylon shook his head as Grant reached for his own hand cart. "Leave that here. It'll slow us down, and you'll need to take turns with me pulling this."

"What? Why?" Grant grumbled at the thought of pulling along that behemoth of a wagon.

"'Cause if we sleep, the Gleam-Fang scent-scouts that are tracking you will tear our necks open." Waylon giggled frantically. "So we're going to be running until we collapse into the arms of a Calendar of Vassals!"

Grant put his head in his hands. "All I wanted to do was find my first elemental spell. Why did this happen?"

"Spell? Why didn't you say so?" Waylon immediately stopped and opened his wagon, *much* too quickly for Grant's liking. He pulled out a book and handed it over. "This is the most terrible spell in the world, and you're gonna want to leave it behind at the first opportunity, but it'll give you a handle on how spells work. Good training; very character building. It'll also help you run."

Grant took the book and stared at it for a moment. Waylon looked at him expectantly, so Grant finally cleared his throat and muttered, "How do I use this?"

"Oh." Waylon pointed at February Twenty Nine. "There's a reason that only Wielders and Vassals are able to learn spells anymore. Your spell slot is not in your mind; it is in your Wielded Weapon. Touch the book to the weapon, then accept it. Also, sorry about this. It's called Spark Shield, and I'm not sure you'd want to use it, but it's the best way to *force* yourself to keep moving."

"Why?" Grant had almost followed the instructions blindly,

and he swore to himself that he was going to stop doing that. "What's the deal?"

Waylon snapped his fingers at him to hurry him up. "It *hurts*. A lot. When your mental cultivation gets high enough, it will kill you after a few seconds of use. Hence the whole 'you'll get rid of this soon enough'. That, and the whole stigma of using spells…"

"Why in the twelve Districts would I want to use Spark Shield?" Grant started to hand it back, feeling frustrated as Waylon ignored his outstretched hand.

"Use it. Like any other elemental spell, it can be cast as active or passive. This particular one can also be used as a training aid. If cast with enough skill to guide it properly, it shocks the body in specific places and makes muscles twitch for hours… potentially. *Ideally*. Great for teaching fast-twitch muscles and reaction speed… but very painful."

Before Grant could say another word, Sarge broke in, <Take it, Grant. It's a training spell, so I'll be able to direct the usage. For you, there are very few choices that would be better. This will give you a feel for how to control mana without having to actually control it yourself.>

"Another benefit," Waylon continued, since Grant wasn't saying anything, "if cast as an active effect, is that it shocks anyone that touches you. As your mental cultivation is probably still low, it won't do too much damage, but it could give you an edge? In a fight, every advantage is important… *an~nd* there're spiders coming to kill you."

"Spark Shield, it is, then." Grant tried to look upbeat as he accepted the spellbook. He didn't relish the prospect of being zapped into action, but he wouldn't know exactly what it was like until he tried it. He ran his hand across the embossed leather cover with the image of a zigzag etched on it. Opening the page, he was presented with details of the spell… and yet, he still couldn't read very well. He shrugged and touched the book to his weapon.

. . .

NEW! Elemental Spell gained: Spark Shield
  <u>*Active Mode*</u>
  Mana cost: 5% per second. Mana regen halted.
  Damage(Self): 25% Mental cultivation per second.
  Damage(Other): 50% Mental cultivation per second.

<u>*Training Mode*</u>
  Mana cost: 1% per second. Mana regen halved while active.
  Damage(self): 10% Mental cultivation per second.
  Cultivation counts as doubled while active and affecting muscles.

Your Wielded Weapon, February Twenty Nine, is equipped with a training ability. It is requesting control of Spark Shield. This permission can be revoked at any time. Allow? Yes / No.

"Yes." As soon as he accepted, Grand could feel something deep within himself shifting, altering pathways and allowing something primal to move through him. "Is this... mana?"

<Yup. Aspected as *lightning*.>

"Yeowch!" Grant bellowed as his limbs locked up.

Damage taken: 0 lightning damage per second! (4 mitigated.) (Continuous.)

<Aren't you so glad your cultivations are so well-balanced? With even *this* characteristic in armor, we can keep this active *all* the *time*!>

CHAPTER FOURTEEN

Grant had a smile on his face as he set off at a brisk pace. He was 'fresh,' thanks to leveling up, so pulling the cart was his responsibility. Waylon kept throwing him strange looks as he jogged alongside. "Okay, I gotta know... how are you smiling? I literally see little lightning bolts jumping between your teeth."

"Face. Isth. Stick like thish," Grant slurred out as his face constantly twitched. "I'll practith more."

"Okay then, listen." Waylon took a deep breath. "I'm going to trust you here, and I need you to trust me as well. Get to the next town. I'm going ahead to warn them and get them evacuated. I'll get us supplies and such; just focus on escaping, buddy."

With that, the Wielder sprinted away and was soon a dot in the distance. Grant felt terror set in, but Sarge jumped in to help keep him sane.

<Keep an eye on your form. Slow down to a pace you can maintain. Don't get sloppy now,> Sarge instructed as Grant barreled down the road. To the wagon's credit, it was well-built and clearly modified with someone pulling it in mind. Every move was smooth, and it hardly pulled on him. Even so, he was

growing exhausted from the constant pain of lightning filling his innards.

He followed his mentor's advice and tried to ignore the pain that he just *knew* would be a constant companion as long as he had this spell. As he jogged, the steady, repetitive motion turned into deep meditation. His mind was calm and clear, with worries miles away. Birds and small critters were startled as he snapped twigs that had fallen on the road.

<Six point two miles in one hour and three minutes. A substantial improvement, but you have a long way to go yet.> Sarge's voice shattered Grant's focus, and he stumbled. Getting back in the groove was a lot harder, but he was determined to find that strange meditative state once more.

Before he could move away mentally, Waylon caught his attention by running back and waving. "They're going. We've got a stockpile getting built in the town center for us; hope you like Beds."

"They're the most disgusting drink I've ever had the misfortune of intentionally swallowing," Grant informed him directly.

"Hah! I know, right?" Waylon's answer wasn't what Grant had been expecting. "Trust a monster hunter; there's only so much you can do for the flavor when you're not allowed to add taste-altering spices to it... or sugar. I miss sugar. So where are you from, Grant?"

"January," Grant puffed out, not exactly comfortable explaining further.

"Oh, neat. Guess we don't have anything else to talk about, then." Waylon squinted and pointed. "There it is! Now, runners have been sent to all connecting towns. We'll never match their speed, so don't expect to see anyone, unless it's a subjugation squad, until we reach Valentine."

"This is so... I don't even know how to describe this place." Grant set the handles down as they reached town center and 'ate' a 'meal'. Waylon took over the cart, and they started off to the next town right away. "Switch every ten miles?"

"*Regent*, yeah! We can keep it up till the *capital* if we gotta!"

Waylon agreed with *far* more enthusiasm than Grant felt the situation warranted. "I've always wondered, what's it like in January? Does everyone do physical cultivation like here, or do they mix it up?"

"Physical cultivation… yes. Like here? No. Not even close." Grant explained a little about the District, the governmental structure, and his personal situation. Waylon listened closely, obviously very interested in the differences.

When Grant couldn't speak *and* run anymore, Waylon took a long minute to think. "So… why are you going to the Valentine tournament? You're already a Wielder, so that can't be it, right?"

"I want to defeat Lady February." Grant explained after deciding there was no reason to lie.

"You want to be her *sparring partner?*" Waylon almost fell out of step as he sputtered the question, certain that no one would be so foolish. "Why in the world would you want to marry that maniac?"

"*Marry* her?" Now Grant was the one being incredulous. "Why would I want to do that? I need to get to March!"

They stared at each other for a moment, and Waylon eventually broke the silence. "Ahem. I, um, think you're under a strange misconception about what this tournament is all about."

"I'm in agreement over here." Grant started coughing as dust particles settled on his face, and he spat some blood onto the road. "Why am I coughing blood?"

<Stress fracture caused some torn tissue in your chest. It happened before you leveled up, so I wasn't going to mention it. Don't worry; it's just your body cleaning itself out at this point.>

Luckily, the Februarian hadn't caught that last part over the rattling of the wagon. "Let me explain a little more clearly. This tournament is to decide the new power structure of the entire District. This will change *everyone's* way of life here. The final slot, the overall winner, becomes the military advisor to Lady February, and her official sparring partner. Sparring is *incredibly* intimate, as you need to be completely open about your strengths and weaknesses. It isn't an *actual* tournament prize, but everyone knows that at the end of all this... whoever wins is likely going to be the Lady's consort."

"What if-"

Grant blushed before he could finish his question, and Waylon caught the drift. "Whatever *male* takes the top spot will likely become her consort. If they come in second or third, that just gives them less political power. In fact, that's one reason that there are so many women aiming for top spot: to make sure they have the highest political positions. But... one of a Lord or Lady's duties is to produce an heir, so..."

"*Okay*, then; this was... informative." Grant couldn't handle the awkwardness any longer. He took the lead just as they passed under the canopy of a tree.

Thud.

Peering around, he couldn't see anything. His sword hilt gripped firmly in his hands, he quietly asked, "Waylon, did you hear-"

"Be quiet," Waylon hissed softly. "A Bastard-Beaked Crow just landed behind you. Any sudden movements, and it'll attack. Don't worry, we can tackle it together."

"Okay." Shivers ran down Grant's spine, and he knew he was being observed.

Skritch-scratch.

Thud. The second sound was more distant. A cold sweat formed and dribbled down his back. From his peripheral vision, he was sure he had glimpsed something spiked swishing around, left, then right. The shuffling noise grew louder until he felt a warm breeze against the back of his neck. Something pointy tapped his leather helmet like it was trying to crack open a nut.

Caw?

The deep bass rumble of the creature reverberated through his eardrum and jangled his nerves. He had to do *something*. He couldn't just stand here until what he assumed was a bird cracked his skull open! The pecking grew more persistent. Finally, he ducked and rolled forward so that he could get a better look at his adversary. Gnarled talons scratched at the ground, and Grant's eyes roved upward to take in oversized chicken feet, topped by ankles laden with ropes of muscle, then feather-covered thighs as thick as a man's waist.

The bird bent over to look *down* at Grant... and tilted its head to the side, more curious than anything about the intruder. It strutted forward to get a closer look, and two itty-bitty black eyes seemed to stare into his soul, yet all he could see was the straight orange beak... which snapped open.

Caw!

"Stay back!" Grant stood up defiantly and brandished February Twenty Nine like a talisman to ward off the creature. Swishing behind the creature caught his attention, and his eyes went wide. The Bastard-Beaked Crow's tail feathers appeared to be hand-and-a-half swords. As he raised his voice, the tail swished, tearing out clumps of the long grass that grew next to the road. "Waylon, what *is* this?"

"Be quiet." Waylon seemed to be trying to force himself to stay calm, and that was doing nothing to help Grant. "They don't *like* loud noises or sudden movements."

Grant stopped waving his sword in front of the Bastard-Beaked Crow's face, but it was far too late. The agitated bird leaped forward and brought its beak down hard and fast. He anticipated the move and beat away the curved beak exactly like he would a sword... with the same effect. There was a clang of bone and steel as the beak raked along the blade. He didn't expect the follow-up attack; the tail lashed out and tried to cut his feet out from under him.

February Twenty Nine was knocked from his hand, sailing off into the undergrowth.

He had to roll to avoid the beak that sliced through the air and took great divots out of the ground. Grant was thankful for all of his additional training as he rolled, and he promised himself to stop complaining entirely. Sarge was his friend and just wanted to see him succeed! Focusing, he pushed the thoughts out of his mind and went on the offensive.

Grant knew he had to end this before the Bastard-Beaked Crow tore into him with those taloned feet, its beak, or its tail. He leaped forward and found himself clinging onto the bird's muscular leg. The creature bounced and flapped in an attempt to throw him off, then angled itself to peck downward. Unable to hang on and call his sword simultaneously, he let go just as the crow's head thrust at him, avoiding the razor-sharp beak. "Time is Space!"

Combining the sword's third ability with the skill Iaijutsu, Grant drew his sword out of the air and attacked in unison, his blade sinking deeply into the undefended bird-head. The Bastard-Beaked Crow's head sat at an unnatural angle for a moment, and then the entire creature fell to the ground.

Head severed, critical strike!

For a few moments, its body flopped around before going limp with a thump. Adrenaline still rushed through Grant's veins, with his eyes darting around in search of other predators. All he found was a sweat-drenched Waylon limping toward him with a grin plastered across his face.

"Well done. I didn't think you had it in you!" Waylon thrust out a hand and assisted Grant to his feet. "I would have helped, but I had my hands full. Mine got a peck in on my leg. The fight would have been over sooner, but my tomahawk wasn't great for a clean kill against him."

Grant gazed around and saw a mound of feathers in the distance from Waylon's kill. "The tails useful for anything?"

"Eh... too flimsy for anything except single-use stuff; certainly not enough to make us stop and clean the kills when stalkers are after us." Waylon's words killed off some of Grant's adrenaline, so the next question took him by surprise. "I hope you like chicken?"

"Wait, we can *eat* these?" Grant regarded the massive bird with new eyes. *Hungry* eyes.

"We'd be feasting for *weeks* if we could keep the meat from going bad. However, there's no room in the wagon, so we leave it to rot. Or… no, sorry to get your hopes up. No room. Gotta run."

The pair left the territory of the Bastard-Beaked Crows behind and followed the road along the boundary of a new-growth forest. Eventually, they reached the next town, and Grant was given the wagon to drag along so they could hope-fully evade the swarm of spiders which they hadn't yet confirmed were after them. His muscles protested every step of the way, but he didn't mind the physical exertion. Still, as he forced down another Bed in hopes that it would give him the energy needed to continue, he regretted ever thinking that adventuring in his free time would be a good idea.

<Feel that wind on your face? It feels like a primal desire for power and growth! Your cultivation progress is *excellent*, I might add. Let's try some new areas,> Sarge bellowed into Grant's mind as he switched the muscle groups that were being 'stimu-lated' by Spark Shield. <High knees, Grant!>

CHAPTER FIFTEEN

Thirty-one hours into their forced march, Grant's stomach began to metaphorically scream and weep as they power-walked through the grasslands. The sun was starting to dip lower in the sky, and dark clouds roiled in the distance as the afternoon shifted toward evening.

"I don't like the look of those clouds," Grant mumbled to himself as he stared at the strange patterns appearing in the heavens.

"Did you say something?" Waylon's tired voice gave Grant a strange sense of vindication. Even though Grant was exhausted, it seemed that he had more staying power and endurance than this Wielder of House Wednesday.

"I was thinking about the clouds. I don't like the look of them," Grant explained, even though he had no real justification for the way he was feeling.

"If we are lucky, they may pass us by. You can go for weeks here without a drop of rain, and then suddenly a downpour comes out of nowhere and soaks you through." Waylon was flagging; clearly he was having trouble staying awake right now.

They had already walked through the fourth town on this

road, which left them with less than ten miles to get to a city—more specifically, a monster-hunting enclave. That made Grant realize that he was woefully uninformed about the politics of this District. Deciding that he could get some information as well as help his traveling companion stay awake, he began quizzing Waylon. "Can you tell me about the Houses?"

"You're a Noble and you don't know about the Houses?" Waylon gave him a strange look that was only tempered by exhaustion. "How is that possible?"

Grant had a ready answer for once. "I do know about the Houses in *January*. I was just wondering if it all worked the same here. In January, people are more focused on feasting and partying than the ins and outs of learning, or... thinking too hard."

Waylon nodded slowly, "That explains... I mean, I see. Where do you want me to start?"

"I know all *about* House Tuesday, the Peacekeepers. For... reasons. Why don't you start with your House, House Wednesday?" Grant figured it would be best to let the man discuss whatever he was most passionate about.

"Alright. I can do that. First off... we're awesome. House Wednesday is focused on logistics; specifically the logistics of hunting monsters and turning them into gear so that, um... so that we can hunt more powerful monsters. To be highly effective, we have to accumulate the best gear, which can only be found by acquiring the rarest beasts and monsters. We don't tend to fight other people, preferring to use our skills against beasts—but we *will*, if needed. As a point of fact, we often train members of House Friday to deal with overwhelming situations, such as their bounties being bandit lords with dozens of subordinates."

"How does that work? The whole turning monsters into gear?" Grant tried to inject enthusiasm into his voice, but he was just too *tired*. Between the sparks racing through his body and the sensory hallucinations from February Twenty Nine, as well as food and sleep deprivation, he just barely had anything left over to think with. Holding a proper conversation? Bah.

"Just like working regular animals or metals into armor and weapons." Waylon had perked up significantly. "You know how more powerful creatures have skills and can use spell-like abilities? That transfers almost directly into the gear we make. Look at the hallmarks of the different gear stages-"

"Wait, wait!" Grant's interruption threw off the twenty-something-year-old. "I know that gear is more powerful in the higher stages, but what are you saying about... hallmarks?"

"Oh, that's easy. Just because you make a snake fang from a Summer-stage monster into a dagger, that doesn't mean the weapon will be a Summer-stage weapon." Waylon didn't make Grant wait for the answer, thankfully. "There are two requirements that must be fulfilled for a weapon or armor to be considered at a new stage. Think about Spring gear; basically just a set of weapons and armor with no special effects, unless you start considering alchemical junk, right?"

"Junk?" Grant was surprised at the dismissive attitude toward life-altering medicines.

"Yeah, we consider anything single-use—consumables—to be junk," Waylon nodded seriously, his lips pressing into a hard line. "It might be useful, even expensive, but at the end of the day, it isn't something you can rely upon for longer than a moment before it's gone. Read as: junk."

"But... a huge amount of alchemical needs are fulfilled with monster parts, right?" Grant peeked back at the wagon full of alchemically-altered rations that Waylon *still* wouldn't let them break into. "Don't you guys do that? Sell the parts to alchemists?"

"Yeah, but House Saturday is all *about* single-use items." Waylon shook his head, even as Grant gave him a sharp glance. "They only produce a single *elixir* to sell per year, and we *know* they could make a ton of them if they wanted to do it. Instead, they make potions and pills that give short-term increases, just to make sure that people always need to keep coming back and buying from them. Such misers."

"That is what House Saturday is known as? Misers and alchemists?" Grant cautiously probed.

"Obviously." Waylon shot Grant an arched brow. "Is it different where you come from?"

"*Nope.*" Grant did his best to put this conversation behind them, already breaking into a sweat thinking about assassins coming after him for letting the Januarian open secret about Saturday out into the population. "Um… in that case, what about Summer gear?"

"Right, right." Waylon's smile returned as he stared dreamily off into the distance. "Spring gear is basically only good as throwaway training material. Not junk, exactly, but close… even though that's pretty much all we have here that isn't a relic from before the District Barriers went up. Summer gear actually offers decent protection and damage, which is the first marker for that type. The lightest weapons have to deal at *least* a base of twenty damage, or damage reduction for armor."

That was stunning to Grant. He took a look at his current weapons and armor, noting that they had a base damage or armor rating of *two*. That was for Early Spring *Medium* armor, so…! "Wait, that actually makes sense. It's an entire large rank, or three small ranks, up from what I've got now."

"Right? I saw that your armor was a little… ratty. Sorry, not trying to be offensive. Just truthful." Waylon shrugged, making the entire wagon bob behind him. "Your sword; is it really a Wielded Weapon? I've never seen one so dull."

"How about you just tell me about the other identifier for high-quality goods?" Grant gripped the hilt of February Twenty Nine defensively, trying not to be offended by this tactless man.

"Right… the single largest change is that there is enough essence, or maybe mana, stuffed into the item that new effects are added to it." Waylon's eyes were bright as he thought about someday seeing such legendary items. "The Summer ranks allow your equipment to have a single-target elemental effect on hit. It's entirely based on what the item was made from, but... fire, earth, water, or wind. That could mean anything, so don't think it's just an elemental blast. For instance, you have these fangs. If they were from a Summer monster, and got made into gear, they might have a water effect of poisoning on hit, or an earth effect of armor penetration."

"How is that 'elemental'?" Grant's question only got him a shrug in reply. "Okay... the armor, then?"

"When *it* gets hit," Waylon explained easily. "Imagine a cuirass that causes a windy knockback if you take a rib-shot."

Grant was silent as he tried to imagine how potent that kind of gear would be if he could wear it right *now*. He'd be unstoppable in January, and nearly so in February. "Then... the higher-ranked gear is even better?"

"But of course." Waylon laughed excitedly. "I've read in the histories that Autumn gear's *weakest* damage or armor base value sits at forty, and Winter at sixty. Now, at each one, a new effect is added. You keep the on-hit elemental effect, but at Autumn, it impacts an area-of-effect. Watch someone strike a shield, and a thirty-foot cone of flames erupts out of the shield in retaliation! At Winter..."

Waylon physically shuddered in excitement at the thought. "An elemental effect, plus area of effect with *no hit needed*. Do you even understand what that means? I would swing my sword through the air, and fireballs would shoot out and explode, same as if I was a pure spellcaster! Someone *tries* to hit my armor, they and their entire group *freeze* solid!"

Grant decided on the spot that the first thing he would be doing whenever he entered a new District was buying the best armor he could possibly find. "They just... function? There has to be a cost, right?"

"Mainly mana; it really depends on what you want out of it." Waylon's explanation was sketchy this time, and Grant realized that it was because the other man didn't know much more information about gear that hadn't been common in this area for a thousand years. "Maybe there's something they can use to power them, if they don't cultivate mental stats?"

Deciding it was time to switch tracks to help his companion save face, Grant asked the first thing that popped into his head. "In January, House Thursday are merchants and are the ones that set up supply lines, but I heard that something changed here?"

"They were stripped of their wealth and status, almost to a man. You may notice me, a Wednesday, doing what was histori- cally their career." Waylon's voice was hard. "The sole focus in House Thursday was maximizing profit. They aren't particu- larly good in combat, but they make up for that by hiring mercenary forces or defending themselves within heavily forti- fied outposts. This translated into letting their people suffer and go unprotected while *they* partied. The restructuring of our District started with them, but they were so well-defended that I think Lady February actually defeated the final member while she was on the mega-marathon route."

"She took time… in the middle of a marathon a hundred miles long… to topple a Wielder?" Grant's awe and fear of this individual only increased each time he heard something new about her.

"Called it her running break, even." Waylon had that dreamy look back on his face. "She's everyone's idol. That's another reason no one wants anyone to win this competition… no one feels like they can match up, but they know that no one *else* will either. No one deserves someone like her!"

"You need a nap," Grant deadpanned.

"Your *face* needs a nap." Waylon giggled wildly at his joke.

Grant snorted at that. "Ugh. Well, at least from what you have told me, there isn't much difference in the Houses between our Districts. One last thing—kinda changing topics here—I was wondering why you were so ready to toss me a spellbook?"

"Well… I…" From his uneasy look, it didn't appear that Waylon wanted to discuss his reasoning. Grant was going to let it go, but the man sighed and shrugged. "Okay… it's just that spells are seen as training tools at best, and a crutch for the weak at worst, unless you *actually* have a mental cultivation manual. Even then, you gain so *little* mana with each increase that they don't become a true threat for *decades*. They are mainly reserved for weak Vassals, or Wielders who get their weapons as children and need a small edge right away. I couldn't *believe* you wanted something like that... until I realized that you, um, need every training tool you can get."

"You Februarians are so funny," Grant chortled as he felt a renewed surge of electricity make his eyes start twitching. "*Winning* is what matters. So *what* if people think spells are useless? I don't have anything to prove. It's actually *nice* to know that while *I'll* do whatever it takes to win..."

"...they'll give up power for no real reason."

CHAPTER SIXTEEN

As it turned out, the new-growth trees the crows had attacked from had been the herald of a deeper and more ancient forest that apparently encircled the city. The setting sun had long since been blotted out by the knots of twisted branches overhead, and the wagon creaked as it moved deeper into the woods. Grant was carrying a torch that had been packed into the wagon, but even so, he struggled to keep the darkness at bay.

Grant.

"What was that?" Grant swung his torch around and peered into the darkness, hunting around with bloodshot eyes. "It sounded like someone was calling me? Did you hear that?"

Waylon slapped Grant's shoulder to catch his attention. "This place is called the Whispering Woods, and it *really* shouldn't be walked through at night. The wind whistling through the trees plays with the mind. Don't listen to the voices; pretty sure they're some kind of monster that convinces you to come off the road and to your doom. No one really knows for sure. The powerful go look and find nothing; the weak just don't come back."

"Come on, Waylon. That's not funny. I... I don't like the dark as it is." Grant eyed the man that was rapidly becoming a good friend, hoping to see mirth filling his face.

Unfortunately, he was deadly serious, and more awake than Grant had seen him in several hours. "I'm *not* joking. Even with the threat of the stalkers behind us, we should have set up camp on the border of the wood and made the journey in the morning."

A large object suddenly loomed large, blocking the road forward. "What is that?"

"Have your sword at the ready, Grant." Waylon slowly set down the wagon and retrieved his tomahawk from the cart. "I'll check it out. Wait here. If I'm not back in *one* minute, come after me and save me, no matter the cost."

Without giving Grant a chance to respond, Waylon strode toward the black object until he was lost to the darkness. "No matter the cost? What? Easy for him to say; that'd mean something went bad for *him*."

After a nail-biting minute, his companion returned with a relieved expression. "Thank Lady February, it's just an old hunting wagon full of skeletons."

It took a moment for Grant to properly register what Waylon had just said. "*Skeletons?*"

"From their size, I'd say they belonged to a variety of beasts. Their bones have long since been cleaned, so I assume these were on their way for processing."

"But... where are the hunters?" Grant peered into the forest, which seemed to have just gotten darker.

That gave Waylon pause. "They could have... taken their horses and bolted?"

"Why would they leave their valuable cargo here?" Grant readied February Twenty Nine as he made another connection. "What could have made what were clearly *experienced* hunters... bolt?"

"Look, we have no information. We've been walking for hours, and I suggest we press on. There could be any *number* of reasons why the hunting wagon was abandoned." Waylon groaned at the thought of continuing further, but he still motioned for Grant to come closer. "Help me shift this off the road."

"Any number of reasons, such as…?" Grant wasn't about to drop his guard. Something didn't feel right.

"I don't know, but let's stop wasting time? We're five miles at *most* from the city." Waylon shook his head at that. "I can't believe we're making such poor time right now; it took us over an hour to walk three miles. I'm gonna light a torch; can you hold it?"

Grant chose not to comment on that, but gave in to Waylon's desire. The pair moved forward and somehow managed to relocate the heavy hunting wagon. The carcasses may have been picked clean to the bone, but up close it didn't look like the result of 'proper care'. Even so, he kept his thoughts to himself. Waylon was more experienced at living in the wilds than he was, so he would trust the Wielder's judgment.

Obstruction cleared, a creeping dread ensured they made brisk progress, further fueled by adrenaline and the need to reach the safe-haven of the upcoming city. Waylon was starting to breathe heavily, the nearly forty hours of marching messing with his ability to function. "Slow down a bit, Grant. We'll reach the city soon enough. Ugh, would you look at that? I hate walking through those things. Mind swiping it with the torch?"

A net of gossamer silk thread hung between the trees, criss-crossing the entire road. Grant held his torch to the silk, and the fire incinerated the complex web.

"Grant, get into the wagon and pull out all the torches." Waylon's voice was calm but demanding. "Light them and place torches around the entire cart as fast as you can."

"What's wrong?" Grant's eyes darted around, but he found no issue. Even so, Waylon was standing stock-still. Following orders with a light grumble, Grant soon produced a ring of fire around the wagon. "Can you *please* let me know what's happening?"

"Well, you see, Grant…" Waylon's eyes never shifted from a point in front of them, "It appears the Gleam-Fangs have caught up to us, and they really don't want us to reach the city. Fun fact: if you stare at one and don't make any sudden motions, they try to remain hidden. That gives you just enough time to attempt to set up a perimeter, if you have a partner."

That was enough to make Grant look *into* the darkness. Now that there was more light, hundreds of eyes reflecting the flickering illumination let him know *exactly* the sort of trouble they were in. He flinched as spider silk sprayed through the air towards them, only for most of it to burn as it passed over the barrier of torches.

"Waylon, what does your armor cultivation look like?" Grant knew that in normal life, it was the height of impropriety to ask this exact question. Luckily, he had a very good reason. "The standard stalkers were unable to break my skin; only the monsters were able to do it when using their skill. If yours is high enough, we have a really good chance of-"

"I'm a Berserker cultivator." Waylon's voice wobbled in fear as the spiders began creeping closer. "Weapon and physical cultivation only. Actual armor is considered… archaic. Almost no one bothers with armor anymore, since converting our standard athletic clothes into proper armor is so expensive that usually only the heads of Houses will do it anymore."

"I don't need a history lesson; I need to know if you can take a *hit*." The first spiders started coming after them, and Grant began putting his sword to good use. "Will you be able to *survive* this?"

Damage dealt: 20 slashing. Overkill!

"I can take hits, but… the poison? It's a paralytic in the small ones, until they reach full-grown. The adult poison is corrosive and-" Waylon was babbling, but luckily, his body had taken over and his tomahawk was whipping through spider bodies almost as fast as it was moving through the air.

Conversation ended as they got to killin'. Spiders were crawling from *everywhere*, and no matter how fast Grant swung, dozens were soon skittering across his body and trying to dig their fangs in. They didn't manage to do so, but not for lack of trying. He even got to experience firsthand that his eyeball was considered armored, thanks to wearing a helmet. He had no idea how that worked, but he was indescribably glad that the fangs simply bounced off. Even so, a paralytic coated his eye, and he was soon unable to properly focus.

In that instant, all the spiders on him suddenly popped, and the smell of burnt hair filled the air as he spasmed in pain.

Damage dealt: 10-20 slashing x111. Overkill x92!

Damage dealt: 20 lightning x35. Overkill x35

Damage taken: 0 lightning (10 mitigated).

Once he noticed that Spark Shield had switched from training mode to active mode, Grant had taken to rolling around to squish the spiders that were on and around him, and was intrigued to note that what he thought was a purely defensive shield came into play at least a *little* when he was using his body as a weapon. As he got to his feet after the most recent roll, he noted that there weren't any spiders coming after him. For a confused moment, he was unsure of why. Then he saw that Waylon had fallen over, and the spiders were going after the downed target. He rushed over and started rolling over them, slapping with the flat of his blade, and in general making a ruckus until the few survivors fled.

Waylon was covered in bites and was spasming as his body attempted to remain breathing through the paralytic rampaging through his blood. Grant slammed February Twenty Nine into its sheath, then reached for his friend. A panicked gurgle was all the warning Grant had, and he whirled around and attacked with a form-perfect Iaijutsu.

Damage dealt: 11 slashing. Overkill!

The spider he slashed looked vastly different than the others. As he bisected it, a surprisingly large amount of fluid splashed onto him. He flinched instinctively and looked at himself. "What-?"

That was all he could get out before the stench hit his nostrils, making him gag. "Was that a *skunk*?"

Coughing and trying to get the feeling of *wet* out of his nostrils, he grabbed Waylon and lifted him onto the wagon. Then he set off as fast as his exhausted body could manage toward the city, hoping that he could make it before his new friend succumbed, or another ambush ended them outright.

CHAPTER SEVENTEEN

As it turned out, Grant did not need to make it the entire way to the city. A subjugation team met them only a mile further down the road, hurrying back toward the initial site of the reports. Grant was seriously concerned to be surrounded by nearly fifty Vassals and Wielders so suddenly, but to his great relief, they were only concerned for his and Waylons' well-being.

While he was unsure if another random civilian would have gotten the immediate treatment that Waylon did, Grant thought it was nice to see the others spring into action to save the poisoned and paralyzed young man. Unfortunately for Grant, the stench coming off of his clothes was so extreme that no one volunteered to come and check in on him, but that was fine with him... all the way until someone explained that he was coated in tracking fluids that wouldn't fade for at least another two weeks unless he received intervention from an alchemist.

The stink *wasn't* why he had been left alone, as he'd initially thought; the fact was that no one wanted to get the smell on them while they were hunting the monsters. It wasn't until they came to a stream and an utterly spent Grant soaked in it for a solid ten minutes that he was reluctantly allowed to join the main group. As they were so close to the city, they decided to send back their fastest people to get Grant and Waylon into the protection of an enclave, while the majority of the group continued onward to go and burn out the nest of Stalkers.

Noticing the state that he was in, they directed Grant to get on top of the wagon, and his soaking wet body was simply strapped to the top with a tarp. After nearly three days of continuous fleeing, filled with intermittent combat and constant pain, he thought that it might have been the most comfortable bed that he had ever slept on. As soon as he was flat, Grant was asleep. His dreams were filled with spiders, bright orange hawks, and shadowy figures digging away at his soul.

Then everything changed.

Grant looked around in the gray world that he was standing in, and tried to puzzle out what was happening. He *knew* he was still asleep, but something told his mind that this was real.

"Hello, Grant. Welcome into February Twenty Nine."

"Sarge?" Grant turned around and stared at the strangest man he had ever seen. He appeared human-ish, but had draconian eyes and muscles that would look more appropriate on a Dire Gorilla. His entire head was hairless, and he easily stood nine feet tall. "What in the name of the Seventh Sword Saint are *you*?"

"I'm *Sarge*, you punk." Sarge growled at him, and a massively oversized version of February Twenty Nine appeared in his hand. "You can only come here two more times after this, but just like every other Wielder out there, you get to use the runoff Quintessence to improve a single skill while you break through a major stage in cultivation."

"I… I broke through?" Grant's eyes lit up. "How? When? Why didn't I know?"

"You broke through on pure cultivation, not by leveling up. You were already close, but doubled cultivation speed, thanks to Spark Shield, helped your mental cultivation a lot." Sarge was clearly impatient. "Listen up: breaking through major ranks can only be done while you sleep, to allow your body to increase in potency without breaking your psyche. You only have a short while where you can direct the overflow into me, so tell me what skill you have that you directly want to increase by one tier."

"That's... I can do that?" Grant's question was met by a nod. "That should be easy, right? Kenjutsu. Always Kenjutsu."

"Hm. Good. That mental cultivation hasn't been going to *waste*, then." Sarge did *something*, and the particle-laden air around them began to swirl and drain away. "While you're still asleep, let me explain what happens at the different tiers. Didn't think this would happen for a long time, so I didn't bother."

"All skills are different, but there is a clear method that each one conforms to at each tier. At tier one—Novice tier—there's a ten percent flat increase. With weapons, this means bonus damage. With something like... let's use alchemy as our example today, it means a more potent effect. Tier two—Beginner tier—gives you a bonus of 'Perfect Aim'. For you, it means that you will be able to put your sword *exactly* where you want it. Might not seem interesting now, but you'll see. It *is* impacted by what your target does, but you'll never need to worry about cutting yourself with a sword again. Continuing our example, an alchemist would be able to place reagents in perfect positions every single time."

"What does-" Grant's interruption was flat-out ignored as Sarge powered on.

"*Tier three*—Apprentice—gives you a Critical Success increase. You put the sword where you want it to go, it has a better chance of *decimating* your target. Tier four—Student—will give you a flat twenty percent increase to all damage. Now we're out of time. Look at how unbalanced you've become." Sarge nodded behind Grant, who turned and saw *inside himself* for the first time ever.

Four enormous orbs were slowly orbiting what had to be his heart. One was steel-grey, the next was leather brown, the third was a radiant deep-water blue, and the final orb was blood-red. The last was enormous, and seemingly strained against the bounds it had been forced into. The sheer size of it was causing the orbits of all of the other spheres to become lopsided as it pulled against them, making Grant wonder where his physical cultivation was actually sitting currently. For the first time ever, attempting to pull his status up gave him nothing.

"Look closely, and discover the ways that what you *do* impacts your *self*." Sarge's words were strange and philosophical, utterly unlike how he usually was. "Look into your mind."

Grant looked at his 'mind' cultivation more closely, and suddenly it was right in front of him. There were odd pathways that connected this orb to other things, and as soon as he noticed the first one, it tried to hide from him. Frowning, he looked closer, and found that the harder he looked... the harder it was to find. "Is that my stealth skill?"

"Correct," Sarge stated simply. "While you're here, I want you to change that skill."

"What? *Change* it?" Grant searched for Sarge or the skill, and yet couldn't find either beyond the shimmering energetic orb. "Why? *How?*"

"Stealth is unbecoming of a samurai-in-training like you," Sarge explained, his voice coming from everywhere. "Unless you want to *kill* all your opponents, you will need to *defeat* them. You will be hunting, chasing, and intentionally drawing their ire so that you can move as fast as possible. Stealth is *not* what I had been attempting to teach you when you went against the Gleam-Fang. I want you to grasp stealth and reel it in. Take that connection away and channel it into your armor cultivation."

"This seems... my mind is *screaming* at me not to do this," Grant admitted cautiously as warning bells seemed to physically resound within his brain. "Also, I'm *not* a samurai. I don't even know what that means. I'm a cultivator."

"You'll lose this skill permanently. There will be no regaining it. This is true." Sarge quietly ignored Grant's protest against the life goal he had set for the young man. "It *hurts* to let go of something that would make your life easier. If it were someone else... never. But you *cannot* increase your stealth and still be the Calendar King. Instead of this skill making a pathway from your mind to your body, sending it into your armor will provide you with defense that is specific to protecting you from those more powerful than yourself."

Grant grabbed stealth, the entire representation of it in his soul... then *tore* it out of his body cultivation with the intention of connecting it to his armor cultivation. Happily, the intent was all that was needed, and the new channel was formed spontaneously, because Grant was in no state to function as he ripped away a part of his soul and attached it elsewhere. It wasn't *pain*; it was an utter feeling of loss. A part of him that had been there was *gone*, and even though he had something else now, it would never be the same.

The strange vision faded, and he opened his eyes to see an unfamiliar thatched ceiling. Grant sat straight up, the sudden motion launching him up from the floor he had been lying on, his body sprawled halfway through the door to the room. He groaned and tried to pull his head back, managing to do so only by absolutely *wrecking* the flimsy wood.

Damage taken: 1 terrain.

An unfamiliar voice crowed, "Called it! He was breaking through a major rank."

"Yeah, but he was out *way* longer than anyone else I've ever seen going through that?" another new voice queried. Grant squinted around for the speakers that sounded like they were right next to him, but couldn't find anyone. They were walking, their steps so loud that it made his head pound. Five seconds later, the ruined door was pushed open, and two people in the heraldry of House Wednesday stepped in. "Hi, there. You okay?"

"Ugh... sorry about the door," Grant whispered, even though it sounded like a shout to his ears.

"You saved one of our boys; a door isn't even worth mentioning." The smaller of the two men stepped forward and gave Grant a once-over. "You look unharmed, but... something is messing with my ability to *see* you clearly. Are you healthy?"

Grant's mind flashed to what had happened in his soul, and he gave a light nod. The larger man smiled warmly. "Besides all the help you've been, this is a room made especially for people that are breaking through into a new major cultivation stage. Everything in here is cheap and easily replaceable so that you can get used to the changes. Figure yourself out, then come down the hall so we can discuss what happens now."

They walked away, and Grant sank his aching head into his hands.

"Display status changes." As the screens appeared, he felt a twinge of loss within himself that swiftly faded.

Name: Grant Monday
Rank: Lord of The Month (January)
Class: Foundation Cultivator
Cultivation Achievement Level: 12
Cultivation Stage: Early Summer NEW!
Inherent Abilities: Swirling Seasons Cultivation
Health: 228/229
Mana: 8.1/9

Characteristics
Physical: 89 -> 119 *Major breakthrough!* (Cultivation Stage Maximized. Gains will be retroactively applied when all stages are aligned.)
Mental: 35 -> 40
Armor Proficiency: 45 -> 51
Weapon Proficiency: 67 -> 75

Skill tier increase: Kenjutsu (2/10).
Tier one effect: All damage dealt when wielding a sword is increased by 10%.
Tier two effect: Your sword will never betray you. When a sword is wielded by you, the blade will always land exactly where you intend.

Skill destroyed: Stealth. This skill has been rejected and altered. As the connection slot is still in use, the original skill can never be regained.

Skill created: Reflective Skin (1/10). Knowing your enemy is half the battle, and you've found a way to make it harder for other people to understand you! As this skill is self-created, it will increase significantly faster than other skills.

Tier one effect: Increases effectiveness of armor cultivation by 10% when interfering with others' abilities to inspect your innards or cultivation ranks.

"Wha... wow." Grant stared at his new characteristics, the changes in his skills, and especially at Reflective Skin. Each time his eyes touched it, he felt the loss of his stealth and a strange yearning to *prove* that this skill was worth having instead. "It'll improve faster? Why don't more people do this?"

<Would *you* ever knowingly go through that again, Grant? I know of some incredibly potent skills you could make.> Sarge's offer reminded Grant of exactly what he'd had to go through to get that rapid-growth skill, and he admitted to himself that *no*, he would never willingly do so a second time. <Best way to get used to your unshackled body is to swing me around. Sword out!>

Grant pulled February Twenty Nine out of its sheath and started moving through sword forms. He marveled at the explosive power of his body, and the fact that the blade would *instantly* come to a halt if he wanted it to do so, no matter how much force he may have put behind the initial swing. It made his forms seem completely inhuman as he swung in perfect lines, zigzags, and varied patterns. His sword seemed to hang in the air as he traded which hand he used to wield it, and he found that it was equally easy to use either when using single-hand attack patterns.

"Sarge... why did that happen? *Any* of that," Grant eventually asked his mentor. "I don't understand why I just *now* broke through a stage, when two of my characteristics were already showing as Early Summer."

<If you were a method cultivator, or a duo cultivator, then that would have been all you needed,> Sarge explained as Grant wiped his sweaty face. <Yet, you are a *Foundation* cultiva-

tor. You have higher heights available for you to reach, but limiters on the speed at which you can achieve them. The short answer? You needed to have an imbalance that broke the deadlock of your various cultivations. The average of all four of your methods is *always* restrained by the lowest possibility. With mental cultivation reaching forty, your physical finally progressed to Mid Summer, and changed what the 'average' lowest bound characteristic was.>

"That's... that was the *short* answer?" Grant's laughter caused Sarge to grumble threateningly at him.

<Looks like you need *spicier* training. Oh, *look*! *Wall krakens!*>

CHAPTER EIGHTEEN

It took Grant well over an hour to get used to the changes that had swept through his body, and he 'died' a few times, but finally, he was ready to re-enter society. He was *pretty* sure he wouldn't accidentally smash anything.

As he walked down the hallway, the whistle of wind drew his attention as it blew through boarded-up windows. Through the gaps in the wood, he could see out into the city and was shocked at the state of the place. Previously vibrantly painted doors and fences had faded, their paint peeling and fluttering off on the breeze. The shocking emptiness felt wrong to Grant and sent shivers down his spine. "What happened here? Did they come under attack?"

He hadn't been expecting an answer, but Waylon came out of one of the doors in the hall just as Grant was muttering to himself. "Kind of? They were 'under attack' by the drive towards physical cultivation. This city was once thriving with industry, and people came from near and far for their expertly crafted goods. When Lady February's father came into power, there was a shift towards improvement via physical cultivation. Any business not aligned with this purpose... suffered."

"Waylon! You're okay!" Grant ran over to his friend and looked him over, noticing a few wounds, but the man was clearly well enough to move. Not wanting to put spidery thoughts in his friend's mind right after their reunion, Grant nodded toward the window. "That makes sense, I suppose...? That's why it was abandoned? Or do people live here still?"

"Normal people, not so much, no. This is now a House Wednesday enclave. Basically, a quick-reaction force that is sent out against monsters and such that are threatening the area. It also serves as a marathon rest stop, but most people try to power through here and get through the woods as fast as possible." Waylon didn't seem sad about the revelation, so Grant assumed he had no real relation to this place. "The final nail in the coffin was when Lady February took over. Businesses not aligned with improving people—pretty much anything leisure-related—were consumed by February-approved establishments to pay for the equipment and supplies required for the numerous updated regulations that swept through the district."

Grant wasn't sure what to make of this information, so he went with the safe option. "That's terrible for them, but... good for people in general? What happened to the people that lived and worked here?"

"Who knows? I assume they traveled to one of the other cities, such as Valentine, for work or training." Waylon smirked slightly at Grant's concern. "We don't need them, Grant. Don't worry."

"Don't need them?" Something about that statement rang false, and Grant felt the need to voice it. "When all the businesses that paid taxes and supported the District are gone... what happens then? Who is growing food? Who is making gear, or selling it? Who repairs buildings, or builds them?"

"The Noble Houses will be in charge of infrastructure. House Wednesday's income depends upon collecting monster parts, and there *is* a huge demand. A quality set of armored running shoes can make all the difference in beating the various dangers during a challenge," Waylon explained proudly.

"What's the end game with all this cultivation, though? When does it end, so people get back to their regular lives? Does it have a point beyond power for power's sake?" Grant's question made Waylon search for an answer, and he failed to find one. "If that's the case… it almost sounds like the entire District is preparing for war. But against who?"

"Um… childhood obesity?" Waylon faltered as they approached the end of the hallway where the pair of men had asked Grant to join them. The older of the two was berating the younger.

"How many times have I told you, boy? *Defense!*" The older gentleman jabbed a finger forward and poked the other in the head. "Seriously… If you weren't my nephew, I'd have given up on you already."

"Defense is just telling the world that you can't take a hit," the younger man muttered as he got back into a ready stance.

"Why does everyone nowadays act like getting hit is such a great proof that you're *strong?*" The older man sighed at his trainee, then his eyes lit up as he noticed Grant and Waylon enter the room. "Good to see you both up and about! First things first: Sir Stinky, this is an alchemical solution that we want you to add to a bath and submerge yourself and your gear in for as long as you can tonight. It's untested, but we *think* it'll remove at least most of the scent marker on you."

He pulled out a bottle and tossed it to Grant, who grimaced as he realized that tonight would be bath night—and tomorrow would be a long day of wet, chafing armor. "Right, introductions are in order. I'm Student Wednesday, and this is Novice Wednesday."

Grant regarded the two men, then their name tags over their heads. Oddly enough, the strange names were confirmed by the system. "That's a unique moniker… is it an, um, family thing?"

"Are you out of your mind?" Waylon questioned harshly, staring daggers at Grant. "Student Wednesday here is actually the Prime Vassal of Heavyweight Wednesday the Sixth. Student has proven his peerless mastery of wrestling time and again, and I *certainly* won't allow you to besmirch-"

"Sir *Waylon*," Student interrupted before the conversation could devolve further. "From the look of things, Grant doesn't come from around these parts, and we certainly can't hold that against him."

"I didn't mean to offend?" Grant's confusion was practically palpable, but it seemed to be too touchy a subject for the older men to comment on. Luckily, Novice seemed to have no qualms about diving in.

"Vassals usually get pulled from the family of current Wielders," Novice explained without looking at the others. "Houses Wednesday, Saturday, and Sunday were practically the *only* Houses that didn't lose positions, having proven to Lady February that they deserve to keep what they've been given. Now… a Wielded Weapon used to go to the direct descendant of the Wielder when they retired; but by order of Lady February, they instead go to the most *qualified* person. Student is by far the most qualified to take over if his Wielder falls, so insulting him-"

"I was only wondering why his name was 'Student'," Grant cut in while waving his hands wildly. "Everything else you're saying makes sense. Why *wouldn't* the weapon go to the person best suited for it?"

The three men looked at him strangely, then Student began to laugh wholeheartedly. "I *like* this one! As to my name, branch family members give up their name when they are in pursuit of power. When their main focus reaches a higher tier, their name changes and they are given consideration for higher positions in their House. They might hold a title if they earn one, such as Heavyweight Wednesday."

"Then… you have a skill at the *Student* rank?" Grant gasped at the man, who nodded proudly.

"You clearly know what *that* means." Student winked at Grant, then bragged, "I'm getting near a name change to 'Journeyman' Wednesday, if you'd believe it. Then there will be almost *nothing* that can't be taken to the ground by me, if I give it my all."

Not knowing where to take the conversation from there, Grant smiled at the man and let the conversation lapse. Student coughed to clear the air, then motioned for them to follow. "The bathhouse is this way. We have your bounty ready and are ready to offer you a fair price for the materials you've collected. Other than that, we had planned to send three Novices and one Beginner with you as an escort to Valentine. Both as a thanks to you for saving our Waylon, as well as protection from Gleam-Fangs, and experience for the chosen Vassals."

The sudden storm of information took Grant off-guard, and he could only agree. Nothing in that deal sounded off to him, and the extra protection would be great. Student smiled as they exited the building, making a motion to someone nearby. They were led directly to the baths, and he showed Grant to a private room. "Use the entire bottle, rub it into every part of yourself, then soak. I'm getting together your rewards now, and I'll send someone with meals to you as soon as they're ready."

Grant walked alone in the small room, with steam curling up around him. Student stopped in the doorway and nodded at the young man. "Thank you, Grant, for your services to House Wednesday. Please relax and recuperate, knowing that you have the full protection and hospitality of House Wednesday to lean on until you leave in the morning."

With that, he shut the door, and Grant poured the bottle of pink fluid into the bath. He eased into the water and fully relaxed for the first time in February.

<You were supposed to rub it onto *yourself* first,> Sarge grumbled at him. <*Sword Saints*, you're bad at following instructions.>

CHAPTER NINETEEN

Clean, well-fed, and rested, and with a tightly bound stack of Time secured in his pack, Grant took one last look at the boarded-up shops and faded signs before leaving the city behind. According to Waylon, the place had once been teeming with life, with craftsmen and shopkeepers hawking their wares to passers-by. He tried to imagine what it was like, the rasping of saws and beating of metal. Physical cultivation and bettering yourself was important, but not if it led to this.

"What a waste." He tore his gaze away and focused on the road ahead. Waylon and their escort trailed behind, and he shouted at them playfully. "Come on, Waylon. We'll never reach the House Wednesday's enclave next to Valentine if you walk at a snail's pace! How am *I* more motivated to get walking than you are?"

"If you hadn't noticed..." Spittle flew as Waylon enunciated the words with faux haughtiness, "I was *injured* during our spidery encounter."

"Why don't you reach into your wagon and put one of those *expensive* poultices on it and get a move on? We don't have all day!" Grant then did something for the first time that he would never forget: a one-handed cartwheel into a front flip. With his body still being larger than healthy, it looked especially impressive. "I think you Februarians might be onto something with this physical cultivation thing!"

"How in the *world*-" Waylon gaped at him.

"Woo-hoo, physical cultivation!" Grant taunted the injured man by flipping again.

<Now *this* gives me ideas.> Sarge's malicious excitement set Grant on edge instantly. <Remember how you were mentioning to me that you thought Lady February's ability to move was impressive? Well... let's just say you don't become a sword saint by ignoring the environment around you. Congratulations! Now that someone else is pulling the wagon, you get to return to practical training! Get up that tree and start learning how to jump between branches. Watch out for regular spiders and all *sorts* of orange menaces!>

"S-Sarge, I was just showing off my-" Grant whimpered, only to be cut off by the sword.

<No, no. You're right. Now that you're at an *acceptable* level of physical cultivation, just being *normal* is beneath you. By the time we reach Valentine, you'll be able to run a tumbler *backward*! I said *up* the *tree*.>

Taking a deep breath, he started climbing and got to the lowest branch. He jumped, missed the next tree over, and hit the ground hard.

Damage taken: 5 terrain.

"Ow."

<Fool. You think you can get to a higher branch by jumping *up* when the branch is twenty feet away? Your cultivation isn't *that* high. Start high, jump *down*, then get enough momentum to be *sent* up.>

"Grant, stop that! I wouldn't want your death on my conscience. Let's just walk, okay?" Waylon trotted forward stiffly in an attempt to catch up with his fallen companion. "We're at least three days from the estate; longer, at my pace."

"No can do." Grant's words revealed such a deep longing

for walking that Waylon was completely confounded. "Walking at the pace of a geriatric turtle just isn't in the cards for me. I'm going for a… jog. *Hurk.* Can't believe I said that out loud. I'll stick next to the main path. If you hear screaming, it's just me screaming, so please send help."

"In that case, I'll enjoy the peace and quiet with our *armed escort.* Hey, if you're gonna be in the trees, be on the lookout for some redcap mushrooms, would you? Do you know what they look like?"

"Mushrooms with a red top, I'm guessing?" Grant paused and rummaged through his pack, pulling out two wilted and slightly smooshed fungi. "I have two here."

"What?" Waylon immediately reached for them. "Do you find pleasure in my suffering or something? I thought we were friends, Grant."

"Of course we are! What are you talking about? Are these hurting you somehow?" Grant's eyes widened in horror. "You're allergic, and the reaction made it so you could barely fight against the spiders!"

"Not cool, Grant. I was fighting as well as I could." Waylon huffed and looked away sharply. "Those mushrooms have medicinal properties. They aren't powerful like full poultices, but they are a base ingredient and will stop bleeding and provide pain relief. I'd *love* to have those, if you don't mind. Some of these gashes have opened already."

Grant couldn't bring himself to explain that he'd had no idea what they were when he plucked them during his travels, though he *slightly* remembered the mushrooms *maybe* being on the stump of the Gleam-Fang nest? "Please, take them if it'll help. I'll leave my pack in the wagon as payment; sound like a plan? Actually, maybe *you* should sit in the wagon?"

"Like a weakling? Waylon scoffed as he accepted both mushrooms and started rubbing them on his injuries.

Not sure what Waylon's comment meant, Grant shrugged, put away his pack, and got back to training. "Hope you feel better. I'll keep an eye out for more redcaps during my jog."

<Enjoy your 'jog',> Sarge cackled as Grant got back into the tree. <Next time you fall, there's a flying orange Vivian-spider coming to nibble on your neck. No teeth, but fourteen tongues.>

"By the Regent...!" With that potent threat, Sarge left him to his thoughts. The warm afternoon February sun warmed Grant's face as he cautiously plotted each individual movement. After the initial terror of flying through the air unsupported finally faded, he was surprised to find that he was relishing the activity. Back in January, he would never have imagined voluntarily swinging through trees to train his reflexes, let alone *enjoying* it.

The odd path brought him across a glade just as the trees ended, and he leapt up onto the upper wall of a humpbacked stone bridge. He marveled at his increased balance as he mimicked the feat he had once seen Lady February accomplish —albeit with far less grace. Everywhere he looked, spring was bursting into life, the harshness of Winter but a memory as frost lost its grip on the land.

If it wasn't for the hilt gripped in one hand to stop it from clattering against his hip, he could have forgotten that he was on a mission to defeat Lady February and move through the world by dancing with his blade. Jumping off the bridge, he landed on a slippery stone only to fall and wind himself. The promised human-torsoed spider jumped at him with a banshee scream, and he nearly matched it with his own. He had completely forgotten the punishment, and had only thought it applied to falling out of a *tree*.

Even so, the bright orange monstrosity was easily defeated —his sword flashed out of its sheath and returned so fast that Grant himself had barely recognized what had happened. He stared at the fading training device, then dropped his stunned gaze to February Twenty Nine. "This is just the *Beginner* tier?"

<It only gets better. Work hard.>

He hadn't needed to use conscious thought to remove the weapon from its sheath, and it was also the first time he hadn't needed to use both hands to carefully put it away. Grant just intrinsically *knew* that the sword would do what he needed. Getting back to the task at hand, he reached the trees on this side of the river and started *moving*.

After bounding along for over an hour in one direction, Grant decided that he either needed to wait for the others or head back. Hopefully, Waylon's injuries would have healed enough that he could make faster progress. Grant entered another glade right next to the road and smiled. This was an ideal place to stop and wait, and he was loath to backtrack and lose his progress. Instead, he came to a halt and started pulling on his sore limbs.

<Behind you!> Grant was too busy stretching after the strenuous exercise to react quickly.

Thud.

Damage taken: 43 blunt (12 mitigated) (Sneak attack).

A spiked log attached to a rope smacked dead-center into his back just between his shoulders, and he went tumbling as half a dozen people erupted from the surrounding woodline with ropes and weapons. "Don't worry, mister. We'll have you out of that armor in a jiffy! Milly, don't just stand there; give me a hand."

Grant was on his feet in a flash, his hand on the hilt of February Twenty Nine. Then he saw who was after him. A young teen girl ran forward with a dark laugh, then did as she was told, making Grant hesitant to attack. He wanted to ask them what they were doing, but it was pretty clear that they were mugging him. After a quick glance around, Grant confirmed that many of his attackers were even younger than his nineteen years. The others, the older ones, let the youngsters go forward to act as shields for them.

The man that had spoken grunted when he realized that Grant was almost entirely unharmed. "Well, isn't that some-thing. Must have a pretty hard head; that gear is nowhere *near* good enough to block a hunting trap to the spine. Normal

person woulda been dead, but I'm guessing that you're important and rich enough to be a real *competitor*."

'Milly' screamed at Grant to get his attention as well as
psych him out, then brandished a sharp dagger in front of her.
"Lose the armor or your life."

Not wanting to fight kids, and uncertain that he could fight
off the full score of people that had spilled out of the woods,
Grant hesitantly pulled off his helmet. When no one moved to
attack, he took off his torso and leg armor, eventually standing
in just his normal clothing and travel-worn boots.

Milly moved forward and patted him down to make sure he
wasn't hiding anything else, then unsheathed February Twenty
Nine. The look of disappointment was etched on all the thieves'
faces. "Scrap metal. Whatever; it's still a sword. *Someone* will buy it."

Confused, Grant eyed the blade. It was as they described,
but...? Then he remembered that without the upgrade
provided by Weapon/Armor Synergy, the blade reverted to its
former rusty appearance.

"Get moving, kids!" The older man sighed in frustration.
"We need to keep moving; this is Wednesday turf."

Milly jammed the helmet onto her head. In different
circumstances, Grant would have laughed at the comical sight
of the young girl wearing his oversized leather skullcap. It was
so big, it almost completely obscured her vision. He stood there
helplessly as the random highwaymen backed away slowly, then
made a mad dash for a deeper area of the Whispering Woods.

It took about a half hour, but Grant had calmed down as
familiar voices began to echo down the road. Thinking that the
robbers had probably been fleeing the entire time, Grant
decided he had waited long enough. He reached toward a wispy
white distorsion in the air. "Time is Space."

He pulled February Twenty Nine out of nothing and let a
small smile grace his lips as he thought about Milly screeching
in fury somewhere. With a sigh, he rubbed at his deeply bruised
back and got onto the road proper. A familiar face was waiting

for him. Waylon struggled to contain his laughter as he caught sight of Grant approaching through the trees.

"Have a… pleasant jog?" Waylon covered his mouth to hide his laughter at Grant's glare. "You appear to be missing your suit of armor."

"It was holding me back, so I took it off," Grant snapped sarcastically. "I got robbed. Bandits using kids to stop me from fighting back took anything that had actual value."

"Bandits?" Waylon glanced sharply at Beginner, who shrugged.

"Unsurprising," Beginner told them apologetically. "We try to patrol the area, but we're a glorified guardhouse. There were *thousands* of people that used to make their living in the city, and not all of them found… gainful employment."

"I've never had issues." Waylon pondered the issue, but shrugged after a long moment. "Sorry, Grant. Not much you can do about it. At least you have a fat sack of Time to spend when we get to Valentine. I'm sure you'll be able to get decent gear. Also, I'm feeling much better, if that helps. Those redcap mushrooms worked wonders."

It was good news, but Grant couldn't find it within himself to make happy noises right at that moment. He walked down the road, rusty sword bared and carried in his hand at all times, due to being down one leather sheath.

CHAPTER TWENTY

They walked in silence through the evening and into the night. Grant was starving but didn't dare suggest they stop, just in case the bandits came back, and he was forced to *actually* fight what had clearly been near-starved children. The next two days passed quickly as Grant practiced moving over rough and strange terrain. Sarge pushed him to try more and more daring feats, to the point that Grant was starting to literally *fear* waking up in the morning.

He was longing for the security he had felt when wearing his armor, even if it had only actually granted him a measly two points of extra damage mitigation. That same fear made him miss what should have been an easy handhold as he jumped over a small ravine, and Sarge was so furious that he swarmed Grant with orange monsters until Grant 'died' to them.

<Are you so weak-willed that the loss of *stuff* breaks you mentally?> Sarge bellowed when Grant came around. <Is it because your sword is less *shiny*? Are you a magpie? Get up and get *good* if you don't want that to happen again!>

"I didn't want to hurt them, Sarge," Grant tried to explain to the furious sword-spirit.

<You're a *Beginner* in Kenjutsu! You literally *can't* hurt them if you don't want to do so!> Sarge's mental bellows almost knocked Grant unconscious. <If you don't want to hurt someone, *don't*! It's *that* easy! Now get up and stop pouting!>

On the fourth day, they started passing estates behind imposing ornate wrought iron gates, with large training facilities attached to the main buildings. In the distance, the lights of the city cast their glow into the night's sky.

The capital city: Valentine.

Unlike Mid January, the air here was clean, not smoggy from countless mills churning out equipment and food. Grant tried to be excited, but his intense training with Sarge had made it nearly impossible for him to feel anything other than exhaustion.

"We're almost there." Waylon sounded almost as weary as Grant felt. He glanced at their escorts and leaned in to whisper, "If anyone asks, you're my direct trainee. Spells may only be training tools, but we don't just hand them out to just anyone. Got that?"

"Is it that big of a deal?" Grant murmured back, only getting a serious nod in reply. Another hour of walking later, and they approached a large estate with the banners of House Wednesday proudly flapping in the wind. The flag showcased a large 'W' made of a single taloned monster foot resting on what Grant now recognized as a spiky cultivation orb, although it was yellow. Had he not broken through to the Summer ranks, he would have thought it was just a neat circle.

"Why is that yellow?" Grant whispered to Waylon, not wanting to step into another social faux pas. "Cultivation spirals are only grey, red, blue, and brown, right?"

"Not everything is about being perfectly accurate, Grant. It's just a representation of our respective position in the Houses of the Week, along with the fact that we cultivate." Waylon could see that Grant didn't understand, so he deigned to give up a little more information. "Humans can see a whole bunch of colors, but someone once made a list of the different organizations of colors. According to them, everything is a variation of seven primary colors, and that matched up with the days of the week."

"Don't tell me." Grant thought about where he had seen seven bands of color in nature. "Monday is red, then it goes orange, yellow, green, blue, indigo, and finally violet for Sunday? Or, *please* tell me someone had more imagination than that?"

"No... what? That's correct; what's the issue with it?" Waylon asked as the gate silently swung open as they entered the estate belonging to House Wednesday. Their boots crunched along the gravel, each step bringing them closer to the looming edifice of stone and wood.

"It's just a rainbow, Waylon." Grant saw understanding appear in his friend's eyes, then a hint of shame that he hadn't realized that till now. "I think someone convinced the Nobles that they were more clever than they actually were, and the Houses all swallowed the bait."

"That's..." Walon started howling with laughter and had to bend over to catch his breath. "*Why* has no one put that together?"

"Misguided pride?" Grant snickered all the way up until they finally stopped before the massive door.

"Ugh... I hate that you told me that. I'm never gonna be able to see all the banners together without looking for rain now." Waylon chuckled a little more, then waved at the building. "We call this place 'The Lodge'. C'mon in."

Grant followed Waylon inside the entrance vestibule, noticing a random dais just... sitting there. Nothing was on it. Why was it here? A conversation starter? He looked closer, noting a small carving on it that read 'For Travis'. "Ah. A... place of honor?"

"Nah. That's where we put our Travis-brand umbrellas when it's raining and they're wet," Waylon clarified for him. Grant nodded in understanding and scanned idly around, almost raising his sword when he saw dozens of monsters in mid-leap! Waylon's hand clamped down on Grant's sword hand, preventing him from attacking what turned out to be taxidermy.

"Calm down. They're stuffed. The only threat they pose is if they fall off the wall and crush you." Waylon's reassurance made the fight go out of him, but he kept a wary eye on the array of magnificent beasts as they made their way along the corridor. The way the things were mounted, they appeared to leap out of the wall with death in their eyes. The beasts had one thing in common: they all looked like deadly foes.

Grant froze as a glass-paneled door swung open, and they were confronted by a balding, beak-nosed man dressed in formal wear. "Master Waylon, will you be joining us for the evening meal?"

"Not tonight, Humphrey. Sir Monday is an expert in logistics and is here to share his insight on our training plans." Waylon offhandedly ignored the man from that point forward, making Grant once more wonder what his actual position was in House Wednesday. "We'll *expect* privacy."

"Very good, sir. Heavyweight Wednesday is currently in a meeting in the War Room. Shall I inform him of your arrival?" Humphrey leadingly offered.

"He's in residence today?" Waylon answered too quickly for Grant to feel comfortable. "*No.* There's no need. Thank you; leave us."

Humphrey bowed, then departed stiffly through another of the many doorways lining the corridor. Waylon gulped heavily. "*Phew.* I thought we were done for. He's *never* here; I guess he's feeling that he should make sure to meet the winners."

Grant wordlessly followed Waylon deep within the compound. Paintings of past heads of House Wednesday observed them, and Grant felt like they were judging him and his companion. Eventually, they stopped before a heavy wooden door. Waylon struggled to unlock the multitude of bolts but finally managed to get into the room behind them. "Wait here.

I'll see what I can find. If I get caught… we'll have to answer to House Wednesday as a whole for giving out rare resources."

"What? Why? What are you doing?" Before Grant got a satisfactory answer, Waylon slipped through the door out of sight. Several agonizing minutes passed, and Grant was sure that Waylon had been caught doing… whatever he had been doing. Finally, the door creaked open, and a triumphant Waylon walked through.

"What took you so long?" Grant let out an exasperated sigh. "What were you even doing?"

"I picked up a selection of elemental spells for you to choose from." Waylon showed Grant a stack of lightly glowing books, making Grant's eyes bug out a little. "I know you were excited about the scraps I handed you, but after everything you've done for me, I thought it'd be only fair to give you a proper selection."

"I'm really happy with this one," Grant lied as his jaw clenched tightly from the static stimulation. "It's *shockingly* effective."

"No way are you happy with that spell," Waylon snorted and offered the books once more. Under the light of a nearby oil lamp, he showed off three leather-bound spellbooks. "The first, the red one, is a flame spell. Cast actively, it heats your body. Perfect when traveling during the freezing days of winter. Cast passively, it adds burning damage to attacks. The damage over time can quickly wear down an opponent."

Grant imagined his sword exploding into flames as he dove into combat. Unfortunately, the thought reminded him that there was a dragon somewhere that was going to turn him into ash. "Not a defense against fire…? Probably a no from me."

Completely undaunted, Waylon showed off the next one. "Wind Walk. Its active ability generates a gust of wind that increases movement speed. How long it lasts depends on your mana reserves, but theoretically—with enough mana—you'd be able to run forever without getting tired. Its passive ability adds a gust of wind to every swing of your weapon, a little bit of knockback, or drying out the eyes of your enemy."

Grant considered it, but slowly shook his head. "For some reason, it just doesn't resonate with me."

"Okay... Earth Slap! It sends a wave of mud-"

Grant cut Waylon off. "No, *thank* you, but I'm actually happy with my spell as it is now. My cultivation is increasing, and I'm learning so much about mana use. Even if it hurts, I can just fight through it. Somehow, I doubt that these other spells scale up like this one does-"

"Yeah, they're all flat damage," Waylon confirmed.

"-which means that this will be more useful as I get better at using it," Grant finished, nodding to acknowledge Waylon's admission. "Who knows? Maybe I'll even figure out how to improve it someday; make it work without frying my eyeballs."

"I have my doubts."

<Seconded.>

"Well *thanks* for the vote of confidence." Grant wasn't sure which of the two he was speaking to, but he felt mildly offended at the lack of trust.

"Well... in that case, I'm not sure what else to say. Um... stay on guard against any Stalkers that snuck past the subjugation squad, and may we meet again?" Waylon scratched his head awkwardly, but Grant slapped it away and glared at the still-outstretched hand.

"I'm not a *pet*, Waylon." Both snorted at the other's antics and started back toward the main corridor containing the stuffed animals. They still freaked Grant out, but he tried to ignore them. Waylon stopped in his tracks. Grant, busy examining the various beasts, bumped into his back.

"Hey. What are we stopping for?" He peered over Waylon's shoulder, finding that the reason was standing right before them. Heavyweight Wednesday waited with his arms folded.

"Waylon, may I have a *word*?" The man's deep voice resonated through the corridor. "Follow me into the War Room, and make *sure* to bring your Monday friend with you."

As Heavyweight Wednesday disappeared into what was apparently the 'War Room', Waylon and Grant shared a concerned look. The gig was up; their goose was cooked. He didn't know how, but House Wednesday had discovered that they'd snuck into the vault.

"Just stay quiet, and only speak if spoken to!" Waylon whispered harshly. Grant nodded and followed him into the War Room. Even more animal busts lined the walls, along with shelves full of hefty tomes.

Heavyweight Wednesday stood over a table, his hands spread wide, with his back to them. "It appears to be weakening further, Waylon. We've received reports from Wielders and Vassals throughout the District. Sir Monday, can you come over here, please? I hear you have good insight into archaic information."

Grant went wide-eyed. Why would such a high-ranking Wednesday want to speak with *him*? Waylon just motioned for him to do as he was told, and the wrong words squeaked out of his mouth. "I can explain."

"Really? I haven't even told you what the problem is yet… perhaps Monday has information they haven't shared? I know Mondays are prized for their informational skills. Please, enlighten me."

Heavyweight moved aside, allowing Grant access to the massive sheet of parchment stretched across the desk. For a moment, he was confused, until he saw a marker highlighting the Whispering Woods. He was looking at a map, but not just any old map; this one had such crisp detail that he expected objects to start moving of their own accord. Even so, he was unfamiliar with the District and therefore struggled to understand what anything represented. Surrounding the District were the shimmering barriers separating January, February, and March.

In a bid for time, he picked up a magnifying glass that lay beside the map. It looked similar to one of Randall's, which he'd played with as a child and had subsequently been punished for using without permission. Staring intently through the glass, he noticed that the barrier between February and March had faded, as though someone had taken an eraser to the oil painting.

Pain shot through his body, and he let out an involuntary yelp as he doubled over. Both Heavyweight Wednesday and Waylon jumped at the sudden noise. Heavyweight leaned over the map and demanded, "What is it? What did you see?"

Sarge's sheepish voice slithered into Grant's mind. <Ah... sorry about that. Was adjusting Spark Shield; didn't mean to make it go through that particular sensitive area. I can confirm that your spell still works.>

Grant was glad they couldn't see his face turn red as he resisted shouting at his sword in front of them. He instead stabbed at the barriers around the District. "Here, and here, the barrier seems to have faded, going by the erasure, but perhaps knowing your specific issue would help me find what you need?"

"Interesting. I didn't notice those spots, but that's what I was afraid of. Who was the last person to alter the map?" Heavyweight Wednesday turned to look at Waylon, then his eyes flicked to the butler, who shook his head minutely. "Hmm... I suppose the regions where the barrier is weakening coincide with the sightings of mutated monsters. We believe that the barriers have begun leaking mana and altering the creatures near them. Waylon, I want you to investigate them further and report back to me. Is that understood?"

"Of course, Father." Waylon went pale as three pairs of eyes stared holes into him. "I-I-I mean, *yes*, Heavyweight! I'll get right on it."

The intimidating elder Wednesday let the awkward silence stretch a moment longer, then turned back to the map. "It doesn't appear to be urgent *yet*, but get on it as soon as you can. Grant, you've been inspected by members of our House, and as far as we can tell... the scent markers from the Stalkers have been fully eradicated by the alchemical soap. I received a report that no less than three subjugation squads reached and burnt out the nest, doubly checking for any additional creatures and finding no survivors. We believe that the threat has passed. In that case, our duty to protect you from being stalked has ended. You may both leave. Thank you for your… *insight*, Sir Monday."

"Before I go…" Grant hesitatingly pulled out the Wielded Weapon he had found in the Gleam-Fang Stalker's nest. "I'd like to give this to you. Your House has aided me beyond what they needed to do, and before anyone ever calls these actions into question, I'd like to absolve any debt between us."

Heavyweight Wednesday stared at the shining rapier, then between Grant and Waylon. "This… good. You are an honorable man, Sir Monday. I thought I was going to have to… no, none of that. Thank you. This will allow me to explain the *gifts* that the *House as a whole* gave you, instead of needing to punish a single *individual* or two for indiscretions. Know that I will speak well of you if it is ever needed."

Waylon gulped deeply as the brooding House Lord locked eyes with him. Leaving the imposing man to his map, the young men closed the door behind them very gently. Grant wiped a small river of sweat from his forehead, then turned to Waylon. "I suppose… we both have places to be, so I'd better get going. Thanks again for your help, and I hope we meet again."

As Grant walked towards the main door, Waylon stopped him with a hesitant call, as though he expected Grant to snap at him. "Wait. You're a man of your word, and you have risked yourself to rescue me on several occasions. You apparently also saved me from the punishment of giving you a spell, as well as sneaking you into restricted areas. Would you… mind continuing to travel together? My mission to the barrier will take me in the same direction anyway…?"

"Waylon…" Grant started slowly, turning to face his contemporary with a feigned look of disgust. "I don't know if I can handle much more of your Lordliness. The *heir* of Heavyweight *Wednesday*? What will the gossips say when I try to make my own name at the tournament?"

<I remember when you could barely spell your own name!>

Sarge chimed in with a touch of snark. <Ah, how much you've *improved* in a month!>

Sarge's cheekiness rolled off Grant like water off a duck, but Waylon looked like he'd been physically struck by the refusal, so Grant reached out to clasp forearms with his friend. "It was a *joke*! Given the option, I'd keep you in my pocket so we could travel the world together!"

That got a laugh out of Waylon, then a snort as he shared the mental image Grant had evoked. "Hopefully your shirt pocket. I've seen *exactly* how often you wash your pants, you filthy monkey."

"Of course my shirt pocket! How else would you enjoy the view as I swing along through the trees?" The outlandish conversation broke all the tension, and they laughingly left the holdings of House Wednesday and walked along the well-made roads. Under the light of the moon, the jovial pair headed out the wrought iron gate and towards the lights of Valentine.

CHAPTER TWENTY-ONE

"We could have spent the night at House Wednesday's estate, you know." Waylon pulled a warm wheatgrass shot out of his pack and downed it with a grimace. Wiping his mouth, he continued with a forlorn expression, "The chefs would have cooked us up a tasty breakfast. As monster hunters, we usually have access to a wider range of food, including meat from all over the District."

"You're telling me this *now*, Waylon? *Hours* after we left?" Grant honestly considered turning back, even though they were finally approaching Valentine proper. He was unable to keep the wistfulness out of his voice. "What kind of... does it taste good?"

"It's amazing. Sometimes, you can eat a single bite and stay full for *days*, if the meat is potent enough." Waylon sighed at the fond memory. "But I realized you needed to get to Valentine, and I just didn't have the heart to stop you."

"I might hate you a little right now, but it'll pass." Grant stomped his feet extra-hard as he walked. "I assumed that all you guys ate was horrid wheatgrass shots and bark-like protein bars, like everyone else."

"Well, we do have those, too. Mainly for guests we don't want sticking around." Waylon shrugged and paused to set his wagon down, taking a long moment to stretch. "It's only illegal to *sell* unverified food; luckily, you can collect and eat all you want. If I recall, the plan for the night was crispy barbecued beast-fowl. Delicious!"

"I'll barbecue *you*, if ya keep this up," Grant muttered darkly.

Waylon was trying to hold back a laugh as he looked over knowingly. "What was that? Didn't catch-"

"I said... I hope there's not a *queue*. You know, to enter the tournament, and we should keep this pace up." Grant silently thanked his increased mental cultivation, promising it that he would learn how to read a book in thanks for the excuse he had just been able to come up with.

"No line? Doubtful. It's still the qualifier for the main event, but the road will still be utterly stuffed with both competitors and spectators." Waylon's casual rebuttal gave him pause.

While he hadn't actually been planning to set up a strategy right now, Grant started considering options. He contemplated the road, and the huge wagon they were going to be pulling by hand. "We could always travel off-road to avoid the crowd? This was the final stop for the wagon, right?"

"True... but that opens us up to all sorts of nasty stuff, Grant." Waylon was apparently not on board with discussing the options right away. "Hey, I'm pretty beat. Why don't we stop for the night? We can stay at an inn; my treat."

The thought of a soft, warm bed in a safe location made Grant's inner lazy man squeal with joy. He tried to feign disinterest. "If you insist, I suppose."

"Then we can say that all between us is settled." Waylon nodded sincerely. "Finally, I can pay off my life-debt!"

"How expensive *is* this hotel?" Grant pretended to be aghast, while actually feeling *delighted* with the prospect of resting his feet. "Or is it just so rough in there that you think you'll need to save my life for us to get some sleep?"

Waylon didn't answer, merely laughing and speeding down the road. A short while later they arrived at the door of the inn. The warm glow from within was enticing and filled Grant with joy. He hadn't realized how weary he truly was. It had been an endless trudge without much of a rest, and the sleep he had gotten had been constantly interrupted by nightmares and the assault of orange attackers so that Grant would 'get used to fending off nighttime assassinations, according to Sarge.

They went inside, and Grant sat down at a round table by the open fire while Waylon got them a room and ordered food. The warmth of the blaze against his face and the chatty banter from the inn's other patrons soothed away his fears and worries to the point that he almost didn't hear Waylon sit down beside him.

"We got the last two rooms. Two Jiggity Jogger specials on the way." Grant smiled and nodded, licking his lips in anticipation. A nudge from Waylon awakened him a short time later, and he groggily pulled his tongue into his mouth and wiped his chin. He looked down at the plate of oats and wheatgrass shots before him and couldn't stop himself from letting out a moan of frustration.

"*No!* I've had enough of this horrid food!" The banter and conversations around them died, and many eyes turned towards the pair at Grant's outburst. "Is it so much to get a grilled steak? A bowl of stew?"

"Keep your voice *down!*" Waylon hissed at Grant, full-on smacking him in the face and getting nods of appreciation from the voyeurs, who turned back to what they were doing. "This is an *establishment* set up to furnish the needs of runners, and it's one of the better ones. Grant, you're in the *Capital City*. This is the seat of Lady February's power; *don't* get us tossed in a jail cell."

"I can't help what I *want*," Grant snapped at Waylon, his eyes locked on the miserable oats that were slowly sucking all the moisture out of the dish. "Back in January-"

"You whine about that place a lot, kid." Waylon's heavy

tone left no room for humor. "If you want January, you could always go *back*."

"No. It's a long story, and not one I feel like explaining right now, but January is lost to me." Grant reluctantly grabbed the spoon and pulled out a glob of mush. He munched on it, not really wanting to admit that with the cinnamon... it wasn't half bad.

"Then I'm off to bed. Here's your key; your room's upstairs, third on the left. When you get up tomorrow, be the young man that saved me. Not the soft brat that whines about his *vegetables*. You don't have a monopoly on suffering." Without another word, Waylon got up and left the table.

"Where did that come from?" Rather than sit there and listen as people whispered about him, Grant decided to retire for the night as soon as he finished his meal.

The following morning, following a much-needed rest, the companions were on their way. Waylon was his usual upbeat self, and the previous night apparently was forgotten. Grant knew that he needed to be more mature, so he put his pride aside. "Sorry about last night. I was tired and grumpy. Thanks for the food and room; it was very kind of you."

"You're a strange man, Grant," Waylon replied with a non sequitur. "When we're in peril, or in hard situations, you're ready for anything. You rush into danger, and you put yourself out there *hard*. Yet, as soon as you're offered a modicum of comfort, you become... whatever *that* was last night."

"That..." Grant felt deflated as he *really* thought about it. "Comfort sends me right back to being a proper *Januarian*. When we have fun, it's supposed to be *leisure*. When we eat, we *feast*. When something isn't *perfect*... we complain. I wanted to be like them so much when I was growing up, but my worldview was shattered. Now I'm in a place that *despises* that lifestyle, and I'm just... I'm *trying* to adjust."

"I can't say I understand," Waylon told him, not unkindly. "I know you're trying, and most of the time you do excellently. Listen, today's an easy day. We just need to get near the assessment fields, which means we'll walk for another four hours, then set up camp. All the fun starts today, which means you only have a few hours to get your head on straight."

"Some time to myself would really help," Grant admitted, while silently wondering if Sarge would be so lenient. A sharp increase in the pain from Spark Shield gave him his answer. "I knew this was big, but I still didn't expect so many *competitors.*"

The road ahead was filled with throngs of people. "So I have to beat all of *them* to progress to the main tournament? I only have a few weeks-"

Waylon let out a bark of a laugh, "Do you even understand how *tournaments* work? If it is like previous years, the top twenty-five that make it through all three stages will go on to the main event. One of those spots is *mine*, so you'll have to fight for one of the other twenty-four."

That brought Grant up short. "You're competing? Why didn't you say so?"

"Wasn't it obvious? I want to win as much as any other Vassal or Wielder in February." Waylon grinned at his travelling partner. "Had to scope out the competition. Let's go pick up our entry tokens."

He waited with the wagon while Waylon went to buy their tokens. The super enthusiastic people of February still freaked him out. They had perpetual grins plastered across their faces, always stretching and smiling... it just wasn't natural.

"Two tokens. One for me..." Waylon appeared next to Grant with a shout, almost getting an Iaijutsu strike to the throat for his trouble. The chipper man withdrew his hand, leaving a shiny token behind. "One for my good friend, Grant Monday. Don't lose it. If you *do* happen to make it through to the main tourney, *don't* lose the token they give you. You can only receive them from coming in as one of the top twenty-five here, and they are used for your entry to the main events."

"Understood." Grant stuffed the token into a small belt pouch, tucking it under his waistband directly after.

Waylon hefted his cart and jerked his head to get Grant to

walk alongside him. "I was told there are three parts to this tournament: endurance, skill, and then a fight for the finish. Anyone with a token from one of the previous small tournaments can choose one of the first two events to skip, but no one can get out of the fighting."

That was certainly news to Grant. "Really? I assumed gaining a token from one of the smaller events guaranteed entry to the main tournament?"

"No, but think about how much fresher those people will be by getting to skip a full third of the trials," Waylon stated knowingly. "That's *almost* as good as a guarantee. The first test begins at noon sharp, *today*. If you're not there, they start without you. Take the time between now and then to prepare. Guard your purse well; there're plenty of people that would happily vanish your bounties."

"Thank you, for everything. I guess that we're against each other from now until this is all over?" Grant bowed to the man that had gotten him this far. "If I don't see you, I'll meet you at the winner's tent after the event."

"That's the spirit!" Waylon looked much more happy after Grant started showing him the proper respect to which he was accustomed. They parted ways, and Grant went off in search of a vendor. The narrow streets were lined with stalls crafted from anything the vendor could use to draw the eye. They contained all manner of goods, from sickly sweet honey to the familiar wheatgrass shots and protein bars.

Competitors and spectators pressed in on him from all sides. He quickly became disoriented and moved to put his back against the wall. Double-checking that a pickpocket hadn't gotten the better of him as he had been gawking, he started moving along the stalls once more, until he finally found what he was looking for: a full-blown armor merchant. After hurrying into the tent, and inspecting the gear and accompanying prices, he was nearly sick.

CHAPTER TWENTY-TWO

The gear was *good*, but the prices would beggar him in one fell swoop for sure. The vendor was staring him down, causing Grant to sweat nervously, even though he wasn't doing anything wrong. Finally his eyes landed on a white robe in the Late Spring section that caught his eye and made his wallet complain… less. "Sir, this young one apologizes for taking your valuable time, but could you explain to me why this robe costs so much for a single article of clothing?"

Grunting at the appropriate manners, the merchant decided to try to make a sale instead of tossing the scruffy beggar out of the area. "I certainly can. That's a Late Spring Light Gi. It's not a robe, though it is a single piece. The gi counts for both your torso and leg armor when worn, and the reason for the low price is twofold."

While the man was holding up two fingers to continue explaining, Grant winced at the fact that the massive price tag was a 'low' price. "First, 'Light' armor is only half as effective at blocking physical blows as 'Heavy' armor at the same tier. It *is* twice as effective at mitigating magical damage, but that just makes two reasons that most people don't want it. Heh. Second is, I don't have any 'Light' helmets or such, and most people want a matching set of gear when they fight."

"Armor Synergy says it'll take the average of my gear and improve my weapon..." Grant muttered to himself while burying his mouth behind a hand. "Sarge?"

<February Twenty Nine will be considered as a Mid Spring Light Weapon. It'll add six points of base damage to your attacks, up from the *zero* your current scraps give ya. That means you'll hit normal attacks as hard as your critical strikes currently do. Not a bad deal, and you'd just need to find a helmet to bump up to a base of eight damage. I say do it.>

Grant pulled out a fistful of Weeks, Days, and a large scattering of minutes. Between himself and the vendor, they counted out the coins and came to an arrangement. The Wielder kept two Week coins and pulled his new white armor onto his frame. It was snug, but nowhere near as tight as it should have been. A quick peek in the vanity mirror next to the shop revealed a man that had practically melted like a candle while undergoing the hardships of February. He nearly didn't recognize himself as he felt at the hard edges of his face.

"Yeah, you'll be a looker when that extra skin is gone," the merchant informed Grant with a small smile. "I saw a lot of that when the cultivation craze was first sweeping across February. The rapid loss makes you look a little... raisin-like, but that'll turn into a physique that the people here are desperate to keep."

"I don't even know who I am anymore." Grant touched his face and the mirror, just to verify whether it was actually a different person mimicking him.

"Well, that's..." Now uncomfortable, the vendor looked outside and caught sight of people flowing in one direction. In an effort to save face, he eyed February Twenty Nine and recognized that Grant had need of a proper sheath. "Take this, on me. It's basic, but it does the—hey now, the first event is about to start."

"*What?* Thank you for the sheath, sir!" Grant scanned the

milling people, then checked the position of the sun and dropped into a full sprint toward the crowd. He passed various groups in mid-conversation as he simultaneously ran and struggled to attach the sheath, catching a strange mix of what information people thought was important.

"Did you say that only a hundred people make it-"

"At least the only people that needed it were in March."

"Kantor! He's a good puppy, but I-"

"Okay, but still, spiders the size of *hunting* hounds-!"

"That's not your *place*, fool! Step aside."

"Announcing the start of the first event! All contestants to the line!" Grant knocked over two people as he smashed through the wall of observers keeping him from the event, skidding to a halt in front of the surprised announcer. He breathlessly pulled out his token, and understanding as well as a hint of mirth appeared in the man's eyes. The official waved for Grant to join the group and got back to calling out to the crowd.

Hundreds of competitors had lined up for the start, and Grant's stomach churned from nerves as he surreptitiously inspected them. One of the conversational snippets made him assume this was going to be a battle where only the longest-lasting one hundred would pass through, but the truth was that no one really knew what to expect.

"Competitors," boomed the announcer, having finished warming up the crowds. "Get *ready*! The event will commence in… *one minute!*"

Glancing around, Grant realized that the competitors stood in a loose ring around a huge muddy field. With nothing else to do, he merely watched and waited. When only thirty seconds remained before the start, the test became painfully obvious: a wall of granite sprouted out of the ground and soared into the sky. A few people around the line started whooping and cheering, "Rock climbing! Woo!"

"First to the top wins!" another competitor bellowed, almost unable to keep themselves from running in.

"The only rule is that if you touch the mud below after you start climbing, you're out! *Go!*" A whistle blew, and the mass of competitors rushed towards the wall. People were screeching in delight that climbing had been picked for the first event. As far as Grant could tell, rock climbing was somehow one of the favorite activities of the residents of February. A few people had apparently been hoping for this and reached into pouches, where they evidently carried a personal supply of chalk with them at all times. This fact made Grant's face twist as if he had bitten into a lemon.

Even so, he wasn't ready to give up before he got started. Following suit, Grant ran towards the rock face. As the other competitors cheerfully dove in and sprinted up the wall, he simply grabbed on and started climbing as well as he could. The first few feet went smoothly, but he was already last, and the gap between him and the nearest competitor, an elderly gentleman, was growing larger by the minute.

<Good thing we've been having you running through trees for the last week. A lot of the same principles apply; watch your form, don't let your hands or legs get hurt, and most of all, *don't fall*.> Sarge was in full encouragement mode, completely aware that training was over and this was the real deal. <No problem with our start. Still, go *up* the wall; don't just cling onto it like it'll give you the love you never got as a child.>

Realizing that he had overestimated Sarge's desire to be nice to him, Grant forced himself to use his legs. He lunged, pushing up to the nearest handhold. His fingers trembled, but he realized that his cultivation made the challenge more than possible: it was easy. The only issue he was *actually* having was nerves and inexperience.

Unfortunately, at that exact moment, he started sliding down as he grabbed the next handhold and found it slick; clearly, a faster climber had left a trap. "I'm going to fall!"

<Not if I can help it!>

Zap.

"*Argh!*" Lightning from Spark Shield lanced through his

hand, forcing it closed and shattering a good chunk of the stone as his grip crushed inward. It did stop him from falling, but it hurt his hand like crazy, even though it hadn't dealt damage, thanks to his new armor.

<That was so fun! Want me to do it again?>

"Only if I'm going to *fall*; that really hurts!" The other issue was that it had left his hand numb for a second or so after the lightning wore off, and he was unable to open or close it with much force.

<Bah, spoilsport. I know *authors* that have been hit by full-power lighting and walked away from it. This is nothing.> Grant ignored the jabs and continued onwards and upwards. Twenty minutes in, the elderly gentleman ahead of Grant was resting against the stone and heaving for breath. He almost felt bad for the surge of accomplishment that roared through him as he passed the old fellow.

Then the man fell, screaming as he plunged toward the ground far below. Grant grabbed for him but missed, since he had been just a *moment* too slow. He watched in horror as he waited for the wet crunch, but instead saw a wave of mud surge up and catch the man, then deposit him into a large puddle where he laughed and swept his limbs around to make a mud angel, much to the delight of the crowd.

Now knowing that there was a safety net in place, a huge amount of tension dropped out of Grant. Able to fully focus on the event, he powered on. Not too fast, so that he could maintain a steady heart rate, he let his adrenaline flow away. Even so, no matter how far he climbed, it seemed that the bulk of the climbers remained far ahead.

The wall shuddered and shook suddenly, so hard that Sarge had to zap him to force him to cling on. The wall transformed as the first climbers got within ten feet of the top; on either side, massive sections of the wall shifted and began dropping downward.

As did the competitors that were climbing.

The moving sections of the wall then regrew from stone

cycled up from the interior of the rock wall, and the fastest competitors were suddenly at the bottom, far below Grant. While he was certainly confused by the turn of events, that only lasted for a moment. He was no longer in last place! That realization—and a few light zaps from Sarge—gave him the motivation to pick up the pace.

Remaining focused, he simply kept going and going. It was only him and the rock, and he would do whatever it took to defeat it. Before he knew it, he was nearly to the top. The sound of cheering suddenly assaulted his ears as he realized that he'd done it. He'd conquered the wall…!

Then it dropped away, and he found himself near the bottom again, scrambling for a better handhold. He looked up, and up, and almost screamed in frustration. Then the words of the announcer reached him, and everything made sense. "That's *right*, everyone! This is the endurance test, and we have a massive swarm of Vassals cycling through to keep that earth moving. With the preparations put in place, this wall can keep going for three full days!"

"No. Please, no," Grant whimpered, not wanting to hear another word the announcer would say.

"Now, just having it move when they've reached the top would incentivize holding still, so now that everyone's been through once… let's start the *real* challenge!" The announcer was answered with screams of enthusiasm from both the audience and participants alike, though Grant kept quiet and focused on putting one hand in front of the other. "From this point on, the walls will sink continuously! Endure till the end, climb fast enough to stay in, and hope that the person next to you doesn't kick!"

"We can kick?" Grant's eyes lit up as he looked down at his belt and saw February Twenty Nine waiting to be swung.

Sarge agreed viciously. <If I remember correctly… the only rule was 'don't touch the mud'.>

CHAPTER TWENTY-THREE

<Someone sliding down on your left, prepare to block a... gonna say, punch?> Sarge commented idly as an utterly exhausted lady with her face pressed against the stone held onto the wall without being able to reach for the next handhold. Her eyes lit up as she saw Grant come in range, and she took a feeble swing at his outstretched hand.

Grant ignored her and slapped the hand she was still using to cling to the wall with the flat of his blade, causing her to release her grip and fall backward. He expected a scream, but a quick glance revealed that she'd fallen asleep halfway to the mud below.

"Look at that! The underdog of the event strikes down yet another competitor!" the announcer's voice boomed, making Grant nervous. The shouting official never spoke up without something *else* being added to the mix. They were now eighteen hours into constant climbing, and anyone without a certain level of physical cultivation had fallen away hours ago. "We call competitor two-nine-two 'The Retaliator', since we haven't ever seen him initiate the first attack! Maybe some other people should try to follow his example of good sportsmanship!

For a long moment, Grant thought the man was done and had just popped in to compliment him. No such luck. "The walls are about to pick up speed. Since we want to make sure all events will be able to be held over the next few days, it looks like our Vassals got an influx of potions from House Saturday: today's event sponsor! Remember the motto of House Saturday: Change Your World."

"Sure, sure," Grant grumbled as he focused on putting one hand in front of the other. "Change your world. Change it for the *better*, House Saturday? For the better, right? *Answer* me, House Saturday."

<You get pretty strange when you get tired,> Sarge informed Grant, as though he didn't already know that. <I don't mind it, frankly. I've always told people it's fine to grumble, so long as you get the job done. Kick coming in on your left.>

Grant moved February Twenty Nine into position to stab into the approaching foot, simply bracing it so that the attacker would impale themself if they continued. They stopped, and the wiry competitor scuttled off around the wall in a fashion far too reminiscent of the spiders Grant had needed to fight off recently. "Method cultivators are so *weird*."

<That guy is pretty strong, Grant,> Sarge warned after a moment of contemplation. <If you have another chance to knock him out of the running, take it. He's one of the most serious competitors I've seen up here.>

"I just wanna climb my rock," Grant puffed as he continued upward. "It's a pretty rock. There are many rocks like it, but this one is mine."

<Someday, when this is all over, you can open a world-renowned Kenjutsu dojo.> Sarge figured that if Grant was getting loopy, he needed to provide a distraction. <You realize that if you ever get a chance to make Vassals, they get a lesser version of me? Imagine that... dozens of *me* surrounding you on all sides.>

"Are… are you trying to make me jump off and aim for a sharp rock on the way down or something?" Grant quipped with a snort, getting a grunting chuckle in return. "On that note, Sarge… can I *have* Vassals?"

<Not unless you restore February Twenty Nine to a full day,> Sarge answered after a moment of thought. <If I become more than I am now—something *real*—you'll be able to have *fifty* Vassals. If you manage to become the Calendar King, you double the number of Vassals you can have, meaning you'd be able to have a full hundred students at any given time.>

"That's…" Grant's eyes shone like stars as he thought of the possibilities. "I'd-"

<Not to mention that you'd likely be able to make some other followers. Not entirely sure, since I'm just a sword spirit that doesn't yet have full access to the capabilities of this weapon.> Sarge took note of a few contestants coming their way slowly. <I guess we'll find out together.>

Now moving with renewed vigour, Grant finally broke his streak of defending only. As other people sank down toward him, he *slapped* them with the flat of his sword. Usually targeting their heinie was enough to make them yelp and fall, but he had severely underestimated the masochism of many of the competitors. A good chunk of them would do their best to endure before fighting back, but oddly enough, not a single one attempted to dodge.

He wasn't sure if this was due to the fact that none of them had ingrained survival instincts, had never been in a fight, or *had* been in a fight; but the Februarian kind, where people just directly traded damage until one passed out. Either way, Grant didn't encounter a single proficient fighter, and soon, there were no more competitors in any kind of realistic range. The fast climbers hurried to move higher, and other people moved into less dangerous areas after they saw people dropping left and right.

<Too bad this doesn't count as defeating Vassals,> Sarge

wistfully mentioned as Grant caught up to an upward-fleeing opponent and smacked him off the rock face. <So I'm guessing your fatigue was more due to boredom than any actual muscle sleepiness?>

"I don't know." Grant realized that his actions were out of the norm for him, but the swell of cheers and people chanting his number... it was *intoxicating.* "See anyone else you think we can take out?"

<I really, *really* don't.> Sarge seemed hesitant about something. <Anyone remaining is almost certainly in the top twenty percent of physical cultivators in the District. Look up at them, and I'm sure you'll see what I'm talking about.>

Grant did so, just in time to see the spidery-guy from earlier get hit *hard.* The man fell off the wall and *caught* himself a half-dozen feet lower. He shot back up the wall, grabbed his assailant, and bodily *chucked* them off. Grant managed to get out of the way of the falling man, then looked up just as another body was being tossed at him. "He's aiming *people* at me!"

<I'll tell you again, take that guy out if you ever get the chance,> Sarge muttered darkly. <The way he moves, he's trained for a long, *long* time. There's no way he's new to all this, like most people are. If you can't get him down, stay out of his way.>

"Don't think that's going to be an option, Sarge." Grant stared up at the man as he searched around for more opponents. Unfortunately, everyone else had scampered away from the duo of competitors knocking other people down, and the man clearly decided it was time to take Grant out of the running.

He was coming down for them. Grant started to get excited.

<You outrange him; we can certainly use that.> Instead of getting worried, Sarge jumped right into strategy. <The biggest issue will be if he gets in your way or decides to try to take you with him. Don't let him get you into a grapple; his grip strength must be *terrifying* in order to allow him to move around the way he is.>

"Keep him out of range, keep climbing, don't let him grab me." Grant adjusted his sheath for easier access to February Twenty Nine, then kept his eye on the competitor as he hurried up. One nice thing about having only one person above him was that he hadn't had any issues with oily traps or the like, though it seemed the difficulty was ramping up again: the wall was becoming smoother, and finding new handholds was becoming more taxing. "*Hey*! Zero-four-two! Go away."

"No can do, two-nine-two!" came the cheery reply. "At this point, all the easy wins are all gone. You've been holding out somehow, but with your size, you've gotta be *just* hanging on."

"I'll *cut* you," Grant warned as competitor zero-four-two drew closer to him. "I don't want to hurt you, but I *will*."

"Ladies and gentleman, it appears we have a situation developing! Competitor zero-four-two and two-nine-two, the favored to win and the underdog, are closing in on each other!" The announcer roared into whatever was amplifying his voice. "Are we going to have an upset on our hands?"

"*Doubt*!" the crowd shouted in reply.

Grant tried to adjust his path when he heard the cry. "Well, *that's* just lovely, isn't it? Zero-four-two, if I throw a protein bar past you, would you go after it?"

He expected the man to be insulted, or to challenge him for thinking he'd take a bribe, but the man laughed instead. "More likely to *fall* if you hit me with one of those bricks than anything else."

"No joke; good thing I left all of them on the ground—*oh wait*." Grant whipped a bar upward, hitting zero-four-two in the foot and actually almost making him lose his foothold.

"Did you *really* just-?" Zero-four-two roared out a laugh and let himself drop, his feet aimed right at Grant.

The young man braced himself and swiped upward with February Twenty Nine as the spidery man's feet closed in, only for the man to glow a soft brown and aggressively slam his hands and feet forward. He came to a perfect stop above the point where the sword was aimed, his limbs partially submerged in the stone. Grant glared upward suspiciously. "Was that a *spell*? Are you already a Wielder?"

"Yup," his opponent confirmed, just before cracks radiated outward and surrounded Grant's position. "Nice to meet you, kid."

With a stomach-turning *slurp*, the land Grant was attached to was cut away and began to fall.

<Oh, *no* you don't.> Grant's leg jerked down, and he kicked off the falling stone as a pinpoint-precision spark jumped into his nerves. He tucked and rolled, slamming into the rocky surface and possibly breaking his nose. No notification appeared, but he chalked that up to likely automatic dismissal due to being in combat and not wanting to be distracted.

A foot lashed out and kicked February Twenty Nine out of his grip, and the blade went spinning toward the ground. Another attack came at him, so Grant yanked his sword out of the air and slashed; leaving a long laceration on the unprotected calf.

They locked eyes, and zero-four-two took that moment to knock the sword out to the ground once again. Grant had it back in his hand the next instant, fending off the follow-up kick. "I can do this all day."

"No need." Zero-four-two shot him a half-smile, then did a backflip off the rock wall.

Ten feet before the spidery man would hit the ground, the announcer called out, "The competition ends! If you are still in the air or on the stone wall, congratulations! You advance to the next round! Please hop off, and we'll record your information right away!"

"Phew... couldn't actually keep that up all day. Twice more, maximum," Grant muttered to himself. His mana pool was already below fifty percent, and each use of that ability cost a quarter of his entire pool. Grant stared at his strange rival, who was the first to get to the announcer and collect his token. "Sword Saints... that man is terrifying."

Then the cheering washed over him, and he looked out over

the crowd. Hundreds of people were chanting his number, and he felt a deep glow in his chest that erupted into a smile on his face. He blinked and found himself falling toward the ground, only to be caught by a wave of muddy water that washed him over to receive his winner's token.

CHAPTER TWENTY-FOUR

"Hey, Grant," Waylon called out to Grant as the young man scanned the mass of competitors lining the tables of the food tent. Fatigue overwhelmed him as he made his way over to Waylon, to the point that he almost considered asking Sarge to zap him to keep his legs moving. "I didn't think you were going to make it."

"Almost didn't," Grant admitted as he flopped onto the seat. "My cultivation was enough to sustain me, but… I just don't have any experience in doing that kind of thing, or working so hard for so long."

Waylon pushed a bar and a Bed over to Grant, who stared hollowly at the 'food'. "Eat. You need to get your energy back before the next event."

"Thanks." He slapped the Bed to his mouth like a salmon popping out of the water and splashing a bear. "Please tell me the next event is, I don't know, a sleeping competition?"

"You're so *funny*." Waylon watched as energy returned to Grant in real time. "No one knows exactly what it will be, but I expect that it will be some form of an assault course."

"All I want to assault is a buffet." Grant's words only earned him a confused look, and he recalled that buffets weren't a 'thing' in February.

Waylon worked to move on and give Grant some actual information. "I'm so happy we both made it through to the second round! I started to get worried when I heard that Goldenseal Sunday was coming after you. How did you make it through?"

He wasn't sure what Waylon was talking about; luckily, the man quickly realized and explained, "Competitor zero-four-two. He's one of the highest-ranked cultivators in the District and is known for his ability to self-heal in almost all circumstances. I heard he was coming after you."

"Oh. Yeah." Grant shrugged and bit into the barely-yielding protein bar. "He threw a few people at me, and we fought until they called the competition."

"Uh-huh. Okay." The smile faded from Waylon's face, and he turned to his own food. "Don't tell me."

"I'm serious."

"It all makes sense now," Waylon deadpanned, "since you fought the highest-favored to win person in the District to a standstill while climbing a rock wall, where he practically *lives*."

"It's what happened." Grant went to push up on his legs, but they refused to move. He tried again, but nothing happened. On the third attempt, Sarge gave a helping hand in the form of a mini zap, forcing Grant to stand bolt-upright. Eyes swiveled towards him at the sudden movement, just as the zap wore off and Grant fell back to his seat. "It appears that I'm going to be sitting here for a little while."

That brought a chuckle out of Waylon, and he gently slapped Grant on the arm. "Recover well. Since the event ended after only half a day, instead of the planned forty-eight hours, Lady February assumes that everyone will be ready to go by the morning. The next event starts at six tomorrow."

For the first time, Grant found a similarity between January and February: nearly everyone that came here to eat after the first event fell asleep at the table after eating. He was no exception, as he directly passed out after drinking nearly a gallon of water. The hours passed swiftly, and soon, a series of horns and bellowing began rousing the people in the impromptu sleeping tent.

"Competitors of the mid-February tournament, this is your thirty-minute warning." The announcer's voice echoed around the site. "The following event will start on time, and any late-comers will be disqualified. There is no time limit to this event; merely complete the course to pass and proceed to the final challenge. Good luck, competitors; District February *believes* in you."

Grant stood, surprised at the lack of pain in his body. Before he could question it, Sarge explained, <I took the time you were sleeping to lightly stimulate all muscle groups to promote healing and reduce acid build-ups. You won't even have a sore neck from sleeping bent over a table.>

"Sarge..." Grant started to get a little choked up. "Thank you. What would I ever do without you?"

<I'm guessing farmwork, until someone snuffed you out by sneezing too hard in your general direction.> Even though he tried to sound grumpy, Sarge was clearly preening under the admiration Grant was showering him with. <As to the lightning massage, I'm glad you enjoyed being lightly fried. It gives me something to do at night until you don't need sleep anymore.>

"Well." Waylon walked out of the outhouse that Grant was waiting on. "It looks like I'll be going before you."

"Good luck. I hope you make it through." Grant nodded at him, ignoring the clearly unwashed outstretched hand and entering the small shack. Contrary to his words a moment before, when Grant came out, Waylon was still there waiting for him. They walked over to the event grounds, only to find that everyone was being lined up by number, and would enter one at a time.

"This is what I've been training for. The assault course should appear any minute now. At least we aren't first!" Waylon was practically drooling as he craned to see what this event would look like.

"Not going first is a good thing?" Grant didn't agree; he had no idea how long they would be forced to wait, while the first people would be fresh.

"We get to watch others attempt to complete it. When they fall, we can learn from their mistakes. Watch. There it is now!" Waylon pointed down the hill they had been lined up on, and the thick fog that had been blocking their view faded away as the start of the event was announced.

"By Regent December…" A complex maze of machinery, nets, and moving platforms materialized, along with huge bonfire spotlights that artfully lit the monstrosity in the pre-dawn light. "What is *that* supposed to be?"

"Assault course!" Waylon patted Grant reassuringly on the shoulder. "There's no shame in failing to win, only in failing to try."

A whistle blew, and the first competitor ran forward. The bare-chested perfect specimen of a man scampered up the initial rock wall. As soon as he stood, he was forced to duck to avoid blunted lances that sprung out of hidden recesses. He dove head-first into a tunnel and crawled along before zip-lining down onto a moving platform. At that point, somewhat familiar dummies sprang up, and Grant realized that they were similar to the enemies that had appeared in his training program back in January.

The competitor clenched his muscles at the incoming blunted blades, barely getting knocked back as a lance shot forward and slammed into his stomach. Seeing the man prove his physical cultivation, the early-morning crowd screamed their excitement and cheered wildly for him. Grant got caught up in it and found himself bellowing enthusiastically along with the others.

Following the dummies, the competitor had to traverse massive drums spinning in the water below. This brought Grant right back to the tumbler he had failed in so spectacularly, with one major difference. Along with the spinning drums, the competitors had to jump over long wooden arms that swept through the air.

It looked like the first competitor was going to make it! After the spinning drum section, climbing a cargo net was the only challenge that remained; however, his luck ran out on the final drum. The drum suddenly stopped, and his mis-timed jump threw him into a pair of rotating arms. There was a collective groan from both the spectators and competitors as the man was slapped into the inky black water below.

Grant and Waylon stood for hours as the sun slowly rose into the sky, watching competitor after competitor attempt to complete the challenge. By his count, perhaps around fifteen percent made it to the end. It appeared to be a highly effective method of weeding out the less skilled or lucky among them.

Waylon stepped forward, and Grant realized that it was his turn directly after. He hadn't thought much of standing next to his friend—who had a number in the high one-hundreds—because they had arrived together. His friend got off to a good start, easily moving up the wall, through the tunnel and down the zipline. Then everything fell apart when he reached the dummies. He successfully used his Tomahawk to deflect a few blows, but the lance proved too long to defend against, and Waylon was jabbed off the arena. Grant forced himself to watch as his friend tumbled off the moving platform and into the water.

The whistle blew, and Grant's legs jerked into action even before he consciously realized that he needed to get moving. He reminded himself of how amazing it felt to win, to receive the adulation of the adoring crowd. If he could do this, it would *prove* that he was a real contender.

Grant had one massive advantage over the others: there was no time limit, and he had no problem abusing that fact. He methodically climbed the wall, patiently waiting for the blunted lances that shot out in front of him to no effect. Several hapless competitors hadn't been so lucky, rushing forward and ensuring that their challenge was over before it had barely started.

At the top of the wall, he had more trouble than most people due to the narrow tunnel. His body had shrunk considerably from the start of the year, but for some reason, the tight space made his heart race. <You'll fit through without issue, Grant. Your cultivation and the prolonged energy usage you've subjected yourself to over the last weeks has changed you.>

He subdued his mounting panic at becoming wedged within the tunnel and edged forward, inch by inch, until he made his way out the other end. At the end, he looked back and realized that there had never been a *chance* he would get stuck. He wasn't a proper Januarian anymore.

That bittersweet thought in mind, he clamped his hands on the zipline handle and dropped like a stone towards the moving platforms. He dropped the last few feet, and found himself on a moving platform consisting of small rollers; needing to maintain a brisk jog just to stay in the same spot as the dummies came to life around him.

This was the most straightforward part of the challenge, and just like all the others, he completed it in a way no other competitor had. He effortlessly ducked, parried, and lunged to dispatch the attacking dummies, his sword moving in straight lines as he maintained a balanced posture.

The lance darted at his chest, and he slashed three times: each cut removing a section of wood that clattered to the ground without causing him issue. The dummies retreated, leaving the path open, and Grant waited to hear cheering like he had for everyone else… nothing. Confused by the lack of sound, he continued forward.

He was onto his nemesis, the most concerning to him of all the trials: the spinning drums. The balance training that Sarge had forced on him by scampering through trees had proved effective, and he easily bounded over the drums and rotating arms. Even as he did so, he marveled at what his body was now capable of, and pushed himself harder. At the last moment, he remembered how the first athletic competitor failed, and put his plan into action.

As the final drum abruptly stopped, he jumped and grabbed onto the spinning arms. Sarge applied Spark Shield to secure his grip on the wet wood and stop him from falling as his legs flailed. Grant strained, and managed to climb on *top* of the arm. When the wooden arms retracted and lined up with the cargo net, he took a leap of faith and clambered onto the rough netting. He hung paralyzed for a long moment, unable to move from laughing so hard at the fact he had succeeded.

<Good job. You did well to get this far.> Sarge's *excited* voice warned of pain to come, <Let me give you a little boost to get up this net. Ready?>

Grant braced himself for the incoming jolts. "Ready as I'll ever be!"

A series of rapid-fire jolts lanced through his muscles, Sarge carefully applying minuscule amounts of charge to specific muscles at *just* the right time. Everyone watching witnessed the unlikely success of underdog two-nine-two as he surged up the multistory cargo net. What they *didn't* see was the massive toll that reaching the top and completing the course took on his body.

To be fair, he also didn't understand the issues inherent in allowing constant lightning to course through his organs.

He stood on top of the course and joined the winner's circle, not even caring that no one was cheering and the other winners were staring at him with something akin to *fear* in their eyes. Upon ensuring he had won, Grant sat down and promptly fell asleep.

CHAPTER TWENTY-FIVE

"What's wrong with him? Is he okay?" Waylon's concerned voice seemed to come from far, far away.

"When we found him, he had passed out and was almost dead. We… can't explain what happened to him. He didn't appear to pick up any injuries during the completion of the course." The healer checked Grant's vitals with a burst of mana, then shrugged. "He *should* be fine. His body has been mended, but it's too early to tell if his mind will recover. We had to strap him down through the night. His body was twitching and flailing around. We were worried he'd hurt himself. Now that he's awake… I see no reason not to discharge him. Keep an eye out for any unusual behavior."

"Thank you, Elder." Waylon bowed to the old man, who nodded and walked away serenely. "Grant? You're awake? We need to get out of here; there's a crowd out front looking for you."

"A crowd? For me?" Grant drowsily struggled to his feet and checked to make sure he had all of his belongings. "I want to greet my fans!"

"You don't understand," Waylon started, but Grant didn't

wait for Waylon and strode out of the medical tent with a dreamy smile on his face, anticipating the outpouring of adoration.

"Boo!"

"You should be *disqualified*!"

"There's no way *you* could complete the course when so many proper competitors failed!"

"*Cheater! Cheater!*" The chant was taken up by hundreds of angry spectators and competitors, and Grant recoiled in confusion. This was *not* the response he'd expected. He raised his arms to protect his face from the sudden hail of projectiles. Protein bars exploded into puffs of oats against his armored gi, and Beds left green stains across his whole body.

"I didn't do anything wrong!" Confusion turned to fury, and Grant reached for his sword. The nearest protestors backed away with a hint of fear in their eyes but were pushed forward as the mob started to surge.

"*Order!*" The thundering of boots echoed across the tournament site. Officials from House Tuesday smashed through the impromptu riot. Fists and feet flew as people attacked House Monday Vassals as if they had somehow colluded with Grant to ensure that he passed the test. "I said *order*!

The senior House Tuesday official clapped two magic-infused billy clubs together, resulting in an earth-shattering *boom* which shook the ground and the eardrums of everyone present. "House *Tuesday* has examined the event in *excruciating* detail. The course was *not* rigged! Grant Monday *legitimately* used his skills and completed the test on his merit alone, without any external help or influence."

"But… it's impossible that *Roderick* failed and *he-*"

"Are you questioning the integrity of *House Tuesday*? Honor From Law!" The crowd disbanded as the Peacekeeper reminded them of the credo of his House. They followed the law *exactly* and were known to be impartial in all matters. With House Tuesday's proclamation, most people were properly chastised. A few nodded to Grant and apologized, but no one seemed *happy*; all they saw was a man new to exercise achieving what they or their favorites could not.

Waylon came over to stand by his side. "I told you we should have taken the back entrance. Listen, you need to hurry... you were out so long that the third test begins in an hour. I'm proud and impressed that you made it past the second test... but I don't know if it's wise that you continue. You almost died, and no one knows why."

"I can't give up, Waylon. It'll end up killing me," Grant tried to explain.

"You *already* almost died, Grant!"

"I didn't go through all that to give up now. Why are you doing this? Did you bet *against* me?" Grant stared his shocked and hurt friend down and tried to turn his accusation into a joke. "I'm kidding, just kidding... I know you *had* to have put some serious money on me right away. I've got great odds if you win. I think. I'm going to clean myself up and prepare for the final round."

Only forty minutes later, Grant had cleaned up and eaten, then gripped the hilt of February Twenty Nine as he awaited the start of the third and final event, which would decide who went forward as a serious competitor in the finals. The assault course had been removed, replaced with a muddy field. More than one hundred athletes lined the perimeter of the field; *far* more than he had expected to make it to the last round.

"Pardon my intrusion," Grant nodded at the man beside him, "but why are there so many competitors? Didn't only thirty or so total make it through the obstacle course?"

It took a long moment to get an answer as the man sized Grant up, "The rest have come from smaller events held throughout the district, and used their token to bypass that stage. I can't say I blame them. Question... should you, um, be here? The spectators are meant to stand over there."

"You know *what*-"

Grant didn't have time to finish his snarl as the announcer began booming instructions. "Competitors, get *ready*! One minute warning. Only *twenty-five* competitors will make it through the Battle Royale and receive a token for the main tournament. District February believes in you!"

"A Battle Royale? We have to fight, I assume?" Grant looked at the huge man right next to him, and was sized up in turn. He really didn't like the gleam in the large man's eye.

"Sure looks like it." The man cracked a broad smile. "From the number of people starting, we'll have to defeat at least four people to make it through."

Grant started subtly edging away from the man, but found that every small step was matched by the person he was attempting to avoid.

"Teaming up is *prohibited!*" the announcer continued to speak, "House Tuesday is standing watch for this event: anyone breaking the rules is out, and no arguments will be heard. This is a free-for-all, but all fighting is strictly one-on-one. Houses Saturday and Sunday are standing by to deal with injuries, but sneak attacks or fatal blows will be punished according to the law, *after* you have been banned from the event! Honor From Law!"

"Honor From Law!" The reply was echoed back from any member of House Tuesday in the area.

Grant's attention was drawn to the muddy field. Patches of red had suddenly sprouted across the area. He squinted to examine a nearby clump, finding that scarlet poppies had started carpeting the field. He didn't want to trample the beautiful floral display but saw no way around them. In the center of the fighting area, a platform appeared out of the ground, covered in a wide array of objects that were too far away to see clearly. He assumed they were things that would help him win, but he didn't know for certain.

"Let the Battle Royale commence!"

Grant's neighbor turned and jumped at him in an attempt to take him to the ground. Having expected this, Grant simply let his Iaijutsu perforate the man's gut.

Damage dealt: 24 penetrating. Debuff added: Bleeding heavily. -5 health per second.

A gout of blood rocketed from the man's mouth as he looked down at the weapon that had penetrated his stomach. "Y-you *stabbed* me!"

"Yes?" Grant pulled his blade free, swiping it to the side to get the blood off. "Non-fatally, if you fix the bleeding. I stabbed you between your organs-"

"How so *much?*" The man whimpered and sank to his knees. "A tenth of my health in an instant? That wasn't even a critical hit! I yield! Help me, *someone!*"

Grant was assaulted by booing from the crowd as a half-dozen people rushed over to remove the fallen competitor. Doing his best to ignore the dissatisfaction of the crowd, he looked to see what else had been happening.

It appeared that the vast majority of the highly trained individuals had sprinted towards the center, and were more focused on getting what was there than defeating each other. Grant was still practically on the sidelines, and he couldn't see a way to reach the center of the field before the others had snatched up all the goodies and fought each other to a standstill. Rather than run in and follow the crowd, he kept his sword unsheathed and chose a nice open area in the poppy field arena.

There was no place to hide, so he might as well claim his territory.

Within thirty seconds, all forms of cultivators were locked in. Batons clashed and clanged, warhammers sparked against shields, and fists found flesh. Cries from the wounded split the air and could be heard over the brutal melee combat. Even with all the confusion, Grant came to a realization: not a single person was using a bladed weapon. "What is happening? Sarge, am I not seeing it, or is everything blunted?"

<Good eye. I'm guessing that no one has confidence in putting a weapon right where they want it. If I were a betting sword, I'd say that there isn't a single Beginner weapon-user among them, at

least not for really *deadly* weapons.> A warhammer strike sent a man flying, and Sarge amended his words. <Not for *sharp* deadly weapons. It's a lot easier for someone to take a fatal blow if you cut up their insides, versus hitting their shield with a hammer.>

Someone with their features hidden behind a dark cloak charged toward Grant and instantly threw all his assumptions out the window. The person's eyes were shadowed deep within the hooded cowl, but a shudder ran through Grant as those eyes locked with his own. A cultivator momentarily got in the person's way, and two curved daggers flashed from within the cloak, leaving the unfortunate competitor a bloody heap that the officials rushed to help.

<There may be *someone* in here with *incautious* aim. Take care, I'm pretty sure that's a Saturday.>

"A *Saturday*?" Grant was out of time to prepare. Without any wasted motions, the totally-not-an-assassin closed in on him. He remembered where he'd seen curved weapons like that before: protruding from the maw of the Gleam-Fang Stalker. Had the fangs already been made into daggers and sold? "Wednesday does quick work."

Grant's training took over as blows rained down on him. No matter how skillfully he managed to deflect one of the blades, he still received nicks and small cuts from the other. These small wounds bled *far* too much; he suspected a poison with an enhanced bleed effect had been coated onto the weapons. Parry, dodge, duck, thrust, slash... no matter what technique he tried, he couldn't get through the swift fighter's defenses—all while the number of cuts was piling up. Grant started to feel light-headed, and he didn't need to check his stats to know that he was suffering from serious blood loss.

Every unsuccessful attack resulted in one more wound to add to his new collection. By this point in the fight, Grant knew that the agile man could have left to fight another competitor and just left him to bleed himself right into disqualification, but his opponent didn't let up. Grant screamed in an attempt to shock the hooded competitor into flinching away, then lunged forward in a perfect attack form. "If I can't defend, I need to make sure he can't *attack!*"

He moved through every pattern that had been ingrained in his muscle memory, his sword so responsive that it felt as though it was literally following his desires instead of his momentum. One pace, two, ten, and his assailant slipped and fell on a group of poppies he had wet with blood earlier. Grant seized upon the opportunity and lunged towards the man, who was trying to recover his footing. February Twenty Nine sliced through the air, coming to a halt against the shocked House Saturday Wielder's neck.

"I… yield," the frustrated man spoke in a gravelly voice as he held up his hands. Grant's blade literally begged for blood as the Saturday finished with, "Well fought."

Do you, Grant Monday, wish to absorb the power of February 13th, 'Razor's Edge'? Accepting 'Razor's Edge' will override any previous wielded weapon power absorbed in the current monthly series. If not over-ridden by another weapon of the same month, this ability will vanish at the end of the year, unless the quest 'Heal The World' has been successfully completed.

Accept / Decline

Grant nodded at the downed man, refusing to take his eyes off him as he silently accepted the new power and relinquished the light ability he had acquired. He had given the rapier away previously, and there would be an issue if it didn't work properly. An official escorted the assassin away, allowing Grant to finally take a breath. Taking stock of his situation, Grant took a deep breath. "So *that* guy was a Wielder. The look of the blades must have been a coincidence?"

<Two things, Grant.> Sarge seemed *wildly* cheerful. <You

just *defeated* a Wielder. Welcome to Cultivation Achievement Level thirteen. You're all healed up, and the ability you just swiped is *delightful*.>

The description appeared without Grant pulling it up, making him question once again how much Sarge *actually* had control of.

Razor's Edge: Any slashing or piercing damage will inflict an additional 25% of the damage dealt as bleeding damage on any targets with blood or vital fluids over five seconds.

The respite from battle lasted only a moment before other competitors were once again charging toward him. Refreshed and renewed, Grant stepped forward to meet the attackers head-on. Leveling up had fixed all of his internal issues, including any hidden injuries he had sustained from his weeks-long intense training.

Now that he was back to top form, fighting against the thinning crowd became far more feasible. He sidestepped a meaty fist before launching a blistering counter-attack. The unfortunate Vassal was clearly wearing Early Spring Heavy armor, yet Grant's blade easily broke through the system-logic barrier and opened a thin wound down his attacker's arm.

Damage dealt: 6 slashing. (14 mitigated.)

The wound *spurted* blood, dealing another point of damage from his new ability as well as from standard bleed damage. Transfixed as he was on the new opening in his skin, the man failed to defend against a trio of blows that Grant put in specifically non-murderous locations. Within moments the competitor was begging for his life and Grant was moving on as a healer rushed over.

"Sarge, is it wrong to love that I feel so much more powerful than them?" Grant muttered as he closed in on the first target he chose for himself.

<You have experience in being *ruthless*.> Sarge's warm and fuzzy tone over that fact gave Grant pause. <I've killed you almost every day for a month and a half, and you've killed or tried to kill a slew of people in January. To help you keep from

getting cocky, let me explain a simple fact to you: these people could *easily* overpower you. You would be a smear in the mud if they would just *commit* to taking you down. In this case, you *aren't* stronger than them. You *do* have skill and experience they lack, and the rules just so happen to be simply skewed heavily in your favor because of that.>

The next competitor, a woman in Early Spring Medium armor, proved a little more challenging, but only because she wielded a shield and short spear. Despite her improved defense, Grant managed to get off a few hits against her forearm and calves as they danced around each other. The small cuts bled *profusely*, eventually forcing her to yield; she wasn't willing to die to secure her position in the Nobility.

Grant was.

<*Down!*> He ducked as an obsidian longsword swept through the air, followed by a howl of frustration. A heavily outfitted member wearing the regalia of House Thursday lumbered towards him, the black armor reminding him of the set that hung in Bob Sunrise's shop in Mid January. There was no obvious way to defeat this person. If he was lucky, he might be able to get his blade between the metal plates or through the visor of his face guard, but he didn't want that imprinted on his memory. He wanted to *defeat* his opponents, not kill them.

Luckily, he didn't need to make that call.

Grant scrambled through the mud, dashing out of the way of the *whooshing* weapon. The competitor didn't miss a step, continuing after Grant as a sharp whistle reached them. Both were too focused on the fight to understand, all the way until the knight was bowled over by three Peacekeepers.

"You violated the law! No sneak attacks were allowed; you will be held for attempted murder!" The struggling armored person was dragged away, and Grant noticed a strange spherical object that had a pin in it.

"Is this from the center area? Why did they all want it?" he wondered as he pulled out the pin and stared at the strange object. "Does it open into a prize?"

<That's an alchemical charge! *Throw* it at someone, you fool!> Sarge screamed into his brain.

In a panic, Grant threw it into a crowd of fighters. It bounced harmlessly off one's armor, and he worried that he had used it wrong. He kept his eye on it for another moment, an exclamation of wonder passing his lips as a blanket of darkness exploded outwards and clouded the vision of everyone in the vicinity.

Grant stumbled to his feet and raised February Twenty Nine in a defensive posture. His only mission now was to get as far away from the blind melee as possible. Screams and shouts assaulted his ears as competitors swung haplessly in the darkness, taking and dealing more damage than they had planned. Grant kept his sword to himself, not wanting to get charged for accidentally killing someone.

The smoke slowly dissipated, revealing a gore-splattered field. Only a small number of people remained standing, and officials rushed to cover the area as the announcer bellowed, "Congratulations to those still standing! The Battle Royale has been completed! All remaining competitors have made it to the main tournament. Please collect your tokens before leaving the site. Remember, District February believes in you, and we look forward to meeting our new Nobility!"

Grant stumbled out of the muddy field and cautiously checked his body. All fingers and toes were accounted for, which was more than many people could say. "That was simultaneously the worst and best of the three events."

<Extra easy for you. You have actual combat and killing experience. The only reason that lasted even *that* long was because of how careful everyone was being *not* to hurt their opponents.> It sounded like the idea of being careful and taking care of one's fellow citizens aggravated Sarge, so Grant tried not to comment on it.

"Grant, you *did* it!" A waving Waylon ran over to him as Grant walked away from the announcer. "Can I see your token?"

There wasn't a shred of hesitation as Grant presented the enamel badge to Waylon. The mother-of-pearl inlay that formed the image of Lady February shimmered in the light. More than a few people eyed the token greedily, and Grant took it back after noting their hungry eyes. "It's *wonderful*. Such a treasure. I can't believe I didn't get through to the main tourney! Still... do you mind if I accompany you?"

"Are you sure?" Grant secured the token and started walking hurriedly away. Waylon caught on to his nervousness around the random assortment of people and kept up. "I'd love to have someone watching my back, but I thought you had an important mission?"

"I'll be heading in that direction anyway." Waylon seemed to be convincing himself instead of just explaining it to Grant. "Heavyweight Wednesday said it wasn't too important, so I'm *sure* it can wait."

"Great. I would be happy to have the company. I'm not exactly sure how to reach the main tournament, but judging by the people jogging on the road, I guess it was— ow! Hey, *watch* it!" Grant received a stray elbow to the face as the crowd pressed closer together and started walking along the road.

"Excellent!" Waylon's general shout of excitement was taken up by the huge crowd; about three-quarters of them abruptly started jogging and running, whooping in excitement. "I think you're making a wise call. The trip is probably more dangerous than the events, since all you need to do to get in is *have* a token... if you catch my drift. Listen, Grant... this is the most important event for February in the last thousand years. Not attending would be considered practically sacrilegious."

"Good thing I know your father. So, if I have any worries about your trustworthiness... I'll just go talk to him?" Grant grinned as his friend blanched.

"Please don't even joke like that. I'm not exactly-" anything else Waylon was going to say was cut off as they were nearly bowled over in the mosh-pit of a crowd. They pushed back against the relentless bodies jostling them, and his good humor began to slip away.

Grant made the judgement call, "This is a *nightmare*, Waylon. Why don't we go off-road? I'd love a moment of peace to think, and I recently found that I... don't like confined spaces."

Waylon pulled him through the crowd and waved at the trees. "Yeah, we can do that. I'd love to try that balance training you were doing."

<Yes! Absolutely, let's get into the trees. My plan to make you a samurai is really coming together. Ninja *would* have been fine too, but stealth isn't right for->

CHAPTER TWENTY-SIX

<*That's* what I like to see,> Sarge screeched in pleasure as Grant threw himself off a thick branch. <You're receiving *serious* training here! Mind for the thought you put into every action, physical is obvious, armor for the falling and scraping, and... oh, you need to start cutting things. Watch for orange birds! Keep it up.>

"How are you *doing* that?" Waylon shouted from well below him.

"Literally just practice!" Grant tried to keep his voice steady as he missed his grip, instead landing awkwardly while swiping up at the expected orange spiders that always swarmed him whenever he messed up. He hauled himself over a new limb and skidded down the steep slope of a huge boulder... then fell forward as a root caught his foot. "*Wah!*"

He landed in a sandpit, followed closely behind by Waylon, who was laughing until they began to sink. Then he became deadly serious. Even the slightest movement caused their bodies to submerge further, as the cloying sand drew them into a warm embrace.

"Stop fighting it," Waylon called out in warning as Grant

attempted to extract himself from the quicksand. "It'll only make it worse, and you don't want to drown."

"A suggestion would be nice!" Panic was welling up within Grant as the sand started to cover his chin. "How can you drown in *sand?*"

"Reach across and grab the vine." Waylon was already out, which both caused Grant to relax a little as well as worry that he would be too slow. "You should be able to pull yourself out. Slowly; don't move too fast."

Grant saw the vine and reached out. His fingers wrapped around it as his head sank beneath the surface. His heart thundered in his ears while the gritty sand clawed at his eyes, seemingly determined to find a way in.

Sarge took over instructing Grant as his ears filled with muck. <Don't panic. Apply steady force to the vine and pull *slowly*. Take your time. Any sudden force risks breaking the plant.>

'Not panicking' was a difficult proposition, but he was determined to survive the stupid *environment*. His lungs burning, Grant tentatively pulled on the vine. Inch by agonizing inch, his body started moving through the sucking sand... then his other hand managed to grasp the vine. The resistance suddenly vanished, and he opened his grit-encrusted eyes to find that he had hauled himself onto a grassy knoll.

"What took you so long?" Waylon laughed as Grant sucked in ragged breaths. "How did you manage to complete the assault course if you struggled with a little *sandpit?*"

"Little! I crossed an ocean of sand!" He looked around to see the short distance he'd covered, finding that he could lay across the entirety of the pit if he stretched. "Fine; it *felt* like an ocean!"

"An ocean of tears, you crybaby. Stop whining about it; you're already safe. It's *meant* to be hard, but you don't need to worry too much in this area. Yeah, you have to be careful, but this entire section has been cultivated by Lady February's people." Waylon paused as Grant sat upright, sending sand flinging off of himself.

"Cultivated? Why is it so challenging? I expected an off-road jaunt, sure, but sand traps? Don't think I didn't see that snake hanging out with the vines, either. It's as if the whole district has been transformed into an obstacle course." Grant spat a wad of gritty mud out of his mouth and flopped back to lay flat.

Waylon was nodding with a knowing smile on his face. "That's *exactly* what's been done. Lady February wants to challenge each and every citizen to push beyond their limits and attain physical perfection-"

"Look what we have here!" A shout came from the suddenly-rustling bushes, followed by around a dozen people. Grant and Waylon were on their feet in an instant, and Waylon proved his situational awareness and forest insight by sweeping his Wielded Weapon through a few vines, which fully freed a previously-fallen tree that had gotten tangled. The falling trunk knocked a few people into the sandpit and trapped another.

"*Run!*" Waylon ordered even before they knew who exactly had come for them. It didn't *particularly* matter: it was clear the attackers were full of ill intent.

The voice that had called out so cheerfully a moment before was now screaming after them as they vanished into the obstacle-wood, "You can run from *us*, but I heard you've got House Saturday after you! I can tell you more, but I want fair compen-"

After that point, the words were too faint to hear as the two companions rushed through the forest. Shortly after that, the crashing sounds of pursuit announced that a little sand hadn't been enough to dissuade the larger group from coming after them. <Don't fall again, Grant. No more sandtraps near here, but I think these people might actually end up burying you in these woods if they get the chance.>

"You think I could fight them off?" Grant mumbled as he heaved for breath.

<I think you could *absolutely* kill them all if you wanted. *Is that what you want?*> It wasn't. They both knew it. The sun traveled through the sky as the chase continued, and before they knew it... hours had passed. Mistakes were bound to happen. Waylon fell and twisted his ankle, then gritted his teeth and urged Grant to push on. "We can't stop now. I'll be fine. Run, survive, and *win*. You're a good man, Grant."

"No. Let's move!" Grant grabbed his friend and pulled him on. Waylon tried to protest, but in truth, he clearly hated the idea of sacrificing himself.

They scrambled through bushes and up a rocky path. Before them lay a stretch of clear ground with trees on either side. Grant certainly didn't complain about the easy terrain, though he *was* concerned that their pursuers would easily be able to catch up to them. Both ran along the grass as quickly as possible, and the pain in Waylon's foot finally receded.

"Grant, you'll have to jump." Waylon leaped into the air and grabbed a branch, then used his momentum to swing from it to the next one.

"Jump? Lord January preserve us...! Feces, that's *me*." The reason became rapidly apparent, but it was also practically insane. Grant skidded to a halt and almost found himself falling into a ravine. He looked up and noted that a series of over-hanging tree limbs spanned the gap. Waylon was almost across the other side while Grant stood there dumbfounded. The group of Vassals came into view, and he gripped the hilt of his sword... but still hesitated to kill if he didn't need to do so.

With a roar of frustration, he slammed the inch of steel that he had drawn back into his scabbard, turned, and sprinted toward the hole in the earth. He launched his body into the air and grabbed the hanging branches. A quick glance below confirmed that if he stopped now, the best result he could hope for was getting horribly maimed from the fall. Once, twice, and after the third branch, he had crossed the expanse. When he landed on the ground on the opposite side, Grant *almost* collapsed onto the ground, laughing with relief.

"There's no time to rest; get up!" Grant followed Waylon's orders and stood without a word, though his arms throbbed from the abuse of the day. He desperately hoped there would be no more swinging. "Follow me. I think I found a path! We just need to make it up to a main road, and then they wouldn't dare try anything!"

"What the…! Up *that*? How is *this* a path?" Grant did a double take as he examined the slick rock face Waylon was already racing up. "Maybe we should double back?"

Waylon wasn't listening, too busy clawing his way up the treacherous surface. Grant had no choice but to follow, and soon, he clung onto clumps of soggy moss as his body became soaked through. Water was dripping down the entire surface, making a difficult climb close to deadly.

His friend was pulling ahead, leaving Grant behind as he struggled to find safe handholds. A glance upward revealed a large overhang that curved out. Going over that would mean dangling over open space with only his hands touching stone. It was *well* beyond his capabilities or experience to climb. Looking down, vertigo overwhelmed him as their pursuers approached the base of the cliff.

Up above, Waylon screamed as he lost his grip. Grant's eyes went wide as his friend tumbled towards him. Without thinking, he reached out and grabbed hold of Waylon's arm before he was lost to the void. <You foolish-!>

Zap.

Both screamed as Spark Shield surged through Grant and forced his fingers to clamp around the stone. Knowing that he only had a bare moment, Grant swung Waylon into the rock face. The man scrabbled for purchase, eyes wide as Grant let go. Somehow, both managed to grab onto the cliff and cling on for dear life.

<There's no time to hang around! Climb!>

Grant surged upwards, focused on overcoming the challenge. His body made it over the top—thanks to the liberal usage of lightning to his nerves each time he almost fell—and he landed in a huge puddle that was slowly draining over the edge. He waited there long enough that he started to wonder where Waylon was. Just then, a hand shot up and grabbed the edge. His soaked friend had made it.

"We survived!" Grant weakly punched at the air. "Good defensive spot, too. Now we can watch over the edge and poke anyone that tries to climb after us.

"Or we can run from *that* group." Waylon's body clearly protested as he rose to his feet with visible effort, and he waved at a group of people that were walking toward them out of the rising mist. "They must have sent some people around to cut us off."

"You've gotta be kidding me." Grant got up and braced his hand on his hilt. "Should we just be done running? I think I'm over my earlier concerns about turning into a bad person. There's only so far they can push us before we *have* to fight, and I'd rather do it now than when I'm *completely* exhausted."

To punctuate his point, he fully unsheathed February Twenty Nine and waited for the attack. Four cultivators calmly walked forward, not bothering to say a word. They knew Grant and Waylon had run before, and from the hard look in their eyes, they meant business. For the moment, they ignored Waylon, knowing that Grant was the real threat.

"Careful! They all have the same weapon, they have to be Vassals!" Waylon warned as he got to his feet and tried to get in a combat stance.

"If you come after me right now… I'm sorry, but you'll all die." The water churned as the Vassals picked up the pace. Grant tried not to feel remorse as he set the tip of February Twenty Nine in the shallow water, flinging his blade up at the last moment to send a spray of water into the Vassals' wide eyes. In that moment, he let his blade flow forward.

"The aorta sits right on the neck, cut it open and hit the deck…!" Grant chanted the song that had been repeating in his head for over a month now. Thanks to reaching the Beginner tier, February Twenty Nine landed exactly where he wanted on his target's neck.

Damage dealt: 8 slashing (18 mitigated). Debuff added: Arterial bleeding. -15 health per second! Razor's Edge will deal an additional 2 damage over five seconds!

Choking wetly, the Vassal grabbed at his damaged throat and tried to stem the bleeding. Grant knew that with the high level of physical cultivation, there was a good chance the man would survive if the others took the time to bind his wounds. He didn't press the attack, instead focusing on the others as they attacked. Only one stopped to try to save his ally.

With a sheer cliff behind him, Grant couldn't maneuver backward and was hard-pressed to hold off the duo of Vassals. Even so, as the fight progressed and he got into the flow of combat, his opponents' lack of skill became evident. Grant knocked the weapon out of the hands of the man on his left and still had time to block the attack from the man on his right. "Last chance to leave. Please, *please* don't make me hurt you. I already have trouble sleeping; I don't want your blood on my hands."

The disarmed man bellowed and bull-rushed Grant, hoping to give his ally an opening. Grant put his sword through the man's chest, spun, and kicked the Vassal off the cliff.

Damage dealt-

Grant couldn't see the rest of the message, since the man's teammate seemed to go berserk with grief. All skill was cast aside as he attempted to murder Grant with brute force blows. Grant wasn't able to get in a clean hit, instead opening cuts all over the man as they danced back and forth for a full thirty seconds. Finally the Vassal collapsed into the now-red puddle, glaring up at Grant as he heaved for breath. "I'll get you for this. You're a dead man. No matter where you run or *hide*—*urk*.*"

Not willing to worry about a knife in the dark, Grant thrust forward and stabbed the man right through his leather chest-piece. The man fell face first into the water… and stayed there.

He looked over to see the other two staring at him in horror. The one with an intact throat spoke, while the other merely trembled and tried to gasp for breath. "Have you no *restraint*, you *monster*?"

"Waylon, run before they recover!" Not wanting to finish the two that were no longer a threat to him, the pair splashed through the water and entered the woods, hurtling past a well-maintained path. Branches and thorns tugged at their clothes as they ran blindly through the forest, and he realized that he hadn't seen Waylon helping. "What were *you* doing?"

"Cutting fingers off hands as people tried to climb up behind us." Waylon's tomahawk was out, and its curved blade still bore a smattering of blood that corroborated his story. "This way! I hear voices, so there must be a road ahead. Listen, I think you did the right thing by letting the other two go. There's no way they will be able to bring the law against us, as they were the aggressors in that situation. I know it might not mean much to you, but it means a lot to me that a few extra of my Districtmen got to live another day."

"It means a lot to me too, I don't *want* to hurt people!" There was no reply to his assertion, so he tried to think about other things. For instance, Grant couldn't *believe* they were going to escape based on the almost pure physicality of running away through the woods. He followed Waylon's path over the multitude of rocks and roots, until his guide's feet suddenly left the ground.

"Waylon!" Grant surged forward as his friend dangled in midair for an unknown reason.

<Down!> Sarge cried, and Grant threw himself to the grass as something whistled through the air.

"Oh, for Regent's sake. Could you be any more annoying?" A new attacker was balanced on a tree branch, pulling her whip back for another strike.

Waylon grasped at his neck as the life was slowly choked out of him by an identical whip held by another woman. She was braced on the nearest tree limb and continued tugging on the whip. Grant panicked as he watched his friend's face turn from red to various shades of purple. "What are you doing? Let him go; he doesn't deserve to die!"

"We're just getting our point across. You're gonna be a *good* boy and hand over that token so Waylon here can keep living, yes?" The woman attacking Grant smiled maliciously.

"That's *our* target, Astrid!" A ringing shout came from the path in the woods that Grant had run past.

"Oh, you spoilsports. Drop him quick, Helga." Astrid's order caused her twin to loosen her grip, and Waylon dropped to the ground, still clawing at the red ring around his neck. Grant glanced around. Helga was right behind him. Nearly a dozen stragglers finally caught up with them, almost all with various injuries. The smug group of cultivators and Vassals surrounded them.

Their time was up. There was nowhere left to run.

"Grant." Waylon croaked the words out. "To me."

The Vassals didn't stop Grant from going to his injured friend's aid. He helped the coughing young man to his feet, and Waylon opened his palm to reveal a collection of small rocks.

"Pocket sand?" Grant didn't understand how a pile of pebbles would help them. Being choked must have damaged his friend's mind.

Waylon let out a strangled snort. "On three, run."

The group closed in, weapons poised and at the ready. Waylon flung the contents of his hand in an arc. Vassals leaped into the air as thunderous noises and light as bright as the sun filled the clearing. The imprint of the incendiary sparks left traces on Grant's vision, and he quickly became disoriented. Waylon tugged on his arm, and he ran where directed. The pair tumbled over a chunky root, and as they rolled to their feet, it became clear that the first of the Vassals was hot on their heels. Desperate, Grant dragged Waylon towards the swelling noise of people nearby.

The pair broke through the tree line, startling the mass of spectators and competitors making their way towards the main tourney. The swarm of people followed behind, but Grant didn't give them the chance to surround the two of them. He swung February Twenty Nine, the blade whistling through the air and cutting off a length of Astrid's whip as it cracked towards his neck.

Another Vassal slammed into his side, and he found himself wrestling on the ground, slamming his fist into the man's ribs. As blood pounded through his ears, Grant could vaguely hear the sound of a persistent whistle. It rapidly grew louder and was joined by marching boots.

The Vassal was jerked away from Grant by a member of the Peacekeepers. As the fight was broken up, Grant expected the group to be more than a little upset that he'd managed to slip through their grasp once again.

"Sorry, officer," one of the Vassals called out. "We were just settling an argument. It's all good."

Grant had a bad feeling, a tingle he got when he felt that something wasn't quite right. He helped Waylon up. The whip had left a nasty red welt around his friend's neck, but at least they had both survived.

"Grant." He turned his head as the House Thursday Vassal, one he didn't recognize, called his name. The Vassal grinned and held up an object he *did* recognize. Mother of Pearl glinted in the light. Panicking, Grant rummaged through his belt pouch. "Thank you for your assistance in the tournament."

Grant went to surge forward and recover his stolen main tournament token, but the iron grip of Waylon stopped him. "Let me *go!*"

"Stop! If you fight them now, you'll end up in chains. House Tuesday is watching us like a hawk right now," Waylon ordered harshly. "They *can't* get that back for you. The law is that whoever is *holding* it is the rightful owner of it. It adds a whole level of intricacy to the events, and you *were* warned about it. Let it go. We just need to find a way to get it back."

Grant had no choice but to stand down and watch the cocky Vassal saunter away with *his* token.

CHAPTER TWENTY-SEVEN

Grant's frustration smoldered like the fire he was sullenly staring into. Waylon had just finished preparing dinner and was now sitting cross-legged, writing in his journal. They had found a secluded spot off the main road, and Grant had attempted to burn off his anger by hauling rocks and building the fire pit. He was still in a bad mood, and Waylon's cheerfulness at getting away from the Vassals was wearing on his nerves.

Just as Grant opened his mouth to give the Wielder a piece of his mind, Waylon put his quill down and smiled. "Thank you. No one has ever stood by my side against other people like that. You came back for me, and put your own safety at risk to do so."

"It's *fine*-"

Waylon held up a hand, though he was clearly reluctant to interrupt. "Please, let me finish. Being a monster hunter is a solitary life. One where you can only trust yourself and your wits. It may be hard to believe... but I don't have many friends."

Grant eyed the man to see if he was jesting. "But you are the son of Heavyweight Wednesday. You're a Wielder, and I've seen at *least* three ladies swoon when you passed them and graced them with your presence."

"Funny. Now stop that; I'm being serious. The fact of the matter is... I haven't been able to earn either a proper combat skill or a Title, which is why I am Waylon Wednesday, near-exiled son of Wednesday, not even in the running for his father's Wielded Weapon. I only have this Weapon of Power now because I've been proving my worth to the District by working for Lady February. Even so, I am my father's child. My status in life only brought me enemies, which is why I was running wagons *alone* when we first met." Waylon looked away, obviously uncomfortable with sharing his emotions to this degree. "Your actions have proven time and again that you are a man of integrity. I just want to say that I'm glad that we met."

A lump formed in Grant's throat at the rapid shift. "I don't... know what to say."

"There's no need to say anything. Drink your District-approved monster-enriched four-ounce Bed. We'll get up early tomorrow and head towards the finals, maybe get a crack at those marauders." Waylon took a shot of the green liquid and shuddered as it oozed down his throat.

Grant nodded and tossed back his own warm and too-salty drink. No matter how hard he tried to empty his mind and focus only on his breath, his mind always returned to the lost token. "How will I get a chance to defeat Lady February now?"

<Not by whining!>

Waylon slurped on his waterskin, applied some rendered fat on his raw neck, and lay down on his bedroll. Grant couldn't blame him. He'd had a challenging day. They both had. A horrifying thought struck him. "Regent's glare, my money pouch! Did they get that *and* my token?"

His hand shot inside his pocket, where he felt the reassuring lump of the pouch... and something else. It crinkled when touched, and his heart beat faster as he pulled out a scrap of paper. He waited until Waylon rolled over and started snoring before reading what it contained.

. . .

Powerlifter Elenor Thursday has your token. Bring Waylon Wednesday to the Red Octagon in the center of Valentine, deliver him, and you'll get it back.

"Red Octagon? Is that a building?" Grant read the note one last time before throwing it into the fire. "Do they really think so little of me? Was this all a ploy to make it look like they wanted the token... just so they could get to the son of Heavyweight Wednesday?"

His head was screaming that he should let the politics of the District play out, that the quest was all that mattered. He watched Waylon sleep, realizing that this was the first night that Waylon had gone straight to sleep. Up until now, he would always toss and turn, waking up intermittently to ensure that Grant was keeping guard during his shift.

<He trusts you. You could *use* that, Grant.> Sarge's offer spoke directly to the darkest part of him, and for a long moment, the young man was frozen with indecision.

"Is that a life worth living?" Grant idly wondered before shaking his head. No matter what, he wasn't going to betray his friend. He stared at the note as it curled and blackened in the flames.

<You pass.>

The crack of a twig late in the night pulled Grant's attention to the opposite side of the fire. He peered around the campsite, still on edge from the previous day's activities. The burning logs had reduced to mere embers, the extra gathered wood having run out hours ago.

A chill ran through his body, growing alongside his sense of unease as a layer of mist suffused the site. He'd seen mist like it before... but couldn't recall *where*. This wasn't the predawn mist that he was used to from his years of carrying out chores at the farm: this was unnatural. Waylon continued to sleep like a log, the steady rhythm of his chest rising and falling the only indication that he was even alive.

The shadows surrounding the trees moved, and he stopped abruptly to rub his eyes. "Please just be seeing things."

The shadows raced towards him. Grant grabbed for his sword, but it lay just out of reach by his bedroll. "*Waylon*! We're under attack!"

His friend bolted upright, only to be knocked down by the butt of a weapon. The owner of the weapon and his companions appeared from the mist. Four figures materialized, their faces concealed within the folds of cowled hoods.

<Forward roll. Get me in your hand. Now!> Grant rolled forward and grabbed for February Twenty Nine.

"Gah!" A boot stomped on his wrist before he could grab his prize, only his cultivation stopping his bones from breaking under the attack. "What do you want? You can have my money pouch!"

He looked up to get a better look at his attacker, and two curved blades slipped out of the hidden folds of the attacker's black cloak to rest against his neck. "House Saturday? Why? I beat you fair and square... are you really going to kill me just because you lost?"

The man leaned down and *hissed*, "I want you to *explain* why my Wielded Weapon has lost its power to deal additional bleed damage. Why *every* Vassal connected to it lost *their* borrowed power?"

"By Lord January... how in the twelve Districts should I know?" Grant's tired thoughts then put together the fact that *he* had taken that power. He tried not to wince as he made the connection, but it seemed the assassin had noticed. Grant opened his status to relinquish the stolen power of February Thirteenth, Razor's Edge... but the option was greyed out. He wasn't able to hand back the power without holding his sword?

"Leave him alone!" Waylon staggered to his knees. "I swear on the name of House Wednesday, Grant Monday did nothing wrong. He certainly didn't steal the power of a Wielded

Weapon. That's *impossible*. Your weapon must have *rejected* you after you lost."

"Shut your filthy mouth." A casual backhand sent Waylon sprawling. Another cloaked figure walked forward and clenched his fists, revealing hidden blades that sprang forward to rest against Waylon's neck. "We recognized the ability being used by Grant during the tournament... after he 'defeated' me."

"A mere coincidence?" Waylon was clearly terrified, but he was also unwilling to back down. "I can name a half-dozen poisons that make clotting impossible."

"Oh, have no fear. We'll get to the bottom of things." The Wielder's teeth reflected the light of the dying fire. "Take them both to Citadel Saturday for *thorough* questioning."

"Please! *No!*" Waylon squealed in terror, to Grant's great dismay. The last thing he wanted was to be taken in for questioning, but the level of terror in Waylon's voice was... concerning. House Saturday weren't even known as assassins in this District. Was their reputation still so terrifying even *without* that knowledge?

While Waylon continued to squeal, Grant surged to his feet. Even without his sword, he wasn't defenseless. He pummeled his fists into the Wielder's stomach and bounced off like he had hit a rock.

Damage dealt: -1 blunt damage

Damage taken: 0 blunt damage (1 mitigated)

<A high enough armor ranking means damage gets reflected if you can't overcome it,> Sarge informed him belatedly. <On the positive side, your own armor will mitigate the reflected damage, so...>

That was all Grant heard before he was rewarded with the back of the assassin's hand across his face, followed by a sweeping kick that brought him to the ground, where he was promptly bound. "If you didn't have anything to hide, then you wouldn't have tried to fight back."

"Literally yes I would." Grant coughed a mouthful of grass

out of his mouth. "You're abducting us against our will, to who knows where, for who knows *what*."

"When, why, who, and you've got them all." The assassin sing-sang as he motioned for the two to be dragged along. "If we are wrong, then you have nothing to fear. You have the word of House Saturday."

More figures emerged from the shadows, apparently distinguished as Vassals by their purple robes. The Wielder walked away after casually stating, "Vassals, take them to the Citadel. Prepare them for some extra special questioning."

CHAPTER TWENTY-EIGHT

The journey from the camp to Valentine was swift, but far from comfortable. Grant's mind was spinning, trying to picture the lengths House Saturday would go to in order to extract the information. Waylon didn't have anything to worry about; the death of the son of Heavyweight Wednesday would cause a House war, and he doubted that anyone wanted that. "What are they gonna do to me?"

<They will need to break you quickly. I expect they will go straight for your fingernails. Works fast, and makes it harder for you to fight back if you get free.>

"Thanks for the information, Sarge." Grant's stomach heaved. It was accompanied by the sound of a gate being raised. "Let's keep the conversation focused on getting free and such?"

<Just don't break too *quickly*. They'll think you're lying and come up with more *convincing* techniques to validate the data.> Sarge was completely serious, and the not-yet-twenty-year-old blanched at the thought of finding the sweet spot of responding to torture so that he would be believed.

Grant was pulled off the back of the small handcart they

had been loaded onto, landing heavily on the flagstones. His bonds were tight, but he could see that they were stopped within a courtyard. Waylon's limp body was dumped right next to him.

"Waylon!" The Monster Hunter lay on the ground unmoving, even as Grant tried to nudge him. There was dried blood down the side of his face. "Are you alright?"

"He'll be fine." A Vassal prodded Waylon with a foot, then turned and kicked Grant in the side, dealing zero damage, to Grant's silent amusement. "You should be worrying about yourself! This fella would be fine if he hadn't struggled so much. Had to clock him a few times to shut him up."

"If you hurt him-" Grant growled upward, getting a shoe to the face for his trouble.

"You'll *what?*" The Vassal's foot ground down on Grant's head, forcing his face into the muck on the road. "Show our guest to his 'room'. I'll be along shortly."

Grant was dragged to his feet and shoved toward a dark entryway. "Start walking."

The tip of a blade pressed into his back, guiding him on the correct path to take. From the closed courtyard, he was forced up a flight of stairs and into the keep. Sconces lit their way. Grant's mind raced, trying to figure out how to escape. If he could make a run for it, he might be able to escape the Vassal, but run *where?* They were inside the House Saturday stronghold. There was no good option to take here, no easy way out.

"We don't have all day. Keep moving, Monday." After numerous dizzying spirals, they exited the stairwell. Grant was forced into a cell at the point of the blade, and the door slammed shut with finality. "Enjoy your stay in Saturday Solitary."

Grant held onto the bars as he turned to watch the Vassal disappear. The man was carrying February Twenty Nine and his backpack. He felt a wave of relief, having assumed they'd left his belongings back at the campsite. Then he saw the ghostly image of his sword in the air, and knew he could retrieve February Twenty Nine if he could just *reach* it.

"Come on…" His fingers *almost* reached the glow, but it was just barely too far away. His hand dropped, and Grant sighed heavily. "Just *had* to keep me a sword-length away, didn't they? *Ironic* is what that is."

The cell was bare, the walls hewn from giant blocks of granite. As he ran his hands across them, he knew there would be no way to escape. He couldn't even fit a fingernail between the tightly fitted blocks. Apart from a stone slab to lie on, the only other contents of the room were a pitcher of water and a barred window above head height. He lay down and tried to center himself.

Hours later, Grant listened carefully to the sound of approaching footsteps and someone dragging what sounded like a heavy sack. He wondered what the contents were. He found out when a cell door slammed shut, followed by a thud, then a familiar groan. "Waylon! You're still alive! Can you hear me?"

"Ugh. I can hear you. So can half the city. Oh… my *head*," came the stressed reply.

"You shouldn't have fought back," Grant chastised the man. "Are you okay?"

"I am *not*," Waylon replied evenly, quietly. "Do you realize where we are? The Citadel, seat of power of House Saturday. No one gets in here that isn't a member of the House. There is no hope of rescue from the outside without a major incident occurring. What did you *do*?"

"How was I supposed to know-" Grant started defensively.

"Regent's saggy… you actually *did* what they're accusing you of?" Waylon started hyperventilating. "How were you supposed to *know* that the Noble House Saturday would seek retaliation for the loss of their Wielded Weapon? *Hmm*. That's a *tricky* one."

"I think-"

"You *think*? No, Grant, you don't. If you *did*, we wouldn't be in this mess; we'd be hunting down those thieves, and you'd be taking part in the tournament two days from now!" Waylon was practically snarling in an attempt to keep his voice down.

"It doesn't matter now. We're probably dead." Grant swallowed hard, looking anywhere besides the direction where his friend's voice was coming from.

"I can't believe I trusted you. If I get the chance to escape this, I will. Even *alone*." The silence stretched after that shocking outburst, and before he knew it, Grant was blinking into wakefulness as the sun lit the corner of his cell wall.

From there, minutes turned into hours. After his outburst, Waylon had remained silent. That suited Grant fine. He had nothing to say to the man that could well betray him to their captors.

<Time to train!> Sarge cheerfully shouted into his mind. Grant was so startled that he fell off his stone bunk and rattled his brain by hitting the ground.

"Sarge! How can I hear you? I don't have my sword." Grant looked around to see if February Twenty Nine was somehow stored nearby, but he found nothing.

<Your sword is part of you. I think. It's bound to you, at least.> They both contemplated that for a long moment. <Anyway, being a captive doesn't get you out of training. Gotta train even *harder* so you can get away. Only through effort and persistence will you achieve your goals. Pushups can be done almost anywhere! Get to 'em.>

Grant did as he was told with minimal groaning. It was something to do, at least. Managing to complete the first fifty in just over a minute, he couldn't suppress a slight smile. <Too easy with your cultivation, huh? Fair enough. Do fifty more, one finger on each hand only. Then the next finger, and so on. I want to see some *enthusiasm*.>

He stifled a groan then started another set. His arms were trembling by the time he reached his ring fingers. "Getting close to finishing, Sarge."

<I'll tell you when you're done! I don't train quitters!> He managed to go until he got to his pinkies. When it was clear to Sarge that he couldn't complete the set, the sword spirit lent a helping hand in the form of precisely timed shocks.

Grant's body sprang up and down as if it had a mind of its own.

"All done?" Grant let just a *hint* too much hope seep into his voice, if the laughter was anything to go by.

<Far from it! We're just getting started. You don't appear to have anything better to do, right? Flip over and give me five hundred sit-ups. Then… I have thoughts on what we can do using those bars.> Rather than debate with the training program, Grant set to work for the next few hours. By the third hour, the burn from headstand planks was becoming unbearable. Sarge provided motivation in the form of shouting and further shocks when Grant rested for too long. By the time he had completed the final set, he was a sopping pile of sweat.

<For the next hour I'll apply a series of modulated shocks to specific muscle groups, varying the intensity and duration. It is… *unorthodox*, but it should provide the required physical cultivation stimulus, along with a boatload of mental cultivation.>

"Mental cultivation? Specifically? Just by itself?"

<You'll soon find out. It's so *exciting*, isn't it? Let's just say… soldiers must be mentally tough to overcome all obstacles.>

The following hour was one of the longest in Grant's life. The shocks started as minute, but they quickly ramped up until his muscles quivered under the load. Sarge was correct; the shock treatment somehow boosted his mental cultivation. He felt like his brain was calloused, toughened from the mental abuse. The shocks were both mentally and physically draining, but he wanted to strengthen his mind for the upcoming interrogation.

Once everything was finally over, he fell asleep on the cold stone floor and didn't wake up again until the next morning, when a bucket of icy water was thrown over him.

"Don't get too comfy in here." The guard laughed as Grant shivered uncontrollably.

"When are you guys gonna *talk* to me?" Grant demanded through chattering teeth.

"That's all part of the fun!" The man snickered again and

walked away, his footfalls echoing down the hall. Rather than cowering in the corner and working himself into a fervor, Grant took control of the time he had left by training for two hours without being forced to do so.

<That's more like it! We'll make a samurai, ahh... a true cultivator out of you yet! Okay, same routine as last night, but this time, we'll push you beyond your breaking point!> Grant didn't answer. There was no point in wasting his breath; Sarge would make sure he needed that soon.

He knew that his mentor had his best interests at heart. As his friend Derek had once told him, with enough hammering, even cold steel could be beaten into shape. He had practically *waltzed* through January, and now he was suffering for his lacking physicality and mentality in February. From here on out, the challenges would only increase in difficulty. If he wanted to make it through them in one piece, he would have to be in *supreme* mental and physical shape.

To that end... two fingered, upside-down push ups. Sit ups using the bars as footholds to keep himself off the ground. He grunted with exertion. "*Ugh!*"

"I have no idea what you've been doing in there," Waylon called out from the adjacent cell. "But I heard a lot of huffing and puffing. There's no point in working yourself into a state. There's no way out, so just accept the situation. Make peace with your inner demons, and go quietly into the light."

"Waylon, please be quiet and listen." When Grant was sure he had his despondent companion's attention, he explained, "I have a plan, and you need to trust me."

"No."

CHAPTER TWENTY-NINE

Footsteps echoed along the corridor, but Grant was ready to put his plan into action. The fingertips of his right hand lightly brushed the metal bars of his cell. To any onlooker, he appeared to be sleeping. "Get up, Monday. You are to be taken to the inquisitor for questioning. Move away from the bars."

"I *know* you're awake!" Grant continued to feign sleep, which infuriated the man. "I think you need some sense beaten into you."

Grant listened to the guard fumbling with the lock. Following the clunk—just as the mechanism opened—Grant switched Spark Shield to active mode.

A bolt of energy surged along the bars and into the body of the unfortunate guard, seizing his muscles so rapidly that he didn't even have a chance to shout. The shocked man collapsed like a sack of potatoes as the ability wore off, but he started getting to his feet almost instantly. The sad fact was that Spark Shield was too weak to do long-term damage. With his current mental cultivation, it was a distraction at best.

Without a second to lose, Grant took a full step out of the

cell and grabbed the illusion that was hanging in the air, visible only to him. *"Time is Space."*

February Twenty Nine coalesced out of the open air, and the point rested against the man's neck in the next instant. "Get in."

After the Vassal had been locked up properly, he grabbed the set of keys off the ground and unlocked Waylon's cell. Waylon looked up at Grant but didn't rush to escape his confinement. "What are you doing?"

"What does it look like?" Grant waved at his companion to hurry up. "I'm getting us out of here. Move it!"

"Not a chance. Are you crazy? There are *dozens* of Vassals, not to mention the Wielders, and probably *hundreds* of cultivator guards between us and freedom. This is *Citadel Saturday*. I'm sitting on my happy rear right here."

"Waylon, *please!*" The young noble vigorously shook his head, and Grant growled. *"Fine.* Be like that. I guess I'll just look after myself. Hope you live long enough that we meet again."

Grant turned to leave and was met by a poison-filled syringe to the side. His armor had been stripped away, so he only had his cultivation to block the attack... and it failed him. He was out cold in mere moments.

The darkness receded an unknown amount of time later. He found himself in a chamber, strapped to a chair and unable to feel his fingers. The leather straps around his wrists had cut off the circulation to his hands, and he struggled to move his head. He felt his gorge rise when he recognized what looked like blood-stains spread across the stone floor and splattered along the walls.

Flicking his eyes to the side, he found a dejected-looking Waylon draped in heavy iron chains. Between them lay a selection of implements on a tray that would look almost normal in a carpenter's shop. Pliers, tongs, tweezers, files, hammers, and other instruments he couldn't identify.

"Grant Monday." The gravelly voice made him flinch as a

cloaked figure emerged from the darkness of the dimly lit chamber, features hidden within the deep folds of the cowl. "Your escape attempt is further proof of your guilt. Confess, and we will gift you a swift death."

Surprisingly, Waylon spoke up for him in a deadpan tone. "He's just a moron from January. A complete and utter fool. His only crime is ignorance."

Grant caught movement out of the corner of his eye. Above and to the left hung a viewing platform, where a line of cowled figures watched the proceedings with interest. He could just make out the black cloaks of Wielders, along with the purple cloaks of multiple rows of Vassals. Their presence concerned him more than the array of unused sharp objects.

"Let's begin." The torturer pulled his hood back to reveal his merciless face and shaved scalp covered in intricate tattoos. Grant wished at that moment that the man's hood was still up. There was no empathy in the cold, piercing eyes, currently observing him. The inquisitor presented a bucket on one hand and gestured to the array of pain-inducing implements with the other. "Make your choice."

"What's in the bucket?"

"Something unpleasant." A dark smile appeared.

"From the look on your face, I don't think I'll enjoy either." Grant thought quickly, "You're alchemists. Whatever's in there can't be fun. I'll take the knife."

"Bucket it is." The man nodded as Grant snorted at the cliche. "Prepare the prisoner."

Vassals leaped to obey, undoing the straps securing Grant's chest. "Hold on. "I'll tell you everything right now, and I can easily prove it instantly! I can even get the ability back, but if you kill me… they get away with it."

"Grant, what are you *doing*?" Waylon was shaking his head in disbelief. He was shocked, thinking that Grant was outing himself.

"Get it back? From who? Who is this 'they'?" The contents

of the bucket sloshed as the man paused, and a single drop fell onto Grant's exposed stomach.

Debuff gained: Nerve Flame. For the next three sec-

Grant couldn't see the rest of the notification through the blinding pain centered on his stomach. Was he actually on fire? The *instant* he could speak, he babbled out, "By the *Regent*! It was House Thursday! They gave me an artifact that would allow me to steal abilities so they could sell them to the highest bidder. As payment, I had to prove my ability to steal them! I liked Razor's Edge so much that I tried to run with the ability, but they chased me down and took the artifact back. Even so, they gave me another chance, since I knew the secret and had enough mana to activate it. They took my tournament token as collateral, so they know I'll have to do as they told me!"

A collective gasp went up from the House Saturday Wielders at the thought of the merchant House being able to acquire and sell their abilities.

The torturer picked up a pair of tweezers encrusted with dried blood and approached Grant. "You're lying! That's *ridiculous*. I will get the truth out of you, one way or another."

Grant dredged up every fact he had heard about the District and spun them into a story. "I'm telling the truth! Waylon and I are expected at the Red Octagon in Valentine before the start of the main tournament, where they will hand over the artifact once more. It will contain Razor's Edge. They want me to capture Lady February's power so they can get back in power themselves! You have to believe me! I'll destroy the artifact and get your power back!"

"Don't worry." The tweezers were clamped over Grant's index finger. "We will *discover* the truth. Pain, I find, has an uncanny knack for loosening the tongue.

"Pause." A booming voice came from the viewing platform. "If he is telling the truth, then we can't risk disfiguring him."

The man stared at the tweezers for a long moment before sighing and looking up. "My lord, his story is *preposterous*. He must be lying."

"Maybe so. Still, one of our Wielded Weapons is powerless. This is a fact. Never in the *history* of the *world* has there been a way to steal abilities from Wielded Weapons. But... if anyone could do it, it would be House Thursday. They have money, and they have access to artifacts that no one has ever seen before. Boy, what is the ability of your Wielded Weapon?"

"I can call it to my hand from anywhere it has been while bonded to me!" Grant nearly shouted, having latched onto this lifeline with all his strength.

Not having any of it, the tattooed man growled, "My *lord*, as you know, there are ways to cause serious pain without inflicting visible injuries. I will get to the bottom of this and discover the real truth!"

Another man stepped forward with a report that he read from. "Professor Saturday. Grant has demonstrated the ability to recall his sword publicly during the final qualifier, as well as to escape his cell only a few hours ago."

Almost throwing a tantrum, the tattooed inquisitor snarled and opened his mouth to interject.

A raised hand stopped all discussion. "Silence. *I* am Saturday, not you, and I have made my decision. Grant Monday, we agree to your plan. Destroy the artifact and restore our weapon power... and you and your friend will go free. Waylon Wednesday will stay here until you have fulfilled your end of the bargain. But let me be clear..."

The head of House Saturday rose to his feet, and a pool of darkness spread from within the hidden folds of his cloak. "If you are lying to us... you will have wished that I had allowed my inquisitor to continue his work."

"Thank you. M'lord," Grant squeaked. "I, um, need Waylon with me. They expect both of us. They want him as additional collateral."

"Excuse *me*?" Waylon hissed at Grant.

"Sorry, Waylon. I had already decided just to run for it, so I didn't bother telling you. It was never supposed to happen for real," Grant admitted to his friend, who luckily took the statement at face value. At least, he said nothing else for the moment.

The four Wielders conferred amongst themselves as Grant mentally chewed on his nails. He wondered if they had bought his story, but it was either that or tell the truth. Better to use two enemies against each other than to take the fall.

Saturday finally came to a decision. "Go to the building, and take Waylon with you. You won't see us... but we will be there. Watching, and *waiting*. Try to run, escape, or warn them... and we will end you both. When you have proved that House Thursday was responsible, we will make them pay. *Then* you run. If they can figure out how to do it once, what's stopping them from doing it again? Give him his sword and pack. You... get out of my sight. For your sake, I hope that we don't meet again."

CHAPTER THIRTY

The two took off running as soon as the portcullis of Citadel Saturday slammed shut. Both of them wanted to get out of the area as quickly as possible, equally eager to put the memories of their time behind them, as well as to be out of the seat of power for House Saturday.

Neither of them had any illusion that they were *safe*, but distance would help. Grant once again felt February Twenty Nine's hilt in his grip and the sheathed blade against his hip. That helped even more.

"I *can't* believe it." Waylon shook his head as he mulled over the events of the last few days over and again. "We got out alive? In one piece? After you somehow used an artifact to steal their power... I don't know if you're a genius or a crazy person. If your plan is successful, you've put Houses Thursday and Saturday on a path to war. A House war here... I have no idea what will happen."

"*I* know." Grant nodded grimly, earning a concerned look from his friend at the anger in the words. The pair made their way towards the center of Valentine, soon finding themselves amongst the heaving crowds arriving for the finals that would restructure the entire District. Revelers, dressed in costumes of their favorite athletes, chugged down green wheatgrass shots. The mouthwatering smell of grilled kale leaves drifted in the breeze, attempting to lure the pair away from their objective. Grant surprised himself by *wanting* to sneak off and gorge himself on the leafy treat, but he knew that wasn't an option.

In his greed, he had stolen the power of a Wielded Weapon, from the most dangerous House, and been *caught*. He resolved to learn from this lesson and be more prudent when using his sword's true capabilities.

"Here we are. The place you are going to trade me for a *chance* at winning an introduction to a pretty lady. I feel so *honored*." Waylon's dry sarcasm didn't stop him from pointing to the red, unusually shaped building. It was heavily fortified with guards positioned on the roof, and burly Vassals guarding the metal braced door. "The Red Octagon. It was once the site of the famous Octagon Theatre. Playwrights would travel from across February to host plays and theatre productions. I have fond memories here with my parents, but I can't wait to exchange that childhood nostalgia for memories of fleeing for my life or being held hostage."

"It isn't going to be that bad, Waylon," Grant grunted as they closed in on the front door. "It's kinda fitting that this is a stage, because we're only here to act out a farce, distract two of the seven most powerful forces in the District, and run for our lives."

<Exit stage left, if you will.>

Not knowing what that meant, Grant still repeated it for his friend. "Exit stage left, if you will."

"Ha!" Waylon barked out a laugh, and just like that, the tension was broken. "Okay. Just… if I'm captured, be prepared to save me at any cost. Powerlifter Thursday is vindictive, and she never forgave my father for defeating her in a brawling tournament. I'd have a better chance at making friends in Saturday and getting out than I have of getting her to let me go."

"I will." Grant strode towards the gold filigree door and the two guards barring their way.

The burly Vassal on the left held out a bronze crowbar, of all things. "No one is allowed in. On your way!"

"I have important business with Lady Powerlifter Thursday?" Grant's statement faltered into a question as the strange title rolled off his tongue.

The Vassal on the right spoke in a softer, but firm voice. "Come back after the tournament. Powerlifter Thursday isn't offering alms today."

Grant looked down at his ragged, filthy clothing and recalled that he hadn't yet put his armor on over it. He tried to lean in to whisper, but the guards raised their crowbars in warning, so he merely spoke quietly. "Tell your boss I have Waylon Wednesday. *Believe* me, she will want to see him."

One of the guards disappeared inside nearly instantly, surprising all three of the others. The remaining guard cast a wary eye at the pair, not letting them out of his sight. He was ready and willing—so *willing*—to brutally retaliate if they tried anything. It dawned on Grant that he didn't know what to do if Powerlifter Thursday declined to see him. For all he knew, she could be at the tournament already, which would certainly shatter his plan; then House Saturday would pulverize his bones one-by-one. He decided that this would be a good time to prepare for attack, so he retrieved his white gi from his bag and pulled it on.

After several nerve-wracking minutes, the guard reappeared and motioned for them to follow. Grant gave Waylon the thumbs up, but the young Noble wasn't in any mood to respond. They were led along an opulent passageway clearly designed to flaunt wealth and the power of the House. Their feet didn't make a sound as they trod along thick carpet, and Grant's nerves started to get the better of him. He had no idea what he was actually leading them into.

Waylon's eyes continuously darted around as he frantically searched for an escape route. Grant felt terrible for what he was putting his friend through, and for what he intended to do. He hoped the young noble would forgive him. A heavy velvet curtain was drawn aside, and they were led inside an enclosed amphitheater. The rows upon rows of plush seats and furnishing were a little faded, but the opulence shone through regardless.

"Don't just stand there." The meatiest woman Grant had ever seen was in the middle of a squat rack, her watermelon-sized leg muscles straining as she smoothly stood up and dropped down. She set down the bar as they approached, the action causing the entire stage to shudder violently. Powerlifter Thursday lived up to her name, so much so that Grant could barely peel his eyes away. When he did, he stumbled to a stop. She was flanked on either side by two *massive* mastiff-monster dogs. "You may approach. They don't bite... without the proper command."

Dozens of Vassals and a couple Wielders sat in the front rows, eying them suspiciously. He had the feeling he'd inter-rupted an important meeting, perhaps a House training session?

"Good puppies." Try as he might, he couldn't contain his nerves as he got closer to the proud canines. "If I knew you were here, I'd have brought a bone? Good boys?"

A nasty snarl was his only reply, and he clenched up as though he had taken a physical blow. He decided to ignore the animals as much as possible from then on.

"I see that you fulfilled your side of the deal. Thank you." Powerlifter flicked Grant's enamel entry token through the air to him. Waylon stared in disbelief as Grant pocketed it without looking at it directly. "You came through for us. Leave now. We don't want any witnesses for the next steps."

Grant nodded and turned to leave, not once looking his friend in the eye. Waylon attempted to follow but was stopped by a pair of Vassals. "Grant? What are you doing? I thought you had a plan to save *both* of us?"

"Not so much." Grant's words came out as a whisper, and he kept moving.

"Excellent; let's get this over with. Keep Waylon quiet, and one of you escort Sir Monday out." Powerlifter sighed happily. Several Vassals rose from their chairs and rushed to obey her with weapons at the ready. Waylon stood alone at the edge of the stage, his tomahawk trembling as he struggled to contain his nerves and anger at being betrayed. "I think a finger with his signet ring will suffice as a message. Then let's head to the tourney!"

Waylon swung his weapon in a wide arc, managing to fend off the attackers for a moment. That was all the distraction Grant needed.

His blade sang as he unsheathed it, forcing all eyes to turn in his direction as he swung at the nearest object, a fist-sized jade statue that could have easily fit in his coin pouch. The blade connected, shattering the sculpture. At the same time, he had his status page ready and relinquished Razor's Edge just as his blade completed its arc.

Powerlifter let out a snarl as jade shrapnel flew, hit the ground, and broke further. "My statue! Why would you *do* that, you deranged fool? We had a deal, and you throw it out like this? We would have both had everything we wanted!"

"You had this figurine on hand, and I know that you have a way of getting or making more." Grant's non sequitur only bought him a moment before an entire Calendar of Vassals surged to put him down. Waylon continued to defend himself in a lackluster manner against a Wielder and two Vassals, but all other eyes were now on Grant. A Vassal lunged forward, aiming his crowbar at Grant's head.

<Behind you!> Grant didn't see the shadow that fell from the upper balcony and saved his unarmored head from being caved in. The person landed behind the House Thursday Vassal, and a thin red line appeared on their neck as a curved dagger sliced. The Vassal collapsed, fruitlessly grasping his slashed neck as his lifeforce drained away in a sanguine pool.

"Better run." Grant was now standing face-to-face with the House Saturday Wielder he had previously fought during the tournament, the man whose weapon ability he had stolen. The Wielder gave a curt nod after his quiet order, then vanished amongst the sudden throng of bodies. House Thursday Vassals went down rapidly, completely unprepared for the surprise slaughter. Grant stared around as if he was trapped in a dream. He had never imagined that his trickery would result in such carnage.

"To me!" Powerlifter yelled as she lifted her crowbar Wielded Weapon. She swung it and impacted the air; the weapon rebounded as if she had struck a stone. A dozen paces away, a thinly-armored assassin practically *splattered* as if he had just had a mountain dropped on him. "Form a defensive line!"

"Time to *go*, Waylon!" Grant's voice hadn't been this high-pitched since he had hit puberty.

The remaining House Thursday cultivators formed a wall between the advancing enemy and Powerlifter. Vassals were cut down mercilessly by the encroaching wall of cloaks. Razor's Edge, the returned weapon power, clearly aided in their vengeful onslaught. Glowing red daggers sliced and diced, even insignificant nicks and cuts resulting in substantial blood loss.

Thursday wasn't taking the attack lying down, even if they were having trouble against their agile foe. Grant was uncertain if it was because Powerlifter was so much more powerful than them, but the Vassal's crowbars only activated the ability when they landed a hit. However, when the blow *did* succeed, the defender would take damage seemingly unproportional to the swing, their body flying across the room as a broken mess.

Waylon stared blankly at the battle raging before him. Mini-earthquakes rocked the once fine theatre, with chunks of plaster falling in a hail of debris as expensive alchemical charges detonated, forcing the attackers to retreat. Unfortunately for House Thursday, House Saturday was who they purchased the alchemical charges *from*. As soon as the combat began to escalate on one side, the other side would immediately bring out more powerful attacks. Despite that, swarms of fresh Vassals leaped from the balcony above and into the fray, and more members of House Thursday entered through the doorways as the sounds of combat grew.

"Grant?" Recognition flooded Waylon's eyes as his friend drew close and grabbed his arm. "You didn't leave me! I thought…"

"All part of the plan, buddy," Grant promised with a weak smile as he yanked on the stunned Noble. "Now come *on*; we're getting caught in the crossfire."

They stumbled over bodies and through a heavy curtain into a corridor. Luckily, they didn't come across—or find themselves forced to fight—any members of either of the warring Houses. Grant ran towards what appeared to be an exit, and a moment later, they burst out of The Octagon, spilling out onto the strangely springy road. They got to their feet unsteadily. Since the building was soundproofed, it was hard to believe that a battle raged within, and that all nearby House Thursday and Saturday members were locked in combat.

"Where is everyone?" Grant blinked the dust out of his eyes. The streets were deserted, with not a soul in sight. "The tourney… it must have started.

"The colosseum! Hurry! Good call; that will be the safest place in the entire District for us right now." Waylon started sprinting down the road, and a moment later, Grant caught up. It was hard to tell which one of them was more surprised. Waylon nodded eagerly. "Follow me. Oh, hey, for future reference, I don't appreciate being used as bait. Cool beans?"

"Never again. I swear it," Grant solemnly promised. "I never wanted to do it this time, and I wouldn't have, if Saturday hadn't forced our hand. I can't imagine that would ever happen again."

"Fair enough." Waylon chuckled lightly. "How are we not dead right now?"

"No idea," Grant laughed along. Soon they were both panic-laughing as they tried to move past the brutal brawl they had just witnessed. The streets remained deserted, so it didn't take long to reach the colosseum. Stone arches soared into the sky... but he wasn't there to admire the building's architecture. In fact, he couldn't care less at that moment. He presented his token to the ticket collector at the entry booth with a shaky hand. "Am I too late?"

"I'm afraid so." The lady nodded sadly as she looked over the beautiful token. Grant almost melted into a puddle of nerves as she continued, "You've missed the entire entertainment segment. An acrobatic troupe was displaying various poses that increase physical cultivation for nearly *any* method. I was told they were *spectacular*. But here I am, stuck in the ticket booth-"

"What about the *tournament?*" Grant grabbed her shoulders and shook her as if that would rattle out the answer for him.

She merely frowned at him, slightly affronted. "Oh, that? Hasn't started yet. It was postponed for an hour, since fewer competitors turned up than were expected. We're just waiting for stragglers such as yourself to arrive. By the way... you don't look so good."

"What?" It was only then that Grant noticed a nasty gash on his side. "When...? What?"

She pointed sharply at a section in the coliseum. "Medical section. Now. You, take him there right away. He'll be seen straight away, since I've never seen competitors get injured *before* the bouts."

With Waylon's help, Grant made it to the onsite House Sunday emergency area. Rows of empty cots lay waiting to hold the inevitable injured competitors during the tournament. The smell of pungent medicinal herbs infused the air, and Grant nearly fell asleep from the pleasant odor, despite the fact that he was still standing. Seeing Grant leaning heavily on Waylon, a House Sunday healer surged to their feet.

"Crumbling caduceus! Come over here and lie down." The healer pulled out their aforementioned caduceus and rushed to the bed that Grant had flopped down on. The damaged

Wielder flinched at the sight of the Wielded Weapon as it swung down toward him.

"It's okay. I'm here to help you." The healer mopped Grant's brow as he triaged the young man. "He has a fever... nasty cut... something is interfering with my ability to see inside him, so I'll need to do a physical inspection. What happened to him?"

"Gleam-Fang Stalkers," Waylon lied instantly. "I'm nearly certain this one had poison, so check that as well, but I think it was a remnant of a nest that was burnt out, since it was alone."

"Gleam-Fangs! I heard about that incident. He survived an encounter with them?" The healer went to slice open Grant's Mid Spring armor with a pair of heavy-duty scissors. "Let's see what we have here-"

"No," Grant mumbled the words in his delirium. "Not my armor-"

"You won't be fighting today, sir." The healer's hand was slapped away as Grant tried to sit up.

"Please." Waylon forced Grant down, but he also prevented the healer from slicing open the armor. "Just undo the straps. Grant is determined to fight, and if he does, he'll need his armor in one piece."

The healer shrugged and untied the binding securing the torso armor. As it fell away, both he and Waylon gasped. The flesh was oozing pus, and blood seeped from the wound and down his side.

"Will he be okay?" Waylon looked green.

"Leave me. This is clearly poison, and it's working fast. We have work to do. Barb, I need your help!" Another healer ran over, this one holding a smaller version of the caduceus; a Vassal, then. A curtain was pulled around the bed, and Waylon nervously waited on the other side, hoping that his friend would pull through.

The minutes turned into half an hour. Waylon could hear the sound of trumpets and shouting coming from the arena. The healer finally appeared from behind the curtain, and

Waylon held his breath as the man spoke. "We have managed to stabilize him and contain the poison."

"That's fantastic news." Waylon smiled; the healer didn't. "The bad news?"

"I removed a foreign body from his stomach." Waylon peered at the razor-sharp object the Wielder was holding up. "This was the source of the damage."

"A... needle?"

"A shard of a thrown weapon, coated in numbing poison as well as a particularly nasty anticoagulant. Not a chance he would notice it, and it nearly took him out. Good thing you got here as quick as you did." The healer looked sharply at Waylon. "Also clearly *not* a Gleam-Fang attack, but I won't even ask. Listen, he is stable at fifty percent health-"

"Why not heal him fully?"

"Ran out of *mana*." This was obviously a sore point, so Waylon held up his hands apologetically.

Grant slapped the curtain out of his way, getting chased by an irate Barb, "I *have* to do this. I have no other choice."

"You're a stubborn fool." She was practically yelling at him. "If you go out there and waste all our hard work, I'm going to find the newest trainees to stitch you up!"

"Healer. Thank you both for your help." Grant ignored the fuming Vassal and turned to face the Wielder. "How much do I owe you?"

"Treatment is free during the tourney, but I *strongly* advise you to sit this one out. Given the circumstances, I can provide a medical pass, allowing you to take part in next year's tourney without having to go through the preliminary stages."

Grant was shaking his head before the offer was even complete. "I have to compete this year."

"Is becoming a Noble worth your life? You're already a Monday!" Barb protested pleadingly, but Grant simply shook his head sadly.

"*Not* participating would cost me my life," Grant half-explained. "Better a chance and failing, than failing for sure. Please... stand aside."

He resolutely walked into the coliseum, with three people watching him go. One's eyes held curiosity, another was tinged with sadness. The last was starting to heat up with interest in this intense young man who had so much to prove to the world.

CHAPTER THIRTY-ONE

At least a hundred athletic bodies in the peak of health filled the arena... and then there was Grant Monday. Overwhelmed, confused, and at half health. The only advantage he had was his Mid Spring Light armor, when almost all the people around him were wearing only regular, unrestrictive clothes. Seeing that, he started to wonder if his armor was *actually* an advantage.

He filtered into the back row, his sunken flesh making it nearly impossible to blend in amongst the proud chins and chiseled jaws. Grant had never seen so many perfect specimens. He knew that each one had passed through a gauntlet of challenges to be here and had been training for this exact event for years. "I feel sick."

Sarge laughed at him in his head, offering no comfort.

The last remnants of fanfare died down, and Grant could feel the anticipation building. The excitement in the air mirrored the fluttering in his chest. *Thousands* of spectators were crammed into the stands surrounding the circular arena. Somewhere out there, Waylon was cheering him on. Knowing that there was at least *one* person rooting for him made him stand tall.

He needed to succeed.

A figure bounded onto the podium, gleaming silver-gauntleted fists pumping in the air. Grant couldn't mistake the patent shocking pink hair belonging to the same person that had zoomed past him as he sat at the foot of a statue in Haji-meni. After an initial burst of whistling and shouting, the chatter from the stands died down.

Lady February's crisp voice pierced the air and the hearts of her fans. "People of February! It is my great honor to open the annual games! My late father held the inaugural games and set February on the path towards success through physical cultivation."

Here she paused for a moment of silence. "Now I, the people's Lady February, am here to continue his legacy and build upon what my father achieved! In the past year, you may have noticed further changes throughout the District. These changes are intended to push each and every *one* of you beyond your perceived limits and towards ever higher heights! Change is not easy, but it is *necessary* if we want to reach our full potential. I believe the citizens of February have what it takes... what in the...? Hey! Where are you all going? What's the meaning of this?"

A call went out, and anyone in the arena or stands belonging to House Thursday or Saturday suddenly stood and just... left. Grant knew why they were leaving; rather than the conflict in The Octagon being the end of the issue, as he had hoped, the war between the two Houses was escalating.

"Turn around and get back to your positions at once!" None of the departing Vassals or Wielders listened to her. She trembled with rage at being ignored. When shouting did nothing, she slammed her suddenly metal-encased fist onto the ground, shattering the stone arena around her. "Anyone who is not present for the start of the games has just forfeited their position!"

The members of both Houses continued to leave, unde-terred by her words. Grant watched around thirty competitors exit the arena, almost a full third of the starting number. As the last of them left, Lady February managed to get herself under control. Speaking to the other competitors, she struggled to maintain a level tone. "Prepare yourself, competitors, mentally and physically for the challenges that lie *ahead*. Only the best amongst you will earn the right to become a Wielder and help to shape and guide the District in the years to come. The very best of you will earn the right to become my personal Sparring Partner! Prove that you have what it takes to keep up with me!"

The wild cheering at these words put a smile back on her face. "Now... let us proceed to the first round. It will be a no-holds-barred melee event. The only rule is: do not kill. Even if the very best are the ones that pass, you are all elites. The loss of any of you will be a loss for the District. Use your strength to make it through to the second round. Even with the *reduction* in expected participants and subsequent scale of the event, only twenty of you will be advancing to the next round."

Grant took a deep breath and slowly exhaled, releasing his pent-up tension. He would have loved to rest and recover fully, but circumstances had led him here. In this arena, he would instead be making his stand. At half health and burdened with weariness, he knew that he didn't have much of a chance. His mind wandered while Lady February droned on, reminiscing about her late father. His goal was simple, to use his Kenjutsu to force as many competitors to yield as possible. Unlike the others, he was fully committed to stabbing someone repeatedly if they didn't submit. He had actual combat experience, and that was something that practice just couldn't prepare people for.

Grant absentmindedly watched as Lady February waved her hands around. A strong gust of wind proceeded to buffet him, forcing him to alter his footing to avoid being swept from his feet. Confused by this, he decided to pay more attention.

"If at any time, a participant forfeits, they will be whisked out of the arena by the wind spell that was applied. However, if they refuse to forfeit, knock 'em out. To yield or forfeit, kneel or lie on the sand and raise your left fist... or go unconscious." This got a smattering of laughter from the crowd, and Lady February grinned. "Now, lords and ladies to be... let the games begin!"

No sooner had Lady February issued the command than guttural cries of competitors rang out and reverberated around the arena, matched only by the jubilant cheers of the ecstatic crowd. Grant unhurriedly unsheathed February Twenty Nine as he tried to get his breathing under control. He had fought before in front of a large audience, but the people of January were always more interested in stuffing their faces on succulent dishes than watching armed combat.

Only the reassuring weight and balance of the uchigatana in his white-knuckled grip grounded him and prevented him from being swept away on a wave of emotion. Right now, he needed to be calm and prepared if he wanted to survive this test. While he *could* kneel on the sand and raise his fist at any time to be whisked away by a blast of wind, failure was not an option.

<Jump. *Duck!*> In his calm moment of contemplation, Grant almost failed to realize that a multitude of battles raged all around. Sarge's barked command instantly brought him to his senses. He didn't have time to question the command as he leaped into the air and simultaneously dropped his head. A blade whistled through the air above his head, while he watched a yari—a spear with a flat double-edged blade affixed to a wooden shaft—sweep under his feet.

The Vassal wielding the blade blinked in surprise and stumbled forward, off-balance. Grant spun and swept the Vassal's leg out from under him before pinning him to the ground with the point of February Twenty Nine. The Vassal groaned and raised a clenched fist, the sign of forfeiture. A gust of wind tugged at Grant's armor, forcing him back a step. The Vassal's disappointed eyes never left him as a miniature tornado swept him up and whisked him out of the arena.

In the next moment, Grant tackled the yari-user and sliced into their neck, just enough to draw blood. The man didn't give up, so Grant shrugged and started to press down. Before the blade could go deeper, wind knocked him back and the man was swept away as he gave up.

Damage taken: 10 blunt (11 mitigated)

Grant cursed and stumbled forward as he was punched in the back of the head. His *unarmored* head. "Thanks for the save, armor cultivation!"

He dropped and rolled, popping to his feet as a one-two combo whiffed through the space he had just vacated. Now facing his opponent, he out-ranged the man significantly. His new opponent didn't seem to mind and closed in a rush. His attacks came thick and fast, but Grant's blade was always there to meet them. Once he had recovered, Grant started sending his own probing attacks.

Damage dealt: 24 slashing.

Damage dealt: 26 slashing.

Damage dealt: 39 slashing. (Critical!)

"You have *no* armor cultivation?" Grant gasped as he opened large wounds across the man with each swipe. Only his *precise* control of his sword allowed him to turn his blade from the far deadlier path it was trying to take. He didn't get an answer, so he flipped his blade and started smashing the blunt edge into the man's head until he passed out. A gust of wind later, and Grant was alone. "How much more till I level, Sarge? >

<Defeat two Vassals,> Sarge ordered his weary student. <Or two Wielders.>

"Either way, huh?" Grant heaved for breath as his stomach wound reopened.

<Technically, yes, though I suggest you pick a few low-level Vassals to fight. There's no need to take unnecessary risks.>

Grant didn't answer, since the circle of competitors was shrinking as they converged on him.

"You *cheat*. Three people in under a minute? Are you a Thursday, promising them a sack of Time if they agree to give up?" A Vassal of House Friday cautiously strode forward. For all his talk of Grant being a cheat, it certainly *appeared* that he was taking him seriously as a fighter. In one hand was a net, the other a trident spear. "*We* deserve to be here, boy. I'll say no more, though I am sure you understand exactly what I mean."

The converging competitors with their perfect physiques nodded in agreement. Grant raised his open hand in supplication. "I'll take you on one at a time; what do you say?"

A low whistle was the only warning he got. He'd heard the noise before, and his hatred of being turned into a worthless, immobile punching bag made him spring into action at full speed. The cast net sailed over him and caught one of the circling men instead. Grant followed the net and slammed his sword into the trapped man's torso. His target gasped and whimpered as their left hand shot up, instantly getting whisked out of the arena… with Grant's sword.

Everyone saw that as their chance, and charged at him. Two blades slammed into Grant, his armor barely slowing them down. A spear poked a fresh hole in his leg, and a new net was tossed up in an attempt to keep him down. He rolled away, leaving a rapidly-growing trail of blood behind.

"Come on, give the *cheater* a chance to prove himself." Grant wheezed a rattling breath as the bombardment of attacks abruptly ended. In a daze, he squinted up into the light to see the owner of the voice who had spoken up for him. A Wielder in shimmering chromatic armor loomed over his prone form. As the Wielder moved, the colorful armor made Grant's head spin. It was hard to focus on his precise location. "I think you are a cheat and a fraud, and I intend to prove it!"

A weapon slashed downwards. Grant clenched his body, preparing himself for the killing blow. It didn't come. Instead, the net around what may have been subordinates was expertly parted with a few deft strokes.

Grant took the chance to scramble to his feet, using a freshly-retrieved February Twenty Nine to pull himself up. Battles continued to rage on, with miniature tornados sweeping defeated competitors away, but this small circle was an arena all its own.

"Nice sword, Grant *Monday*." The chromatic armor owner looked down on him, both figuratively and literally. "Does it collect its own rust, or do you just never clean your weapon?"

Grant pretended that he was going to exchange more insults, but instead slammed the hilt of his sword into the head of one of the newly freed subordinates. Once, twice, a third time, so rapidly and violently that no one could react in time. The man fell unconscious and was whisked away.

Instantly, Grant felt his wounds stitch themselves as his Cultivation Achievement Level increased to fourteen, and he burst out laughing as he began moving at full speed. The chromatic man roared, "You were *feigning* your injuries? You have no honor!"

"Competitors!" The cheerful voice of Lady February bellowed across the arena. "Twenty-one competitors remain, but only twenty will make it through to the next round. Good luck!"

<Careful, Grant. You can currently strike with a force that these unarmored fools cannot withstand. If you critically hit one, you'll deal up to forty-five damage. That's almost enough to kill a level one in a single blow. It's *certainly* enough to open arteries and finish a human post-combat. Choose your point of attack *carefully*.>

"Understood." While Lady February and Sarge spoke, Grant took a moment to prepare mentally for the fight ahead. The Wielder didn't look like he would back down. Now that Grant had been boosted, they were the same level. Even so, his opponent's armor was superior, and it looked like he was a duo cultivator at a minimum. Grant had witnessed firsthand how poor Early Spring armor was compared to Mid Spring armor. This time, though, he was at a major disadvantage.

<I said to pick a low-level Vassal to fight... I love that you're up to the challenge that a proper Wielder offers! He's wearing spiffy chromatic armor, but I wonder how well he can use it! Take 'im down, samurai!> The double-bladed sword his opponent was wielding zipped through the air. <*Parry*! Good luck; you got this.>

The razor-sharp blade slid along the edge of February Twenty Nine as Grant reflexively parried and stepped forward to counter, striking the Wielder on the arm.

Damage dealt: 2 slashing. (28 mitigated.)

"Maybe you do have some skill after all." Before Grant could do more than gasp at the fact that his attack did practically nothing, his lightning-fast opponent spun counterclockwise. The other end of the bladed weapon sliced through Grant's torso armor and bit into his back. For a moment, he felt no pain. He pressed a hand to his back. A slick of sticky, hot blood coated his hand. He stumbled away from his opponent in shock at both his opponent's speed and the severity of the injury.

Damage taken: 5 slashing (33 mitigated.) Bleeding: -1 health per second for eight seconds.

<Power through, Grant. It's only a flesh wound. Get back in the fight.> Grant nodded and clenched his teeth. Like him, his opponent had no qualms about breaking his opponent to prove his point.

"You're an interesting fellow! How about I put a word in with Lady February? Maybe you can be a jester in her court, entertaining the masses as they become powerful? What do you say?"

Grant knew better than to get caught up in the distraction. His sword moved through the air, rebounding off the wall of armor three times before his opponent reacted.

"Yawn. If you want to *play* the part of a Noble, you have to start acting like one. I suggest-" The Wielder stumbled back as

Grant leaped into the air and brought February Twenty Nine down on his helm. The force of the impact left a dent in the helm and rang the man's bell.

Damage dealt: 10 slashing (33 mitigated).

"Seriously? You *dented* my helm! Do you know how much chromatic armor costs to repair? I, Vanguard Sunday, am gonna *cut* you up!" Grant wasn't listening. He slid the edge of his blade along the Wielder's cuirass, yet the multi-colored surface remained pristine. Vanguard spun his razor in a figure eight, and the blade glancingly cut into the soft flesh of Grant's thigh as he danced away. Any deeper, and he risked losing the use of his leg; with it, the fight.

"Sarge, options?" Grant muttered as the encirclement laughed at the wild fight.

<Hmm... he's too well protected, but I think you're getting to him. The sparks that flew when your sword took the helmet dead on->

"Sparks! That's it! Sarge, use Spark Shield on my sword."

<Not a thing, Grant. It's a *defensive* spell; the logic of the system makes you hitting him *not* apply the damage.>

"Fine, put it on *me*!" Grant snapped and almost continued shouting, but the pain of lightning coursing through him forced his jaw to clench.

Vanguard went in for the killing blow. Grant knew that if the fight dragged on, both of them would make it through to the next round, and neither of them wanted to face the other again at this point. Grant sidestepped the blow, but he allowed his sword to partially block it.

Damage dealt: 11 lightning (12 mitigated)

"Heavy armor is twice as effective against physical blows, but only half as good against magical damage." Grant smiled grimly as he used the moment of surprise to lock their weapons together. Since he was still *technically* blocking, lightning surged into Vanguard Sunday ceaselessly. The cultivator shook as the energy surged through him, his teeth chattering together as the vibrations grew in intensity. Grant swung around and swept the feet out from beneath his opponent, then jammed his sword into the hollow of the man's throat and started pressing down until his sword overcame the system barrier of armor and began to draw blood.

Then he pogo-hopped on it, jamming the blade down further. The fight went out of his opponent, and a blast of wind sent Grant reeling backward as the Wielder was swept away.

Do you, Grant Monday, wish to absorb the power of February 14th, 'Live by the Sword'? Accepting 'Live by the Sword' will override any previous wielded weapon power absorbed in the current monthly series. If not over-ridden by another weapon of the same month, this ability will vanish at the end of the year, unless the quest 'Heal The World' has been completed.

Accept / Decline

"Not like he can tattle on me before I get to March, right? I accept." Grant felt a jolt of energy rush through him as he accepted the ability.

CHAPTER THIRTY-TWO

The wind howled, battering his ears and tugging at his sword and armor. Grant looked up into the air as a tornado made contact with the ground, greedily sucking up sand from the arena floor. The turbulent winds grew in magnitude until Grant's feet left the safety of the solid ground. "I made it through to the next round! Didn't I? Let me continue!"

His voice was but a whisper as the screaming wind assaulted his ears. Looking down, he felt a wave of vertigo overtake him as the arena and spectators sank away. From this high up, he couldn't even make out individuals in the crowd. They were insignificant specks. Peering through the swirling mass of debris captured by the tornado, he could see other bodies joining him on this journey. He didn't know where they were going, but at least he wasn't alone. He fought to sheathe February Twenty Nine to prevent it from being wrenched from his grasp. He didn't want to be remembered as the competitor who committed seppuku in mid-air.

Sword secured, Grant peered down at the landscape of February as it zipped past. From this vantage point, the land resembled that of the map at the estate of House Wednesday.

He could see the dark spread of the Whispering Woods, farm-land, and the sprawling metropolis of Valentine. Even the city faded away from sight as he sped upward and eastward.

"I feel sick." Spinning within the vortex, the contents of his stomach threatened to join him.

<It looks like we're really going places! By the way, you're looking a little rough. Use your new ability while we're in transit; this was an *awesome* steal.>

Grant didn't answer Sarge but took the opportunity to check his stats. He wanted to see what shape he was in and get further details on his newly acquired ability.

Name: Grant Monday
Rank: Lord of The Month (January)
Class: Foundation Cultivator
Cultivation Achievement Level: 14
Cultivation Stage: Late Spring
Inherent Abilities: Swirling Seasons Cultivation
Health: 197/228
Mana: 10.8/12

Characteristics
Physical: 119
Mental: 46
Armor Proficiency: 63
Weapon Proficiency: 88

Wielded Weapon: "February 29"

Weapon Inherent abilities:
1) Weapon Absorption: This sword has the ability to absorb another Wielded Weapon's power, taking its ability into itself. Restriction: Only one weapon per Monthly series.
2) Weapon/Armor Synergy: When the Wielder is equipped with armor, this sword increases in potency and gains power. Increase is capped at the Weilder's cultivation stage, or average armor stage, whichever is lower.

February 29 is currently considered a Mid Spring Light' sword. Current maximum damage is: 29 (23 from weapon cultivation, 6 from base weapon stage damage, rounded up.) Damage type is 'piercing', 'slashing', or 'blunt' depending on how February 29 is used.
3) Time is Space: you now have access to any of the powers of February Twenty Nine, no matter where the Weapon is. You may also call your Weapon to you so long as you touch upon a place in the world where it once was while in your possession. Cost: 25% of mana pool.
4) Locked

Weapon Absorbed abilities:
1) Sword Grandmastery: Imbue your weapon with a Sword Spirit that creates a model that allows for enhanced physical, mental, and weapon cultivation. Restriction: the training plan must be followed, else the ability locks for 24 hours. There is only one warning given per day.
2) Live by the Sword: Pause and meditate on the failures of your combat ability, healing up to 30% of all damage taken within the last 10 minutes, over one full minute. This ability will increase with physical cultivation.

"I'm beaten up and bleeding, but not as bad as I feared. I've taken thirty-two damage… let's see if this new weapon ability will make a real difference." He closed his eyes and activated *Live by the Sword*, and for a moment, he was aware of both the outside world, and each point in the previous battle where he had taken damage. In his mind's eye, he saw how he could have done better, and practiced avoiding the blows.

Grant started shivering involuntarily, and came back to himself to discover that he had regained eleven health. It was incredible to suddenly have lessened pain, like a mini-level-up. Yet, he could no longer feel his hands or feet. More worryingly, his vision had become cloudy. He wiped at his eyes and squinted at the ice crystals that had formed. Windswept tears instantly solidified into a shower of perfectly formed snowflakes.

The tornado that had been his companion suddenly abated. He found himself falling towards a sea of whiteness. He couldn't fathom what was happening, only that he was falling.

Then there was a blanket of silence as he slammed into something.

<Up we go! There's people to slap around!> Sarge's voice startled Grant back to reality. For a moment, he thought he was dead, ensnared in a world of whiteness, but the aches and pains and the biting of searing cold against exposed flesh reminded him that he was very much alive. After several attempts at standing in the pillowy snow, he managed to get to his feet.

"S... s... snow in February?" His teeth chattered and he searched for any explanation. "I don't understand."

"Lords and ladies to be, thank you for joining me here." Grant followed the voice that he could barely hear over the clatter of his teeth. Lady February stood on a mountain peak ahead of him, her shocking pink hair in stark contrast to the snow blanketing wherever they were. Her cheeks were rosy as she snuggled within her cloak of arctic fox fur. "I'm proud of each one of you. The trials are far from over; the next..."

"Where *is* here?" Grant found the courage to speak up. Lady February glared at him, while the other competitors dotted around the snowy peak gasped at his audacity at speaking out. "I was just wondering."

When it was clear that Grant had got the message, she continued. "We are at the highest point in February, the peak of Mount Segatakai. As I was saying, the next stage of the trial will begin shortly. This test is a *race*. To qualify for the third and final stage, you can either make it to the end of the race, or defeat everyone else in combat. A maximum of five competitors can pass and continue onto the final round. Follow the pink light to the end. Ready, set, *go!*"

A huge pillar of light shot up into the sky from... somewhere. Competitors grunted as they waded through the waist-high snow towards a clearing next to the peak. Lady February clapped in appreciation as a Vassal of House Monday unsheathed her sword and cut down the man next to her without hesitation. The ring of steel was joined by other competitors as they engaged in combat and eagerly attempted to impress Lady February.

<Tell me your plan.>

Grant thought about joining them in combat, but he was numb and freezing. He knew they wouldn't be much better, but he at least had a gi, while the rest of them were almost all in form-fitting athletic gear. "I just have to finish the race in the top five, or survive till then. I'll only fight when I have to against mostly-frozen Vassals."

He turned and took in the epic sight before him. Candyfloss clouds blanketed the world. Shivering and sucking in a lungful of frigid air, he started running toward the pink beacon off in the distance. He had gotten an almost five-minute head start when he heard a voice on the wind. "*Hey*, he's trying to skip the fighting!"

There was a pause in the brawl as the pack realized that Grant was trying to slip by and get an easy win, and their fights broke off as they started following after him. Grimacing, he picked up the pace. He didn't have to turn around to realize they were on his tail. Fourteen ambitious competitors were hot on his heels. All he had to do was stay ahead of them... but he had a feeling that might be more difficult than it sounded in his head.

A person appeared next to him, screaming as they cut down with meteoric power. Grant flinched out of the way and followed up with a form-perfect Iaijutsu, his sword taking the woman in the chest. She choked as she stared at the sword, then up at him, before being whisked away in a tiny tornado.

<Nice one! Brace yourself!>

Golden power flooding his body took the young man by surprise, and he missed his step as he reached level fifteen. The slope abruptly fell away, and Grant found himself falling head over heels. There was nothing to stop his fall or to grab onto, at least not until he landed in a thick blanket of snow and came to a halt. He shook the snow off as he exploded out of the snowbank, clearing his ice-encrusted eyes.

A huge storm was brewing, making it difficult to tell which direction to go unless he got a clear view of the light. He forced himself free of the snow and to his feet, resuming his running pace as he spotted a group of rapidly growing dark spots on the pristine white snow closing on his position.

The first among them caught up and launched themself at him. Grant was done playing nice; while the person was in the air, he put his sword through them and used his blade to empower their jump and slam them on the icy ground beside him. The others slowed down with fear in their eyes as Grant stabbed down again, but a gust of wind vanished his target and sent their large, round shield skidding atop the icy snow. Grant watched it move and already knew what he needed to do.

He charged the shield and jumped onto it, pulling the front edge up and holding on for dear life as it *shot* down the slope. Grant knew it was childish, but he turned around and blew a raspberry at the others. There was no *way* they would catch him now! It was impossible to tell how fast he was traveling, apart from 'breakneck speed'. His grin twisted when his glance back revealed that he wasn't the only person who'd had this idea. Three other people on makeshift sleds were keeping pace, but not keeping up—a silver blur sped past the other competitors. Grant's sled bounced along, but he couldn't take his eyes off the unusual sight. A Vassal was balanced atop a gleaming silver tower shield.

Grant found himself hurtling through the air. He had passed the edge of the snow line, and with it, his sled had met resistance in the form of a rocky scree. The sled may have stopped if he had been going any slower, but due to his momentum, he had been flung skyward.

<Tuck and roll!> He didn't have to be told twice. He tucked in his head protectively and curled into a ball. Only by sheer luck did he narrowly avoid cracking himself open like an egg on a nearby rock. Pain from the impact still ripped through him as he rolled to a halt, but his armor and cultivation saved him from any major wounds.

He stood shakily, missing his new shield but not his life. The tower-shield-surfing Vassal was the first to join him on the rocky slope. Scanning the area, Grant spotted the finish line at least a couple of miles away and started running as soon as he was sure he wouldn't fall over. He was still in the lead, but the race was far from over. As it was all downhill against the wind, his size was an advantage. Even so, the other competitors were fitter, with a lifetime of training and the stamina that comes with it. It was still *really* funny to look back and see them get pushed back a few feet every time there was a particularly strong gust.

No trees grew at this altitude, which was a great boon to his reckless descent. It would likely become an issue later as he barreled down the precipitous slope, since it wouldn't be long before he breached the treeline and perhaps encountered less dangerous terrain. A thundering roar from behind startled him. He risked a glance back to see that the closest Vassal had kicked a boulder at him, much to Grant's dismay. One boulder became ten, and ten became hundreds as the loose rocks collided with others, creating a landslide.

Adrenaline surged through his muscles at the terrifying sight, but he knew that no matter how fast he ran, he likely wouldn't outrun the wall of rocks. "Gonna have to take a few hits."

<Try to avoid them!>

"*Obviously*, Sarge!" A rain of missiles peppered Grant's armor while larger boulders bounced past. Despite the relentless barrage of rocks, the finish line loomed ever closer. Grant could even make out the silhouette of Lady February and her shocking pink hair amongst a sea of spectators. She was standing on the other side of the ribbon, awaiting the five competitors who would make it into the final round.

He *would* be one of them.

CHAPTER THIRTY-THREE

With the finish line in sight, he couldn't help but feel a sliver of hope wash over him. Just a few minutes more, and he would beat the best that February had to offer.

Smack.

A stray boulder the size of his fist slammed into the side of his head. Momentarily dazed from the impact, he stumbled over the loose rocks and lost his footing. Grant made it to the bottom of the mountain, almost exactly one hundred yards from the finish line. The only problem? He was officially swept up within the landslide and currently entombed in what might become a rocky grave as the fist-sized boulder was followed up by what felt like half the mountain.

Blood spurting out of torn lips was accompanied by spasms from his lungs. A short while later, he heard the crunch of boots nearby and hoped that someone had arrived to rescue him. Help didn't come. The crunching was followed in quick succession by two more pairs of footsteps. He rightly guessed that they didn't belong to a rescue party. A loud cheer erupted from nearby as the first three competitors crossed the finish line, and

Grant's chances of reaching the final stage in the tournament started to vanish.

<It seems like you're going through a rocky patch, Grant! You really shouldn't take things for granite like this.> Grant groaned and swore unintelligibly at Sarge's attempt at humor. <You know, there was once a poll of people about their favorite natural disaster. Avalanche won by a landslide.>

"Noo…" If he was going to die, he would do so with a view of the sky, and perhaps whoever found his body would hold a respectful funeral in his honor. It was all he could hope for at this point. With the solitary goal of breaking free of the pile of rubble, he used his one good arm to pull himself out inch by excruciating inch.

His moaning figure wrenched itself free from the rubble, but no one came to help. Grant flipped onto his side. The crowd was too busy celebrating to notice the final moments of his existence. The finish line was tantalizingly close, and despite his broken body, for the moment, he was still alive. If only he could force his body into action. "Sarge… apply… Spark Shield. Walk… me."

His body jerked into motion. All his limbs had been dislocated by the slide, and the muscles in his neck were failing to support him. His head lolled to the side as he heard a cheer for two competitors that were racing towards the finish line to claim the remaining spots.

"The *dead* have risen!" Cries erupted from the crowd, replacing the jubilant cheering. Panic spread, and spectators scrambled to get away from the marionette dancing towards them, its movement powered by unnatural forces. Arms and legs spun in circles as the groaning figure jerkily approached. "Run for your life! Lady February, protect us!"

Five yards from the finish line, and people still weren't rushing to help, instead seeing him as a monster. Lady February and his fellow competitors, who had finished the race, had their weapons at the ready but stood their ground, unwilling to approach the unidentified target. Grant checked his stats, focusing only on his health parameter, to verify just how bad a state he was in.

Health: 12/229

His body walked itself across the line, then sat down as gently as possible. <Heal, Grant! Now!>

Grant's fluttering eyes closed, and he just *barely* managed to activate Live by the Sword before he would have succumbed to his injuries. He relived the landslide as he lay there, once more feeling the pain and horror for the first time and seeing how he could have done better.

Over the course of the next minute, his arms and legs wrenched back into position with a meaty **pop**. He sucked in a deep lungful of crisp alpine air as the hole in his chest closed. The spell wasn't a panacea for all injuries, but it had miraculously healed his mortal wounds. From the startled looks of the crowd, he still looked like garbage, but he was now up to seventy-seven health. He might only be a third healed, but he felt better than he had ever expected to again.

"Grant Monday narrowly secures the fourth position!" an announcer called to the crowd, which was cheering wildly.

He had no idea where they had come from, but it was nice to hear the happy sounds at his success. <Well done. You woke from death and returned to life. I knew you could do it! Grant? *Grant!*>

The young Wielder's eyes fluttered closed, and he fell over.

———

Grant awoke in a panic, sucking wind. For a moment, he thought he was still trapped under the pile of rocks. Recollection abruptly flooded over him, and he blinked and took in his surroundings. His jaw dropped so far that he thought he might have dislocated it. From the bars lining his window, he realized that he was in a cell.

"*What?* I made it to the final. You've gotta let me out!" An unblinking Vassal on the other side of the bars was watching his every move but declined to respond. "Hey! Is this for *real?* Answer me! Are you deaf? I don't belong here!"

"Give it a rest, Monday," a voice called out from nearby, "Some of us are trying to get a little shuteye. The Vassal is one of Lady February's. He's there to make sure you don't keep cheating."

"I'm not a *cheat!*" Grant roared as he jumped to his feet, wobbling since he expected pain but getting a pleasant surprise in the form of being in peak condition.

"Shut it already. We are all in the same boat as you. There's a Vassal outside my cell too," the voice called to him sleepily.

"We're on a boat? There's an *ocean* in February?" Grant's mind was spinning, and he sat down to try and collect himself. "How big *is* this place?"

"Good one, Monday. I'm glad to see you have a sense of humor, and not just a murderer's cold stare!" This time the voice was mocking; clearly the man didn't like being woken up.

Sarge saved him from any more faux pas. <It's a figure of speech. You're being held at Lady February's villa outside of Valentine after being healed for a full day by three healers.>

Grant, face burning, didn't bother to reply at all. Instead, he sat up in his cot and took in his surroundings once more. This wasn't any ordinary prison cell, and it certainly was not dark and oppressive like the one belonging to House Saturday. Colored light flooded the six-by-nine cell through an intricate stained glass window. It illuminated an oil painting of someone standing triumphantly at the top of a hill. Grant's memory was a little hazy, but the figure seemed to resemble the statue in Hajimeni of Lord February, Lady February's father, which would make sense, considering he was in her villa.

He was starting to understand why the district was the way it was: Lady February idolized her father and appeared to be on a mission to take his love of physical cultivation to the next level by forcing the population to be more like him. Even in his short time in the district, Grant had seen the negative consequences of these actions. All industries not directly supporting the numerous events and races had ground to a halt, and full towns and communities had been destroyed. Banditry was running rampant, and even though various monsters were being used as a main food source, the creatures were expanding into dangerously high numbers.

As he sat motionless on the stone cot, Grant wondered if Lady February realized the impact of her decisions, or if she even cared.

Clink. Clink. Clink.

The metallic ring of metal on metal wrenched his thoughts away from his pathetic state. The clinking grew louder until a figure was visible on the other side of the bars. It seemed that she had been trailing a metal-clad finger along the bars as she walked. Grant struggled to focus, but the spiky, shockingly pink hair could only belong to one person, Lady February. "What do we have here? Relaxing instead of working hard once more, I see."

Grant's eyes drifted shut as if his mind refused to focus on her. He forced them open and found a figure in white robes looming over him. He didn't need to check the name tag to know that it was a Wielder from House Sunday. "I'm fine…"

"Hush, now; there is nothing you need to say. Rest, recover, and fight to grow stronger." The Wielder felt Grant's forehead. "I'm here to ensure that you will be able to function tomorrow. Though your body is healed, the mind needs time and rest, or it will fracture beyond repair."

"Thank you, Lord Sunday. I will do my best." Grant shifted to stand and show his thanks.

"No! You must remain immobile." The healer pushed him down gently. "To speed up your recovery, I have applied rapid-acting potions, along with soothing oils and a dream-weave that will allow you to grieve and heal from your incurred heart demons rapidly. I daresay you'd be able to go *spelunking* as soon as tomorrow, if you wish."

"O-oh. All that? I won't move." Grant promised as he

worked to hold still, though he felt that he should smile at what he was almost certain was a joke.

"No." The Sunday Wielder pressed an alchemically-infused cloth firmly against Grant's nose and mouth. The young cultivator struggled, but it was too late to resist the older man's iron grip. "You won't."

Lady February watched the proceedings with *great* interest… and a small smile.

CHAPTER THIRTY-FOUR

A fragment of Grant's awareness remained in the darkness of his unconsciousness and traveled inward to places normally inaccessible within the human mind. Isolated from the world, a mental representation of Grant walked through darkness. Curiously, he didn't feel fear as his bare feet trod across the expanse.

He should have, because what waited for him would have sent him reeling into a panic if he were fully awake. Everything he had experienced thus far in his life that left scars on his psyche was here in this room with him.

Randall, Lord January, and the horrors they had inflicted on the population while seeking out ever-greater entertainment. Grant's first kill, and the way it felt. Every kill after that, which had hardened and stunted his ability to reach out and connect with people.

His terror from monsters, rats, spiders, and other scurrying things. Grant's failures and burning desires... his near-death by avalanche, and the crushing stones that had trapped him and filled him with a deep terror for enclosed spaces.

They aren't here to destroy you. They couldn't care less about you personally.

Instead of breaking him, an external influence allowed him to recognize each of these things for what they were and accept that they were now a part of him. Able to contemplate the issues safely like this, Grant started to understand them.

"They just *are*."

Grant's moment of realization opened a new part of him, a part that was vulnerable, and *needed* to be. The part of himself that had always held others at arm's length, even after they had tried to reach out to him. New rings rippled out from under him as healing tears rolled down his cheeks and struck the water below.

The abomination that was Sarge's spirit form appeared next to him and offered an arm over Grant's shoulders. Grant looked up to the spirit and voiced his doubts, "How do I beat them all, Sarge? Even if they are just being themselves... I need to go against them. Destroy them. Or... I need to be *better* than them."

"There is nothing outside yourself that will allow you to be better, faster, stronger, or smarter. *Everything* is within." Sarge stayed silent for a long moment as the representations of Grant's mental scars grew blurry and dim, their previously *sharp* imagery fading as the young man was given the accelerated ability to stop letting them have power over him. When the sword spirit spoke again, it was slow and careful. "I know *nothing* about working to surpass others. I only know how to outdo *myself*, day after day. I work hard to pass that on to you. Over time, other things just... stop *mattering* so much. I look back at my past, I see how I can be better, and I live that way."

They stood together in silence as the darkness closed in and the color began to leech out of the now-hazy images. Grant sighed as he pondered Sarge's words.

"I can live with that."

Slowly the area brightened, and soon, Grant's real eyes opened. He looked around the cell, and for the first time... felt no anxiety from his situation. "I'll either succeed, or I'll do my *best* to succeed."

The guard outside his cell noticed that Grant was awake and slid a covered tray across the floor without a word. The young cultivator's mouth watered as he wondered what delights Lady February's chef had cooked up. "Wheatgrass shot and protein bar. *Delicious*."

The food was scarfed down with a smile. He'd built up quite the appetite after… he wasn't sure how long it had been. At least several days since the last time he'd eaten. The bars slid open with a clunk as he popped the last piece of food into his mouth.

"The final round will commence shortly." The Vassal stood to the side and motioned for Grant to leave his cell. "I will take you to the courtyard. Do *not* speak to Lady February unless spoken to first. Do *exactly* as you are told. Do you understand?"

Grant nodded as he exited the cell. Six of Lady February's Vassals led the group of competitors through the vast estate and towards the courtyard. They passed staff toiling away, scrubbing floors, and scampering to complete tasks. Grant couldn't shake the feeling that he was being led to the executioner's block. One false move or improper response would likely be the end of him.

His sense of unease grew as he passed a long line of statues. All were men—apparently previous Lords of February—with defined chests puffed out above chiseled abs. He couldn't fathom the cost of transporting, then refining the stone into such exquisite works of art. He was startled when he looked up at the final plinth before the entrance to the courtyard. Lady February stood atop the pedestal, holding a heroic pose. An artist furiously worked on her portrait, capturing her black skirt and white shirt, while a blob of shocking pink paint, prepared for painting the section of the canvas had been allocated for her hair, which was unbound in her standard pixie-cut style.

"Oh, it's time! Wonderful!" She bounded down from the plinth, fizzing with energy and vitality. Grant couldn't help but grin as her presence lifted his stoic mood following the troubled dream. "Come, come. Follow me. Oh, I'm so *excited!*"

Only Grant, out of all the competitors, was grinning. The others looked directly intimidated to be in the presence of Lady February. To them, she was royalty, ruler of the district, so he could understand their trepidation, although he didn't share it.

"Is there something *amusing*, Grant Monday?" She turned to observe him like a cat would a mouse. "If there is, please share it with the group and our honored assembled guests? I *do* love a good joke. You wouldn't be poking fun at me, would you?"

There was a sharp intake of breath before silence fell over both spectators and competitors. Grant merely smiled further and shrugged. "I like your energy and enthusiasm, Lady February. It lifts my spirits."

"*You*... have the right idea. This *is* supposed to be fun, for all that it changes the whole District." The group let out a sigh of relief at her words. "Follow me, competitors, and I will explain the rules."

Grant and the other four competitors were led onto a stage in the center of a spacious courtyard. Around the perimeter sat all the Wielders of February, apart from those of House Saturday and House Thursday. Grant presumed that they had been banned from attending due to their behavior at the arena. Scanning the spectators, he caught sight of Heavyweight Wednesday, yet realized that Waylon was nowhere in sight. There was no one more excited about the tournament than him, so Grant couldn't imagine why he wasn't here.

"It is time for the event you have all been eagerly waiting for." A shaft of light broke through the cloudy sky, illuminating Lady February as she stepped onto the stage. The light shining on her gleaming white gloves gave every motion additional gravitas, as though the heavens themselves were accepting her words as law. "A chance for us all to be better, and to guide the District to the highest heights."

"It is with great pleasure that I announce the final round of the tournament. My father valued physical cultivation above all else and passed that drive on to me. From me... to the entire District. Competitors, I'm sure you are eager to compete against one another and secure your position in society." A hint of a mischievous smile appeared on her lips.

"Yet, you won't get the chance."

As intended, a confused muttering filled the area. "Instead, *I* will be fighting each one of you individually and assessing where you belong." Grant noticed Lady February's Vassals share a look of confusion. They weren't expecting this development. "As a Wielder, a Vassal, an advisor, or a combination of those."

Grant wasn't the only person a little uneasy with this change of circumstances. He, like the others, had anticipated fighting one another for the chance to become the *winner*. Not to get *assessed*. Not only that, but Lady February had a brutal reputation; none of the competitors were eager to fight her. "Now that you have all had time to digest this change, let us begin. Who amongst you wishes the honor of fighting me first?"

The kite shield-wielding Vassal that had sent an avalanche at Grant strode forward. "Ahh, Shieldnovice. Vassal of Shield-student Perceval of House Tuesday. I should have known you would be the first to accept the opportunity to prove yourself after your indiscretions nearly had you disqualified. You should take the time to thank Grant Monday for surviving, else you'd be in a hole somewhere, guarded by Tuesday."

"Thanks, Grant." Shieldnovice's grin was almost as wide as his kite shield, since Grant had taken a step forward just a *heartbeat* after him, and *he* had been chosen. The three remaining competitors were Vassals of Houses Monday and Friday, and a Wielder from House Wednesday. At that moment, Grant was simply glad that he was not the last to move. Grinning at Lady February had given him more exposure than he'd wanted. His blood was boiling, and now he just wanted to *fight*.

Even so, he outranged her. Grant was *certain* he could win, even though he'd heard that her Wielded Weapon, a pair of gauntlets he couldn't see anywhere, allowed her to put her considerable body and weapon cultivation to great use.

"Whoever defeats me in fair combat wins. If you do so, you

pick your own spot. Otherwise, *I* choose. Easy, huh?" Lady February's words weren't cocky, they were *confident*. Grant wondered what would happen if more than one competitor beat her; would they have to face off against each other? "With the eyes of the District upon us to ensure total fairness, *begin!*"

Lady February backflipped to the other side of the stage, overflowing with energy as her shining gloves bloomed out and transformed into massive gauntlets that covered from past her elbow to her now-oversized fists.. Shieldnovice brought up his shield and attacked head-on with his long sword. Like most of the fights Grant had seen in both January and February, there was no finesse to the fight. He just hacked away with little regard for his safety.

Sarge had taught Grant to watch his opponent carefully, only attacking once he had identified his enemy's weakness. Lady February's metal fists hammered into the Vassal's shield, again and again. To Shieldnovice's credit, he managed to get his shield in the path of her fists every single time.

The shield started to hum. Grant assumed that it was normal, or perhaps the Vassal's ability... and then Shieldnovice spat out a mouthful of blood. He coughed out a command, "*Return!*"

The shield hummed and shook, and Lady February was abruptly sent flying. This, Grant realized, was the Vassal's lesser ability. Perhaps taking energy from his opponent and using it against them? In Lady February's case, the energy generated was *substantial*, with the Vassal struggling to hold onto his shield as it nearly rattled out of his hands. Shieldnovice, despite his best efforts, couldn't manage to land any blows against Lady February as she landed and charged right back at him. He was back to defending himself, but he didn't appear to want to seriously wound the Lady of the Month.

His reluctance to commit to an attack was his downfall.

Lady February's fists rained down, fully ignoring the now-deafening tone emitting from the shield. It didn't take long for the barrage of blows to break through the defense, and the shield was slapped to the side. The shield bounced to the ground. Blissful silence followed. For a moment, a look of horror crossed the Vassal's face, but he didn't let it dissuade him from fighting onwards. He swung his sword directly at his opponent, but without the defensive ability of the kite shield, he was vulnerable to assault. By contrast, Lady February's speed and agility meant that she easily dodged his lackluster, unskilled blows.

Even wearing full plate armor, the Vassal was hardly defenseless against the relentless rain of blows from the Lady's fists. The rapid-fire hammering reverberated around the courtyard, and the Vassal wilted as the damage from each impact increased. Grant couldn't understand why, but his sense of unease grew as the man was beat down to the point of finally surrendering with a raised fist and coughing blood near-continuously.

"Nice try, Shieldnovice. For making it to the final stage in the tournament and for putting on a good show, I offer you a position as Standard-bearer, currently ranked as Tuesday the sixteenth. May a deeper calling to the law allow you to choose your future actions more cautiously." Shieldnovice's wild smile —bloodsoaked as it was—showcased his excitement as he agreed. A huge flag with the heraldry of House Tuesday was pulled onstage and handed to the man, who traded his sword and shield to take it up, at the same time trading Vassalhood for becoming a full Wielder.

Tears of joy ran down his face, leaving clear trails through slowly-drying blood. Despite losing, he had achieved the goal he'd set out to complete. "You will be in charge of creating a group dedicated to improving our competitors. Congratulations; the District expects great things from you."

The resulting cheering that rose up was out of proportion to the gathering, and Grant realized that there was a wind spell augmenting the cheers of those listening to the proclamation from a distance. "How in the District do they know what's going on? Or... they're just *cheering*, aren't they?"

<No way to shape elemental light into illusions. Not till you get your fifth spell-slot,> Sarge confirmed. <They just know *something* impressive is happening.>

"Who's next?" Lady February lifted her fists into a perfect boxing pose. Grant stepped forward; it was his time to shine. "Oh… I've been looking forward to this. I've seen your skill several times now, and I'm intrigued by the challenge."

A few other people were laughing at Grant's sunken skin, proof that he had only recently been serious about his physical training. The Lady of the Month's words brought them up short, laughter turning into confusion, then expectation. Grant bowed lightly. "Thank you, my Lady."

"I'm not your lady… not unless you earn it!" She gave him a wink, then looked him up and down. "I'm only confused about one thing. I have only seen you fighting with a sword, but do you intend to fight hand-to-hand combat? You can if you wish, but I prefer to fight you at your strongest."

"My sword? It's right…?" A wave of nausea passed over him as his hand went to the place on his hip where February Twenty Nine should have been fastened. Had he left his weapon in the cell? "I appear to have… misplaced my sword? Please allow me a moment; I'll run back and get it?"

"*Will* you now?" Try as she might, his opponent couldn't hide her amusement, and neither could any of the spectators. The Nobles roared with laughter, and he felt his cheeks burn with embarrassment.

<Nah, I dropped myself off back there because I wanted you to go last. Study her movements and prepare yourself accordingly.>

"Sarge…!" Grant hissed in a fury. "How can you *do* that?"

Lady February waved her hand magnanimously. "Grant, my Vassal will collect your weapon. For wasting my time and that of our guests… you will go last."

He shuffled to rejoin the line, his face burning with shame. There was no point in arguing, and he didn't want to weaken himself by expending his mana to pull the sword out of the air. By the time a Vassal returned with his sword, Grant had witnessed Lady February dispatch yet another competitor.

The Vassal's Mid Spring Medium armor did very little to protect her against Lady February's devastating blows. The woman had started enthusiastically, but it was clear after a few minutes that she was distinctly outclassed. By the end of the fight, she was rolling around the stage and screaming as she tried to avoid blows. Rather than being upset about how events had played out, Grant took Sarge's advice and used the extra time as an opportunity to study Lady February. How she moved, fought, and defended.

He winced: there was *very* little defending.

She, like the others, used her sheer cultivation prowess to overpower her foes and beat them into submission. Between her weapon and physical cultivation, she simply moved to deal as much damage in as little an amount of time as possible. She clearly enjoyed fighting, to the point that Grant was *sure* that he saw a hint of disappointment in her face after beating both competitors so easily.

His eyes locked onto Lady February as he caught a repeated combo, just as the Vassal surrendered.

<Did you see it?> Sarge didn't even bother waiting for a reply. <You totally saw it. Knowing your enemy means you will enter the fight with far less uncertainty. Good work.>

Grant slowly nodded. Lady February would land a series of five blows, leading with her right fist, before retreating to recover her stance. He didn't know how this information would help him, but he would soon find out. "Do you think I'll be able to move fast enough to knock her off-guard?"

<That's really on *you*, isn't it?> Their conversation ended as a Wielder from House Wednesday stepped forward. He held a spear and proved himself different from the previous competitors simply by the fact that he didn't charge forward. Lady February threw a testing punch, but the House Wednesday Wielder easily sidestepped it. He half-heartedly lurched forward

with his spear, the clear telegraphing of the blow allowing Lady February ample time to dodge.

Grant couldn't understand *why*; the Wielder had the opportunity to get a strike in against her. From what he had seen so far, that might have been his *only* opportunity. Then it clicked. The Wielder from House Wednesday was only there to bring honor to his House, not to become Lady February's sparring partner. He didn't *want* to win or get Lady February too excited about his prospects. When he had gone for slightly longer in the fight than the others, the Wielder surrendered, then graciously accepted the offer of a position on her advisory counsel. There were no outcries of shock, so this was an expected—if boring—outcome.

The fourth competitor, a Vassal from House Friday, stepped forward. She held a longsword. As Lady February bounded forward, Grant heard a familiar whistling noise. After hearing it directed toward him several times in deadly situations, he nearly dove out of the way, even though this thrown net *wasn't* coming for him.

He watched as the net sailed through the air and perfectly encircled the Lady of the Month. She struggled briefly as it tightened itself, before clenching her fists and explosively breaking free. The shredded net fell apart, accompanied by clapping from the assembled audience.

Pow!

Lady February's right fist shot forward, slamming into the Vassal's middle. The impact launched the woman into the air and sent her skidding backward across the marble floor. Lady February hopped over and helped the House Friday Vassal up, before offering her a position as a personal Vassal and a spot on the counsel. She happily accepted the offered position, as had each fighter previously.

"Last but *hopefully* not least, we have Grant Monday." Lady February turned to face him with bloodlust in her eyes. "You haven't also forgotten how to *swing* that sword of yours, right? Know what... don't answer. Let's find out together."

CHAPTER THIRTY-FIVE

Grant nodded and stepped forward to face down his opponent. He'd be lying if he'd stated that he was ready to take her on. After watching her easily defeat three Vassals and one Wielder without breaking a sweat, he knew better than to hand her another easy win. Rather than running to share the fate of his fellow competitors, he stood in a defensive guard position. Immediately, people started to boo him.

"Your booing means nothing to me," Grant snorted defiantly, "I've seen what makes you cheer."

No one except Lady February heard him, but luckily, his words only made her chuckle. Silence slowly fell among the assembled guests. The defeated competitors sat on the sidelines, pleased with how things had turned out; they didn't stand a chance against Lady February, particularly if they weren't willing to inflict mortal wounds.

Grant held no loyalty for the woman standing before him. He would do whatever it took to defeat her and travel onwards. He unsheathed February Twenty Nine with a smooth motion, the steel ringing out across the courtyard. "I'm prepared, Lady February."

"Nice sword. Do you know how to use it?" She lowered her voice so that her words wouldn't carry, and Grant couldn't detect sarcasm this time. "I hope that you do... *Lord January*. Come now, show me what you're made of. I also hope you understand what's at stake here."

"Regent's fury." Grant cursed softly. If she knew who he was, there was no way she hadn't learned nearly everything he was capable of doing. Lady February circled him, a cat ready to pounce on its prey. Like a cat, she would likely toy with her prey first before landing a deadly blow. As his nerves settled, he let his training soothe his thoughts. She had endless stamina, but there were a few areas of weakness which Grant had identified.

Her Wielded Weapon, the massive metal gauntlets, were powerful at extremely close range. If he properly used his ability to place his sword precisely, he should be able to keep her at bay, due to the difference in their ranges. The only other aspect of what he had seen her do that could possibly be seen as a weakness was her repeating pattern of strikes. He had no reason to believe she would change her fighting style, which meant there was an opportunity.

Grant's mental preparation nearly cost him the fight in the first move.

A wind-wrapped fist flew towards his face, and only instinct led to him dodging the lightning-quick opening strike. Her metal gauntlet skimmed harmlessly across the top of his head, somehow still dealing two points of blunt damage. He recovered his stance and let his blade flash out, creating some distance between himself and those fists.

He instantly reevaluated what he had thought of as a weakness: the lack of reach *wasn't* a problem for her. What she lacked in reach, she made up for with pure speed. In the blink of an eye, her left fist flowed forward around his outstretched blade. He was ready this time. He cleanly dodged to the side and sliced the edge of February Twenty Nine across her back with an underhand sweep.

Damage dealt: 28 slashing. Debuff added: Heavy bleeding. -7 health per second for four seconds.

Blood erupted into the air, a gasp went up from the crowd, and a Calendar of Vassals surged to their feet, ready to put an end to the threat.

"That was… unexpected." A slight smile spread across Lady February's lips, and her stance shifted away from her standard open and unguarded position. "Let's see if you can do that again?"

She shot forward, her movement incomparable to what it had been only a moment before. Blade and gauntlets collided in showers of sparks again and again. It took every ounce of skill he had to keep her at bay, and even then, he wasn't able to do so perfectly. She was suddenly crouched in front of him, and an uppercut slammed into his gut and sent him flying.

Damage taken: 23 blunt (33 mitigated, 11 penetrated.)

"Wh-what was *that?*" Grant coughed as he read over a message he had never seen before.

<She did forty-five damage outright.> Sarge snapped out the explanation. <Twelve wasn't blocked by your armor, thirty-three *was*, and eleven of that *still* hit you. If you get hit again, I'll be able to tell you if a third of the blocked damage gets through, or a quarter of the total, but just *don't* get hit!>

That was certainly easier said than done. After Grant had bloodied her, Lady February was far more careful. She also mixed up her movement patterns, so he wasn't able to damage her in the same manner a second time. Grant's strategy at this point was to wear her down, but he wasn't sure if that was going to be possible, knowing that she could sprint for one hundred miles straight.

Even so, there was a difference between running and fighting. Her movements had started to become slightly more sluggish; she hadn't taken a break once since fighting Shieldnovice, the Vassal that was now walking around with a flag strapped to him. It was imperceptible to those watching, but Grant could tell she was finally beginning to tire. Then she disengaged and opened a good distance between them.

Lady February slowly exhaled and briefly closed her eyes. His eyes could have been deceiving him, but her gauntlets appeared to sparkle for a moment. Her next movements were lightning quick. Fatigued as he was, he couldn't dodge the sudden burst of blows that rained down on him. Despite wearing armor, he was shocked to discover that his health had dropped by twenty-five percent in those few seconds.

Health: 149/229

<Got it. As far as I can tell, a quarter of the total damage goes right through your armor. Try parrying instead of tanking; perhaps weapon-on-weapon will deal no damage to you.> Sarge's voice remained calm and analytical, the words giving Grant's churning thoughts an anchor.

He considered the situation carefully as Lady February got back in position. As she stepped forward, it dawned on him that this was *exactly* what had happened to the previous competitors. The more armor they had, the more they ignored the attacks... and the faster they fell.

Despite *her* strange recovery, Grant's energy certainly wasn't coming back. His best bet was to continue to keep her at arm's length. As she darted forward, Grant shifted from a defensive stance to an offensive one. She tried to veer away, noticing his plan, and his blade bit into her calf instead of her side. A damage notification appeared, but Grant wasn't about to make the mistake of looking away from her. Not a third time.

Her previous playfulness had vanished. Grant knew she had no armor cultivation, which meant that whenever he hit her, she took full damage. Yet, all she showed him was a wild battle fervor, a massive grin stretching across her face. Lady February surged forward and landed an uppercut which he barely managed to block.

His sword completely took the hit, and yet his body was launched into the air. The jarring impact rattled his head, and his mind still hadn't comprehended what had just happened as the back of his head cracked off the marble tiles. How he *hated* that he didn't have any armor on his head for this. The round of applause was instantaneous, as if the fight was over. Anger flooded through him, despite the fact that he was in a daze. Grant watched as the assembled nobles leaped to their feet to congratulate their ruler on yet another well-deserved win.

<Back on your feet! We may encounter defeat, but we must not be defeated!> He wanted to lie there and close his eyes, but he knew that Sarge was right. He got up on all fours before unsteadily forcing himself back onto his feet.

A gasp came from the audience, disrupting the start of Lady February's self-congratulatory speech. She frowned at him, but motioned away the healers. "Have you not suffered enough, Grant? There is no dishonor in conceding now. I will gladly make you one of my Vassals. You have more than earned that right."

"Thank you for your offer." Grant gave a sketchy bow, then firmly set his stance. "I'm here to win. Losing is not an option."

"Suit yourself. I'll make it quick." Disregarding all tact and skillfulness, she rushed in to grapple with him. She took two deep slashes to her arm and torso before she got her hands on his wrists. February Twenty-Nine fell to the ground with a clatter as she squeezed. Somewhere in his addled mind, he remembered that he wasn't defenseless. Lady February flinched backward as if bitten by a snake as Spark Shield activated at full capacity. Grant used the moment of her confusion to recover his weapon as though it had never dropped to the ground.

A moment was all the respite she offered before she surged toward him once again.

Now prepared, he successfully parried her metallic fists while applying a substantial amount of shock through blocking with his sword, forcing her to retreat and regroup. She raised her fists, and Grant could tell she was about to use her power to rapidly recover. Grant, now on the offensive, sprinted forward. Her eyes went wide at the unexpected attack; any normal opponent would have used the moment of respite to recover—but not Grant. He was wise to her attacks, and under *no* circumstances would he allow her to replenish herself.

She lifted her hands to block the attack, and at the last moment, he dropped down and slid across the sweat-slicked tiles, knocking Lady February's feet out from under her. She collapsed in a heap with her pink hair in disarray. Both of them were on their backs, so before she could recover, Grant had the tip of February Twenty Nine pressed firmly against the base of her neck.

If she didn't concede the fight, he wouldn't hesitate to end her life.

The courtyard erupted into mayhem. Wielders unsheathed their weapons, ready to defend their leader at a moment's notice. Even so, Grant knew that they didn't stand a chance of stopping him if he decided to follow through. Then he would be the Lord of this month as well and could escape in an instant.

Surprising everyone, Lady February *laughed*. Not a cackle, nor a shrill cry against loss, but a delightfully cheerful laugh.

"I give up, Grant. You win. I accept that, and all the consequences therein. Now please put your sword away."

CHAPTER THIRTY-SIX

Do you, Grant Monday, wish to absorb the power of February 1: Power Through? Accepting Power Through will override any previous Wielded Weapon power absorbed in the current monthly series. If not overridden by another weapon of the same month, this ability will return to its current Wielded Weapon at the end of the year, unless the quest 'Heal The World' has been successfully completed.

Accept / Decline

Grant dropped his sword to the ground as golden light suffused him. Even Sarge seemed taken aback, <Would you look at *that?* A double level up, one from defeating a Lady of the Month, and one from a cultivation threshold. Fun timing. Welcome to Cultivation Achievement Level seventeen. Oh, also, that puts your mental cultivation into Early Summer, so... you may notice some overall changes.>

He lay there and contemplated his options as his flesh returned to whole; better than ever, in fact. The process this time was... *intense*. He blacked out several times as his brain seemed to change, and his body was wracked with seizures that should have destroyed his ability to process, but the energy that moved through him allowed only pleasure to be felt as every cell in his body was suffused with energy.

When everything ended, he simply lay on the ground in shock. The strangeness of it all was almost unbearable, and he found that he could only focus on the notification waiting for him asking if he wanted the new power. He could take Lady February's Wielded Weapon ability, but she was working hard to give her people a better life... even if the way she was doing it was hurting a whole lot of people. Even so, the vast majority of people loved her. Taking her ability to protect them away would be too selfish by far. He hit 'decline'.

Even so, a nimbus of light surrounded both Grant and Lady February, and he whimpered as energy started to move into him once more.

A wild, vibrant pink—the exact color of her hair—was drawn out of Lady February and created a huge swirling array of power on the ground that expanded rapidly into a massive spell circle. In the next instant, the focal point shifted away from her and onto Grant. February Twenty-Nine once more shifted into an intensely beautiful sword, and the dragon's mouth stretched wide to suck in the pink power.

The entire process took only a moment, but everyone that saw what had happened was utterly dumbfounded. Happily for Grant, the 'Fragment' he had absorbed didn't want to send off any messages, so the population didn't instantly know that a transfer of power had occurred.

Quest Update: Heal the World (Legendary)

Congratulations, Grant Leap, you have defeated the Lady of the Month, Lady February, and have been granted her Fragment. As the new Lord February:

1) You have inherited the power of the Februarian Fragment of

Vibrancy, the ability to restore your energy and mana to full whenever the month you are a Lord of is in its ascendency. Each use costs 10 per restore and requires three seconds to activate. Charge: 99,110/100,000.

2) You have gained the ability to open the boundary separating February and March by utilizing the Februarian Fragment of Vibrancy. Each use costs 1 per person. Charge: 99,110/100,000.

3) You have gained the ability to send a message to anyone within the District of February by utilizing the Februarian Fragment of Vibrancy. Each use costs .1 per message. Charge: 99,110/100,000.

4) You have the ability to switch your name from Grant Monday to Lord February at will.

"This is an *outrage!*" A powerfully-built man stormed forward, his weapon a strange sword-length calligraphy brush. "You *dare* to pull apart our District like this? This will change *every-thing*; it will throw us into civil war! *How* did you just become the Lord of the Month? That's not something that can be *stolen!*"

Grant looked at his status sheet and noted that his name had automatically shifted to 'Lord February'. There was no hiding it at this point, so he decided not to try. With that thought in his mind, he looked at his opponent and realized that her name was now displayed as 'Pugilist Friday'.

"Calm down, Bureaucrat Monday." No-longer-Lady-February ordered as both she and Grant lurched to their feet. "I'll explain-"

Bureaucrat Monday barged past the front line of Wielders. The Head of House Monday for the District of February was *seething* with rage, his bloodshot eyes and surprisingly concerning brush leveled at Grant. His formal kimono and ornate Wielded Weapon were in stark contrast to his barrel-chested physique. "Grant didn't win *fairly*. I demand that he is stripped of his victory while we investigate this matter."

"Oh, get over yourself," Pugilist Friday interrupted. "If this is *my* reaction, why is yours so extreme? I thought you would be the *first* to congratulate Grant on his unexpected win, with him being a member of House Monday, after all."

"He may somehow bear the Monday name, but I have never seen this man before. As far as I know, he is an *imposter*; not a member of my House! Take him for questioning! We will get to the bottom...!"

"Be *quiet*. Does anyone here vote for the integrity of Lord Grant *February*?" Pugilist Friday looked around with a raised eyebrow. "I would like him to become my Sparring Partner, but not at the expense of distressing my trusted Nobles into doing something rash. Doing so would ease this transition and cease all concerns of rebellion."

"I will speak for him." A chorus of grumbling grew from the spectators as Heavyweight Wednesday stepped forward. "I know this man, and I vouch for him. He returned a priceless lost Wielded Weapon to House Wednesday, and for that, I am forever in his debt. He has also saved the life of one of my Wielders, Waylon Wednesday. If Waylon were here, I am positive that he would also vouch for him."

"A House Lord vouching for him? Good enough for me. It's settled." Pugilist Friday clapped delightedly. "Grant will become my Sparring Partner!"

She turned to look at Grant for the first time since they had fought, and her next words caught in her throat; she nearly choked. Then she started blushing furiously. "What happened to *you*?"

"But my Lady..." Bureaucrat Monday wasn't finished yet. "This doesn't answer the question of where he came from, what he is doing here, and why he *immediately* attempted to grab power. Between the insurrectionists and the halting of foodstuffs from District January-"

"Enough. I have my reasons for accepting this, and I'm certain the rest of what you are concerned with has an easy explanation. *No* more; I won't hear another *word*!" Pugilist Friday raised her voice and managed to tear her eyes off Grant, silencing the slew of critics. "Lord February won fair and square. There were no rules against anything he did. In fact, the *way* he won is the entire reason I am excited about this outcome."

"My lady..." Bureaucrat Monday weakly tried one last time.

"I need someone with intelligence who will be able to run the district while I focus on physical cultivation. Every day I need to work to fix the issues of making a District filled only with Elites. Lack of jobs, high prices, and other such tedious nonsense. I'm *decent* at it, but the attention needed to complete everything, plus meeting my own standards? I need a consort that can run things without me. Is that so hard to comprehend? Every moment I spend on the mundane is time I don't have to work on my cultivation! Everything has been arranged. We will have a ceremony here in the courtyard later to seal our union."

"Um... about that, Lady February." Grant's interruption caused Pugilist Friday to turn hard eyes on him, and he feared that her explosive anger would soon be vented upon his person. Several Wielders stepped back, anticipating the worst. Even so, her face shifted as she once more focused on Grant's face. "While I appreciate the... loveless marriage proposal to drop the tedium of your life onto my shoulders, I already have what I came here for. I have no intention of eschewing my *own* goals. I have to go further into the Districts-"

"Nonsense." She looked genuinely hurt at the rejection, and reached out as if to touch him. "No one would *dare* reject the Lady of the Month. What could be more important than staying here and making life better for tens of thousands of people?"

He had wanted to keep the details to himself, but the look of hurt and confusion on the eighteen-year-old's face pushed him to tell her the truth. "I'm working to better the entire *world*. I have the potential to become the Calendar King, and a quest to make it happen."

Silence reigned for a long moment, then the Nobility and audience as a whole started laughing. Grant got to his feet and quietly sheathed his sword. He didn't need this; it was time to move on. Just as he decided to use the Fragment to step away and leave the District, Pugilist Friday waved him down. Her face was red, but not a *hint* of laughter could be seen.

"Well… that *does* sound rather important. I have to admit that if you're serious, this changes things. I just need time to think." The Noble Wielders shared a look, unsure of what she was going to say or do next. They didn't have long to wait for an answer; only a half-minute later, she bounced on her feet and confidently marched back to the center of the stage. "Grant, when your quest is over, you will become my Sparring Partner, Consort, and Co-ruler. Is that understood?"

CHAPTER THIRTY-SEVEN

"I think you... *misunderstand*." Grant shook his head as the assembled people sucked in a collective breath. With a simple thought, his name changed from Lord February to Lord January. Names could be hidden or changed, but only minorly. The system wouldn't allow someone to falsify a Lord or Lady of the Month's title; it had been attempted for a millennium. "I am not going to be just a Lord of the Month. I cannot co-rule a single District when I am the Calendar King. I have no idea what my responsibilities will be."

This time there was no laughter from the audience at his admission: only fear.

"It appears we now know why the transport of goods from District January has halted," Bureaucrat Monday muttered. "Go back to your District and reopen *trade*, you barbarian."

Lady February, that is... Pugilist Friday... was shaking her head as things came together for her. "Ah... as you know, I knew of your real title. Still, I thought you were merely here to join two Districts closer together. I had no idea you were actually planning to press further. A question then: is the position of Calendar *Queen* available?"

Grant was shocked beyond belief at her directness. "I don't even *know* you."

"Political marriages rarely allow for that anyway. I can tell you that I'd be a staunch supporter, and a close ally," Pugilist Friday explained carefully, not pressing too much. When Grant continued to hesitate, she continued a small amount more, "Perhaps if I traveled with you for a time, we could come to an arrangement? Besides that..."

She swallowed as her eyes once again studied him carefully.

<Heh. Don't think you've realized it yet, Grant, but now that your cultivation is all in the Summer ranks... anything not *perfect* has been washed off. All impurities were consumed in order to facilitate the change, which is why you don't reek right now. You should still shower, though; I bet your clothes look like a snake shed all over them on the inside.>

"I don't-" Grant started to speak, but his confused reply was instantly cut off amidst the uproar of the Nobility.

"Lady *February!*" Her Prime Vassal spoke up, unable to hold his tongue any further. "I will prepare the entire Vassal force for departure. One Wielder from each of the Houses will also join you as chaperones and protection-"

"No need for any of that." Pugilist Friday stood and stretched. "We'll be departing immediately."

"My Lady..." The Vassal's voice wavered, but the direct stare that drilled into him a moment later made him gulp and nod. "Of course."

"Grant." Pugilist Friday turned to him and looked him over. "You clearly cultivate armor; do you prefer the gear you are wearing or would you be open to an upgrade? Any skills that require a certain type of armor?"

"I..." Grant hesitated to refuse her. An upgrade would be welcome, but he didn't want her to think she could buy a position as his *Queen*. The thought made his head spin; *he* certainly hadn't thought that far out.

Before Grant could finish his thought, the Prime Vassal dropped to a knee and begged, "Please, my Lady... I *insist.*

Allow at least a *small* contingent of guards. I can have the carriage ready to go in under an hour."

"A carriage will only slow us down and bring unwanted attention. Beginner Friday, I know that you worry about my safety, but I'll be fine. I have to do this. There are no challenges left for me in February beyond challenges that, frankly, I am unsuited for. If I want to push myself beyond all perceived limits, then I must leave and cultivate in the wider world."

The Prime Vassal opened his mouth before closing it and slowly nodding. "Yes, my Lady."

"On that note... while I am away," She swept her gaze across the eager Nobles, "Bureaucrat Monday will govern the District in my stead. Bureaucrat Monday... in pushing so many of our people to be the best they possibly could be, I realize that I have failed to administrate effectively. Until such a time as I have the experience to guide my people as I should... I humbly grant you regeny of District February. Please do right by the people I've failed."

"Surely you *jest*! Leaving the Head of a Noble House, someone from a *competing* House, in charge? Are you *mad*? You should-" a voice called out, clearly intending to go on a tirade against her. She never gave them the chance.

"Are you challenging my decree?" Her metal gauntlets began trembling as the power built up within them. "I know it is a little unorthodox, but the fact *is*... Bureaucrat Monday has been performing the majority of my administrative duties for years now. That was the entire *point* of this competition! Putting power into the hands of the people that can use it to help people the *best*. Not giving it to the strongest or the most *powerful*! I can see no one better suited to take on this role, and if *you* can, tell me now!"

Silence swept the area, and she nodded at Bureaucrat Monday. The man's eyes were filled with shock, despair; not even a *hint* of greed shone through. "No... I don't *want* to work for the District! I refuse!"

"Ha! By the Regent, that's just too bad! This isn't a post you

can turn down; you've been *appointed*. Report to your new housing, Regent Monday." Pugilist Friday chortled as a few other
people started to get wise to what was happening. "If you're
gonna serve the people as their ruler, you need to act like it."

"I like having nice *things*! I don't *want*... you *can't* put this on
me!" Bureaucrat Monday swiped at the ground with his brush,
leaving empty space wherever the bristles touched.

Grant watched the proceedings with great confusion.
Heavyweight Wednesday quietly stepped toward him as he
watched people argue, and decided to explain the situation to
Grant. "I see you are confused. You see, while she was still Lady
February, she made the law very... straightforward. If you are
in a governmental position that dictates the rules for a section
of the District beyond just the Houses, either elected or
appointed, you have to live in the District-provided housing."

"That doesn't sound too bad?" Grant shrugged at the
thought. "Having a house is already a luxury, in my mind."

"Heh. You two might *actually* get on well." Heavyweight
Wednesday snorted at the thought. "You are also unable to
accept income or use Time from any source beyond your
stipend. You cannot make any contracts that benefit you, or live
anywhere except District-provided housing, for five years after
you leave your position. Oh, also, all matters involving your
Noble House must be handled by a separate official. Though
getting outfitted is the responsibility of the District, all individual purchases with District Time must be approved by two
peers. The only person that can rescind these orders are the
Lady... or Lord... of the Month."

Grant thought about that; *really* thought about it. "That
sounds *awful*. Why would anyone ever want to get a District
job?"

"*Exactly.*" Heavyweight nodded and smiled as Grant walked
right into the question he wanted him to ask. "Two reasons
only: you actually care about the people and want to put them
first, or you need a job and don't mind being forced to do it
well. Quarterly reviews mean that you might lose your job,

which usually means a prison sentence, since they can't live anywhere but government housing."

"Sword Saints. You guys don't mess around here. How did you get people to agree to that? Seems like a lot of power to give up... oh." Grant's skin prickled and he shivered as he regarded Pugilist Friday with new eyes. "They *didn't* give it up or agree, did they? It was *taken* from them. That's what this whole thing was all about, wasn't it? So House Thursday...?"

"Almost entirely wiped out. In exile, that is. You catch on quick. Listen..." Heavyweight Wednesday stood straighter and formally began, "My Lord. I have an important request to beg of you."

"It's Waylon, isn't it?" Heavyweight's jaw worked soundlessly as Grant reached an arm out and clasped the larger man's shoulder. "Is he alright? I didn't see him during the finals."

"Of course... you've seen our journals before?" Heavyweight Wednesday pulled out a large book and opened it to show Grant before writing in it. "They are made from a monster that has the ability to replicate itself perfectly, which means we can harness that ability to make books that write in each other as one is written in. As to my request, Waylon has identified numerous monster nests near the March barrier. I had *hoped* they were only isolated incidents, but the sheer number has been increasing lately, and I don't know why."

"I don't mean to offend, but Waylon is more than capable of looking after himself." Grant shrugged and tried to get the man to move to his main point. "What do you need from me?"

"The lad would never complain, but... bloodstains appear on the paper occasionally as he writes." Heavyweight Wednesday grimaced as he looked down at the book. "His words are dire, but he's been holding out. Two towns along the border have stopped reporting recently, and our main forces and myself are needed in order to restore contact... and possibly human control. Since he's *surviving*, I can't ethically divert forces to his location."

"It won't take you out of your way. Take this," Heavyweight

Wednesday pleaded as he presented the leather-bound journal and elegant quill to Grant. "The journal is part of a matching set of three. Whatever you, I, or Waylon write will be mirrored across all three journals."

<*I don't need this.*> Grant used his Fragment of Vibrancy to send a message to the man even as he pushed the book back into his hands.

Heavyweight Wednesday flinched back in surprise as a notification appeared in his vision. "Ah. I see. However, can I send a message *back*? From what you have said, you will be traveling to and possibly beyond March. I need you to inform us of any disturbances you come across. There has been no word from beyond the borders of March, other than terrified gibberish, for more than three hundred years. As you go further, we need to know more… so we can prepare for when the barriers come down."

Grant was too embarrassed to share that he couldn't write more than a few words at best. Still… since picking up February Twenty Nine, his mental cultivation had come on in leaps and bounds. Perhaps he could pick up the skill quickly? He *had* noticed that he'd been able to functionally use an increased vocabulary, and Sarge didn't make fun of him for his flubs as he had done in the past. With a grunt of annoyance, he took the book. "Where's Waylon now?"

"I…" Heavyweight's eyes went wide, and he cleared his throat before answering. "Thank you, my Lord. Please rescue my boy. He's been operating in a border town named 'Kurai Ana', which is famous for their mushrooms and elementally dark monsters. They produce some of the best hide for stealth in the entire district."

"Hide… for stealth." Grant chuckled at the unintentional pun but only got a stone-faced stare in reply. He coughed lightly and nodded. "I'll make sure to seek him out."

With that, Heavyweight Wednesday left with a slight spring in his step and went to mingle with his fellow Nobles. Grant stood silently examining the leather journal.

"There you are!" Lady February playfully slammed her fist into Grant's shoulder, staggering him and making him drop his newly acquired journal and quill. "Right, sorry. I don't know my strength sometimes. Anyway... got that all taken care of. The District is in good hands, even if Monday is gonna whine and groan about it for the next half-decade. About that gear... any preferences?"

"Yes." Grant's head drooped even as she perked up. They both knew that meant he was going to let her join him. "I greatly prefer medium armor, and I'll take the best you can get. Other than that, traveling gear. Bedroll, toiletries, healing potions, food, anything we need for an extended trip. I've recently started to appreciate soap, so if that's available...?"

"Is there *soap*?" Pugilist Friday snorted and smiled, though it faded as she realized he wasn't joking. "I'm starting to get the feeling that I wouldn't enjoy District January very much."

"I *really* think that's probably true, um, Pugilist Friday-" Grant was cut off as she held up a silk-gloved hand.

She looked around to make sure no one was looking at them, then leaned in. "Call me 'Suki' when we're alone. That was my name before we put the changes in place. Before my father... before I became Lady February. We're supposed to forget who we were before we started serving our District... but I've only been doing this for a few years, and I've been in training for only a decade."

"Suki." Grant tried out the name, finding that it fit the pink-haired powerhouse well. "It's nice to meet you. Officially."

She smiled brightly, and Grant felt his heart catch. Luckily, Sarge was there to give him a small reminder in the form of a shock and shout. As Grant convulsed, Sarge bellowed in his head, <You have *time* to be playing doe-eye, Grant? Get. Your. Self. *Together*!>

Each word was punctuated with a shock, and left Grant panting for air. He looked up at Suki, managing to request one more thing. "Any chance you've got spells I can replace Spark Shield with?"

"There are, but a question for you..." Suki watched as sweat rolled down Grant's face. "How long have you been using that for? It appears that you have *really* good control of the spell, which means you likely have nearly-aspected mana channels by now. If you push through long enough, you'll gain a skill for lightning-based spells."

Grant's head jerked up in excitement. "That's a *thing*? I thought you just had to find stronger spells!"

"You *do*, but you can get skills related to their use," she started to explain as a runner came over with two large packs. "Ah, the gear is here. Here's the armor we've been able to acquire for you, befitting a Lord of the Month. Runner, go pull three offensive lightning spells from the stacks as well, and meet us back here."

Grant accepted the worked chainmail-and-leather armor, inspecting it with awe. It was composed of overlapping horizontal strips of laminated metal sewn over a backing of normal chain mail and soft leather... and it made everything he had used before look like castoffs. There was only one problem, "Suki... this is tiny."

"How about you just try it all on." Suki motioned for an attendant to guide Grant away.

"All?" He checked the pack and found several sets of clothing that he could wear under his armor and was confused for a moment. Then he recalled that most people tended to have at least three sets of clothing so they could be washing two and still remain socially acceptable.

Grant was led into a secluded bathing area and took off his gi, then literally tore off the remaining clothing. It was so damaged and worn from his heavy usage of it over the month that it took almost no effort at all. As it turned out, Sarge had been correct. As soon as his skin was exposed, a massive amount of shed skin scattered across the floor, as though he had dumped a wheelbarrow full of leaves into the changing room.

After a liberal application of soap and pumice, Grant felt clean again. A few moments later, he was fully dressed and somehow fit into his new armor. He checked his armor and weapon status, and nearly broke his jaw from smiling so hard.

Name: Grant Monday
Rank: Lord of The Month (January, February)
Class: Foundation Cultivator
Cultivation Achievement Level: 17
Cultivation Stage: Early Summer
Inherent Abilities: Swirling Seasons Cultivation
Health: 228/228 -> 347/347
Mana: 12/12 -> 19/19

Characteristics
Physical: 119 -> 198
Mental: 46 -> 73
Armor Proficiency: 63 -> 108
Weapon Proficiency: 88 -> 140

Late Spring Medium Ornate Banded Mail armor. Full set: Head, Torso, Legs.
Each piece offers:
Total Physical Damage Decrease: 50. (Base Armor: 14. Armor Cultivation bonus: 36)
Total Magical Damage Decrease: 50

February Twenty Nine (Considered as a Late Spring Medium weapon due to Weapon/Armor synergy)
Total Damage increase: 61. (Base weapon increase: 14. Weapon Cultivation increase: 47.)
Critical hit maximum damage: 93

<All of a sudden, you hit like a draft horse kicks. Congratulations on your advancement.> Sarge's levity faded momentarily, <Careful where you swing me; a casual strike has a good chance of just flat-out killing even a weak cultivator.>

"How did I gain so *much* in three levels?" Grant couldn't

stop grinning: here was perfect proof that he had changed so much as to be unrecognizable. *Finally*.

<You didn't. You got access to all the withheld points. This might be a good time to explain the Autumn bottleneck. While you only need *sixty* points to reach Early Summer cultivation, you need *two hundred and forty* to break into Early Autumn. So… while you got a huge boost for breaking through all the way, that's *nothing* compared to what you'll get if you ever manage to bust through that bottleneck.> Sarge paused, having expected an outcry or something about fairness. <Grant, are you listening?>

He wasn't. Grant was staring into the mirror that had just unfogged, trying to figure out why the beautiful man on the other side of it was able to mimic his movements so well. "Is that… *me?*"

<Let's see… fresh-washed long black hair. Breakthrough-perfect skin. Fixed teeth… no residual adipose stores or extra skin at all. Yup, that's you.> Sarge allowed Grant another moment to admire the impressive man, then hit him with a surge of lightning that didn't even make Grant flinch. <Oh, *great*. You're too resistant to this for me to even make your external muscles *twitch* now. Any chance I could convince you to take off the new gear so I can zap you properly?>

CHAPTER THIRTY-EIGHT

Grant peered at the map Suki was showing him and found the closest point to their destination as he remembered ever going. His sword lashed out, and a hole appeared, hanging in the air. She stepped through, holding his hand so they could travel together. An infinite moment passed in this place between places, and Grant felt a moment of fear as time seemed to stretch. He blinked, and they were suddenly standing next to the site of a recent avalanche.

"Great memories here," he commented breezily. "I think *that*'s the rock that punctured my lung. Oh, look! That one still has my blood on it."

"Stop complaining about the past; we've got places to be *now*." Suki chuckled at his strained features. "I want to see how you can move now that there's... nothing getting in the way."

Grant looked down at his refurbished body, then into the woods surrounding them. Suki pointed into the distance, then took off in a sprint. "Road's this way!"

After a moment, he realized that she was trying to race him. He felt his face stretch into a wild smile as he started running after her. "Massively better gear, yes. Perfectly sculpted body, yup. Running speed, thanks to body cultivation…?"

His pink-haired target appeared to slow down, then resumed what seemed like a normal running pace as he charged after her. The miles flashed by, and he was suddenly beside her… then in *front* of her and gaining ground. He threw a look behind himself, and felt gratification to see that she was showing as much shock as he felt. She narrowed her eyes and sped up, and soon they were thundering down the road at a pace that humans had never been made to move.

The most impressive thing to him was that they kept that pace up, and it felt as easy as going for a moderately long walk; his armor cultivation seemed to have made it so that his body didn't even get sore from the strain anymore. A small building appeared in the distance, and Suki grabbed his arm. Moments later, he found himself racing through a hamlet while trying to figure out how to slow down without falling flat on his face.

There were no lights within the windows or smoke from chimneys. The smattering of abandoned wooden shacks sent shivers down his spine. He had to admit, he was glad to have Suki as company; it was invaluable to travel with a capable fighter to watch his back in an area where monsters were known to roam.

A sea of unnatural fog swirled past their legs, adding to the strangely otherworldly feel of the place. "I visited this place once, long ago. Father would take me hunting in the woods to hone my ability to notice detail. Nothing quite like hunting creatures in stealth to become a detail-oriented individual."

After she finished speaking, they walked in silence in an attempt to find any sign of life in the area. Grant listened intently—so much so that, when a soft scratching came from his backpack, he nearly jumped to the top of one of the small buildings. He shifted his new gear out of the way and found that the journal was attempting to impart the message currently being written by someone else.

Surrounded. Doesn't look good. Won't survive. Monster wave. Will hide Wielded Weapon in dead tree next to barrier. Send full calendar.

Grant stared dumbfounded by the words. He snatched up the quill and, in his terrible handwriting, replied: *Survive! On my way. -Grant*

"*Suki!*" He slammed the journal shut and looked around for the barrier, only to be stymied by the omnipresent fog. "The barrier! Which direction?"

She understood his concern and instantly turned to run. "That way. What's the situation?"

"Monster wave! Waylon's almost down!" The pair sprinted through the fog, and soon terrible bellowing roars were echoing strangely through the haze. A light appeared through the mist. "The barrier! He's gotta be near the... Regent's icy stare, that's not good."

Between the barrier and a group of terrified villagers stood Waylon Wednesday. He leaned heavily on a stout villager as blood streamed from numerous lacerations. At first, Grant couldn't tell if his friend still lived, or if the man next to him was just propping up his body. Then the young Lord Wednesday lashed out and slammed his weapon into the skull of a charging... thing.

"Those are Early Summer beasts! *How?*" Suki surged towards the heart of the danger, forcing Grant to keep up. By now, he could tell what the creatures were from their tags: Beastmen. Beyond walking on two legs, there was little else that resembled humans. Their bodies were hairy and heavily muscled; their heads sported intricate horns. Two beastmen focused their attention on Suki, who launched herself into the air and slammed her fist down on one's head. It let out a mewling cry as it stumbled backward, a few of its horns snapped clean off.

Grant winced at the sight. On a human, a blow like that would have easily snapped a neck, possibly knocked the head clean off. Clearly, their heads were well protected, and yet Suki's fists unerringly slammed into them instead of going for less-armored portions. At first, he thought it was due to the unsettling focus he had seen in people to simply trade blows; then he recalled that she was able to power right through armor. With such high defense on their skulls, it rapidly became apparent that the Beastmen hadn't ever needed to defend that area.

Even so, it wasn't anything Grant could take advantage of. In one smooth motion, Grant unsheathed February Twenty Nine and slashed across the chest of another Beastman.

Blood *showered* from the wound.

Damage dealt: 52 slashing. (41 mitigated. Critical! Massive blood loss: -25 health per second.)

The Beastman stumbled back and gaped at its wound in horror. The powerful strike had torn through the tough hide and shaved off nearly a quarter of its total health. Grant stared at his sword for a beat too long.

<If you do *not* follow up on that, I am going to figure out how to shock you through your armor when you go to relieve yourself.> Sarge's bellow burst the strange moment of stillness that had overcome Grant, and the young man darted forward to turn the Beastman into venison.

A cloven hoof dented his chest armor and sent him sailing in a perfect parabolic arc before he slammed into the wet earth. He coughed lightly as the damage notification rolled in.

Damage taken: 5 blunt (50 mitigated)

Grant glanced to the side to check on Suki, and instantly found himself in awe of her power. Her metal fists slammed again and again into muscle and bone, forcing the beast to the ground. Grant couldn't just sit and admire her skills; the Beastman he had wounded had dropped to all fours and thrown itself after him. A cloven hoof landed next to his left thigh right between his legs as he rolled. <One second later, and you wouldn't have needed to worry about marrying Suki next year!>

"Not helpful!" Grant slammed his sword up, hoping that this creature's arteries would behave the same as a human's. February Twenty Nine sliced point-first into the area where the superficial femoral artery would be on a human; thanks to the attempt to crush him, Grant had a perfect target to aim for. The Beastman screamed as Grant shredded its inner thigh, and by the sheer volume of blood… "Arteries are in the same spot."

Damage dealt: 61 slashing. (32 mitigated. Critical! Massive blood loss: -30 health per second.)

The monster stumbled a few steps toward Grant, then dropped to the ground, unconscious and rapidly headed toward death. Grant didn't wait for the creature to expire naturally, driving February Twenty Nine through its heart and earning another monster kill toward his next Cultivation Achievement Level.

Waylon slumped onto the ground just as Grant rolled to his feet, desperately hoping that his friend was still alive. There were no monsters going for the downed man, so Grant couldn't justify running to check on him. He instead turned back towards Suki, who was still hammering on the other Beastman. Grant sprinted forward and joined the fight, swordpoint leading. His weapon met resistance for a moment, then the sharpened blade slid through and wrought carnage on the soft organs, and debuffs started piling on rapidly. The creature bellowed in rage and pain, the vibration shaking the nearby trees and pulling the attention of the other Beastman.

Boom. Grant's attention was pulled to a thunderous discharge of energy from the barrier that struck a stock animal which was fleeing the fighting. The domesticated bovine screamed as it was warped, and the animalistic cry became a full-throated scream of rage and hunger. The newly-minted minotaur charged at the nearby people, scattering them in its rampage.

Another Beastman leaped into the air and brought his hooves down on Suki, who blocked the blows by punching the hooves so rapidly that the creature was knocked out of the air. Grant pointed at the minotaur. "Suki, did you see that?"

She jumped onto the Beastman and beat it to death in the next two seconds, and the remaining Beastmen scampered backward. "What a rush! That's the most fun I've had in *years*! I always have to hold back when I'm fighting-"

"Grant...!" The shout and wet cough refocused Grant. Waylon was trying to pull himself to his feet. In the mayhem, Grant had almost forgotten about his wounded friend. "All Wielders can... reinforce! You need to... the fluctuation-!"

Grant charged at his friend, murder in his eyes. Waylon watched him advance, confusion the only thing in his mind as he slowly slumped to the ground. The Lord of the Month jumped over the collapsed human, slashing into the arm of the minotaur that had nearly crushed his friend's skull without even being noticed. His attack tore open a wide wound on the monster, but its follow-up punch sent blood flying from Grant's mouth, eyes, and nose as the intense blunt damage transferred from his chest to the rest of his body.

Damage taken: 85 blunt. (50 mitigated.)
Health: 257/347.

Furious at the damage to his new gear, and confused as to the massive amount of damage, Grant struggled to his feet and prepared himself to meet the charging monster. He moved into a defensive pose as the creature tucked its head and charged like a bull. Every step shook the earth, and Grant tried to decide how he would manage to both attack and evade at the same time.

He shouldn't have worried.

Suki blazed past him, appearing low in front of the minotaur, a move she had managed to pull off on Grant during the tournament. Her unexpected massive uppercut forced the creature into an upright position with its head thrown back.

During the moment that the monster was undefended, Grant leapt forward and slammed the point of his sword into the hollow of its neck. He met resistance for a moment too long to be comfortable, but then February Twenty Nine pushed through the beast.

Grant was *slapped* away by a huge hoof-fist, taking another hundred points of blunt damage and sending notifications of broken bones and ruptured organs scrawling across his vision. He squinted up through blurry eyes to see the minotaur still moving, still fighting.

<The sword is blocking the blood flow!> Sarge's words were all the hint he needed.

Grant raised his hand, and called his sword back to himself with blood-flecked lips. "Time… is Space…"

His sword appeared in his hand, and blood fountained from the deep wound he'd carved into the creature's lungs and airway. There was only one message that Grant saw before his vision went black.

Caution! Your heart has stopped!

CHAPTER THIRTY-NINE

"You. Aren't. *Allowed* to die!" Grant came out of the darkness of unconsciousness to terrible pain. Suki's fists were rhythmically beating on his now-unarmored chest, alternating with lightning surging directly into his heart, now that he had no resistance to the spell.

Skill gained: Lightning attunement (1/10). Power literally flows through you, becoming one with the person you show the world. Masters of this skill can empower natural lightning bolts to shatter mountaintops. Saints are *the storm.*

Tier one effect: Increases damage of all lightning-attuned spells by 10%.

<Oh, good. Hey, I figured out what you needed in order to get the skill for lightning spells. Gotta run lightning directly through your heart. There were, ah, *complications*. Better stop her from hitting you. She and I were turning your heart on, then off, back and forth pretty bad.>

"I'm back." Each word was soft, and blood streamed out of his mouth each time his lips parted. "Stop…"

His health was below fifty, something he hadn't seen since before he'd started increasing his Cultivation Achievement

Level. No… since he had gotten crushed by an avalanche. He'd seen this *far* too recently. Suki stopped punching him, and it was only now that he could see tears sparkling down her cheeks. He closed his eyes and took a deep inhale. *"Live by the Sword."*

In his mind, he was back fighting the minotaur. The bulk of the damage he had taken had been from this monster alone, so that wasn't terribly surprising. The fight happened over and over, and he saw how he could have moved to avoid attacks. How he could have mitigated extra damage by moving his body *with* the blow. Over and over, until the skill moved on to show how he could have staunched his blood flow, though he felt this wasn't as fair; he'd been unconscious.

Then as it turned out, Suki's attempts to save him had nearly finished him off. He almost laughed when the skill-version of him didn't try to dodge or ignore; instead, he saw himself giving her instructions on how to apply pressure firmly and calmly to circulate blood until the heart had gotten back into rhythm.

Health: 48/347 -> 153/347. Critical areas focused. Bones reset. Organs repaired. Soft tissue still severely damaged.

Grant opened his eyes and gazed into Suki's. "Thank you. I'm all set."

"You don't *look* all set." She wiped her eyes, then scanned the area. "Waylon's getting fixed up by the locals, but I need you on your feet to help me fix this barrier. Two Wielders stabilizing it will have way more impact than just one."

He stood gingerly and walked with her toward the sparking barrier. They passed the corpses of creatures large and small, and his feet squelched as they sank into bloody mud. "What happened here?"

"Waylon happened. He had a whole bunch of his Vassals with him when this started, and… I don't think they made it." Suki swallowed back the roughness in her voice. "His weapon allows him to gain temporary characteristics when he gets the last hit in on a creature, so by the time he got to these last chunky ones, he was able to stand against them practically toe-to-toe. The issue was that he got so beat-up getting to them that he wasn't able to finish the job."

"*That's* what his Wielded Weapon does?" For three beats of his heart, Grant was upset that he hadn't taken that power for himself. Then he recalled that Waylon was his *friend* that had suffered tremendously in order to save a town's worth of people.

"Sure is." Suki winced at the admission. "It's one of the reasons his relationship with his father is so strained. Waylon got a Berserker's weapon, but he's a meticulous and thoughtful person. Combine that with the fact that there are a good half-dozen Wednesdays in the world that have a variation on that power, a *better* variant, and you can see why an heir apparent is instead an unnamed Wednesday, all but exiled from the House."

"Wait... *what?*" Grant went *very* still at that declaration. "I thought they... unnamed? His name is Waylon."

"The barrier to entry for skills is incredibly high. Almost all skills have terrifying prerequisites that have to be fulfilled to gain them." Suki shrugged and waved at the barrier. "Can we *please* stabilize this now?"

"I thought that people that went by their skill names were the ones that were seen as branch family, or hopefuls at best. Are you telling me that losing your name is a badge of *honor?*" Grant was still frozen, but a crackling like a massive buildup of static lightning made him start moving to the shimmering barrier once more.

"Why would you think *that?*" Suki reared back and slammed both gauntlets directly into the barrier. It rang with a sound like a gong being struck, and the wavy curtain of energy took on a more rigid form. For a moment, Grant could see *through* the barrier; thousands of multicolored lights on beautiful houses shimmered, then vanished. "Don't you remember me telling you that you could only call me Suki in private? If the Lady of the... that is... if even *I* think that way, imagine the Noble Houses."

"I see. Question. Do I just... stab the barrier?" Grant was

holding February Twenty Nine in one hand and applying pressure to his bruised abdomen with the other.

"Yes."

Since he had no energy to shrug, Grant merely nodded and stabbed forward. Unlike when Suki had hit the barrier, when his sword hit the shifting energy wall… it *screeched*. Brown and pink swirled out of his sword and into the colorless, translucent wall, dyeing it as if he had touched oil to water.

The barrier didn't just firm up. Instead, hexagons dozens of meters wide appeared along the shifting curtain as far as the eye could see, fitting together perfectly over and over. When Grant could pull his sword back, the barrier seemed practically reforged by plate armor. "That worked?"

"You have a gift for understatement." Suki turned to him and grinned ruefully. "I like that you don't do anything by half measures, but I *had* been hoping to join my people to District March in my lifetime."

"Lady February!" A woman's shrill cry echoed through the fog that had been creeping ever closer as day shifted toward night. "Sir Waylon's taken a turn for the worse!"

A quick glance between the two cultivators was all that was required before they turned and ran to the area where the wounded were being kept. When they arrived, Grant was pleasantly surprised to find that only a small number of people had been wounded. He cheerfully remarked on that fact, only to earn a glare of pure rage from the man tending Waylon. "Yup. Only a few *wounded*. The monsters didn't care to leave survivors."

"Grant, we can bring them directly to Valentine. Aim for the site of the tournament; it's directly adjacent to House Sunday." Suki's orders were crisp and direct, and in an instant, Grant had opened a hole in the air. He shuddered as he watched the fog being drawn in, as if the hole were a mouth in the sky sucking in pasta, and he started to get hungry. He shook himself, then yelped as a shock caused his arm to jerk.

<The mind goes to strange places when terrible things are

happening, Grant. If you are terribly, *terribly* unlucky… you'll get a skill that allows you to ignore the worst of it. Until then, try to keep your head on straight. Not only do you need to help people, you need to get yourself patched up.>

The young lord nodded sharply and hurried to get everyone through. All the wounded, and a few people that were brought along to move them gently, were followed by Suki, and lastly, Grant. Soon the previously empty arena floor was bustling with activity, and healers were attending to everyone that needed help.

Grant blinked as people swarmed them and mana was poured into various healing spells and Wielded Weapon abilities. His tired eyes closed, and when they reopened, the sun was hanging low in the sky. Somehow the night had passed in almost no time at all.

"Here, Grant." Suki smiled sweetly at Grant as she handed over a thick tome. "I *think* this is something that you can use. Good morning. Everyone survived. We managed to save them all, and Heavyweight Wednesday reported late last night to inform us that all known mutated monster nests have been destroyed, and the barrier has been fully stabilized, as far as his scouts can find. It's all thanks to you. District February thanks you and believes… *I* believe in you."

Having just woken up, Grant wasn't quite sure whether to thank her or run to find a latrine. He could also go for food. However it worked out, his mind was a little foggy. Deciding against making a fool out of himself, he simply took the tome and looked it over.

Elemental Spell: Thundering Step
Prerequisites: 65 Mind. Two feet. Metallic weapon.
Active Mode: Create a static field in a five foot radius around you that damages others when they move through the area. Does not move from the point it was set. Lasts five seconds.
Mana cost: 10 per use.

Damage(Self): 0% Mental cultivation.
Damage(Other): 100% Mental cultivation per second.

Training Mode: Increase movement speed by 50% while out of combat. Combat is considered ended when you have not dealt or taken damage from an opponent for five seconds.
Mana cost: 10% per second. Mana regen halted while active.

Grant couldn't find any words to express how much he loved the new spell. He could use it while running to push himself faster, or leave a trap that would blast enemies to bits if they were chasing after him. As he wasn't able to make his muscles twitch with his current spell when wearing armor—which meant no more bonus to mental cultivation speed—this couldn't have come at a better time. "Are you sure? This seems… potent."

"There's no one in the District that we would both trust to use it, and who *can* use it," Suki told him bluntly. "If you like it, it's yours."

He looked at the powerful woman that wanted to marry him at the end of the year, his friend that was recovering after not being expected to survive the night, and the Wielded Weapon that had given him power beyond his wildest dreams. "You know what today is?"

"Awesome?" Waylon called weakly from a cot nearby. "Look at that sunlight. Regent's *smile*, that's some beautiful grass. I really like what they did with that grass. So green."

"Healer, lower the dose of whatever you have him on for the pain? Thanks," Suki called while pointing at Waylon. "It's the twenty-ninth. Why?"

Grant simply smiled at his friends as he touched the grimoire to February Twenty-Nine and replaced Spark Shield with Thundering Step.

"Best. Birthday. *Ever.*"

EPILOGUE

"There's been an incident at the barrier." A huge man that wouldn't look out of place in District January suddenly appeared next to his golden-haired master.

The Wielder in question was watching a card game through one-way glass, his position allowing him to use the filtered panes, set in the eye-holes of his jester mask, to see all the marks on the cards that were in use.

"Which one?" came the bored reply, "The one that's accidentally raising an army and recently stopped selling us food, or the one with all the refugees that never last the night?"

"The food one, Lord March." The huge man's voice, already high-pitched, suddenly took on a new tone. "T-that is-"

"*What* did you just call me, Cuddles?" The Lord of March's words were a bare whisper. A baton appeared in his hand, and a light flashed deep within the brilliant diamond that sat atop it. "You know *The Rules*! I. Am. *Dokeshi* March!"

The huge man with a comically tiny head began to scream as bruises appeared all over his body, as though he were suffering a terrible beating at double the speed of real life. Dokeshi March tossed a Day into the air and muttered something, then looked at the coin as it landed in his palm. He grunted, and Cuddles collapsed to the ground as he lowered his baton. "You've won a stay of execution. Do not test me again."

"Yes, Dokeshi!" Cuddles squealed as he bowed to the ruler, who turned his attention back to the game and pressed a button. As the next hand was dealt, a card in the dealer's hand shifted what was shown on its face and was passed out without the dealer batting an eye. Both players smiled at their hands, and a round of furious betting ensued.

"Tell me the problem," Dokeshi March demanded without taking his eyes off the match below.

Cuddles shuddered and carefully wiped a line of blood from his mouth. It wouldn't do to spray blood all over the Lord. The *Dokeshi*. Cuddles swallowed the iron tang and pressed forward. "The barrier shifted in configuration. House Thursday thinks that this may signify trade restarting, but the spies you dispatched from House Saturday warn that this may simply be a precursor to war. If the barriers *do* drop, as the alarmists warn, it could-"

"Enough; I'm bored already. District February can do anything they want, and it just won't *matter*." Dokeshi March waved off the rest of the report, watching placidly as the man that had gained the altered card collapsed into despair. "After all…"

The crying man was surrounded by a handful of Peace-keepers, who led him away. Dokeshi March let his perfect teeth show as a warm smile oozed across his face.

"The House *always* wins."

ABOUT DAKOTA KROUT

Associated Press best-selling author, Dakota has been a top 5 bestseller on Amazon, a top 6 bestseller on Audible, and his first book, Dungeon Born, was chosen as one of Audible's top 5 fantasy picks in 2017.

He draws on his experience in the military to create vast terrains and intricate systems, and his history in programming and information technology helps him bring a logical aspect to both his writing and his company while giving him a unique perspective for future challenges.

"Publishing my stories has been an incredible blessing thus far, and I hope to keep you entertained for years to come!" -Dakota

Connect with Dakota:
MountaindalePress.com
Patreon.com/DakotaKrout
Facebook.com/TheDivineDungeon
Twitter.com/DakotaKrout
Discord.gg/mdp

ABOUT MOUNTAINDALE PRESS

Dakota and Danielle Krout, a husband and wife team, strive to create as well as publish excellent fantasy and science fiction novels. Self-publishing *The Divine Dungeon: Dungeon Born* in 2016 transformed their careers from Dakota's military and programming background and Danielle's Ph.D. in pharmacology to President and CEO, respectively, of a small press. Their goal is to share their success with other authors and provide captivating fiction to readers with the purpose of solidifying Mountaindale Press as the place 'Where Fantasy Transforms Reality.'

Connect with Mountaindale Press:
MountaindalePress.com
Facebook.com/MountaindalePress
Twitter.com/_Mountaindale
Instagram.com/MountaindalePress

MOUNTAINDALE PRESS TITLES
GameLit and LitRPG

The Completionist Chronicles,
The Divine Dungeon,
Full Murderhobo, and
Year of the Sword by Dakota Krout

Arcana Unlocked by Gregory Blackburn

A Touch of Power by Jay Boyce

Red Mage and
Farming Livia by Xander Boyce

Space Seasons by Dawn Chapman

Ether Collapse and
Ether Flows by Ryan DeBruyn

Dr. Druid by Maxwell Farmer

Bloodgames by Christian J. Gilliland

Threads of Fate by Michael Head

Lion's Lineage by Rohan Hublikar and Dakota Krout

Wolfman Warlock by James Hunter and Dakota Krout

Axe Druid,
Mephisto's Magic Online, and
High Table Hijinks by Christopher Johns

Skeleton in Space by Andries Louws

Chronicles of Ethan by John L. Monk

Pixel Dust and
Necrotic Apocalypse by David Petrie

Viceroy's Pride by Cale Plamann

Henchman by Carl Stubblefield

Artorian's Archives by Dennis Vanderkerken and Dakota Krout